outskirts press

Shiny in the Shade

v2.0

Outskirts Press, Inc.
http://www.outskirtspress.com

ISBN: 978-1-9772-4911-1

Library of Congress Control Number: 2021922004

Cover Image by Jay Nordgaard

PRINTED IN THE UNITED STATES OF AMERICA

Acknowledgment

When I embarked on writing this first novel I reached across the pond to Dorothy Davies. Dorothy shared stories and writing tools. Among many gifts were her books *Skullface Chronicles* and *A Long way to Babylon*. Many thanks to her!

My wife, Kari, likes a clean and neat kitchen table. The better part of this production was typed at that table - she put up with the chaos for way too long and with little in the way of complaints. Thank you.

Thank you to my readers. My brother, Eric, not only was a reader but also made inspiring suggestions. Janice, my dear mother, had a go at it and stitches books as well as quilts. Many thanks to Kirsten, my sister. She found time to give it a very good shake and also helped with graphics! Aliyus, my son, was a wonderful sounding board, thanks for listening!

When I asked my daughter, Nissa, if she would be willing to take a look at my manuscript I don't think I knew what I was getting myself into. The girl can carve - she put a chisel in my hand. Thank you so much for all your help!

Thanks to Jay for cover art and Casey, for the graphics.

Thank you Kenny for your fun artwork on the back cover.

I like to finish what I start. Sometimes that doesn't happen but I'm delighted that this novel came to fruition. I hope you find *Shiny in the Shade* engaging.

Part One
MANAGE

Chapter I
Mirror Mirror

Jon Rawling walked the riverbank of the Platte north from the boat dock. Trees shaded the path after midday and a gentle breeze followed him. Sun on the water tinted the river's gray to olive green and he welcomed the serene view. Above, a kingfisher circled, dove to the river, and returned with a silver minnow in its beak. From a naked bleached branch, it eyed him, tilted a scruffy crest, and the minnow vanished.

The archaic path trailed the river's edge, low and close to water, or rising well above water, on a ridge, and sometimes mid-bank as terrain allowed trek. Once a cow path or hewn by a thousand exterminated bison, he didn't know, but this half-mile endured clear by their use, as did a section trailing south from the couple's home.

Mental fissures needed mending, patching, and Jon's walks had become frequent.

The current ran opposite and he imagined shrugging off anxieties. Let the river float them away. Let stress flow south, mix with worries and cares of others, melding with those discarded by North and South Dakotans. Worries of Minnesotans and Iowans merging.

The Platte drains to the Missouri, the Missouri joins the Mississippi. And farther south, troubled waters fraternize with eastern turbulence delivered by the Ohio. Don't fret -- the particularly sad Arkansas gets to dump its load. The concoction – a hirsute Mississippi, teaming sorrow, grief, torment. All those troubles – all those states. And *Flush* – a huge toilet, down the Louisiana sewer pipe. Despair broils brackish into the Gulf of Mexico. Then what? Does it dissipate, does despair settle to the bottom, or does grief flow out again? Picked up by the Gulf Stream, redistributed, recycled. Maybe it flows back up the coast to tetchy New York to repatriate, loops across the Atlantic, landing on gloomy old England to emigrate. Maybe some evaporates and rains right back down on my shoulders? *Nah – bullshit – sometimes it just helps to walk.*

And sometimes it doesn't. Nothing good in Jon's convolutes of gray – *out of perorations – out of pep talks.*

The tamped stretch of river trail ended. Here, another path cut up the bank and wound west into the woods. Agitations hooked left with him, no gravitas sluffed to the currents. *Hail Dale, goddamn son of a shit-sack – If I had a nickel for every…* Jon slashed a stick through low-hanging leaves. *They keep stacking the deck – I'm the Joker.*

A rutted road intersected the ending path and a left pointed him home. *Myopic consortium above – disgruntled employees below,* his stick he tossed to the woods, *Jon Poo-pon shit sandwich.* Fifteen minutes he walked in and out of canopy on the ruddy road south, and played word association, *Dale* – ***bastard*** – *Breakdowns* – ***daily*** – *Business* – ***expenses*** – *Accountant* – ***poof*** – *Employees* – ***blue*** – *Consortium* – ***greed*** – *Money* – ***grubbers*** – *Shit* – ***stack*** – *Sleep* – ***deprived*** . . . *Mass* – ***grave***. At the last curve, Jon traded road for shortcut and hiked up Smokehouse Hill.

At the summit sat the shack.

The elevated rest-stop provided a view and a minute to stow embitterment. Through failing fall leaves he could see their house more clearly than in the summer.

A stout breeze pushed uphill and puffed his hair back. Leaves swirled around the smokehouse and the late-day wind whistled on the shed's vertical boards. Directionless notes sauntered up and down the second octave below middle C.

The breeze fell off.

The rustic shed creaked.

He turned and his reflection, disjointed in four window panes, beckoned and hissed, "Hey, Joker, guess who?"

As Jon stepped closer the evening breeze rushed again and a chill passed through him. Above shake-shingled roof, the stained black chimney pipe seized an uneasy E-flat. He blinked firmly, cleared his mind, and slowly opened his eyes. The vision absolved. "Whooh," relief leaked in his exhale.

Better – one restful night – that's all he needed – one good night's sleep.

He locked eyes on the window and squinted. *Quite the trick.* It scared him. *What kind of weak-minded person could that even happen to?* Then a deeper thought numbed his knees, *the mind of a fuckin crazy person.*

A concerted exercise shoring up mental consternation; he took a minute to reflect on the physical, to feel body, heartbeat, breath, and he concentrated on strength. *I'm strong – surely the mind follows.*

His calm meter gained altitude, *what the hell was that – this isn't cartoon land . . . Hello Descartes?*

"I think therefore I am," he said aloud. Again, he slowly looked side to side. The reflection followed in silent serious serenity. Relieved, he turned and waved off the aberration.

"Harrumph, Don't try to ignore me now, Johnny Boy. We have some things to talk about, don't we? You've been riding in the back of the bus long enough, haven't ya? Come up – sit by the driver." Otherjon's spell exuded; tamping Jon's independence. Magnetic flux lines held him in orbit, and shrugging shoulders, Jon gave Mr. Reflection an apprehensive nod. *I think, therefore we are.*

Secrets needed conveying. High eyebrows twitched and Mr. Reflection said, "Now, listen up, cause I don't have all day."

Rebellious Child Jon crossed his arms. "I'm thinking, maybe you don't have anything I wanna hear."

TAh-kish – lower windowpanes cracked. With mismatched jaw-line, Mr. Reflection yelled, "SHUT UP! *Core* isn't paying you to think, and neither am I."

"Who do you think you're talking to?" For a brief moment, all eyes questioningly shifted about.

A squirrel jumped from a limb to the top of the shed and ran across. No one noticed.

Most fatherly, Mr. R continued, "Come, come, now, Johnny Boy. You know you have to stop cutting. I'm here to help. Anyway, how are we going to get anything done with that kinda attitude?"

Jon tumbled down the rabbit hole, solidifying the acquaintance.

Rigorous conversation ensued. For Jon, no verbal response required. Otherjon, animated and flamboyant, commander in chief, spouted.

Sun setting, Jon stumbled down the hill. Long shadows, he recognized. Of time spent and fractured line walked, he comprehended little.

Chapter 2
S & W

One week later

"My back hurts, I'm going to try the other bed."

"What time is it?" Jon asked.

"Almost midnight. Would you like one of my sleeping pills?"

He waved her off. It felt good to stretch across her warmed portion of the bed.

She pulled the curtains tight, blocking the inch of dissecting yard-light, then felt her way around the bed, and kissed him good night. Rebecca left him alone to sleep and snore or batter about. Battering about had become the norm.

More comfortable now – it was the flock at the plant he counted. Around 1:00 a.m. he fell asleep . . . and dreamt . . .

The game, Roulette: Russian style.

"One for the money." Jon blinked slowly. – Click! – The snap echoed. He took the Smith and Wesson from his temple, pulled the release, and dropped open the polished cylinder. He removed the lonely cartridge and inspected the lead head, a smiley face of sorts, with two small hollow points drilled off-center for eyes, and a smile scratched in the malleable metal opposite the nosey tip.

He fit the cartridge to a new chamber, and holding it with his finger, turned the gun to look in from the other side. "Good Luck," he wished it and smiled at the happy little lead head. The lead reciprocated.

A flick of the wrist and the Three-Fifty-Seven snapped to the ready. Light in the room strobed with the spin he applied to the cylinder. Clickity clickity tickity tickity tick. Jon tilted his head back. Then, taking his time, lifted the inverted tool, and fit it under his chin.

"Two for the show."

Red spray-painted a cartoonish elliptical bullseye on the white wall. The bang he didn't hear. The percussion rocked him, and he was awake.

Jon rolled out of bed and looked at the clock. It flipped to 3:33, halfway to hell, but regarding the night terror, he felt alright. He shuffled to the bathroom to splash his face. Cool – refreshing. In his hands, he cupped some and sipped – *nothin like cold country well water*, and splashed again. A white and blue-striped hand towel lay near on the vanity, and after drying, he returned it to the hanger. The towel had spotted red and he checked himself in the mirror.

A grotesque reflection met him. Damn – I've done it now. Blood ran down the side of his head – more dripped from his nose. Mr. Reflection flipped a palm up, raised an eyebrow, and said, "Whaaat?"

"I was playing."

"And a charming game of finality it was."

"I'm still dreaming, right?"

"Screaming, dreaming," Otherjon shrugged, "Try leaning."

Half full of blood, Otherjon's eyes bobbed. Jon curiously tilted his topless head side to side, and as liquid in a level, watched red pour back and forth. Cute. He pinched off the nosebleed, turned from the mirror, and removed his skivvies. In the shower, water fell like rain, and in its rising steam, he felt for an intact cranium.

Burrerrerr . . . Jon woke, slapped the clock – a small faux wood-grain job. It read 7:00 a.m. For five minutes he lay, listening to it hum, and each minute its little electric motor flipped a numerated panel behind a clear plastic window. Like most on dressers and nightstands in nineteen-eighty-nine, it had snooze. Again, he used it.

One leg at a time, like everyone else, Jon. One leg at a time. At the dresser, nauseous, head pounding, he wavered. *Hangover? No – like I blew my brains out. Only had two – Okay – who am I kidding – three – Oh yeah – one in the boathouse – four self-medicators last night.*

"Rebecca," he called, but not loud enough for her to hear. Downstairs, she worked on breakfast. It smelled like onions sautéing. *Omelets?* His stomach cramped. He needed the bathroom, and in the mirror, a recap of his fleeting nightmare flashed. His head pounded front, back, center. *Hercules! – Please – stop milking my brain.* Pink puffy eyelids and bloodshot eyes reflected in the mirror. *Aspirin.* From the medicine cabinet, he grabbed the bottle and shook out a helping. Mouth under faucet, he gulped them down.

They sat across from one another. Rebecca didn't say a thing when he pushed the half-consumed breakfast aside. She'd try harder. Better ingredients, better man. He looked peaked.

Rebecca took plates to the sink. "How'd you sleep last night?"

"Fair to middlin. How's your back?"

She ignored his question. "Nightmares?"

"Some."

"Again? What this time?"

"Can't remember. I think there was blood."

"Uhf, Jon."

Jon cruised ***Core*** *Fuels* parking lot, *gotta get this place back on track – coach up my team.* He parked up front next to the visitor slots in his spot and the sign read – Manager.

His old Impala looked good; Nebraska winters, seldom extreme, had been kind, and he'd too, been easy on it. The ashtray, open and clean, held a familiar curiosity. Jon picked out a razor blade – sharp as new and destined a loner; removed from an industrial pack of fifty. *Hello little buddy.* He slid his pant leg up and tested the edge on exposed skin. Hair shaved loose he brushed away. He cut and watched blood well in an inch slice. A drip left the incision and angled down his leg. From the glove box, he fumbled out first aid and covered it, then adjusted the rearview mirror.

Otherjon advised, "Calm down. Managers manage – plan and execute."

Jon repeated, "Manage," and finger-combed his graying hair. Mr. R did the same.

"Manage then, Captain Corn. You know they call you that?"

"I've heard em, Captain Corn, Colonel Corn, Colonel Klink. Other things, probably."

"Hapless Kernel Klink, why do you keep up this ruse? Who are you trying to impress? All this effort for those shits?"

"Must be the quarterback in me; never give up if there's still time on the clock."

Otherjon chuckled and adjusted his tie.

Jon got out. He was in his head, but not alone, and of the good September morn they were oblivious.

The thick glass plant doors were closed. Weather permitting, maintenance opened them, flipped the stops, and let fresh air in. Not this fall; August brought flies – sticky bloodsuckers. Now, in September, the hungry vamps sucked insanely.

At the door, he focused on his reflection.

Mr. R asked, "We cool?"

Jon nodded and going in, checked the time – 8:10. By twos, he counted floor tile, walked the short distance to the first doorway, and entered the offices.

"Good morning," Bernice said.

"Good morning," he said loudly for all in the room.

Drawn across the small labyrinth of low fabric-covered cubicles, his attention settled on Teri's station, and her company. Henry, visiting, rested one cheek on her desk. The intrusion – not a first – and Teri didn't look thrilled.

"Mr. Rothness, please stop pontificating with Ms. Thompson. She has work to do. I'm sure there are responsibilities in need of your expertise."

"Just giving Teri the load-out numbers for the . . ."

"Monday." Jon wasn't taking Henry's load-out of B.S.

Henry lightly rapped huge knuckles on Teri's desk to say goodbye. He gave her a smile and lifted his big frame. Jon waited. Henry ignored him as best he could and gave Bernice a surreptitious wave. Jon proceeded to his office proper in back.

Bernice's chin crinkled, she pursed her lips and cut Teri an ugly get-busy mien.

Teri looked away.

Big Bernice adjusted her plus dress for a sit. And though she spun the scale, like Henry, few women as large wore robust better. Her face didn't have a wrinkle, defied gravity, and she was pretty – when she slept. It was the mean inside, the mean she spit through her tiny teeth that made her ugly, not her looks, for nothing on her really bulged, her skin looked like a commercial, and from skirt-hem down, no cellulite. Unencumbered by size, she used her attributes well, and if you didn't know her, Bernice could love ya to death. But she dared few men and few men dared.

Never an implication that office personnel need wait on Jon, but shortly after Henry's departure, Teri entered with a cup of coffee in hand. She'd astutely prepared it as Jon preferred. Cream for color and she delivered it with her sweet smile.

He looked up from the report on his desk. "Well, thank you, Ms. Thompson."

"No, thank you, Mr. Rawling." Teri placed the cup on the coaster in front of Jon's work.

"How's it goin?"

Teri didn't want to say, 'easy'. "Smooth enough – busy."

"And with Bernice?" Jon hadn't deviated from the norm when he placed Teri under her supervision. Bernice, lead for the office staff, the sole human resource person, and now, second in command. Queen of *Core Fuels*.

"Fine." It came out opaque, but she couldn't help it.

"Good. The numbers must not be too daunting. You seem to be well in control of the ledgers."

Teri gave him another warm smile – not that there wasn't plenty to do – but if they knew how overqualified she . . . Something else had been bugging her.

Was it the time, did it matter? She threw it out, "Did you hire Ms. Bernice?"

Everyone except Teri knew the answer to the question. Jon also knew what she was asking – without asking. The real question; how did *Core* get so lucky to find a bitch like her?

"Ms. Jorgen? She was here when I started."

"Oh," Teri said in high tone. Mesmerized, she paused and felt a sweep of relief. It had been a question gnawing at her soul, she should've known. "Okay, thanks again, with Henry – I'm gonna get back to it."

"Ms. Thompson, would you remind Bernice that I'll be out this afternoon?"

"Will do." She turned her little tail and left.

Chapter 3

On the Green

Tee-time, 2:00 p.m., and at twenty of, Jon entered the clubhouse.

"Good afternoon, Mr. Rawling."

"Monroe." Jon reached across the counter and shook the young man's hand.

Manny Monroe – the closest thing to a golf-pro at *Prairie Rose Public.* The 23-year-old didn't look the part; stout, big around the middle, large undefined upper arms. But when it came to golf, Manny carried a big stick.

"You gonna compete today?"

"I don't know." Jon gave him a wink. "You know how it is."

Manny smiled. "Do I?"

"Aw, it's so nice out. I don't think I should upset their rickety cart of apples. Maybe down the road a-tish."

"So it's politics? Do those guys really shoot eighties?"

Jon turned. "I'm sure you've watched em tee off a few times." He looked to the number one tee box. "Whatta you think?"

"Mm, Michael, maybe."

"Yeah, he's good enough." Maybe on a good day Mick the Prick could match him – but one of these days – one of these god-damn days . . . before age caught up, he'd kick his ass – with the rest.

"Don't you ever look at the stat board and you're shooting way up in the nineties?" Manny smiled, shaking his head.

Jon strolled to the handicap board and looked at the recorded scores. "About right. Has Lon been writing em down?"

"I think it was Lon, sometimes Michael, maybe."

"You done with college?"

"I wish. No, I head to Lincoln for Chiropractic, next."

"Gonna be a back-crackin Cornhusker, eh?"

"Ha, guess so."

"And you gonna golf at Lincoln?"

He laughed. "I remember last year, when you invited me to play a round, you outshot me. I think if middle-aged guys are beating up on me, it might be time to set aside dreams of golf grandeur."

"Middle-aged? Well, thanks, a bit past, but isn't that the beauty of golf, you can play well later into life? And I don't think I really won that round. If I remember correctly, you gave me a couple mulligans. You're good, Monroe, I think I'd stick with it if I were you."

"Thanks, Mr. Rawling. I'll have to think on it. Those classes won't be easy, not sure if I can afford the time, and who says I'd even make the team?" Manny pointed to the parking lot. "Looks like your competition's arrived."

Michael, in a new Corvette, followed close behind Larry's Wagoneer. Lon sat in Larry's passenger seat, riding shotgun in the amenity-filled Jeep. He looked past the recently removed window sticker's tape-line and, in the side mirror, watched Michael find a safe parking spot.

"How's the remodeling going?" Larry asked.

"Alright. It wouldn't hurt for the corn price to drop back down," said Lon.

"We can't control corn prices, but Jon'll squeeze it outta *Core*."

"Kristy's talkin new pool."

"You've got a pool."

"I guess we need a bigger one."

"Janie's not even a swimmer."

"Doesn't mean she won't be needing a pool, though, does it?"

Michael parked the Vette and walked to the Wagoneer to meet the men and his clubs.

"Hey Mick, how's the Vette?" Larry asked, opening the back of the Wagoneer.

"One-forty like a damn."

"That's movin." Larry slid Michael his clubs. The old guys sat on the end gate and changed shoes. Michael strapped his clubs to a pull cart.

Lon said, "You wreck this one, Kid, you're walkin."

Chapter 4
Side Job

The truck driver checked his watch. "Right on the nuts." He looked back to the battered two-lane blacktop, swerved, and straddled a pothole. The bulk truck found another. *Wham.* "Jesus!" The jolt knocked a lengthy ash from his cigarette. He brushed it from his lap. Another drag, and he mashed his fag in the ashtray.

He grabbed another gear and rolled south on *Core Fuels'* mile-long service road. The weaving and swearing continued as he dodged last spring's frost boils and summer's newly-formed mini-craters. Not all could be avoided; the truck's alignment took some hits.

In the plant, Malcolm cleaned sinks in the men's room next to the offices.

Bernice cornered the lackey. "Are you watching the clock?"

"Oh, yeah, I was gittin there now." He'd been watching the clock all right, but hey, what's five or ten minutes? He didn't say that aloud, he didn't dare; Bernice wasn't one to argue with. It was an easy task, actually, a job that needed doing anyway, and he was becoming quite comfortable with the crisp Jackson he found in his locker every Friday.

"Well, get movin. I've told you to be punctual. If you can't keep an eye on your watch, I'll make sure Bobby knows how much you'd like to clean the pit. Or better yet, scrub down that nasty bathroom out back. Now, remember what I told you?"

"Keep em off and keep em out. No one leaves tracks on my wet floor," Malcolm recited.

Bernice continued to prompt. "What do you tell them if they still want to pass?"

"Waxin; ya gotta stay off."

"And you show them what?"

"The bottle of wax . . ."

"That you . . . ?"

"Set on top of my cart."

"And last but not least . . ."

"West door stays shut. I don't open the door, go outside, or let fresh air in or anything. Just guard my floor."

"Right, you're not as slow as you look. I think I see another fiver in your future – if you can be punctual. Now hop along. I'll have Bobby or Henry come by and inspect to see how it looks, then ya can go on break, not before, right?"

"Yes, Ms. Jorgen, just like always."

And always, it was Henry that stopped by and gave him the dismissal. Johnson could see Henry and Bernice were kinda chummy. He figured it a platonic relationship. Frequently together, they looked affable, but not in an affectionate way. And he was a little grossed out thinking of them doing – doing something.

The truck passed a laden and leaning signpost, DOCKING AREA AHEAD. Under that, a smaller horizontal sign announced, FLAMMABLES, and lower still, a third, NO SMOKING! Through a freshly washed windshield, the driver surveyed the plant, fidgeted in the truck's worn seat, and inhaled its fresh blue and white paint job. *Core Fuels* loomed ahead, large and dark, the north side shaded from the tilting September sun. A small industrial water tower stood at the compound's southwest corner. A row of silos on steroids lined the northeast side. Behind them, and extending west, sprawled the main structure with two gray stacks towering skyward, steam and smoke billowing. Ethanol, *fabricatio exquisitus.*

Malcolm Johnson left the office restrooms; *I wish her well – I wish her in a well.* Bernice's little job was across the plant. He walked with a hitch, pushing his cleaning cart as the left front wheel oscillated a speed wobble. Occasionally, shoving off with his good leg, he stepped up, copping a short ride. Malcolm, on cart, rolled by the hammer mill. He peered in. Gene, the foreman, was giving someone the What-For. None of his business, but he got the gist. "How many times do I have to tell ya? Look here, you're gonna get hurt or you're gonna get someone else hurt. Now you've been here how many months and…"

Malcolm trundled west and hummed a blue tune of his own making. An odd duck, Johnson didn't have any friends at the plant. He didn't have any friends out of the plant, either. He hung a right and headed north up an open corridor formed by milling equipment on the right and fermentation, with its massive vats, on the left.

He kept the cart rolling, staying close to the blue tapeline at the walkway's edge. Malcolm stopped humming.

Bryce in Malting heard the rattle of Johnson's approaching cart. To Mark, the area lead, he said, "Here comes Mop Man Malcolm again."

"Give it a rest, he's just doin his job."

"I hate him. Look at the little beady-eyed weasel."

There was plenty of sitting around time in fermentation; Bryce had time to hate a lot of things.

"Hey Mop Man. How's it hangin?" Bryce chided as Malcolm passed.

Malcolm kept his gaze low and hugged the line, cravenly limping by as far from Bryce as possible.

Bryce looked to Mark, rolled his eyes back in his head, stuck his tongue half out, and launched his acting career; a full-on dramatization – 'Mop Man' humping his cleaning cart.

Mark shook his head, a most unprofessional laugh escaped. "You're cracked."

Malcolm took three, CAUTION – WET FLOOR, signs from the

cart bracket and evenly spaced them across the entrance of the west hallway. He set the orange Willie's Wax bottle on top of the cart and unloaded his metal mop bucket.

A shudder passed through the bulk truck's entirety as it traversed the railroad spur line. It looped in the lot, pulled to the dock, and stopped, air-brakes hissing. Henry stood on the deck, thick black fuel hose snaked over his shoulder. The driver dismounted, leaned against the freshly painted blue fender, pulled a pack of Winstons from his shirt pocket, and lit up.

Again, Henry scanned the area, then climbed down and attached the brass nozzle to a receptacle on the fuel truck. "What's up, Bud?"

He didn't know the driver's name and the driver didn't know Henry's, exactly as Bernice wanted.

"Nothing much, just enjoying the hell out of this beautiful afternoon. How's about you?"

Henry took another look around. "Same."

The men stood in silence and watched gallons click the meter under the deck's corrugated metal awning.

Front Nine – sixth hole at *Prairie Rose Public.*

"Jesus H Christopher Columbus! You couldn't discover the fuck'n green from a hundred yards out, you hopeless son of a Bee-otch." Larry's temper took hold, big time. He felt scalp tingling and sank his nine iron into the fairway.

Nothing others in the group didn't have the urge to do from time to time, but Larry, with lax control, would let-er-blow.

Jon raised an eyebrow. *So much for a Gentleman's game.*

Larry's angry red face went well with his end-of-summer, sunbaked, pink, skinhead. Wound tight, he could explode in board meetings, most everywhere else, but especially on the links. Larry, a steaming pile of emotional dung, flung it from a slop bucket, splashing everyone with verbal manure.

The seventh – a short par 4.

Time to school these dolts. I'm putting this one on the green – right from the t-box. Jon had done it, numerous times, but never in present company. An aggressive backswing and he uncorked, keeping head down. He pivoted, spine shifting. Something unhinged. The club duffed ground, sending the white *Titleist* straight out, but a weak 80 yards. Jon slid the shaft behind his waist, inhaled, and with the one-wood, pushed hips forward. He blew, "Whoooh."

Larry grinned. "Almost a dick-out, huh Jon?

Mick said, "Lordy, Lordy, look who's waaay past forty."

Jon replied, "Your time's coming, Mick," which he left for Michael to interpret however he wanted.

Michael's dad, Lon Peck, rounded out today's party, but all owners in the consortium took turns going on the monthly outings, cajoling Jon. Lon walked one loose, took respite at the seventh-hole facilities, and returned. He approached, pointing over his shoulder, and with a big dopey grin, said, "If anyone else wants to use the pooper, I gotta' say, better give it a couple'a minutes. I didn't peel the paint off the walls, but pretty sure I softened it up."

"NICE … DAD," Mick said.

Larry said, "Well Lon, your tee, try not to stink it up, eh Buddy."

Lon bent down, and with a blast of gas, teed up a shiny new *Pinnacle.* Same dopey grin. "Guess one got stuck."

Larry recovered from his tantrum on the sixth, and having a good round, golfed the seventh and eighth well. Jon, with back out of sorts, decided today wouldn't be 'his day'.

It was time for Lon and Larry to start in. It would be butthead training for Mick. Consortium members knew the song when it came to working Jon over. Now is when it got interesting. A *pas de chata* with a *pirouette* for Jon. What a pleasure, dancing for the owners.

"Had some downtime, we heard. Maintenance not able to keep up?"

Larry asked. He didn't like brown people. The rest of the consortium was okay with brown if they made green.

"Lots of moving parts, Bobby keeps up." Jon knew where they got their info. *Bernice's unmitigated floodgate.* The next board meeting was looking u-ug-ly. A long expense column and ledgers don't lie, usually.

"Some hefty repair costs on the books last quarter, too. Maybe your little Mexican could fix a thing or two. Seems exorbitant to replace every little thing that fucks up."

"Bobby saves us a lot. Things wear out. We're lucky to have him." *Damn lucky to find a guy that can change out shitty second-rate parts your cheap-ass contractors built the place with.*

"Those are some nasty-looking clouds," Lon said.

A black sky, creeping over the tree-line and distant rumbles hinted of things to come.

The ninth hole ended near the clubhouse. Monroe yelled from the Pro-Shop door, "Storms comin!"

"How about a rain check on the back nine, guys?" Lon said.

Larry said, "Soon, though, I don't want you guys forget'n who's kicking your asses. Monday?"

Jon and his back were afforded a reprieve, but the dry ground was not. The storm had some bark but rumbled on past. Another bust for thirsty fall soil.

Rebecca watched the news and weather with Jon, but when sports came on, she went up to read. After, he too went upstairs and readied for bed.

"No rain in the forecast," he said.

Rebecca closed her book. "Saw that. We could use a shot."

"I know, been good for the harvest, though, farmers are rolling in with product."

"My canning's going good. Eight quarts of pickles."

"You're a pro." Jon joined her in bed.

Rebecca placed her book on the nightstand and turned off the lamp.

"The river's getting a little low. We should take the boat for a cruise tomorrow evening."

"Okay." Rebecca put her leg over Jon's. She fell asleep.

Again, sleep wouldn't come for Jon. *Pushy prejudice pricks.* At one in the morning, he got up for a drink of water. *Sick of golfing with those whizzers – yo-yos.* At three he slipped downstairs and tried the recliner. *Sucking the life out of Core – Sucking the life out of me.* Four a.m. he returned to their bed and tossed a short while longer. Sleep came – and a dark dream – *Culinary Delight.*

St. Mary's Church construction included a two-story Sunday-school wing. *Jon stood on the second floor. He peered down the hall, past open and closed classroom doors. 'Hide!' 'Where?'*

'Something – someone – below – behind? It's coming – It's hungry.'

A stairway at the end of the hall and Jon ran the other way, looking over his shoulder. 'It's coming – up – for me – a pack – a swarm.'

In a small windowless classroom, perfect for delivering Bible lessons, he crouched behind a low wooden table. 'Too big – I'm too big.' He prostrated. 'Bad idea – Hard to run laying down.' He moved behind the door. 'No – they'll smell me? – My blood? – They smell blood!'

'Go!'

'Hide!'

Down the hall and to another door, and the plaque on it read: Storage. He opened it and stepped in. 'It smells like shit in here.' Jon looked down. Dim yellow light from dusty hallway bulb illuminated an underfoot topography, a piled carpet of floor guano. Eyes adjusting, he looked up, peering into his cast shadow. Stalactites. Bodies hanging. Un-dead night creatures. Michael at the fore hung by curled feet, claws deep in plaster ceiling. Close, a bad breath away, and Jon took a slow step back. The light passed over his shoulder, moved down the body and fell on Mick's face. Michael's eyelids dropped; yellow bloodshot rings surrounded gaping black pupils. Others opened their thirsty eyes.

Michael unfolded his arms and reached wide. He smiled, fangs up. "Look Ma, no hands!"

Jon stepped back, stumbling into the hall.

Mick dropped, easily landing erect. The hanging mates followed his lead.

A gray-faced family emerged from the stairwell. The man in front, another Core Fuels owner, stopped and stood silent. A thin child moved from behind and slipped under her father's arm. She pulled at his sleeve. "Can I go first?" Fangs exposed and white as a new stove, she asked again, "May I go first?"

The father calmly brushed her hair back. He didn't answer, but addressed Jon instead, "We've come for you, Rawling."

Jon shot across the hall, what's behind door number two? He flung it open – slammed it behind him.

Class in session. Enthused young ones sat at the table in little wooden chairs. Larry had their attention, and held a pointer in one hand, a remote in the other. On the table lay Timmy the Victim, St. Mary's very own blood dummy.

"Children, we have a guest, so please, manners," Larry said. "Jon, Jon, Jon, they're learning so fast. Watch."

Jon backed himself into the corner next to the door. The children's pupils, like Mick's and Larry's, were gaping and black. Unlike the adults, the rings around theirs' were clean white, matching nubbin fangs.

Larry pressed the remote. Timmy the dummy's eyes bulged. Timmy's mouth popped open. Timmy emitted a low-fidelity scream.

"He's scaret, he's scaret," laughed a seven-year-old. Others laughed, too.

"Make him do it again," a little girl demanded.

"Make him do it again – PLEASE," Larry said.

"Please, please," the youngsters rallied.

Larry pressed the remote, again Timmy's eyes pushed outward and the dummy barked.

The children roared.

Larry let them have their moment, then tapped his pointer on Timmy's neck. He aimed the remote, pressed another button. A pump started and sounded from deep in Timmy's chest. A jitter passed through the rubber figurine. Pressure surged, circulating rub-a-dub-dummy's red plasma. Wrist and forearm veins expanded. Pressure unfolded Timmy's arms a smidge.

"Ohoo," a young one cooed.

Timmy's neck expanded and the veins in it stretched, pulsating with the flow. 'Whurrr-err-err-err.' Under pressure, Timmy's heart pump groaned palpitations.

Giddy children laughed and drooled and clapped and drooled and drooled.

A short boy, the youngest, stood, folded at the waist, bending to Timmy. He bit hard. Sharp nubbins pierced the dummy's pulsating wrist. Blood squirted from the wound, spraying his nearest classmates.

They laughed and licked at the spray.

It was Larry's turn to chuckle. "So cute at this age, wouldn't you agree? Ya know what I think? They need some hands-on training. How about it, Jon? And don't tell me you gave at the office."

Larry pressed the remote again.

'My heart,' Jon felt it race. 'My neck,' arteries bulged.

The children quieted, sensing something better – something real – real tasty. They turned, some eyes opened wide, others squinted. Some rolled clenched fists in anticipation. Others showed virgin fangs behind taut smiles, and some, sniffing, twitched sensitive little noses.

Larry turned a knob at the top of the hand-held controller. PSI rose and Jon's eyes bulged, neck veins strained – firehoses of blood ready to burst. He covered the pulsating pipes from youngsters' lust.

The door opened – adults grabbed him.

"Help! Help! Rebecca, someone, Help Me!" Owners lifted Jon on their shoulders and carried him down the hall to the stairs. Children, chins up, noses twitching, trailed behind. The procession descended the stairway and entered the sanctuary near the altar.

Grandma Falkher waited their arrival. "Put him here." She patted the destination.

Michael, Larry, and other Owners stretched Jon out on the marble slab. A groove cut around the border drained into a relief at the end of the altar. Near the altar's base, a mid-scream frozen face directed flow to cascade off a suspended tongue into a basin. The hopeful children gathered, fingers clutching rim.

"Ladies first," the Matriarch said.

Her daughters and ladies-in-law took to securing Jon, holding him by the limbs, teaming up on his legs. The stalwart men stepped back to watch.

Jon struggled. "Let go! I'm sure we can come to some arrangement!"

"Arrangements have been made," Grandma said and pointed.

Near the lectern, Lon held Rebecca from behind, and he sucked – deep in a meal. Rebecca reached overhead, pulling him tighter to her neck. He pulled at her hair. She moaned small ecstasies. Lon sucked harder – Rebecca held fast. Aged wrinkles deepened on her face and she pressed her other hand firm, low at the front of her skirt. Lon slid his hand down her arm and pressed atop her fingers. She inhaled, and inhaled. Through her, orgasms quaked.

"I haven't been to the Well for a while." Grandma used the back of her hand, dragging ashen fingernails across Jon's neck.

"Drink him, Dinette," said the daughter-in-law. "We've got him."

"Sorry, Jon, we're thirsty. I'm afraid we'll have to suck you dry. Dry, my sweet boy, oh so dry. Humph-ha-ha-ha." Her slight shoulders wiggled as she chuckled.

Jon heaved, jerked, and tried to kick.

Grandma Dinette slid a hand behind Jon's neck. "Hold him tight, he's a little bucky."

In a panic twist, Jon freed an arm. Liberated fist met Grandma Dinette's wrinkled nose.

Jon yelled, "Whack-O!"

'Crack'. The punch flattened Dinette's antediluvian beak and sent the twanky old witch sprawling. Her girls tried to catch her and Jon wrestled free. He stood on the altar. Delivered with precision, a stomp kick landed most squarely to a Falkher lady's face. "Aaaaha." She framed her facade and crashed into the men.

A two-step launch and Jon leaped Mick. He ran the aisle, sprinting free toward the door. He turned, looked. The brood roared laughter. Larry called, "Aren't you going to say goodbye to your girlfriend?" Lon let spent Rebecca slip to the floor.

Jon burst out the church doors, extricating himself into the sun's bright salvation.

Light burst into the bedroom and the sound of the opening shades stirred him.

Rebecca said, "Time to wake up, Whack-O."

"Whack-O?" Jon mumbled.

"I could hear you yelling all the way from downstairs."

Chapter 5

Rings and Things

Late Thursday afternoon, Teri laid on the horn, Whaank, Wha-whaank.

Leia scampered down apartment stairs and flung open the door. "I'm coming."

Parked across the street, Teri leaned out of her Camaro window, shielded her eyes from late day sun. "Drink specials end at six."

"We've got time." Leia skipped down the short walk, putting on a shoe. The lawn, short cut, looked crunchy, smelled dry, not fresh like in summer. Warm air, trending cooler, breezed, tumbling leaves to the curb.

Teri checked her makeup. Leia circled and got in.

"Let's go," Leia said, and they exchanged a high ten. She turned up Teri's radio. One of their favorites played, *Girls Just Want to Have Fun.*

Together, the girls sang with Cyndi. Both slightly off-key; the two wrongs almost made it right.

"*Cold Spot*?" Teri asked.

"Sh-yeah."

Teri pulled into *Cold Spot's* congested lot. "Looks busy."

"Ten to six, see, still happy hour."

"And ten-to-one everyone will have left by seven."

A familiar black Jeep Wrangler sat in the row on the side of the establishment. Teri noticed, *Doodie doodie do, don't say a thing. She can suck it up*.

The girls budged in along the bar-maids' station. "Holy busy," Leia said. A sign mounted above on the decorative awning read:

Cold Spot
Your
Libation Station

The bartender placed his hands on the bar across from the ladies and leaned.

Leia said, "I'm looking for libations, two PBRs, Dave."

One hand already in the cooler, digging for red, white and blue. He asked, "And what can I get Teri, whisky-Diet-Coke?" The girls weren't strangers at *Cold Spot.*

"Better make it two, time's-a-tickin." Teri spotted the Wrangler owner's *Stetson* topping a booth in back and took a position, blocking Leia's view best she could. Seats up front looked well separate – *those should do.*

"Let's sit," Teri suggested, leading her comrade to the tables near the front. High windows illuminated the otherwise shadowy bar. The sun's rays amplified the smoky ambiance and light penetrated wafting wisps. The amber-gold shafts reached the floor, exposing *Cold Spot's* stained and dated mauve carpet.

"Hi Teri," said Bryce, her *Core Fuels* co-worker. He sat with another man who also looked to be early thirties. "Come sit with us."

Teri looked to Leia for approval, but it wasn't much of a question. Guys buy girls drinks, and usually, that's a good thing. *They look tolerable?*

"Bryce, right?" She knew him from timecards and payroll, but they hadn't conversed other than, 'hi' or 'good morning' in passing.

"Right. And this is my friend, Orrin."

"Hi Orrin, I'm Teri, this is Leia."

"Hi."

Orrin half stood and slid two chairs to accommodating positions. "Pull up a seat, ladies. You guys work with Bryce?" His focus shifted to

Bryce as the girls piled their happy-hour drinks on the table. Both men thought the same. *Lucky night.*

Teri said, "Just me. Leia works at *Seed Genetics.*"

"Isn't that where you used to work?" Bryce asked.

"Used to, but I left Leia to hold down the fort." *He's been asking around about me.* She felt mildly flattered.

Cold Spot's coolers were cold, but cans of PBR warm quickly. Leia finished her first beer and traded it for the full one.

"Here's to Leia – holding 'er down at *Seed Genetics,*" Orrin toasted, lifting his half-full mug to meet Leia's. Teri and Bryce joined the salute. The guys were cracking the ice.

Teri missed it. Leia didn't, *nice white circle around Orrin's ring finger – ass-hole. Try to be nice – Leia plays well with others,* and said, "To *Seed Genetics*, eh?"

"Eh," Bryce repeated.

"Eh," Orrin repeated.

"Eh, aren't you a long way from Canada?" Bryce chided.

Leia thought, *Stupid . . . don't say that. Eh! Eh! Eh!*

"Her mom's from Canada," Teri defended.

"Your daddy couldn't find any nice American girls?" Bryce asked.

"Hello, Canada is America . . . North America, duh!" Leia said.

The guys, keeping it playful, were all smiles.

Time to change the subject. "So, how long you been at Corny, now?" Bryce asked Teri.

"Oh, almost four months."

"A couple more months and you get your first review."

"And health insurance." Teri finished her half-off well and lit a *Virginia Slim.*

The barmaid passed close; Orrin made eye contact and circled his finger for another round.

Bryce continued, "Right, if the place hasn't gone belly-up by then. Won't be any raise, either. Captain Corn has everyone on wage freeze. Is Bernice your boss, or the Captain?"

"Bernice, but my reports go to Mr. Rawling."

Leia's eyes narrowed; she took a pull off her PBR.

"Oh, ha, I don't envy you, up there with the snakes," Bryce said.

"I thought *Core Fuels* was the best place to work in the whole county," Leia said.

"Corny? Ho, Ho, Ho, we haven't had a Christmas bonus in two years. The place is rotting from the inside out. If we're lucky, somebody with a clue'll buy us out."

Leia had had about enough, but pressed further, "Doesn't sound like you're too fond of management?" and with the question gave Teri a quick glance.

"Can't stand the two-faced brass-tards. Bernice has her little cadre, but as for the Kernel? Nope, nobody outs theres haves any love loss for that A-hole. And, we've had about all the pep talks and promiseses we can take." Bryce had started early; speech command starting to slip.

Talk, cheaper by the drink, and Teri dug another hole. "How did Bernice end up at *Core*?" She took a deep drag on her *Slim* and waited for the answer.

"You should ask her."

"Not me. No way." She shook her head and spoke as she blew. Smoke, expelled in breathy spurts, swirled in intersecting light.

"She's been there from day one, a niece of the Falkher's, you know . . . the owners, well, some of the owners, anyway. She's from money, but not – 'in' – the money," Bryce added air quotes for emphasis. "Know what I mean?" – She didn't.

"Aren't you a wealth of information? How ya know all this?"

"Stick around sweeeetheart, you'll be privy to all of Corny's dirty little secrettis . . . *Buh-hurrrt.*" Bryce squelched a belch.

Leia was full. "I need to use the ladies' room."

Teri, too, had noticed Orrin's missing ring and found Bryce, informative, but . . . *just another smart ass 'boy' – shouldn't be allowed to partake – If you can't handle your booze – give it up – or stay on the porch. No wonder I'm not married.*

Orrin's round of drinks arrived but good times weren't about to roll.

Teri crushed out her cigarette. "I'm going to join," she stood, "Ms. Rawling."

Jon's boat floated over lowered lift, bobbing in the river beside the dock. He reached to help Rebecca aboard. She placed a foot on the gunwale and stepped. The boat heeled. And balance lost, Rebecca teetered. Jon grabbed her wrist, drawing her harshly onto the craft.

"Whew!" she said. "Close one."

"I got ya." Jon stabilized her; one arm around her waist and she slid down his front.

"I almost went for a swim."

"Ker-splat in the Platte." Jon repeated their twenty years on the river family axiom. He loosened his embrace.

"Mm, my hero," she kidded, holding his arm around her, and waited. She wanted a kiss and would use the excuse. Jon obliged.

How about a little enthusiasm? She thought, longing for sparks that had become few and far between.

I care – of course, I do – this distance –why can't I get past it? Jon looked in the convex mirror mounted in the windscreen's crux. Rebecca was making herself comfortable on the cushioned bench astern. Otherjon at the edge of the panorama, raised an eyebrow, about to say something.

Don't answer that.

"But, you know what we could do, if you . . ." Jon cut him off.

"Zip it!"

"What was that, Hon?" Rebecca said.

"How about we zip down around the island and back?" *Boat'll be fine – just fine – she's running perfect.* They usually went north – upriver in the evenings, just in case. Easier to get your ass home with the current if the classic conked out.

"South? Yeah, sounds like a plan." She could care less. To be with Jon, that's all she wanted. Floating on a rock in a lava flow would do if they were together.

Jon idled *Baby Cakes* in reverse to the center of the river. "What an evening. Suppose we won't get many more of these. I'm not looking forward to pulling her out."

"Where has summer gone?"

Throttle, reverse to neutral, and Jon let current swing the bow around, then bumped it to engage.

"The colors are spectacular. We should take Leia out this weekend."

"Hmm, she coming home again this weekend?" Jon palmed the lever ahead, nudged it again, bringing the RPMs up a grand.

Rebecca reached overboard and let her fingers drag the swirling water. "I guess so. No man."

"No hurry, is it? Only twenty-four."

Rebecca scooped at fallen leaves on the water. "Twenty-six," she said and thought of baby lost and said no more. For all her effort, Leia could keep little from a mother's prying ear.

Teri hoped to catch Leia before she spotted the Stetson in back. I should've at least warned her. Teri didn't need to pee, but . . . somebody's going to need moral support in about five seconds.

The line for the Ladies' Room spilled out into the bar. The girls merged uncomfortably close to the booth with the *Stetson*, and the man under the hat.

Leia locked eyes with Teri.

Teri spoke first. "Yeah, I see em."

Reserved, yet loud enough, Leia said, "*Cold Spot's* full of pricks tonight."

Jason in the hat sat all married up with his petite Cowgirl. Across, sat his brother, with another, this one not so pretty, not so petite.

They look a little too comfortable, a little too smug. Stir the pot. "Hi Pete," Teri said.

Pete made glancing eye contact and with a low-key wave acknowledged her existence. His big blue-eyed heifer shifted closer, sliding in tight across the red vinyl whoopie-cushion. She stared attractive Teri a new one.

Teri never loved Pete. Teri didn't hate Pete. He had been a date of convenience, more or less for Leia's sake. The rodeos had been fun.

Teri laughed silently at the protective bovine. *Never gave two licks about Cowboy – never licked him once, actually.* The line moved and the girls advanced past the tall booth and near the bathroom door.

Leia paid little attention to Pete and his gal, she was all in on Jason's high-maintenance bride. "Holy shit, did you see her diamond? If any sunlight gets back here and touches that rock we'll all be lasered to pieces."

Teri nodded, confirming she hadn't missed it, then lobbed a grenade back at the booth, "Hey Pete, remember the last time you and I were in this bathroom?"

Checkmate. No reply.

The girls went in.

"Fucking Jason! As soon as I pee I want outta here," mercurial Leia said.

"Yeah, absolutely, no men here." *Why is it always about men?*

"*Cold Spot* sucks tonight. Take me home, I'm not sharing Hot Shot's air."

"Forget him." *Role reversal night? – I'm the one that's supposed to be high-strung.*

What was said in the booth while the girls were in the ladies' room, they couldn't know.

Another gal exited, Leia looked out the swinging door. The tall booth hid the occupants but she imagined them all cozied up. After their break-up and her breakdown she had found solace in Joe Jackson's ditty, *Happy Loving Couples,* and it now struck her, she had no friends in that booth.

Teri, washing, said, "When we leave, don't even look at him."

"I'm not saying a word."

And as they approached the booth, she tried not to look.

Mrs. Petite sat tapping her middle finger on the table, her left middle finger, and with the giant diamond riding the finger next to it. Distracted, Leia slowed. She looked. Jason reached to cover his Mrs.'s hand. She wasn't having it and rotated the bird skyward, then extended her arm, placing the finger fancy as close to the passing girls as she could. Jason pressed his hand on her arm. Cowgirl wasn't done: she lowered the middle finger, made a fist, then raised her ring finger, the real eff you. The big laser caught bar-light and flashed Leia. It seared her heart.

She ran for the door.

Teri stopped, *I'm snapping that little bitch's finger off!* She didn't, but returned the gesture, flipping the party her own circling bird.

Twenty quiet minutes on the Platte and the Rawlings rounded the island. They turned northward and south breeze pushed engine exhaust back at the stern. Jon didn't mind but ran the RPMs up to keep ahead of it for Rebecca's sake. The low sun glinted off the water in steps as the boat passed through the west bank's cottonwood shadows. It would soon be dusk.

*I'm with him – but – where is h*e? Rebecca thought.

Jon kept *Baby Cakes* in the middle where there wasn't much to navigate. Mentally, he let go and tuned in on other things.

Myopic consortium above – Angry. Disgruntled employees below – Angry. Take a bite, Jon. Right here. Take a bite out of your shit sandwich! Mm-mm good. Take another. Out of the middle – Tastes like . . . no Christmas bonuses at Core, eh? Chomp chomp. What's that? A McMansion makeover? Mm-mm, creamy – plant breakdowns, a repair budget? Ha ha ha, but Naa. Try this instead, a bite of greasy shit – Mm-num-num – here, have another – shitty, huh? Three years – no raises for my boys and girls at Core. Tasty poop? What else for my team? Walking papers – Benefit cuts. Full yet? Swallow. And for the owners? Remodels. Vacations. Country clubs. 'Show us the money, Jon.'

"What you thinking about over there?"

"Ah, not much, zoning."

"Jon, come on, talk to me."

"Things aren't going that great at *Core,* right now."

"They aren't?" Rebecca didn't get out much, but rumors run.

"And stewing about Michael a bit." Rarely would he talk shop with Rebecca. Why should he, his friend in the mirror had the answers, but this played into their lives together. Longer-term. About retirement, pulling the plug at some point.

"Lon's boy? Why?" Rebecca knew the consortium heads and most of the families. "What about him? Isn't he, like, twenty-five? What's he got to do with anything? He isn't on the board is he?"

"Here's the deal. Owners don't think I'd quit on em, and before you get your panties in a loop, don't worry, I'm not quitting."

Rebecca sat up. *He never shares.*

"They see our white picket fence, our home on the river, your big garden. The boat. We're not going anywhere, right? They know the economy's not so hot, too. So they push and they push and they don't know what the hell they're doing. I could fold em, we have a good bit squirreled away. Another chunk when they settle your dad's estate . . . "

"A little bit, maybe."

"And what do we spend? Jack. You with the canning jars – a subscription to *Mother Earth News*. I've spent a bit on the boats."

Rebecca smiled. "Bring On Another Thousand."

"Yeah, once in a while, but really mostly just sweat equity.

"So, you're thinking about it . . . you kinda wanna quit?"

Jon paused. "No." He shook his head and turned a hand up. "Not yet. Owe it to my guys – and gals – to see it through. I'm not giving up, there's time on the clock – I wanna turn it around for them."

"Still team captain, eh? So what does this have to do with Michael?"

"He's done with school and I can see what's up. They're grooming him, to put him at my desk – keep it a family affair."

"He's so young."

"And, oh boy, he's got a mouth!"

"Sounds like real leadership material."

"I know. He acts like he wants to run it now, and not only is he not ready, never will be. Total butt-head. Mick the Prick. First time I met em, wanted to pull the silver spoon out of his mouth and stick it up the brat's ass." With a free hand, Jon jabbed upward. "If he gets in there, it'll go right down the flusher. Another pile'a people on unemployment."

Rebecca crossed the deck and rubbed his back. "If I know Jon Rawling, he'll have it running smooth in no time."

Teri caught Leia in the parking lot. In sync, they slammed Camaro doors.

Tears welled in Leia's eyes and Teri leaned across the console to console. Cohesion let loose; salty drops rolled down Leia's cheeks.

"You okay?"

"I'm over him."

Obviously not, "You know what I did with Pete in the bathroom?"

Hope it wasn't . . . "Uh-uh?" It came out broken with a hard swallow. "What?"

"Held Cowboy's hat while he was on his knees, puking. A little boy, hanging onto the toilet, retching his guts in the girl's bathroom."

Leia tried to laugh but wasn't ready to let go, *Teri doesn't need this – I'm so stupid.* "You're the best."

"It's not just Jason is it?"

Leia hugged tighter and shook her head.

"The baby?"

Leia sniffled, inhaled fully, and hugged tighter still. Her inhale whimpered out and broke into an airy sob.

"Go on, let it out." *Again. Have to find this girl a distraction. Someone kind – for a change.*

"He didn't even know I was . . . Dropped me like an obsolete kitchen gadget. Already on to his next infatuation, it wasn't that one in there, either."

"I know. You've broke some hearts too, though."

"You saw it comin, didn't you?"

"Maybe . . . your head was kind of up in the clouds. I didn't want to say it, just hoped and prayed it'd work out for ya. But, Hot Shot – self-proclaimed god's gift to women – has a Mrs., now, and it looks like Pete found a winner."

Her crying mellowed. "Roped himself a whopper," she said in a sniffling laugh and tried to sleeve-dry her leaking eyes. "Not an ice cube's chance in hell Jason and I would end up together, was there? All those dolled-up cowgirls, little whores, flinging themselves at him. Wasn't I the silly one with blinders on? All for Hot Shot. And a cowboy at that. I don't even like horses."

"You don't like horses?"

Leia shook her head and did laugh.

"Not fond of the saying, but like my Grandma says, 'you're footloose and fancy-free. Got your whole life ahead of you.' Let's let the cowboys ride into the sunset."

Leia gave her a small nod. *How? – Losing a baby sticks with you – Weighs.* She paused. "I like that your grandma-ma doesn't ride you about finding a man like our moms do."

"Nobody here is desperate. We've learned some lessons, and who knows, Mr. Right might be right around the corner. We'll have babies someday, when we're good and ready, right? We'll have girls and it'll be fun and they'll grow up sweet and be best friends."

"Girls want to have fun." *I'm not much fun.*

"Just fun." *Take her home.*

Chapter 6
Pulp – No Jail for Dale

Friday, Harrison stepped into the office. He wasn't enthused.

The Boss's secretary brushed past on her way out. "Hi, Ellen," he said. She gave him a woeful look, her *dog in the street, about to be run over,* look. Ellen closed the door behind her, shutting him in.

The burnt-down cigar smell punched him in the nose. Everything in the room smelled of it, including the Boss, loving on his *King Edward.*

Cigars weren't Detective Harrison's thing, and the blue haze bothered him. He looked out the window. With better news, he might have gone over and opened it.

"Grab a seat, Harrison. Where we at on the *Core Fuels* deal?"

"Chief, we got a Sum-of-a-bitch, clues add up to zip."

"Come again? Tell me ya got – something – something for me to chew on."

"Dead ends, lots of dead ends. Kinda exhausted my leads, Sheriff." Harrison cocked his head and slipped his manicured fingernails into well-conditioned hair. Like a confused monkey, he almost scratched, caught himself, and pushed his brown locks back.

"Listen, nobody's getting away with-uh sweet 180,000 dollar severance package. Not in Saunders County and definitely not on our watch. This has gone on long enough. How about go grab your folder. I wanna see what ya got, take a look at your homework."

Notches in Harrison's belt were few, at least recently. He wasn't slow, but the win column looked short. He'd solved some cases, others were pending, pending on a lucky break. Riding a rough patch, 'this has gone on long enough,' didn't sit well.

"What about his history?" O'Leary continued.

Harrison's shoulder holster was also digging in. He adjusted it as he stood to retrieve his folder. "He's got a nifty little dossier. A closet full of skeletons."

O'Leary's detective made a quick loop to his desk, returning with a tattered manila binder and a shot of fresh air in his lungs. He laid it in front of the Sheriff, and announced, "Dale S Higgus. I say, S for 'Smoke'." Again, he adjusted the shoulder holster and his sleek new Walther in it. *If it's good enough for Bond . . .*

O'Leary, unimpressed, watched the adjustment. "Smoke, like poof into thin air?"

"Yeah, well, poof," Harrison flipped hands up into the blue haze, "but more like smoke and mirrors. After the interviews, I walked away thinking, that con artist's been blowing smoke up everybody's ass."

"That's all well-and-good, but he didn't con *us*. He embezzled the shit outta *Core Fuels* and it's our job," O'Leary jabbed his middle finger at the detective – knuckle in his index finger had been shot out. Every time, an unintentional eff you, "Let me rephrase that, 'your job', Harrison, to smoke Smokey out."

"I hear ya, maybe just missing something. Never said I was giving up."

The Chief sucked a big hit on his *King Ed* and huffed a stinky gray ring, sending it up into the haze. "Let's see if we can figure out where the hell Dale's run to." He felt himself waffling between good-Chief bad-Chief, and said, "Let's take a look." O'Leary flipped the folder's beat-up cover back, exposing an explosion of papers.

"Okay, the top ones are interviews from out at the plant."

"Je-sus," another puff of smoke escaped, "for a guy that's so particular about suits and boots, you sure keep some slop-the-hog notes." (Not the first time O'Leary had chided him on either account.)

Harrison adjusted his tie, considered O'Leary's marginal hygiene, and decided to take the remark as a wash; yep – messy notes, but looking sharp while I'm takin'em.

"I got some pictures, too."

"Well, go get em. This a game of Simon says?"

Ellen had been trying not to listen, but it was too good. She gave Harrison an empathetic smile as he passed with retrieved photos.

Harrison liked her a little and felt the chemistry, but wouldn't ask her out. A previous office romance ended on a sour note. *The last thing I need right now is another failed chemistry experiment.*

He handed O'Leary photos. A five-by-seven of twenty-nine-year-old Dale Higgus lay on top.

"Did he have any help?"

"Only getting hired, I think. He hoodwinked the human resource person. Here, Bernice Jorgen." He didn't have her photo but pointed to her name on the list of people interviewed. "She's a smart one, probably knows damn near everything about everybody out there. Nosey bitch for sure, but he got her good."

"How's that?" O'Leary cocked back. His old oak office chair started with a creak, then groaned.

"References, dubious references. She did a once-over before putting Dale's app in front of Rawling, the Head-Honcho."

"I know Jon, we played ball. Way back." O'Leary bit down on the cigar and rubbed his shoulder. It seldom hurt, unless he used it. "Go on."

"Except – the phone numbers were for people he was drugging with, all supporting his bullshit history. Higgus slid in there with an Accounting degree. Looked legit, right? Trouble is, it was conjured up out of thin air, and, well, probably a damn good printer."

Harrison had been doing his homework, and though the case wasn't going great, he was pleased he had a good morsel to report. "Oh, Higgus had accounting alright, one class in college, and here, look, he took an incomplete. Dropped out, or drugged out, I suspect. It was those references that duped em at *Core*. Jorgen bit, hook, line, and for Rawling and *Core Fuels*, it was the big sinker."

O'Leary, generally impressed by Harrison's precocity for storytelling, sat up to take a look. "Keep going."

Harrison spun a copy of Dale's application from the folder and pointed. "So, I tracked down this first number, 'Professor Lowman.' That was Higgus's college roommate. Lowman, yes; professor, no. Another druggie that didn't make it a year at the U. He claims he hasn't seen nor heard from Higgus in forever." Harrison slid his finger down the page and tapped another name. "Then this guy, Dihms, supposedly an old boss. He gave Bernice a spectacular review of Dale's attributes, work ethic, etc... We couldn't find Dihms, from Cali, probably moved back out there."

He could feel the Chief's stare peeling open the top of his head. It itched; he scratched, but didn't look up and flipped to the next picture. "Finally, we go see this gal, Melissa Swank. She's as high as a turnip when we talked to her. Told us Dale gave those guys scripts. *Core Fuels* probably wasn't his only application at the time. She laughed about it and flat out admitted he gave the boys baggies of delish old Mary Jane for their efforts. But, this is a good one, she said, 'I was in drama', and, 'just did it for kicks'. I think she smoked her baggie, and then some."

"Knee-deep in horse shit."

"Grab your waders, it gets deeper." The room's blue-gray haze was killing Harrison and his sinuses were closing up shop.

O'Leary set the smoldering turd on the edge of the ashtray between them. He clasped his fingers, placing hands on the desk, and leaned into it. "I'm sure it does."

"Look at these bank statements. *Pro Rail and Trucking, Inc.*"

O'Leary finally snuffed out his soggy nub, picked up reading glasses, and the statement for closer inspection. "*True Trust State Bank.* In Wymore – what's that, about ninety miles?"

"Yeah." A thick dry layer of nose goblins, crusty, way deep, were assembling. Harrison worked his nose back and forth, pinching. "These are copies of the canceled checks made out to *Pro Rail.* And the President? Yours truly, Dale *Smokin* Higgus."

"*Pro Rail and Trucking*, huh?"

"Look at the address. Down the block from the bank. An upstairs office suite."

"Right, I guess if you're going to run a bogus logistics company, an upstairs suite is as inconspicuous as it gets." (O'Leary was looking for opportunities to use "bogus," the cool new word with the younger gen.)

"Same company name Dihms pretended to be from. Now, look at the dates and amounts, bigger and bigger, moving money in through and back out. Higgus to *Pro Rail*, *Core* to *Pro Rail*, *Pro Rail* to Higgus, Round and round, getting the staff at True Trust softened up for bigger and bigger transactions. Some checks, but, look at these slips, lots of cash. Can't you just see the bank president sitting in his office, rubbing his hands together, *Cash Cow – in the House*?"

"So what did they say at the bank?"

"Of course, he's anxious for us to catch him, but knew little. I think he's worried the bank'll still be sued over it, too. He just said, 'Higgus built up a congenial rapport with our staff', then turned me over to Lester, his loan officer. 'Maybe Lester knows more about, *Your Dale*,' he said. Basically, another dead end, but Lester wanted Higgus to take out a loan."

"Why?"

Harrison shrugged. "He's a loan officer. That's what they do."

"Well, did he give him one?"

Lester said, "No, thank God, he didn't want or need a loan."

"Screwing the bank would have taken more than charisma. Charisma only takes you so far, and the bank would've been more scrutinizing. They would've wanted tax statements, everything. Smoke and mirrors I doubt even Mr. Higgus and his good copier could have come up with."

"Chicanery of that magnitude probably beyond his skill set. I bet he thought about it."

"I'd guess he came to the conclusion that *Core's* 180,000 smackeroos would have to do. Not dumb at all."

"One weird thing, though,"

"What's that?"

"There's still thirty-two-hundred in the account."

"Buying time, leaving it open and funded."

"That's some expensive time, don't ya think? This ain't the roarin twenties."

"Time enough to get away, wasn't it? Sounds pretty cheap to me. He went missing when?"

Harrison shuffled into the stack, spilling chaos from the tattered folder onto O'Leary's desk. "It was at the end of *Core's* fiscal quarter, around May fifth, I think. I got it here somewhere." His scalp was crawling.

"You and I are going out to the plant." *I'm not taking the investigation over, but I can sacrifice an afternoon, see if I can get Harrison back on track. Besides, a little fresh air wouldn't hurt.* He pressed the intercom. "Ellen, would you call *Core Fuels*, set up a meeting with Jon Rawling, please. Say, two o'clock this afternoon."

Ellen crackled back, "I'll call, Sir."

"Harrison, you'll be back by one?"

"No problem. Pudge and I are going for lunch. We taking him with?"

"No, and you might want to slow down on those lunches with Pearson, or pick out another suit. Looks like this one's bout ready to pop, and your PP-K'*s* showin."

Harrison sucked it in and, turning to leave, gave the jacket a furtive tug. O'Leary smiled. Poor policy to rip on him, but it was so easy and fun.

The detective, almost out his door, and O'Leary said, "Harrison."

He spun on his heel. "Yeah, Chief?"

"When you guys get back from lunch, send Pearson down to Wymore. Tell him to grill-em at *True Trust* again. Tell him to latch on like a bulldog and bring us back a bone."

Leia stopped her Ford in the gravel parking lot. The Futura was blue, the economy model with the sparsest options. A lesser model would be of the fleet type; hers wasn't one of those. Lemonade had carpet.

She was taking it to a familiar place, *Jake's Garage*, for the Ford's latest trick; coaxing it to start. Multiple attempts at the ignition until the starter engaged, and each failed synchronization produced a screech that woke the dead.

She scrunched her empty sandwich bag, smiled, and tossed it over her shoulder to the back. This lunch hour was about multitasking. She brushed crumbs off her blouse and opened the door. On exit, her heel caught the sill plate and snapped off. *Good, I've been nursing-em long enough*, she picked it up and aimlessly flipped it into the back seat with the previously discarded trash. In high spirits, she wouldn't sweat the small stuff. She seldom did.

Mushy September clouds hung in the sky, long disintegrating contrails just higher. Midday sun dried the gravel lot, but whispering breeze and old oil leaks held the dust down. Leia felt better about this visit to *Jake's* than the last. She had a job, a couple hundred in savings, and the rent was paid. For a change, she wouldn't need Dad's largesse to settle up.

The block station's dirty, peeling white paint wasn't easy on the eyes. Jake didn't seem to notice or care. But Jake did notice, as usual, how easy Leia was on the eyes. He emerged from the dark center bay to greet his favorite and most frequent customer. He wiped his hands on an orange shop rag, wobbled his head back and forth, and with a smile, said, "If I was twenty-five years younger."

"Oh, Mr. Kenzie, you're too funny." Half the sign on the building had let loose since Leia's last visit. GARAGE, of *Jake's Garage,* hung low, resting on the trim board above the bay door. She pointed, "Looks like your sign's about-ta-fall."

"Ah, it was that damn twister end'uh June. Waitin on the insurance cause the roof got-er too." He pointed to the peak where a spattering of shingles were missing tabs. "And poor Carl Holt."

June's town-bruising twister snapped trees, damaged buildings, and left one Mr. Carl Holt dead, but no other loss of life, this year.

"I heard the neighbors found him face-down in their kiddie pool," said Leia.

"That's no rumor. He didn't drown though. They said, 'maybe

suffocated, maybe couldn't catch a breath.' Not a mark on him, cept his shirt was mostly ripped off."

"Oh? I heard when they flipped him over, his eyes had been sucked out. Just dangling." Leia held hands up to her face and wiggled her index fingers.

"Twisters do the damnedest things . . ." Jake made his way to the front of the car, slid his hand, found the latch.

"So Lemonade has problems again . . . let's take a listen." He lifted the faded Ford's sunbaked hood. "Okay, bring it."

She turned the key. The starter's unsuccessful attempt at flywheel engagement announced itself. The horrific grinding sonically removed a layer of enamel from Leia's teeth.

Jake smiled. "How long did you say it's been doing it?"

"Just a few weeks."

"My goodness, girl, lucky you made it here." Jake shook his head.

"At least I didn't need a tow this time."

"Well, she's going to need a starter, and more than likely I'll have to R&R the flex-plate."

Leia had no idea what a flex-plate was, but knew it wasn't a Greek salad. It sounded more expensive than Greek salad, but she had a job and needed wheels.

"How long will it be in, you think?"

Jake pointed to the empty third bay. "I'll get her in this afternoon. Get some slick-em on the bolts. Tear her apart tomorrow. Parts – Monday – and she should be ready to pick up on Tuesday, or Wednesday, yup, yup."

"You always say '*she*' . . . I've always thought of Lemonade as gender-neutral."

"Oh no, this patina covered Ford's of the feminine persuasion – B-type personality, don't ya think?" Jake felt it suited Leia and figured her the same, minus the advanced case of patina, of course. No A-types would put up with a piece of shit like this sunbaked pile of repair-prone dung.

Leia was still under the impression that if she kept pumping Aid into the Lemon it would start treating her better. A relationship attuned to an abused girlfriend that can't quit it. And she'd done that well.

"Just leave the keys in'er and we'll get you back to . . . what's the place?"

"*Seed Genetics,*" Leia reminded him.

"Yeah, on the radio every spring with the plantin ads. 'Try our seeds. Seeds with good Genes'."

"And, 'Great Seeds, What's in Your Genes?'" Leia added.

Jake remembered that ad too, but the gruff mechanic wasn't repeating it to the young lady. That might be one innuendo too far. He wasn't going to be known around town as the DOM.

Leia returned keys on the smiley-face keychain to the ignition, "You don't think anyone will steal it . . . Her?"

Jake twisted a smile and lifted an eyebrow.

Leia got it, and they shared a laugh.

The pair walked across the parking lot to Jake's truck. Leia wobbling, less an inch of heel on the right shoe, and Jake, a bit hunched over from thirty-some years in the wrench swinging business.

"Shall we?" Jake pressed the old tow-truck door handle's button. The door dropped an inch and swung open on distressed hinges. He helped Leia step up and into the dusty cab, then closed the inglorious door for her.

"I really appreciate the ride, Mr. Kenzie."

"Not a problem, I was just about to go grab a little lunch."

Jake turned the key. The tow truck purred. He thought *I'm not doing a tow – but using the truck to give her a ride – Somehow this doesn't quite add up.* He chuckled at himself, he had yet to charge the pretty young thing for a hook.

Harrison returned from lunch. He had refrained from ordering the special. The chef salad was good – Person's Hot Pork looked better. He popped a couple of Tic-Tacs, masking his onion and ranch breath.

O'Leary was waiting. "Ready? Ellen set us up with Rawling. I see you have your folder. Good, I was looking at some more of your notes. You can tell me about Higgus's residence on the way."

Out the door, and a breeze shifted O'Leary's comb-over. He patted it back reasonably well.

"When da'ya get your new cruiser?" Harrison asked.

"Cancelled it."

"Cancelled it?"

"I didn't requisition it, the county did. Waste ah money."

"Not giving up on the Bronco, huh?"

"Not yet." O'Leary liked his four-wheel drive, aggressive tread at the four corners, and traction-lock rear differential. He liked the roll bar, the big ashtray, and the classic light bar on top. He loved the power. He'd had Jake fit the 351ci engine with a big four-barrel carb and a camshaft ground for torque. And he liked to say, 'Screw OPEC. Eleven miles to the gallon, loaded or empty.'

Harrison took his boss's lead and buckled. "I was surprised the seat-belt law got rescinded."

"Nebraskans are ruggedly independent by nature. We just don't like being told what to do. Still, looks like more and more are buckling up."

"I don't think I ever had one on til I got my badge."

"Gives ya a different perspective after seeing a few fatalities, don't it?"

"I was called out to thirty-six roadside wrecks when I patrolled – five fatalities. Two kids; that was the worst. Still see em in my dreams."

"I wouldn't mention that at your annual physical. Not during your psych eval, anyway. Those shrinks gotta way of twisting nothin into somethin."

As they left the lot, O'Leary pulled the cellophane off a new *King Edward*. He stoked it and immediately a blue haze filled the cab. Harrison popped more Tic-Tacs.

"All I saw was his address in your folder, 2020 Oaknut Ave. Apartment B3, wasn't it? And Manager James Skogan."

Harrison nodded. "How about the receipt from *Gambles*?" He dug in the folder. "Here it is. I shit you not, found it in his kitchen garbage can."

At thirty mph, the Bronco's *Trail Hog* grippers and high flow exhaust howled. On the highway, at sixty, it was almost unbearable. The men talked over the roar.

"Look here. *Gambles*, for two duffle bags and a candy bar."

"Did you check out the store?"

"Yeah, Mom and Pop operation. The owner recognized Higgus when I showed him the photo but said they didn't talk. Bought two big duffle bags, gray, paid cash and out the door. I did learn one thing."

"What's that?"

"*Snickers*, Higgus likes *Snickers*."

"Uh-ha."

Harrison's prayers answered: O'leary cracked his window. He thought about the PPK in his holster and wondered if Bond ever used a smoke-screen thick as his boss was releasing from the Bronco.

"How about the apartment?"

"A dank shithole. Basement style, ground-level windows. His raggy thrift store furniture molding away as we speak."

"I suppose they're anxious for us to release the unit?"

"Not particularly. The manager, Skogan, says it's no rush. Apparently, he's got a few empty apartments. Says the lack of jobs has sucked the life out of town. Oh, and we can call him Jimmy."

"Well, that's nice."

"Isn't it?"

O'Leary turned east on ninety-two. The day heated up, and the Bronco's A.C. was cranked. Harrison rolled his window down a couple of inches to match O'Leary's and bolster the oxygen level.

"Skogan said he liked Dale: 'good renter'."

"Anything else?"

"Higgus informed him that he wasn't renewing his lease, told him, 'I'm buying a house – movin out in sixty days. As soon as I get settled in, though, I'm throw'n a big party. Lotsa girls, and ya know the first person I'm inviting? My good buddy, Jimmy.' Bet the smoke's still tickling Jimmy's sphincter."

"Probably waitin for a call…"

"Dale's little pickup was still in its usual parking spot, too. Faded yellow Ford Courier – sagging in the middle, looked like King Kong stepped on it – banana on wheels."

"Have you asked around at the car lots?"

"Pudge and I've been to em all. Here, in Wymore, everywhere. No luck. We tried the bus stops, too. Got this vision stuck in my head," Harrison tapped index finger to his temple, "Higgus, straps over his shoulders, crisscrossing his chest, and at his sides, he's patting those two big gray bill-packed duffle bags, then, with all the fifties and hundreds a guy could ever want, he just evaporates into the night."

"I think your brain is evaporating. You checked with DMV to make sure he didn't have another vehicle registered in his name?"

Harrison hadn't, and perjured, "First thing we did, nothing else, just the banana."

"He might have bought a car from someone at the plant."

"Maybe, hard to run away in a Chiquita."

Nancy and Deb sat across from Teri in the cafeteria.

"I have to get back." Teri placed garbage on her tray.

"Bernice going ta write you up? You barely sat down," Deb said.

"I'm getting along with her – I'd like to keep it that way. I've seen her when she's mad."

"Yeah, but have you seen her when she's hungry?" Nancy said.

"Isn't she always?" Teri whispered.

"I'm taking an extra ten. I *hope* she fires me," Deb said. "That would be a great day to be done working at this funny farm."

"Fire you? She might sit on you, and that would be the end of little Debbie," Nancy joked, but no one was laughing, and they sat, envisioning the horror, the possibility.

"I like it here, so far," Teri said.

"You do?" Nancy asked.

"Well, at least you're relatively safe up in the offices," Deb said.

"You guys . . . this place has a good record, no accidents, for what? Forty some days? And what was that, a sprain?"

"Believe me, somebody's gonna get hurt, *bad.* Things out there are breaking all the time. I see Bobby running around the place, putting Band-Aids on everything. I heard him talkin, hardly gets any new parts, 'no money for nothin," Deb said.

"That's cheap Kernel Corn for ya," Nancy added. "Lining his pockets at our expense."

"And putting all of us at risk," Deb said. "Someday, *Ka-blewy*, we'll be wiped right off the map. Office or production – won't matter, we'll all be blown to smithereens."

"We'll see how long you like it, working up there with Captain Greedy, Kernel Ignoramus." . . . 'I have a bit of bad news, guys, we have to temporarily suspend Christmas bonuses.' . . . "Tell that to my kids, like you can suspend Christmas." . . . 'You've been doin a great job for us, Nancy, but unfortunately we're right in the middle of a wage freeze, but as soon as I can . . . yada-yada-yada.' "You'll see."

"Some of that might have to do with the reason I was hired, you know?"

"We know, all right, but don't kid yourself, Honey, it started *way* before *that* incident," Deb said. "Anyway, who left the door to the vault hanging open? Rawling, Kernel Dipshit."

"You guys sound almost as angry as Bernice, sometimes. I'm off, she isn't big on answering the phone."

Nancy and Deb looked at each other. "She's – Just – Big," they said it together, laughing.

Chapter 7
Star Status

Core Fuels' smoke stacks grew as the Bronco clicked off miles. O'Leary took a final puff off his cigar and threw it out.

Harrison asked, "So you know Rawling?"

"We went to school together. Jags – the Jaguars. Jon made the team his sophomore year. I shot up over summer, putting my sophomore slump behind me. The next year I was running-back and he played quarterback as a junior."

"You were a senior?"

O'Leary nodded, "We almost went to state. A couple of good years, Jon was something."

"Not very big, is he? Five-eight, five-ten?"

"Tough though. Core strength. While us town kids were lifting weights, Jon spent summers on his grandparents' farm. Carrying milk cans, pitchin' shit, baling – farming – back in the fifties – when farming wasn't all machines like today." And, using his middle finger, he pointed at a massive combine gobbling field to the south.

The roar of *Trail Hogs* on blacktop was blowing in with hot September air. Harrison rolled his window up, letting the AC do its work.

"Doesn't sound like any fun at-all."

"Some people seem to love it, the animals, fresh produce . . ."

"Yeah – romantic, till your back goes out."

O'Leary dug his *Ray-Bans* out of the console. "No . . . farming wouldn't be for me, either. But, anyway, his granddad retired. Jon finally tried out, and that's when our coach, Hendersheen, discovered Jon's attribute."

"What was that?"

O'Leary rolled his window up, the cab noise ratcheted down a few decibels; he wanted a turn at storytelling.

"Tell you what happened. We were in tryout week, maybe our third or fourth day. Jerry lined the whole team up behind the goal line and started feeding us pigskins. We were supposed to try and hit Lenny Kratz, the assistant coach, at the forty."

"So, I take it Rawling was the only one that could?"

"No, a few of us hurled it out to the Lenny, that's what we called Kratz. Jerry sent everyone else to the sideline and the Lenny out another ten yards. First, our quarterback and I tried the fifty-yard toss, then Jon."

"How did that go?"

"Farren, the quarterback, he's a senior, pumps it out there but comes up a few yards shy. I did, too. Then Rawling gets the ball. He gives the assistant coach a playful wave, like, go out further. Lenny pretends he's going to do just that. So, Jon falls back a step. Then, a firm stride to the goal line and he let'r rip." O'Leary pointed his middle finger up at the sky, well above the horizon. "The perfect spiral, thirty-degree angle, and it just kept climbin like it came out a cannon." O'Leary, smiled, recounting the scene. "By the time Kratz realized he needed to sprint to catch the missile, it was too late. With flailing legs and upside-down smile, he stabbed at it. Ball spanked off his fingertips somewheres around the opposite forty."

"Really? You shittin me?"

"There were hoots-n-hollers, guys with jaws dropped down, gasping. One kid, trying to make the team, Hallgeson, says, 'Holy Hail Mary', and Farren, our quarterback, worried or dissed, I don't know, looks at me and says, 'Freaking Freakoid'."

Harrison gave his boss an entertained sniff.

"Coach comes over with his patented one raised eyebrow, gives Rawling a slap on the helmet, and asks, 'You got a license to fly that thing, kid?' The Lenny, joggin in, hears Jerry's comment and piles on, says something like, FAA might be calling with some questions. Then when we get to the locker room that Hallgeson kid pulls out a camera and says, 'Gotta get a picture of *The Arm*', flash went off right as Jon was flipping him the double bird."

"Standard fare in male high school photography."

"Standard fare."

Three visitor spots open and O'Leary parked next to the sidewalk.

Jon's intercom lit up. "Mr. Rawling, your appointment's here."

"Send them in."

"Jon Rawling. How ya doin?"

"Kelly, Kelly O'Leary, come on in. Hey, guys, come on in. Good to see you, Sheriff. It's been a while." Kelly's firm handshake met Jon's. "I'm okay, and how's it with you, Kelly?" *Either good news or they don't have jack-shit.*

"Well, Jon, more office time than I'd like, god-damn paperwork and reports. Don't get time to follow my guys out all that often." O'Leary nodded to his detective.

"You're preachin to the choir, Buddy."

The plant smelled like fresh-popped popcorn. Harrison took in a deep breath. He looked at Jon's neat desk, expensive European shoes, pressed shirt, Windsor knotted tie, and his jacket hanging neatly on coat hook at shelving's end. The top shelf supported a wave of trophies. O'Leary had a couple of trophies in his office, but that's where the comparison ended. *They might be about the same age – but they sure weren't cut from the same cloth.*

"Harrison's been investigating some leads. He'd like to talk with Bernice again, and some of the others that knew Higgus. Maybe I could get you to go over it with me, since I'm here."

"Yeah, sure, since you're here. No one here's too busy that they don't have time to help you track down that son-of-a-bitch. But you know, he was like an assistant manager, everybody out here knew him well enough. Except for Teri Thompson, she replaced him."

"Sounds like you got more interviewing to do, Harrison." It came out gruff, more so than O'Leary wanted it to.

"I have some more questions for Ms. Jorgen, then, anyone, in particular, I should start with, Mr. Rawling?" Harrison knew from the initial investigation that *Core* employed a lot of people. *Damn – need a good lead. Wish we'd brought Pearson.*

Jon scratched the three foremen and Bobby's name on a pad, "These are the guys he interacted with on a daily basis, and Bernice, of course. Bobby's repairing a mill and we need that back online, so even though I said no one's too busy to help out, best if we let him do his thing and start with the others."

"Okay, great, I better get to it." Harrison looked to O'Leary. "Maybe we should have drove separate?"

"Well, see if you can get something to work on over the weekend and come back out Monday." O'Leary turned to Jon. "Maybe we could get some phone numbers and Harrison could catch a couple of them at home tonight, or tomorrow?"

"I'll have Bernice find em before ya leave."

"Take an hour and meet back here," O'Leary instructed Harrison.

"Could you close the door behind you, Detective?" And Jon had to ask, "So, Kelly, you taking over the case?"

"Helping out. Right now all I got are a couple of overweight investigators with fewer hair follicles. Getting tired of all the head-scratching. Looks bad for our office, not to mention *your* losses. They need something. A win, a good story for their Sunday afternoon barbeques."

Jon envisioned a backyard full of overweight kids running amuck, wives bringing out the potato salad, bars, buns, condiments. The Porky Pigs at the grill, jawing it up, sucking down their *Scores Lite* and flippin big sizzly burgers.

Jon shook his head. "Dale, going missing with all that money, damn it. I needed someone to back me up. Someone to help mind the store. Higgus seemed to be one of the few around here with potential. A new guy making things click, and good with people." Jon took a breath. "I can't be here all day, every day. There's meetings with the Board. Running after the farmers, procuring corn contracts." Jon pointed about. "Government Ethanol program meetings, golf outing once a month with the consortium. There's another half-day shot."

"Well, Jon, that's a nice perk. Golfing and all."

"Nothing nice about it. I'm sure even the County Sheriff, with his own detectives and a slew of deputies, has someone to answer to."

"Hmm."

"Some folks, up above, expecting more – pushing for more?"

"Like a Commissioner, Governor, my wife."

"Ha, ya, get where I'm coming from? The consortium's putting this Dale thing on me. They expect me to 'make it up to them' – and what-the-hell's that mean? Dale was my Yes-Man. I knew he was young, but he really had his shit together, bright, and getting along so well with everybody. What do ya do? I needed someone, why not the Yes-Man?"

"You didn't notice anything unusual, then?"

"There's no business-as-usual around this place. Rough seas are the norm, here. I always took a quick look over the ledgers, never felt the need to check em super close cause they're audited at the end of the year. Didn't occur to me someone would dare try something this nuts."

"Quite the job he pulled, really. I haven't seen another like it. Patience, planning. *Big* Balls. Not some teller skimming a bill here and there, or some family antics, power of attorney, or some such bull."

"Even if I'd been checking the books closer, looking back at entries, I'm not so sure I would've spotted it. Unless you really examined it, everything basically looked legitimate."

"Harrison doesn't think he had any help, and considering it's all about accounting, I would tend to agree, but I want to know what you think, your gut feeling?"

"Hell, I don't know what to think anymore." Jon swept his hand in the general direction of the plant floor. "Is anyone trustworthy? Well, other than Ms. Thompson. It was good to see her resume in the stack of applications when we were looking for Higgus' replacement."

"Why's that, girls don't embezzle?"

"No, they can. Teri is a family friend, my daughter's close friend. She practically grew up at our house."

"I see."

"She won't exactly be replacing Dale, though, and she won't be in any management position. Ms. Thompson doesn't have any real-world experience in the accounting field, but, turns out, other than balancing his checkbook, neither did Dale."

"He has experience now. Well, Jon, hopefully, your new accountant can keep the books."

"I think she'll do fine. It's just adding and subtracting, not rocket science for crying-out-loud."

"And what about now? When you're out, who runs the show?"

"Those responsibilities have been passed to Bernice."

"Your Yes-Woman."

"Not *my* Yes-Woman, she got the job perforce. Bernice the Niece. If there was an application it didn't pass my desk. Not to sound too disparaging, but the Yes-Woman mostly just says 'yes' when it suits her."

"Harrison said Bernice never caught on that his diploma was faked. Didn't ask the U to send his records."

"Yeah, well, it's on me too, of course, but if I could, I would have sent her packing. Her, being related, my hands were tied. Word came down, and instead of getting fired, she got half his responsibilities and a raise. Not my first choice to help run the plant, but at least they have someone that won't be ripping them off."

***Cold Spot's* tip** jar filled quickly on Saturday nights.

Harrison squeezed her muffin top, Ellen jerked. He passed behind and took the barstool next to her. She laughed and tried to poke him in the ribs. He let her.

Bryce helped himself onto the stool next to Harrison and set his drink on the bar. "I saw you at the plant yesterday."

"Likewise, what was your name?"

"Bryce Ross."

"Roy Harrison, Buck."

"Lookin for Dale, Buck?"

"High and low."

"I tipped a few with him here at *Cold Spot*."

"You knew him well?"

"I tipped a few with him here at *Cold Spot*." Bryce sucked down his drink and set it on the bar a little to his right, encroaching Harrison's space.

"Fair enough," Harrison said. "Can I get a round, Dave? What you drinking, Bryce?"

Bryce pushed the glass, redirecting it to the bartender. Dave didn't have to ask what he was drinking and made another rum and coke to set up with the beers.

"When was it you shared these potations?"

"Not after he disappeared, if that's what you mean."

Chapter 8

Red Flag

The employees didn't see it. Folks in the surrounding small towns didn't see it. Rebecca noticed little, but Leia perceived changes, and disturbing they were.

Now, in her twenties, she was reconnecting with parents that might not be that dumb after all. Mom was Mom. But Dad, well, it had been working on her all summer.

Forty-nine by a few months and he was okay before, but now? Something. Hard to put a name to it, but something nonetheless. Age-related? Maybe, but was it? Or the realization you're no big deal and never will be. No, he must be past that. Not the cynical, crabby, 'old man', either. Dad probably isn't that kind of old yet, anyways. A bit of evil? No, not Dad. Surely not '*Here's Johnny*' evil.

She spent Sunday home with her parents. They did the river. *Baby Cakes*, back on the lift, and the sun slipped away.

After the evening meal, Rebecca and Leia loaded the dishwasher. Rebecca latched the door and hit start.

"Is that thing getting louder?" Leia asked. "Sounds like a thunderstorm twisting a cat in there."

"Like it's gonna take off. Jon, does the dishwasher sound louder to you?"

"Yeah . . . that's not good. Let's see how it does tonight and we'll call Darrin tomorrow."

"What would you say to a new one, eh? Ward's has them on sale, I think," Rebecca said, and not thinking too hard – flyer in the magazine rack.

Leia tried to help Mom. "You've had this one as long as I can remember, and didn't you have Darrin out looking at it not that long ago?"

"He fixed it fine, didn't he?" Jon stated.

"He did. Smelled a little boozy, though," Rebecca said.

"Did he make you nervous?"

"No, of course not, just saying."

"Oh, that reminds me, I met one of your employees at Cold Spot the other day, Dad," Leia said.

"Yeah?"

"Bryce. Seems to like his drinks well enough. Not tattling or anything." Leia wasn't sure where she was going with it, but Bryce's comments had pissed her off and animosity lingered.

Oh god – please don't tell me you're into him. "Bryce, he's our thirty-something teenager. I got a little Bryce story for ya. You weren't planning on dating were you?"

"Ah – I think not."

A jittering vibration passed through the dishwasher, rattling a crock of utensils on the countertop. Rebecca steadied it. *Should I get the flyer, now?*

Jon started, "Would have been two years ago, well, three in December. An overzealous board member had the wonky idea that I personally hand-deliver Christmas bonuses, and not just around the plant, but to their homes, with gifts. Treats and some *Core Fuels* trinkets, pens, ashtrays and such, and the bonus check, of course."

"I don't remember that," Rebecca said. "Was I in Winnipeg?"

"Yeah, that's right, you went up a couple weeks early that year." Jon continued, "Bernice mapped me a route the day before. Anyway, so when I pull up to Bryce's place, oh my god. I took a look at my list to see about hitting him up later. But that wasn't going to work, he was my last stop in Wahoo and I was headed east after that, so, no way I'd make all my stops if I didn't stick to the plan."

"Was everybody home, on all those stops, I mean?" Rebecca asked.

"Of course not. That was just one of the stupid things about it. All those stops, a couple Saturdays before Christmas? How many are going to be home? Most likely out shopping."

"That's the first thing that popped into my head, eh?"

"Well, Bryce's house is one of those run-down ramblers on Biscuit Knoll, and his yard's covered in party trash, lawn chairs overturned, beer cans everywhere, *Busch* I think, probably a hundred. Empty bottles, Jim, Jack, the Captain. A deep scar in the lawn – looked like a trailer or vehicle had bottomed out and furrowed into the dead December grass. Oh, and there was a smoldering umbrella sticking out a rusted iron patio table. I'm not kidding, it was still smoking. The party had to have been an all-nighter and I couldn't have missed it by much. Looked like the place had been *Busch*-wacked."

"I would have left," Leia said.

"You left, didn't you?" Rebecca asked.

"Kind of wish I had, but the goodies were in the back seat and his envelope on top the pile next to me."

Rebecca smiled. "Couldn't help yourself."

"The house had *one* new attachment, a deck, with an incline down to the sidewalk. I started across, trying not to trip on the dead soldiers."

"Dead soldiers?" Leia asked.

"Empties."

"Oh."

"And I have to go by the picture window, and I look in. It's the living room, and Bryce is naked, half on the couch, and I suppose he heard me so he's stirring. I'm pretending I didn't see. Get to the door, and look at the doorbell. It's hanging out the socket by the wires. I'd been shocked enough for one morning but knocked. There's a banging scramble inside, then Bryce opens the door dressed in some saggy pajama bottoms."

"Nice, well, you asked for it," Rebecca said.

"A sweaty beer-fart stench wafts out his front door and then Bryce hits me with his zackly breath.

"Hey Captain, bringing me out lunch or my homework?" he asks.

I told him I was making the rounds with company gift bags and

Core bonuses. "Got yours right here," I say. He looked at me like he's still drunk, head drifting one way then jerking back like a typewriter. He kept himself from puking, anyway, and mumbled something like, "For little old me? Thank you."

I was starting to feel his pain, and told him, "No problem, thanks again from *Core*. You take care now."

He says, "Don't worry about me, see ya Monday, Captain," and slowly shuts the door in my face. I couldn't help it – leaving, I had to look again. He stumbles back to the couch and grabs up a makeshift spew bucket, an ice cream pail. Fortunately, I didn't see anymore, but he was in Monday. I know, cause I checked. That was the last time I delivered bonus checks."

Leia squinted. "What a loser."

The dishwasher, in a death throe, screeched. Water poured from beneath, pooling onto the kitchen floor. Rebecca went for the advertisement.

When she returned, Leia held a towel, Jon, the mop, and working it. A few minutes and the flood was contained.

"It's getting late, Dear, and somebody's gotta get up for work in the morning," Rebecca said to Jon but looking to their daughter.

"I suppose. You ready to go, kiddo?"

"I am." Leia rounded the table and gave Rebecca a hug. "Thanks, Mom."

"Love you, have a good week. Will we see you next weekend?"

"I think so. Jake is supposed to have my car done on Tuesday or Wednesday. I can't keep buggin you guys for rides," she said, mostly to Dad.

"Not a bother, and when it's about getting you home, all the better; but maybe you should start looking for something a little more reliable."

"I like my little *Lemonade*."

Jon smiled and shook his head.

"Don't forget your leftovers."

Leia thanked Mom again and gathered parting Tupperware.

They turned from the driveway and Jon stepped on the gas. The tan Impala's modest V-8 had good compression. It pulled hard.

Too fast, she thought. But then again, rural drivers drove fast, even on gravel . . . especially on gravel. If there's ever a place to put the hammer down, country gravel's where it's at. No secret – troopers seldom drove the dirt, wouldn't want shiny cruisers all scuzzed up, now, would they?

It was darker and they were moving. Tall ditch grass, due a fall haircut, waved at their passing. Dirty Impala headlights pierced the night but a short distance beyond its heady speed. The needle bounced at seventy-five. Conditions made it feel faster and Leia thought, *Crazy – Are we late for something?* She kept her lip zipped and reminded herself, Dad too, worked come morning and had to drive home after dropping her off.

"Looks like the grader went by," Leia said.

"A day late. Usually, Saturdays, remember?"

"Oh yeah."

The steel blade had left a substantial gravel wake just right of the driving lane, if one could call it a lane. Generally, ruralites drove well over center, and at times right down the middle. Tonight was a down-the-middle night; when speeding, down the middle was the way to do it. The left tires ran on hard-pack where the grader had shaved the road clean to clay. Right tires floated true, near the gravel mound parallel to the ditch. Occasionally, tread grabbed a stone, sending it into the wheel well with a *ting-tang* and *bang*, or *bapped* one on the undercarriage, causing Leia a start. The first mile ran straight – the second mostly so, but with long sweeping curves snaking between twin sloughs known by the locals as Kissin Cousins. At seventy-five the full-sized sedan coursed stable, but in the curves, not so much. *If we even start to slide – we're goners!* Jon negotiated the cousin's cambers. Leia pressed the door, then pressed left, body in seatbelt. All was fine. Moon, full and bright, reflected off the still black water. *Beautiful night – to die in a wreck.*

Sometimes placid isn't placid. Dad's silence felt icky, but she, too, spent from a day visiting, had little to say and supposed he was talked out.

A day with Mom and her? That'd do it, two against one. Uncomfortable speed and uncomfortable silence grated her nerves.

We're gonna die on a Sunday. In her side mirror, Leia watched rain-deprived Nebraska billow. The speeding Impala woke a dust cloud, clay powder, rolling, rising in the night. *This is nuts.* Taillights illuminated the chasing dirt beast. *Better to be hypnotized by dust monster than face the black hole we're racing into.*

The speedometer nipped eighty.

Not saying a word – shit. Not a backseat driver – shit. Not when riding with the man that taught me to drive – shit! Should I ask, where's the damn fire?

From the cousins they raced, and the crossroad ahead didn't make for a smooth intersection. The junction crested and the Impala jolted. Leia snuck a look. Dad didn't flinch.

She thought of the heavily wooded hills that lay ahead. *He has to slow down, now.* With her right hand, Leia gripped the armrest and her left restlessly checked the seat belt. *Small hills, but steep.* The first mogul came with an exclamation. Antiquated suspension stretched its full expanse, tires scratching ground, and weightless they went.

"Ooh," Leia exhaled, mostly out of fear, but also a hint, telling Jon to slow down. *Maybe he drives like this alone, but never with Mom or me in the car.* Pale, and about to say something, they hit the second hill – fast as hell.

She knew its steepness, front and off the backside as well. They took air, truly took air, this time. She felt her feet drifting, arms rising. Her feathered hair floated and her body tried to follow. Restrained by the seatbelt, her rear remained benched. Airborne, the nose-heavy car tilted. And standing center-road downhill, a yearling to view. A true *deer in the headlights* moment.

Touchdown! Deer sausage. An Impala '*meat and greet.*' *BangBang*, double indemnity; car slamming *terra firma* – Bambi exploding off old Chev like a water balloon. Leia braced the dash and stared through a red mist-covered windshield. A smashed header, fiberglass shards at the hood's front, and tufts of fur fluttered in the cracks. She realized she had actually screamed "Oh Shi---it" – and wet herself a bit, too.

The teeth-jarring massacre fazed her pilot little. Dad stuck the landing and let off the gas. He turned on the wipers. Washers cleared the mist of blood.

She looked at him.

"Okay?" he asked.

"I think so."

He didn't stop, only slowed. Then she saw something truly amiss, the glitch.

Jon wore a two-tone smirk. There – she could just make it out – adorned by red moonlight reflecting off the bloodied hood and green instrument cluster glow. The smirk one gets when their head's a pressure cooker brimming crazy, letting off a steamy release. Leia quickly looked away. Hair on her arms stood. Peripherally, she glanced. It looked like he was trying to wipe it from his face, but the smirk, lifted by glowing cheeks below glassy eyes, wanted to stay on a bit. *Never ever have I seen that look. – That's not Dad.*

The putrid rank of deer crap permeated the car. Dad didn't seem to notice. Leia bit her tongue.

Chapter 9

Santa's Clause

Past eleven, and Jon parked the smashed Impala. It smelled horrendous. A rain would be nice. Nothing looked to be leaking from the damaged beak.

Rebecca slept, but Mr. R in the bathroom was up.

"Nice shot," Otherjon said.

"You again?"

"Don't get defensive. You were just feeling angst about the bonus thing, were you not?"

"You a mind reader?"

"Ha, ha. You should have told Rebecca what happened the next year."

"What I do with my bonus is my business."

"What bonus is that – you don't get those anymore, and what *did* you do with that last one? Gave it away to those worthless shits at the plant. Cashed it – split it. We could've had some fun with four grand."

"What's the diff'? If they found out I got one and theirs were cut, they'da strung me up by my . . . Just tried to keep some semblance of normalcy."

"Great. How did that work out for ya? The consortium's money vacuum came for yours next year, didn't it? – Sorry Jon, but things are really tight; let's see how it's going next year.' They couldn't leave a nickel on the table and you took it like a beaten dog. If we're going to work together you'll have to man-up."

"Are you talking to me?" Rebecca asked from the bedroom.

Jon removed the razor blade from under his fingernail. "No sweetheart, getting ready for bed. I'll be in in a minute." Otherjon smiled, shook his head.

In bed, Rebecca snuggled him, then turned to get comfortable. Jon stared at the clock until two-something and, finally, slipped into his dream machine.

He ran downstairs; it was Christmas morning. Santa had left gifts and got the hell out of Dodge. He felt his face, looked at his hands; am I forty-nine, or ten? A spiffy toy train circled the tree – hopper-cars full, brimming corn. He knelt next to the transformer and cranked the dial to FAST. Black smoke puffed from the miniature steam engine's stack and it smelled like popcorn, burnt popcorn. The speedy train steamed past, rattling precariously. Cars rocked. Loads shifted. A tiny engineer leaned out the locomotive window. His little striped hat blew off as he flipped Jon the bird. Round and round the "Big O" raced, hoppers dripping kernels with each vibration.

On every gift, his name, and Jon picked a red package. Damp blood-soaked paper pealed wet and fell apart in his fingers. He opened the soggy box. Inside, the haunting blade lay waiting. Onion Slayer, the knife that's hard to be rid of. Jon jumped, slapped shut the box and a wild pitch derailed the racing train. Corn spilled across the Christmas rug and the tumble catapulted mini engineer from his window. He flipped long rotations through the air, arms out in an iron cross. Striped bib-overall pant-legs fluttered in the air and he lost a boot. Smack! The little body piled into the transformer, slid, landing in a crumpled muddle. Jon looked at the incapacitated miniature, smiled, and thought; little corn haulin bastard got his up-n-cumins.

Jon deliberated and chose another gift, an expensive-looking white velvet jewelry box, and removed the ribbon. He opened it slowly, carefully, and peeked inside. A pair of shiny chromed handcuffs lay on red silk. He picked the love bracelets from the case, and read engravings, a script on each, "Santa's Little Helper," and, "Mi Maquina de Amor."

He heard a low, but sweet, two-syllable whistle. A "Here I Am," whistle.

"Whooot-wooo."

Jon looked. Bernice, positioned atop the chaise, lay on her side. She wore red lace garter stockings and a Santa four-yard mini-dress adorned with white furry cuffs, matching deep-V collar, and fluffy white skirt fringe. Bernice smiled her best baby-teeth smile. She leaned on her forearm, and positioning a leg up, rested her foot behind a knee. Cleavage, cushioned in white fluff, strained the Santa suit and her panties said, 'peek-a-boo.' She placed a red fingernail to pursed lipstick-red lips and gave Jon her big naughty girl look.

Jon shook his head; neg-a-tivo.

Bernice motioned; come closer, beckoning him with her stout index finger. Then onto her back with a spin, and she threw both legs over the chaise's backrest. She hung her head off the front, stuck her wrists out to be handcuffed, and said, "I knew you couldn't quit Bernicie."

Jon thrashed. He woke.

Rebecca mumbled, "Bad dream?"

He stumbled for the bathroom, blowing deep exhales. Hearty slaps to the cheek; Reality check. "Horrible!"

Monday morning, Bernice at her station, greeted him as on any other Monday, or Tuesday, or whenever. The difference – her blouse. Red, an extremely low-cut sort. Jon swallowed hard, nodded good morning, and bee-lined for his office.

Notes from Friday lay on his desk and the afternoon schedule looked exasperating.

And Harrison, at his desk, waited for O'Leary's arrival. Ellen, at her desk, was a mess but glowed.

He intercepted O'Leary before he had a chance to sit. "Got a lead. What kind of travel leeway do I have?"

"Where you going?" O'Leary poured Harrison a cup of joe, then another for himself.

"Vegas."

O'Leary settled behind his desk and indicated for Harrison to take a seat. "Let's hear it."

"It wasn't the interviews at the plant or my Friday evening visit with Roberto Alvaro, the maintenance dude, but Saturday night I was at *Cold*

Spot and a guy from the plant sat down next to us. He had some interesting things to say."

"Who was that, then?"

"Bryce Ross. (Harrison wasn't forgetting any last names this round.) Said he had run into Dale at the bar a couple times. So I lubed him up with some drinks and, it turns out, Dale told Bryce that he could change the odds in Vegas, that he had it all figured. When Bryce asked him, 'How you going to do that?' Dale said, 'With a van and a plan'."

"A van and a plan?"

"Bryce said it intrigued him – so he pressed him on it another night, but Dale just smiled and repeated what he already told him, 'A van and a plan, Baby, a van and a plan'."

"It's a lead, I guess. Enough to send ya? I don't know." O'Leary squinted an eye. "Too much time's passed, don't ya think?"

"I know, but there's something else. Pudge and I've been up and down the shortlist of Dale's relatives, but I took it a step further. Started splitting logs on the old family tree," Harrison handed O'Leary a note, "He's got an eighty-six-year-old great aunt that lives in Vegas. It should be worth a look, at least."

"I suppose it wouldn't do to pass it to Vegas PD. If he *is* there, you can bet, sure as shit, he won't be when they start stumbling around."

"Drive or fly?"

"Two-day drive, or a couple of hours, if we can get you on a plane. Going to cost the department a grand any way we cut it. Ellen," he yelled, "see if you can find Harrison a flight to Vegas. Pack your bag, Harrison, an git!"

Chapter 10
Big Shot

Degenisis
On the seventh day he rested,
and on the eighth he slept in.
"Man must be tested."
And the Devil took his turn.
"Look what I've invented,"
the dark angel proclaimed.
"It'll beat you like a mule rented,
no matter bags, and balls, and clubs retained.
No coincidence a word of four letters,
I used in the naming of my game.
Misfortune will propagate the others,
tongues impossible to tame.
Searching for the green,
rolling past the cup,
they'll call out his name,
with all their bad luck."

Like the first hole, the tenth tee-box sat near the clubhouse. Clear, winds light and variable. Jon thought, perfect day to clean their clocks.

Larry stood on the practice green, waving last outing's carefully preserved scorecard. And, like the taunting brat he was raised to be, said, "You girls ready?"

Behind Larry, shooting a 40, and down 5 strokes, Jon stretched, preparing. *Today I am gonna give ema lesson in golf. And soon . . .*

Otherjon interjected, *We'll give ema lesson in life – and death. Rawling . . . send these dweebs to hell.*

Not getting their licks in last week, the boys had pent-up grievances at the ready. Jon knew the owners well, and, like clockwork, they'd pick up where they left off. It was their time to push. They'd slide in smooth, building to a galling crescendo, then bring it back down going into the clubhouse. The consortium had Jon's number.

Tenth hole, par 4:

Larry's low score from the ninth gave him honors. He teed up, stepped back for a couple of practice swings, and gave Lon a discrete nod; the start in-on-Jon signal.

"How's everything lookin this month, Jon?" Lon asked.

"Real good." Habitually offering little more than necessary.

The group walked their way out to the shots.

Larry asked, "How's the JIT?" (Just in time, inventory)

"Getting there." Jon paused, cut grass with a practice swing, and continued, "Bins are filling and the semis are coming in from the farms, we're building up the three-hundred-thousand bushel piles in the lot. They're almost ready to be covered."

Lon nodded.

Mick had to throw in his couple of cents. "Better cover em soon. Another storm's a'brewin," and pointed his club to the western sky where fall weather generally came from, "they're saying on the radio."

Not looking up from his chip, Jon replied through gritted teeth, "Oh yeah . . . Henry and his guys'll be on it." With beautiful backspin, the ball bit and laid on the green. A three-foot sinker got him off the tenth.

Eleventh, par 4:

Old Money Lon and his new custom *TaylorMade* ten-degree one-wood smashed a drive out of the park. It rolled twenty yards past Jon's well-hit ball. Lon turned to the group, and in a faintly disguised brag, said, "Well, if that wasn't luck?"

"Good shot, Lon," Larry congratulated him and, readying to tee-up, he looked to Jon and said to the group, "That's what we need at *Core*, a home run, eh Boys?"

Jon didn't comment, but instead, joyfully watched expletive-barking Larry slam club head as his *Titleist* skipped into the bunker.

Mick enjoyed the results almost as much as Jon. "Your ball likes the beach today. You should buy it a little umbrella drink." Mick had no qualms goading Larry or any other elder. He knew he was the future, regarded respect an inconvenience, and grooved on acting the big shot he was soon sure to be.

They moved out to their shots. Heated Larry converted to his mission walk.

"Got a battery up your vagina, your ball isn't going anywhere, is it?" Jon pushed. *With a little luck, Larry will go down with an aneurism.*

Taken aback by the comment, coming from their slave, Larry slowed. *Did I hear that – or did my brain just play a weird trick on me?*

It looked to be a beauty. With five-wood, Larry clacked a hell of a long ball clean off the sand, but the little white globe managed a slice, as they often do, and found trees a hundred and fifty yards down-field. It nestled in a challenging lie 30 yards right of the green. Verbal color added, Larry chased, unconsciously returning to his mission walk.

The others hit safely and waited for Larry to chip out of trouble. A crack followed a click. Quiet seconds passed, and then the sound of ugly emanated from the tree line. Intensive chopping accompanied a burst of well-connected cursing. Larry emerged empty-handed, nine-iron apparently consumed by the woods.

Lon, deflecting Larry's temper, dropped a ball a few feet from the trees. "Here ya go." He gave Larry a pat on the shoulder and redirected their attention to Jon. "Jon, we've been hoping you could move some older guys along, you know, get some new young blood in there. Blow out some chaff, so to speak."

Not new news, ideas expressed and pressed at previous board meetings. Push out older tenured folk, bring in new low starting wage people.

Lower payroll, lower employment tax, lower health insurance premiums. *Good Business – for the consortium. Good Business – when plant manager gets the community ire – consortium hides in his shadow. Good Business – when I have to come up with an excuse to terminate. Then, Nice Business – when I see the guy I axed in town, certainly won't be asking Joe Blow, 'How's it go?' Other than Bobby, Bernice, and their Johnny Boy, I doubt any owner could name five employees.*

Twelfth, par 5:

After parring the eleventh, Jon led with a smash. The blast served the extended party a slice of humble pie. They offered shallow congratulatory remarks. Jon returned a two-eyed wink with a thin smile and nod.

The long 540-yard twelfth was a challenge. Mick and Larry found water, both put up snowmen. Jon did everything right.

Thirteenth, par 4:

The men watched Jon drive the green. To Larry and Dad, Mick said, "Well, stroke my *balls*."

With a helping of ugly bluster, the others crashed the course. Drives in neighboring fairways, shots in trees, hooking, slicing, duffing – golfing. Jon two-putted. Nearly audible, were the gnashing of teeth.

Consternation kept them quiet over the next few holes. Jon continued outshooting owners and caught another reprieve as Lon, Mick, and Larry spent time excusing dismal play.

Lon putted the sixteenth, counted, and said, "Don't ask." Larry scribbled Jon's comeback on the card and forced his hand to circle another par. "*God Damn*," Larry huffed. He leaned to Lon, and murmured, "Jon must've got into his Wheaties this morning, let's pull it together – salvage this thing."

Seventeenth, par 4:

Mick purchased a *Michelob* from Missy, the perky cart girl, and at the apex of Jon's backswing came a loud, *Pusheet*. Jon sent a grounder skipping a hundred yards out.

Mick guzzled, grinned, and said, "Better keep your head down, Jon," this time for Jon to take however *he* wanted.

Mr. R broiled in Jon's frontal lobe, *Take his head off.*

Jon fought back steam, and as Michael teed up, said, "You too, Mick, you too."

All chipping near the seventeenth green and the overdue owners started, anew.

"Jon, what's with *Core* expenses – keep going up?" said Larry.

"Corn prices."

"Yeah, we know, not talking corn prices, everything else.

"Upgraded a few things, valves, leaky junk made in China."

"Sherbt's not happy with the bottom line, Jon, and frankly, neither are we."

Here it comes, Joker.

Abandoning pleasantries, Lon added, "See Jon, we've about run outta patience, the numbers just suck . . . We're lookin at you, Jon. We're lookin at you to un-suck em."

Mick let the old guys work. He kept his mouth shut; it wasn't easy.

Now, Mr. R was giving Jon the aneurism. The pulsating pressure coursed into his putt and he ran the ball well past the hole and onto the opposite skirt.

Mick turned to Dad, and loud enough that Jon would be sure to catch it, said, "That's the Jon we know and love." Getting in digs – Mick's specialty.

Jon bit hard, tongue nearly bleeding.

The Eighteenth, par 4;

The last link coursed substantial left around a stand of trees. The strong and the brave might hook left, circumventing forest, or drive over it, but those who misfired paid dearly. All in the party felt confident today, but two stroppy strokes put Lon and Jon in the oaks.

Larry's curveball hooked left, skipped around the bend. He postured a tilted pose, applying imagined follow-through. "Lon, I hope that fancy *TailorMade* club of yours came with a return policy."

"Yeah, yeah, yeah."

Mick nearly swung free of his hundred-dollar golf shoes. *Th-wacK.* "Oh, *yeah.* That's it," Michael gloated. They watched his towering teeshot easily clear the grove. He adjusted his hat, and to Jon and his dad, said, "You lumberjacks have fun in the woods." He supplied them an exaggerated swagger, chasing ball around the bend. Larry, back in mission mode, accompanied him. Mick looked back at Jon entering the woods in search of the wayward *Titleist*, and said, "Looks like you're gonna be a loser today, after all."

A short search ensued – Jon found his ball a few trees shy the fairway. He peered out the arboreal canopy into the light. Mick and Larry stood on groomed grass, boasting near their safe drives.

Half obscured, Michael's backside was visible through a narrow opening between oaks. It looked . . . *Playable*, and Mr. R came-a-knockin.

Jon pulled out Big Bertha and teed up a *Pink Lady* recovered from the ruff.

Mr. R whispered a jingle, "*Take his head off. Take his head off. Take his head right off!*"

"*KerrrraacK.*"

Perfecto, right up the bunghole. The trick shot of his life with a slice of spice. Like he just eagled the 18th at the Masters, Jon pumped fist, lifted a knee, and with eyes bulging, roared, "*FORE!*" Jon, or Mr. R, smiled and leaned against a close oak, giggling, hand over mouth.

Taken to the turf by the 150 MPH *Pink Lady*, Mick, writhing in agony, screamed, "Son of a mother-fuckin goat!"

Not exactly up the bunghole. An expanding weal pulsated high on his upper thigh just below the left butt cheek. He pulled his Dockers low, exposing an enormous bleeding welt. Eyes watering, he twisted and stared, but dared not touch. Larry leaned in, shielded a look, and said, "Ooh, kiss my pattookas."

Jon played skilled politician, deflecting blame to the ball. "Holy Shit! Sorry bout that, Mick. Honestly, I think you saved me, though. That little son-of-a-gun would have been across the fairway and into the rough for sure had your leg not been there to stop the damn thing."

"His leg? More like his ass," Larry said, kneeling to help Mick to his feet.

Michael limped a circle. "Go get a damn cart, I'm riding in."

Larry said, "Yep, we better call it a day, get Mitchy up to the clubhouse – get some ice on that thing before it gives birth." Forty yards ahead, Lon came out of the woods. Larry, ecstatic, saving face with an incomplete outing, waved him to the clubhouse, and yelled, "Go up, get a cart. Mitchy got a boo-boo."

Larry – (85), Lon – (86), Mick – (fat ass), Mr. R – (apple pie)

Chapter 11

Crazy Train

Mr. R took the night off and Jon hoped for quality rest to follow up his qualifying round of golf. He applied sleepy-time pressure with Rebecca's pills and washed away any guilt with a shot of JD. But it wasn't to be. Bernice's new blouse dominated disturbed thinking as well as the push from Lon and Larry. Sleep came in fits and starts and, shortly before dawn, Jon settled into REM.

"All aboard." A full-scale version of the steam locomotive from last night's Christmas celebration was leaving the dreary station. "Hurry." A day late and a dollar short, Jon ran to catch it. "Come on," the conductor said, waving, and reached with a white-gloved hand.

Jon leapt, grabbed the help, and pulled himself up. "Thanks, buddy."

White wispy hair, matching his gloves, stuck out from under the Conductor's garrison hat. Old, lanky, and sunken cheeks accentuated his thinness. They stood on the stepped deck between two cars, clung a short iron rail, and watched the dilapidated station disappear in a swirl of smoky coal dust. Jon caught his breath.

"Well, old chap, we're glad you could make it." He brushed a presumptive dusting from Jon's shoulder. "You're quite a sprinter, Mr. Rawling."

"Have we met, sir?"

"No, but you're reputation precedes you, Jon. You don't mind if I call you Jon?"

"That's fine, and you are?"

"Well, I'm Mr. Conductor, here to make sure your dream goes smooth as Olay. And guess what?" He removed an oversized discombobulated pocket watch from his vest. The halves hung together by springs hooked in gears. The

minute hand fell off, landing at their feet. "Oops." He fetched it up and stuck it to the center stem. "There, all set. Two minutes to six, Jon. You made it just in time for dinner."

Sparks between wheels and rails strobed the ties below them. Building size Christmas presents loomed in the night vista.

"I seem to have forgotten where I'm going . . ."

"The destination isn't important, but enjoying the ride, that's mandatory. You best be off, if you're going to make dinner. This is the diner car, the one farther ahead, the birther – if you want to rest up after dinner." He opened the door and showed Jon in. "They're serving beef tonight."

A bushel of corn spilled from the door. Jon stepped in and waded down the aisle, shuffling through shin-deep kernels. Tall, cherry-wood booths with ornate carvings celebrated the aisle-side panels. Passengers filled bolstered seats covered in rich leather. Consortium couples with uppity friends feasted. Gluttonous, they ate turkey, roast, potatoes, and cake from silver platters. They swilled coffee and cocktails. As Jon passed, the consortium greeted. Their comments were snide and numerous.

"Love to have you – onboard – Jon." Stifled snickers passed up and down the car.

"Hi, Jon. Enjoy your ride." Ladies giggled.

"Hope you brought your appetite." The car erupted in laughter.

A guest's portly shoulders trembled. A mouthful, and he nose-laughed. Pressure rose – he sprayed the woman across from him, showering her in a fine merlot.

"Business or pleasure?" And again, they roared.

In the last booth, one person sat facing away. This booth, stitched in jewelry-box red velvet held a lonely lady with familiar hair resting on bare milky-white shoulders. Bernice sat alone – naked and waiting.

She looked up with desiring eyes and repeated the previous greeting, "Business or pleasure?"

Jon gulped and stepped ahead, looking to the birther car.

Bernice blocked the alley with her ample pin, huge on top, tapering to a narrow ankle and smallish foot. "Got a spot all warmed up for you," she said, patting the seat. She tugged Jon's sleeve and welcomed him in as she slid over a tish. And placing a hand on his knee, asked, "Did the conductor mention – this trip's about fulfilling Jon's dreams?"

"I think I'd prefer to wake up now."

"Oh, don't be that way." Her other hand plucked a steaming corn-on-the-cob from the surfeit mound in front of them. She rubbed it in a vulva of butter sticks, looked him in the eye, and with a teasing twinkle slid her hand on his inner thigh. Three-quarters of the way to Johnsonville, she stopped, gave a gentle squeeze, and glided the cob into her mouth. Butter dripped from her chin. Jon blinked and looked past Bernice to the reflecting black window behind. Mr. Reflection blew him a kiss, and with a squirrelly nod, whispered, "Go for it!"

Guests tinged spoons on highballs and coffee cups.

Rebecca rolled away, sliding her leg off Jon's. His dream flashed ahead.

The half-happy couple, now in a sleeper car . . .

They swam in corn, more under the kernels than not, just head and shoulders above. Bernice smoked a Virginia Slim and flicked Teri's 'Grease' lighter for fun. A small peep-door slid open and Jon's conductor friend peeked in. "Atta boy, Jon." The door snapped shut, restoring privacy.

She placed her hands on Jon's head and hoisted her milky shoulders upward, exposing her big girls. She bit the grit in baby-teeth, and using her lips, spoke around the smoldering fag, "Get back down there, Butter Boy," and pressed Jon's head deep into the corn.

"Nooooo," echoed through the Rawling house and bedroom windows vibrated on a like frequency. Jon's sweaty body thrashed wet twisted covers.

Thwump. Rebecca, deposited on the floor, yelled, "Ouch!"

Tuesday brought challenges that frequently came with Tuesdays. Challenges similar to Mondays, Wednesdays, Thursdays, and Fridays at Corny. Word leaked regarding employee revelry. Morning rumors sparked, flared, and spread like fire into the afternoon. Eventually, 5:00 p.m. rolled around, and Jon drove home, stewing.

It had been a day babysitting. Tension boiled up the back of his neck and into the base of his skull. Jon went for his favorite escape. Time for a trip down the hill to the boathouse.

Before going in, he looked down the bank out onto the gray-green river and endearingly checked his boat. Above the water, adjacent to the lengthy wooden dock, the mini cabin-cruiser waited on the steel lift. "Not tonight, *Baby Cakes.*" Late afternoon sun glinted off the boat's windowpanes. Jon, feeling the love, winked back.

The block boathouse protruded from the hillside with its top and front clearing the surrounding sod. Wisely constructed, it sat a good, safe distance up the bank. Steel trolley rails ran from under a pair of hinged cedar doors and continued down the bank to the water. Jon used the side door and entered the dark building. The familiar musty smell hit, then escaping chemical and sawdust odors brushed past. He pressed an old light switch and the "ON" button clicked in with a snap. The structure, built in the forties with fabric-wrapped wiring leading to and fro, was sparse on sockets. Above, in exposed rafters, two large incandescents circulated current through the switch's copper contacts.

Glowing bright, the clear bulbs illuminated his multiyear project. Jon stood, inspecting the antique mahogany hull, evaluating past progress. He rubbed his hand down the side and over a recent repair, then clapped, producing a small gray storm. The urge to work on the dusty mess quickly passed. Around the boat and against the back wall, stood a small, battered, round-top fridge. Jon pulled out a bottle. "Hello, Wonderful." A sanding block holding down his stool needed moving. He sat for a bump, glanced at his watch – *It's after five* – and touched his bottle to the bow – *I'm not drinking alone – I'm drinking with you.*

Jon thought about the rail job Bernice had typed up per his instruction. A schedule to ram down everyone's throat. And he recalled the day with a bristle. . .

Bryce heard about the introduction of twelve-hour shifts and fumed, anger pumping up his blood pressure. Already looking for deliverance from a head-pounding hangover, he went to the basement to visit Stillman, the still.

Stillman, acting company psychologist, hid in a defunct oil furnace and had tapped into the 190-proof flowing between Fermentation and the Beer Well a floor above. After additional filtering, Stillman freely dispensed shine to employees in the know, (most everyone in the plant.) And those, 'in the know', talked code about their colleague.

'You better go see Stillman on your break.'

'Stillman wants us to stop in later.'

'Did you say Stillman wants to see me?'

Stillman always had the right tool for the job, or with a sympathetic ear, metes out his best advice. What a mate.

A two-snoot binge and Bryce flowed through the men's locker room and up the stairway. *Hair of the Dog*. The headache moderated, but his vocal cords were all tuned up. Loud and belligerent, Bryce returned, revved, and ready to stir the pot.

"If they think I am working twelves they better think again. Tell me, tell me again, please, how you *idiots* didn't think we needed a union."

Not long and he had half the production floor joining in.

Mark: "This place sucks, I might call in sick next week."

Nancy: "I heard they're cutting paid sick time, too."

Bryce: "Captain Corn's lost his marbles. This place is falling apart as it is. How in the hell? Wheels are gonna come off the whole damn works."

Mark: "We should all call in sick for a week – see who needs who. First, they cut bonuses. Then came the pay freeze, and now they want us working like dogs. Just. Like. Dogs."

Cecil: "Piss poor benefits."

JR: "Time clock, don't forget about that. Now we're punching that damn thing, no trust I tell you, and no appreciation. *Time Clock*."

Gene, from Milling, walked by, catching the rant. He nodded, pointing his head at his department, and announced, "I guess we're only going to be working tens in Milling."

Bryce said, "That does it! I'm going right up to the office and take a dump on Jon's desk."

"Gross," Nancy said.

Bryce glared at Gene and lashed out with his whiskey-tongue. "Better get back to your crew, Gene-o."

"I'll get back to them when I feel like it, Stillman," Gene shot back, suspecting Bryce's earlier-than-usual indulgence.

Deb attempted sheepish mitigation, adding, "It's a free country."

Bryce gave her a 'zip it' look, then nudged Gene and said, "Free to be a KISS ASS."

Bill, in the control room, watched the scuffle develop on the grainy monitor. He keyed up the microphone for Jon's office. "Hey, Mr. Rawling, there's a disturbance on the production floor."

Jon depressed the com. "Yeah?"

"Looks like, well, I don't know, some pushing – shoving . . ."

Jon arrived, finding half of Gene's crew now in fermentation, bickering with Bryce, Mark, and the others. He cleared his throat, and the few that hadn't noticed his appearance trailed off.

As if speaking to kindergarteners, he asked, "Who's in charge of Milling?"

Gene bobbled his head.

"Who's in charge of Fermentation?"

Behind Bryce, Mark shifted and slid hands in his pockets. He tilted his head back to the side, and breathed, "Yo," looking away from the obvious question.

With the team's attention and figuring the cat's out of the bag, Jon said, "Bernice'll be distributing new schedules tomorrow. It goes into effect next Monday. We're going to buckle down and make this place hum."

Gene asked, "What about my people with kids at home? Lots'a folks can't work longer hours, they got families."

Now, Bryce, flipping sides, slapped the vat he leaned on and added, "Yeah."

Deb, with kids in school and a husband at home in a wheelchair, sounded worried, "Yeah, easy for you to say, Jon," and with voice barely audible, little more than a whisper, added, "Not everyone has it so smooth, like you."

"First off, Bryce, you're single, so . . ." waving a finger at him, then let it slide. Jon addressed Deb next. "There'll be room for adjustments to accommodate parental needs, but you'll have to work that out with Bernice. Anyone that can't work it out is obliged to ask her for a freshly printed, no-expense, resignation form."

Jon paused to let it sink in and to wait for any other dissatisfactions.

"Lest we not forget, here, how you all balked last year when I suggested everyone cross-train. Okay, so we see how that eventuated. Now, back to your battle stations, let's see what this place can do." And with that, Jon did a military about-face and walked out as the screwed crew burned holes in his back.

When out of earshot, Bryce turned to Mark and mockingly repeated, "Make it *hum*. Make It *HUM!*"

Jon poured a river of booze down his throat. He remembered, *I'm in the boathouse to forget, not rehash, the day.*

Ring-ity Ding Ding Ding, Rebecca rang the seldom-used dinner bell. Up more as a decoration than its triangular forged function, but when Jon lost track of time, she rang it with vigor.

Jon thought, *sometimes you just can't drink enough.* Tonight was going to be one of those nights.

As so many nights last year, while attending college, Teri sat on her bed, smoked, and worked a TI 55 calculator. Monday, Henry hadn't missed his legitimate opportunity to visit her with the previous week's load-out numbers. And Tuesday, Core Fuels' sneaky ledgers hitched a ride home in Teri's purse. Neat columns developed on yellow notepad pages. Adding and subtracting weren't her only attributes; other tricks in Teri's bag included algebra, statistics, and she was damn good at calculus, too.

I kind of miss Calculus – hmm – I'm weird?

After supper, Rebecca asked, "How's the old boat project coming along?"

"I'm out of dust masks, so didn't get much done tonight. I have-ta start another list, stuff to pick up."

"How long before we christen her?" she asked, and could give two shits, but it certainly was important to him. *It better not be Baby Cakes II.* "Something a bit more posh than *Baby Cakes*, maybe, eh?" But, just a little, she hoped that Jon had named *Baby Cakes* after her. (Which, of course, he had.)

"Haven't thought much about it, but I've a feeling the second it hits the water, we'll know. Anyway, I was thinking you should name this one."

"It's your project, your boat. I'm leaving that entirely up to you."

"It's our boat, we'll think of something. How about Hard Wood? Just kidding, no, really, let's wait till it hits the river, we'll think of something awesome."

Rebecca retired early. Jon quietly handled a bottle out of the cupboard and emptied the remnants into a tumbler. He downed it and checked his secret stash – both of them. Bottles previously expunged, and Jon discovered the Rawling residence a house low on booze, more so than remembered. *I guess I CAN'T drink enough.* He passed on Rebecca's wine, put the bottle in the boathouse out of mind, and tried healthy, for a change. Jon watched TV with water on ice.

The news, cheery as usual, included homicides in Omaha: a mother and infant.

Chapter 12
Bundle-O-Joy

He slept like a baby, until about six . . .

Jon ran down the hospital corridor. The thick air, a median, slowing progress.

An orderly yelled, "Hurry, you're missing it!"

He wiped perspiration from brow. With each stride, the floor and ceiling moved, but walls, attached insecurely at the top and base, slowly crept by.

He checked doors, right, left. At the end of the passage, their pediatrician emerged, and exclaimed, "You made it!"

"I did?"

Sunburned, as if he had been boating on a clear day in hades, Doc's face peeled. He wore a headband reflector and singed gray hair curled out from under.

"You look like you've been to hell and back."

The doc nodded. "A unique delivery." With bloody hands and smock, he presented Jon a newborn. The devil baby, wrapped in cozy chiffon hospital blanket, smiled baby baby-teeth. Jon recognized them well enough; Bernice's.

"Congratulations Jon, it's a boy."

Ancient scraggy nurses, one at each side of Doc, assisted with infant presentation. A click-ity-click tap-dance and they leaned forward, reached out, and, "Ta-da," gave Jon congratulatory salutations. The hoary gals curtsied, sporting Jon grim grins, less a handful of prongs.

He cradled the child. The munchkin chomped and swiveled his head toward Jon's grip. Like a set of wind-up dentures, two perfect rows chattered. The little monster flashed eyes of fury. Upset, not able to bite, he ripped his blue hospital-issue onesie, exposing a burly baby chest.

Doc snorted at the infant's antics. "Better watch your fingers."

"Hungry little bugger, ain't he?"

Jon entered the room with infant in arms. Rebecca lay in bed, unbuttoned her top, and reached for baby smiles. He handed her the bundle of joy. The infant twisted and looked back at an angle ridiculously inhuman, giving Jon a nod and an affirmative grin. "Hahahaha," prattled Baby Teeth.

Doctor and nurses explained neo-natal care, and after the extended diversion, Jon returned to the suite. Rebecca's milky, dead eyes stared at the ceiling. The bloody little shit, all filled up, gleefully squirmed in a pool of red.

Jon held his little monster down by stringy, plasma-soaked chest hair. From the operating stand, between scalpel and such, he found Onion Slayer.

The neonate growled, "Up yours, Dad, up yours!"

Jon woke with a start.

Mid-morning Wednesday, Teri knocked on the door-jamb of Jon's office. "Would you have a minute or two?"

"Sure. Come on in." He reminded himself of the years she had spent growing up at their home, how proud he was of her as well as his own daughter, how damn forty-nine he was. But fuck, she looked good.

"Mr. Rawling, I have some numbers to show you." She cocked her head and quietly asked, "Would you mind if we closed the door?"

She wore a sharp business suit with thin pinstripes, her hair was up with a stick, and she had glasses on. The ones she had worn to her interview – prescription zero. In her arm, she held a company ledger and a yellow tablet with it.

Jon, already up and passing, said, "Sit down, I'll get it."

Teri sat uncomfortably in the chair near the front of Jon's desk. Her slacks and top fit fine, but doubt was creeping in. *My math is spot on – hope I'm not a nosey fool.* Jon pulled the other guest chair next to her to sit where he'd rather.

"I'm not sure where to start, but we have a lopsided ledger."

"How can that be? You have the checkbook and I've signed every check leaving the place. No new rail or trucking companies in the mix."

"It's not exactly that."

"Well, I should hope not. You know we had an extra audit right before you started – figured to the penny how bad Higgus pummeled us."

Teri slid the notebook aside. "It's not that ledger, it's this one. The production figures."

"Pugh," Jon puffed. "Production hasn't been a problem, incrementally increasing two years now. And it should take another jump as we implement the extended hours." Defending the new schedule wasn't easy. His doubts had been reinforced by Mark, Gene, and especially Bobby, who had reiterated concern about the precarious condition of their rapidly aging and failing equipment.

"Someone," she meant Jon, "must be calculating the output to input ratio. Gallons out per bushel. Right?"

"Well, it's about a bushel to three gallons. That doesn't change, hasn't changed, has it?"

"It's fractional, Jon." She suddenly felt sorry for him and almost wished she could go back in time, about ten minutes, sitting at her desk, minding her own business. But understanding, too, that it wasn't something a person would notice, or even think to look twice at unless that someone liked numbers as much as she did. "It's in the hundredths, second number right of the decimal."

Jon shook his head, not in disbelief, and he knew very well what 'in the hundredths' meant, but how, why, or what Teri was talking about, escaped him. "Is that something we know, or even keep track of?"

Teri opened the ledger. "Entries have always been made in whole numbers and rounded off to the hundredths, that is. In July I noticed the notation was different. In August, with production being a bit higher, the numbers all changed again, and I didn't think much more about it." They stared at the ledger that meant nothing to Jon, all he could see was the production increases. His ray of pride in *Gloomsville*.

Teri felt herself spinning and backed up. "We actually make 2.8

gallons from each bushel." She handed Jon the yellow notepad and flipped the top page. "September came and we didn't change input, but my fraction decreased." She turned more pages on the notebook, exposing column after column of her bedroom calculations. "I went back a few years . . . the numbers – ratios – so solid, consistent, I mean, up until . . ." She stopped at May 1988 and pointed. "It starts here, about a year and a half ago."

"What started?"

"Gallons per week compared to the input."

"How much of a discrepancy are we talking about?"

"This column, May 1988 through the end of last year, looks, by my calculation, about five hundred gallons a week are missing." She turned the page. "Starting this year, almost exactly seven-hundred-fifty gallons a week, and last week a thousand gallons. Could we be losing efficiency, or is there any place *Core* could be leaking product?"

Jon knew of a leak, but not five hundred or a thousand gallons a week. *Maybe a couple of gallons a week – five, at the most, not hundreds.* "No, I don't think so, but I do have one idea . . ."

Teri jumped in, "It's evaporating?"

Jon almost laughed, *great with numbers but she doesn't understand the processes down the hall.* "No, not evaporating, but possibly a change in the brew recipe. Seems unlikely – unless someone took it upon themselves to do so. But the lab's always testing, always one-ninety proof."

"We shouldn't jump to conclusions, is what you're saying?"

"Too late for that I'd think, but I'll talk to Mark. See if the Brewmaster can shed any light on possible fluctuations." He stood to dismiss her. "Thank you, and in the meantime, discretion, please."

"Not a word."

"Next Monday, let's see what your math tells us about this week." Jon tapped on the notepad and handed it back. "I don't think anyone would know what they were looking at, but best not leave this lying about."

At noon Jon waited for Mark in the cafeteria. "Join me. I'm buying." He handed him a tray.

"Sure, but we have schedules worked out in Fermentation. Even Deb squared things with Bernice."

"That's my team . . . But it's not about that, I have some production questions."

Mark explained recipes, corn moisture content, mill grind, fermentation times, and more. Jon knew most of it, only asking a couple of questions when he fell behind.

"You know this stuff, I know you do. This isn't just about wanting to better understand working details, is it?"

"If we came up five hundred gallons short, where might it go?"

"A year?"

Jon had some doubts about Teri's conclusions and nodded. "Could we have a leak?"

"Hell no, Bobby would be on it in a minute. We couldn't leak without seeing it. If it was under a vat, it would seep to the locker room. Be an ethanol swimming pool."

"Evaporation?" Didn't know why he asked that.

"You know it's basically a closed system, right?"

"Right. Thanks, Mark, *Core's* lucky to have ya."

Chapter 13

The Accident

Dry weather pushed harvests ahead of schedule. Farmers trucked in local contracts and two corn piles grew fifty feet high on the south side of the plant. On Core's north side, via spur line, corn arrived by the trainload. In reverse order, six and down, bins filled, 260,000 bushels each.

"Bin Two's still missing the diffuser," said Bobby, Roberto Álvaro, the company tech.

Control Room Bill said, "Yeah, I know. Can't believe how fast grain can wear through steel. No wonder the dragline's screwing up, too much corn falling in the middle. . . You shoulda called em again."

"I did. Told *GRS*, when the train comes, we can't wait. Don't know what's going on, they're usually here in a day or two."

"Someone got their wires crossed," Bill huffed. "Probably forgot us. Hopeless – they know we can't go in there."

"*GRS, Government Regulated Services*, more like Mentally Regulated Services. I should've tried cleaning the rotor contacts before you started filling it."

"OSHA, you get caught in the bin and we'd both get fired. Anyway, dragline's working fine now. I ran it back and forth a few times before I started the fill. Call *GRS* again in the spring."

"I bet it was losing signal from the remote."

Bill shrugged.

Bobby rolled his chair close and watched the monitor over Bill's shoulder. "Lookin good, Bill."

"Four down, this one today, and tomorrow, Bin One; almost a wrap."

Bill squeaked past, rolled across the tight control room, and grabbed his mug.

"Almost full, ninety-five percent. I'll probably shove off after this. Leave you to it."

Bill rolled back, spilling coffee on his shirt en route. He brushed at it, took a sip, and set his mug on the counter. They watched, waited. "Ninety-nine percent." Bill pressed the icon. The drag auger stopped on queue.

"Well, that does it. Good deal." Bobby gave Bill a thumbs up.

Bill returned Bobby a smug smile, then touched the control screen to divert flow to Bin One. The monitor didn't change, the flow volume did not change, and flow destination to bin one, instead of bin two, didn't happen. Bill gave Bobby an anxious glance and pressed the icon a second time. The icon flashed. And, no change.

Bobby said, "Ya know, if the dragline gets covered it won't be good; press it again."

Bill's pissy internal voice repeated it, '*Ya know, if the dragline gets covered it won't be good.' Don't think I know that, I'm the Control Operator for Christ-sakes.*

He hit the icon again, this time loudly tapping the screen as if extra pressure affected software. The icon flashed, and nothing. Only the bin's level changed. Capacity, 102 percent. The dragline was covered.

Bobby yelled, "Kill it!"

Bill hit the 'Emergency Stop' icon and the massive input auger fell silent. "Crap, now what?"

"Shit, I'll call Jon, this is going to suck." Bobby hated involving *El jefe*.

Smoke rolling off the soles of his shoes, Jon said, "*Now*, what happened?"

"Flow won't switch to Bin One." Bobby pointed to the screen. "Bin Two's at a-hundred-n-three percent . . . dragline's buried. Bill had to kill it."

"What can we do?"

"Well, we'll have to call Dezers, they'll have to suck out some product cause . . .

Jon cut him off. "No, what can *we* do? We can't be down that long; more cars'll be here in the morning – and as long as it stays in this room." Jon shot Bill a glance and repeated in a softer, fresh tone, "What can we do?"

"I can figure it out, but I might need help. Can I take Bill up with me?"

Jon didn't have to think long. "No, Bill stays here. It'd look weird if I'm at the controls. I'll go with ya. He can watch us on the monitor. We wouldn't want someone coming in here and touching anything while we're up there, would we?"

Corpulent Bernice marched by the control-room window as *'Would we?'* echoed around the cramped room. She stared in. Jon, masking concern, turned a neat smile toward Bobby. Bill waved. "Ugh," Bernice grunted and passed.

"Your tie, Sir," Bobby said. Ties and manual labor mix poorly. Dragline augers and ladders screamed deadly. Jon removed it to leave with Bill for safekeeping.

Bobby stopped in Maintenance, grabbed his pack, and the two made their way through the plant, nonchalant as possible. They exited the north door and walked toward the outside repair shed.

"Want *tu* grab a scoop shovel; should be one leaning on Black Magic." Bobby pointed.

"I'll just be a minute." Jon entered the tin shed. Black Magic was initially company slang for an *American Standard* fitted in a small room in the back. Eventually, the shed in general had picked up the moniker. Jon lifted the stool's tainted lid and cringed. How many months, years, since it had been cleaned properly, he wondered. Black coated the bowl's inner, and as he whizzed, pieces broke loose and floated in the urine. Jon discovered the *Magic*, it miraculously flushed.

Two men, one with tools in a green canvas backpack, the other carrying a red-handled aluminum scoop shovel, entered Bin Two's top hatch and climbed down onto the landing. Bobby flipped on the food lights, illuminating a dusty haze. From the backpack, he pulled thin paper dust masks and handed one to Jon. The men descended the ladder to the golden sea of corn below.

Bill guarded the control room.

In the office, Bernice babbled to Henry and Teri. "You know what? Call it my crazy-good intuition, but I think something's shaking."

Teri wondered if it was something other than the flab hanging off Bernice's upper arms as she watched her rip cellophane off a bacon-ranch sandwich.

"Which way is the dragline?" Jon asked. Though, somewhat in a dome, the corn lay smooth and concealed it completely.

"Not sure. Already in too deep to tell."

The men waded to the center of the bin to investigate. "I'll start digging if you wanna try to figure out what's up with the input shoot."

Bobby gave him a cheap left-hand salute and waded back to the ladder. From the deck, he climbed the steep gangway that followed the slope of the roof. Jon shoveled around the spine, the center corkscrew on which the auger rotated. Bobby pulled the walkie-talkie from his utility belt to check in with Bill. "Eh Bill, we're in, *tu* see us *en su* remote?"

Startled, Bill jerked, banging his head. "Damn-it!" He re-plugged the power cord into the socket and skivvied out from under the desk. *Who knows, the infamous, 'did you try restarting it?' might help.* He got up, rubbed his noggin, and keyed the mic. "Bill here, the cam isn't on yet – hang on a sec." Bill ejected the Employee Safety video looping on *Core Fuel's* monitors and selected; Camera – Bin Two. A grainy picture unscrambled and 'Bin Two' in green bold font appeared on the upper right corner.

"Okay, I got ya." What Bill didn't do was select "Control Room Viewing," and anyone that bothered to look at one of the six, still operational, monitors throughout the plant also watched Bin Two indiscretions. Vigilant Bernice, between bites, noticed. Two men in a bin added up to trouble, and everyone knew the rules. She pointed at the monitor, looked over her shoulder, and gushed.

Henry strolled to the monitor. "What the heck? What's Bobby doin in there? Is that Mr. Rawling down in the corn? Rawling in the corn!" Henry slapped his thigh, chuckled at the pun, and hoping to impress, looked to Teri for approval.

As the words left Henry's lips, Bill's brilliant 'reboot' idea kicked the system into motion. Full augers groaned under duress and Bobby, wide-eyed, drew a sharp breath.

A few kernels dribbled, plipping off Bobby's face like raindrops. He turned to run and augers spun – the corn poured – thirty bushels a second.

Jon looked at his ankles and listened. *RrrrRrruh.* Deep in the kernels, an angry dragline strained to move. It lurched, sending a ripple through the granule sea. A dense corn tsunami stole Jon's balance. He toppled back, looked up. The fresh flow gurgitated. "What the FU . . ." and the golden falls hit.

The gusher ripped Bobby's walkie-talkie from his grip and sent him scrambling down the gangway, riding an amber wave of grain. He peered through billowing dust, and yelled, *"Vamanos* Sr. Rawling, *Vamanos!"* but it was too late. Jon was gone. Without walkie-talkie, Bobby screamed into the camera's cyclops eye. "Kill it, Kill it, Kill it!" waving fingers across his throat.

The restarting augers groaned and shuddered through the plant. Employees stopped, eyes landing on monitors. Most in the plant, now watched Bobby's distorted convex face, lipping, "Kill it," over and over.

No one better understood what the shudder meant than Bill. A depth-charge went off in his coffee-filled stomach. He turned to the monitor as Bobby the Mime frantically flailed. Bill spun, hit the Emergency Stop icon for the second time (The second time in his life for that matter). An inverted groan . . . and augers fell silent. Bill paled. Big, cohesive sweat beads formed on his clammy forehead. In frozen panic, he thought, *who coded this piece of shit software?* And in a bar near Lake Tahoe, Van Chung flaunted cash at a barmaid in a low-cut blouse.

Most opposite Bill's reaction, Bernice snorted a puffy chortle. A chunk of chewed sandwich shot out, landing on paperwork. It crossed her mind if uncle Falkher might give her a shot at running the show.

Bobby weighed options. Get help, or try to get to Jon himself. Either way, *time ticked.* Swirling dust slowed. Down the ladder and through the hanging haze he climbed, to the new, higher level of corn. He waded to the center and knelt where he last saw his boss slammed by the golden belch. After pulling a few armfuls of grain back and around, he realized the futility of one man groping. *Help – I need help – now!* Like quicksand, the corn sucked as he hastened to the ladder. Finally, the rungs, and Bobby was up and out.

Jon's battle for air began. The corn crushed like a kid mashing a sandwich, and, on his back, Jon struggled. *Move arms – Hands to face – Make a space? – Take a Breath! – Thank God I'm wearing the dust mask.* It had kept grain out of his nose and mouth, but the weight was unbearable. His eyes hurt, he tried to close them tighter. Corn in his ears, and it pressed his throat like an enemy boot. He fought for each breath; the pressure on his chest, a python's coil.

Bernice looked to Teri and Henry. "Let's see what's happening."

The three walked the hall past the control room window. Inside, Bill stared at his monitor, clutching tufts, and above, sweat glistened on baldness. Damp, expanding rings showed at soggy pits.

Bernice threw open the door. Guilty Bill spun in his chair.

Bernice snorteled, "What have you done, *now*, idiot." She smiled at Henry and slammed the door. Bill, through watery eyes, blinked empty, staring at no one. Teri watched the little round man from the hall window, the scolded child in the corner, missing only the dunce hat.

A curious crowd from malting, cleaning, and cracking made way toward Bin Two. Bernice's stream of three merged with the others and they filed out the north door. Past Black Magic, and on Bin Two's steps, they climbed the circumference. Bobby, heading down, shrieked, "Bring shovels! Hurry!" And Bobby had an idea. *The aerators.*

Empathy for Jon Rawling didn't run deep in the *Corny* crowd. Other than Bobby, only the newbie in accounting had help on her mind. *Hope he's okay*. Teri knew Jon and had spent the summer ignoring her crassitude workmates.

Two men near the tail end of the climbers turned, headed down for shovels. Bobby pointed. "Quick. Check in Black Magic."

The hand-rail spiraled the side, and for rapid descent, Bobby positioned himself on it, released his grip, and slid. Halfway down, Bobby met the up-crowd. He boosted himself off railing, stumbled onto the steps, and took an inside line, trying not to dance with ascending co-workers.

I'll hotwire the aerators – MacGyver em. Mark and Bryce will find shovels – they'll grab a few – won't they? Bobby touched ground and met the men coming with five-gallon pails and one shovel.

He spat orders, "Keep everyone out. He's near the center. Start five feet from the spine opposite the landing – move the corn outwards. I'll be right up . . . *Run, pinche cabrones!*"

Another quarter breath. *I'm going to die – Where are you now, Otherjon?*

Electric screwdriver whined, screws dropped and Bobby threw the cover panel. He ripped out the guts, snipping and stripping wires recklessly, only slowing, at last, to carefully insert two heavy black wires in a bright-yellow wire-nut. (Many-an unsuspecting homeowners had been lit up touching black. Bobby knew long before technical training, black meant death.) Hot, white, wedding sparks flashed from wires in their new yellow bungalow; loud and powerful aerators on Bin Two spooled up. "*Si!*" *Espero que no sea demasiado poco tarde*. And, vaulting stairs, he raced to the top.

Jon recognized the humming, felt the vibration, and battled for another half breath. The freshness of it elevated hope.

Mark and Bryce, the bucket-crew of two, squeezed between gawkers at the entrance. Then down, and they shoved past a tight crowd on the landing. An ascending line of spectators stood on the inside catwalk, peering down like a row of buzzards. With pails and a shovel, the men clunked to the sea of corn below. Teri gripped the handrail, and yelled, "What the *fuck*? Hurry!"

From the landing, Henry blurted, "Probably too late, anyway."

Two *Corny* lifers, on the catwalk, low-fived one another.

Bobby, climbing in, with legs of rubber and chest on fire, heard Henry's comment. "Is *NO* too late. We get him out, *pronto!*"

Bryce, not looking up, whispered to Mark, "Take your time, he's a goner."

Jon heard scooping and gulped for a puff of air. He also could make out most of the rhetoric. He was in deep, but not *that* deep.

"More that way," Bobby yelled, one arm flailing, one clinging to the ladder. Mark used the shovel, Bryce, a pail, and unattended, lay the other bucket. Five rungs above the granulated sea, Bobby pushed off, leaping into the corn below. In like a *Jart.* Knee deep, and resembling a dwarf, he pointed at the pail and glared at the jaded crowd above. "Really?"

Bobby started for it. A muffled comment from the gallery didn't escape him. "Oh-oh, lookout. His Mexican jumping beans are gettin steamed now."

A throttled laugh went viral.

Teri, appalled, felt she'd just witnessed one of humanity's new lows. She wanted out and Bobby gave her motive.

He looked up. "Somebody get the de-fib. Who knows where it's at?"

Like a schoolgirl, Teri raised her hand. She said nothing, nodded, and shuffled left. Nobody was forcing her to be there, but the cohesion of a group works in a peculiar manner.

Bobby looked at her, eyes pleading, voice cracking. "Seconds count!"

Teri spun, squeezed past Bernice's heft, and climbed.

Mark's eyes shifted to Bryce. "Hope springs eternal."

Jon heard scooping, *close, so close*, and he strained for a breath. The python coiled. *I don't want to die. Rebecca.* Again, he tried to inhale.

Strength spent, air expelled, and through him, a searing pain pulsed. A tear squeezed out and moistened the dusted hair pressed to his temple. Another minute ticked and the dormant form seized an involuntary breath. His heart clutched, pumping an oxygen-deprived final surge. Frontal cortex – sputtering on bad gas.

Jon let go. The golden beast received her due.

With Bobby's help, the corn crater grew. A couple of minutes and the tip of Jon's blucher said hello.

Frantic, Bobby dug with his less-enthusiastic cohorts. "Pull," he groaned.

Three sweaty men pulled their lifeless boss up and free. The gallery gave a light round of applause. Jon's subconscious sparked on scraps of oxygen lingering in a nonfunctioning system. In a dream state, he knew he was dead. He had felt his last heartbeat. The burning had passed, his mind drifted, dried leaves blowing down a gray street. Yet, the applause registered as a cheer of his passing, which it very well may have been. His final cranial imprint – Bryce, asking no one, "Wonder who they'll get to run the shit-show now?"

Bobby slapped Jon's dusty cheek. "*Jefe, jefe.*"

No response – he pumped Jon's chest. Each compression, pushing Jon back into the corn whence he came.

Bobby turned to Bryce. "Can you give him air?"

Bryce looked at Jon's death mask, slowly shaking his head.

Mark reluctantly pushed Bryce aside. "Move over, Sally, I'll do it."

Teri, returning with the de-fib, waded across the corn. She shuffled it from the bag, and pleaded, "Help!"

A couple of puffs in, Mark decided CPR wasn't much fun. "Here, give it to me." He reached and pulled Teri to the party. The idea of running the de-fib on Jon sparked rapture.

Bobby pulled at Jon's dress shirt, sending buttons flying. Teri tried to look at the de-fib instructions through a steady flow of tears. She gave up; holding them out for whom they may concern. Mark held the paddles, rubbing them together with anticipation. Bryce deciphered the illustrations, took initiative and gave Mark orders.

Mark waited for the tone.

Whwwhhwut.

Bryce said, "Hit it!"

Excited Mark pulled the triggers.

The jolt popped Jon's eyes open. Bobby peered into the lifeless pupils, no movement ensued. He felt for a pulse. Nothing. He gave Mark a determined look. "Again!"

The second jolt slammed Jon's eyes shut, body jumping. Teri looked away. Bobby checked for a pulse. "No go."

Mark, enjoying himself, cocked his eyebrows. "I'll try again."

Bryce waved him off. "Forget it."

"One more! Let me do it," Bobby said, prying the paddles from Mark's zealous grip. He spat on one and rubbed them together, then placed them on Jon.

Whwwhhwut, and Bobby stared at Bryce. "Recycle it, like glow plugs starting a Diesel in January."

The defibrillator said, "Hello everyone," and, with a high-pitched whine, spooled up on itself.

"Ouch." Teri put her hands over her ears and squinted.

WWWWuT. The signal blared.

Bobby gave him the lightning.

The ashen body arched like a suspension bridge, then fell to the corn.

Jon opened one bloodshot eye. It spun, scanning sweet Teri, the three sweaty diggers, and the crows in the peanut gallery. Wide-eyed, they all stared at him. Another lap and the eye landed on Bryce, and winked. Jon cracked a thin Cool Hand Luke-warm smile. With one watery eye glaring through Bryce, and in a dry raspy voice, Jon declared,

"*The Shit Show* has *JUST* begun."

Part Two
PLAN

Chapter 14
Take Stock

Larry parked the Wagoneer, picked his nose, and wiped the winner under the cuff of his slacks.

Sherbt's doorbell was a knocker and the butler answering wore a three-piece. "Mr. Falkher, Mr. Sherbt and the others are in the billiards room. I believe they are waiting on you."

"Maybe Sherbt could invest in some parking, had to walk halfway up the drive."

"Yes Sir, the fountain did take up more yard than expected. You have some perspiration on your forehead. May I suggest a trip to the restroom, Sir?"

"Screw that, is Lon here?"

"You're the last, the others are waiting. May I show you the way, Sir?"

"Out of my way, billiards room. Got it."

A minute later, Larry caught the butler in the kitchen chumming with the cook. "Could you show me where they've moved the god-damn game room to?"

Sherbt sunk the eight and tucked Mick's hundred in his shirt pocket.

"Larry's here." Lon used tongs to drop an ice cube in his drink.

Sherbt moved the group to the adjoining study and positioned himself at the head of the table. Some brought their drinks, and Lon, with his, sat at the opposite end of the glistening mahogany slab. Mick sat askew, keeping weight to one side.

"Has anyone not read the agenda?" Lon asked. Whether or not they had, no one spoke up. "Okay, thank you Sherbt, for getting this together." He patted it like a puppy.

Sherbt's lawyer whispered something in his ear. Sherbt smiled.

"You all have the preliminaries for the quarterly?" Lon held up a thin green binder like those placed at the other nine seats. "Alright, let's start with series A and B preferred."

Grumbles circled the table and back to Lon. Undisturbed, Sherbt sat, folder closed.

Mick pulled out a calculator, and, figuring off his 6200 B Shares, he'd deposit just shy of five grand for the quarter. He slid the calculator to the other young man at the table, showing his cousin the total. They looked to one another and shrugged. *Nice check for a round or two of golf.* And the cousin thought, *Membership has its privileges.*

Lon droned on, "Federal credits this, preliminaries that."

"I know you're looking at production climb and wondering how the hell your check could be less? It's all about the rising corn prices. Yes, our bottom line's off a few percent, but don't sweat it, Larry and I have Jon implementing a new schedule as we speak. . ."

"Actually, Bernice said she posted it yesterday," Larry interjected.

"Good." – "Sounds good." – "Excellent." – "Oh, good." Anticipation, confidence and pleased visages worked back and forth across the table.

Sherbt gave his lawyer a nod.

The lawyer stood. "Two things for you today. First, not in the folder, but just to let you know, litigation will be served to True Trust Bank on the second of October. I'm sure I don't have to tell you to keep that under wraps, but keep *that* under wraps." Chuckles circled. "Okay, now, if you'll turn to page seven, you'll find the proposal Mr. Sherbt has put together. Read it through and see what you think."

Lon interrupted. "This is a no-brainer, men. I want the go-ahead before the end of the month."

Sherbt's lawyer continued. "We would like to offer preferred commons to our *Core* employees. We call the shares *Core Commons*, or *CCs*.

And they'll be matched by the company, one for one with each share purchased. Share cost deducted from their paycheck, or offered for direct purchase at fifteen dollars a share."

"With dividends?" Larry asked, almost blubbering.

Sherbt sniggered and the lawyer answered, "With – the prospect – for future dividends."

"Christ, sounds like a giveaway to me," Larry said.

"Can we offer shares like that . . . if we aren't publicly traded?" Mick asked.

The lawyer let Lon field his son's question. "These are private offerings, direct from the company. An offer for labor to buy in, to participate."

"What the fuck are you talking about! Participate?" Larry went off.

Lon paused and looked across the table to Sherbt. Sherbt, happily unresponsive, looked at his lawyer.

"Yes, participate . . . Hmm. That might be putting it in an overly generous light. Read it through, everyone. And for you on the board, remember, you decide when and if you ever pay a dividend, and employee purchases should cover *Core's* note, well, the interest anyway."

"How many shares you printing? Larry stoked.

"As many as they'll buy," said the lawyer, and stared at Larry, like it was he who owned a fat slice of Nebraska. "One last thing, look." The lawyer flipped pages, "Here, bottom of page ten. The company's matched shares go into holding, can only be sold after the employee is vested – that's seven years." The lawyer tried not to smile. Communicating his crafty work out loud delighted him. Pleasure glands overflowed; he pushed his glasses up and sneered.

Lon placed a reassuring hand on Larry's shoulder. "Think about it, the motivation. Way better than the out-of-pocket bonuses we used to give. They'll work hard as hell, and for what? Nothing, some pieces of paper with *Core Fuels* printed on top. Maybe we give em a couple pennies a share, half a percent? And so what if it's worth a couple of bucks down the road, meanwhile, we make bank."

Larry fumed in silence, half soothed, a quarter consoled.

"Should we call an ambulance?" Teri asked. With Bryce and Mark's help, Jon sat up, grimacing. Again, she asked, "Should we call the ambulance?"

Everyone above gazed down in disbelief – Bernice wishing they would have put the paddles on his temples.

Jon coughed, took another look around, and gaining his bearings, waved Teri off. His chest burned, head pounded – every heartbeat smashing a starved, blood-lapping brain. *Worst hangover known to man – picked it up in hell – brought it back.* A painful heat surged, burning into every cell. And he felt heavy, weighed down, full of half-dead tissue.

He tried to get up but wavered. Bobby grabbed him and the other two men helped lift. They got him moving.

To the four near him, he breathed, "This never happened."

His open dress shirt, dust-coated and with splotches of damp grime, looked a sweaty blue-gray camouflage. His hair struck an oily pose. And after adjusting the button-less shirt, he looked up, shielding his eyes from floodlights. A silent audience stood above. Jon looked at the silhouettes, winced from the glare, and growled, "Get back to work, you sons-a-bitches."

Monitors throughout the plant, the rugged six, broadcast the action and the score. Employees who hadn't made the pilgrimage watched with indifference as Jon placed hand and foot on the ladder to climb out. In the control room, the seventh working monitor no longer glowed. A white smoke tendril rose from a gaping hole. Bill's chair lay toppled on the floor in front of the imploded cathode-ray tube. The other chair hung between the room and the hall. The shattered viewing window lay distributed across the floors, some in the control room, more in the hall.

Bill hid in the basement.

Two drawers, and below them, two sliding doors fit under the shelving in Jon's office. From the left drawer, he took a white shirt in clear factory wrap and went to the bathroom to change.

"How we doin, Johnny Boy?" Mr. R asked.

Jon gave him a look, *how ya think*. Gingerly, off with the button-less blues, and he laid the tatter on the counter next to the sink.

"Did you hear those shits? I did, I heard those shits."

Jon turned, lifted his arm, inspecting the red blotch on his side. He touched the one on his chest. "Ooh." *Tender.*

"A real eye-opener, that defibrillator, eh, Joker?" Mr. R chuckled.

Faucet on, and hot water steamed the mirror, shielding Otherjon's view. Jon removed stick pins from the new shirt and stuck them well into his thigh.

"What's up? – You better not be taking it out on us."

Jon buttoned the crisp shirt and with the soiled blues, cleared the steam for Mr. R. *It's what we do – isn't it?*

"Kill Bill."

"No." Jon pulled out a pin and tossed it in the waste.

"Kill Bill."

"No." Another, out and in the bin.

"Your tie's in the control room, go strangle Bill."

"I'm not killing Bill." Jon pulled two more.

"Kill Mark."

"I'm not killing anyone."

"Bryce."

"I don't think so."

"Henry? Bernice? How about Mick the Prick? Larry? Or Lon!"

"I said, I'm not killing anyone – right now." Jon placed three remaining pins between fingers and pulled with a jerk.

"Later then?"

"Maybe."

Otherjon pouted, then declared, "Rebecca!" like it was an epiphany.

At the mirror, Jon glared.

"You're such a pussy."

Jon spiked the blue shirt in the waste as he left the men's room.

"Wait!" Otherjon begged.

More agreeable than he imagined, Bernice, willing, almost jovial, went with it.

He closed the office door behind her. "Seeing's that I brought this teeny mishap upon myself and no employees were injured, I see no reason we need to file an accident report."

"Oh, no, that would just gum up the works. The thought hadn't even crossed my mind, Mr. Rawling," and she smoothed her somewhat inappropriately-short plus size dress. "No one would benefit from a temporary shutdown, some silly old investigation, or such, now would they? Tomorrow, if you don't feel like coming in, I'll cover, it'd be fine. Business as usual."

"Thanks for the offer, but I'll be in bright and early. A couple of things before I go. You'll take care of the sign in the front hall?"

"No accidents at *Core Fuels* in a long, long, time." She loved leverage and filed Jon's untruth for future use. *Uncle Falkher, Jon's having problems following protocol.* She had an angle, and not just over a peon, this time. Lubed gears turned. *The mileage I'll wring out of this.*

"Good, and could you find Bobby? Tell him to stop in right away; I want a quick word with him before I head home. See if he can get Dezers out here tomorrow, or ASAP."

Bobby visited. Jon left early.

It happened, and with a plant full of witnesses, Jon's cover-up would be superficial. Bernice flexed her muscle, warning of consequences as she made the rounds, and by late Wednesday, everyone understood. 'Gossipers will be outed, condemned, put to death.' Well, not to death, but she had a knack: if she wanted you miserable, you were miserable.

Jon's drive home could have been better. Stagnant blood clotted his thinking and felt like a dagger twisting in his forehead. An occasional spasm jolted him. They felt like spears, piercing his lungs from behind. A coughing fit seized him and his mouth tasted of burned flesh. The Impala swerved, in puffs of tuft a rabbit life ended – *thumpity thump* Thumper.

"Did a little oil change for you while I was under there."

"Thank you, Mr. Kenzie," and hoping to sound intelligent, Leia asked, "How was the flex plate?"

"Chewed to shit, like I figured. Saved you on it, though, old mechanic trick, flipped the ring gear and welded it back on. Probably outlast the rest of the driveline. Here's the warranty card for the new starter." He slid it across the counter with the bill.

Leia made out the check for damages and handed it to Jake. "Would you mind if I used your phone to call out to the folks?"

"Mom, hi, just got my car back. How about I bring out KFC?"

"Oh, please, do come out, but forget the chicken. I've got chops thawed in the fridge that need to be made and I dug some fresh little potatoes this morning."

"Mmm, num, fresh potatoes. What time?"

"Whenever, we'll start them when you get here."

Leia didn't bother knocking and Rebecca was in the kitchen. "Looks like Dad beat me home."

"He changed and went right back out. I told him not to be too long, that you were on your way."

"You saw the front of the car," Leia asked.

"Oh, yes, he told me all about it."

I bet he did. "Is it fixable?"

"I think so, he mentioned something about getting used parts." Rebecca turned the burner up and flames licked the kettle of scrubbed red-russets. "These won't take long. How about you go out and round him up, eh?"

Leia walked down the bank to the boathouse and knocked. "Dad?"

No answer, so she pushed in. *I love this old switch.* She clicked it, then made a trip around the boat-in-waiting. *It's getting close – next summer – I bet.*

The dirt path from the boathouse intersected steps leading directly from their yard down to the dock. Built before the Rawlings, flat field rock, collected and dug in place, made an iconic stairway. They'd been told the visionary builder's name, who left his mark in stone, and for fifty years now, owned a slab of granite. Leia had shamefully forgotten the name.

Dad wasn't on the dock, but she chanced a look in *Baby Cakes'* cramped cabin. On the lift, the boat's windows sat eye-level and she found the cabin empty as she guessed it would be. She stood a minute on the end of the dock and looked out over the *Platte. God, I love this spot – the view – the river.* Books read, thousands of pages turned. Summers sitting there in a lawn chair. Sometimes with her legs over the edge, and sometimes, when the river was high, feet swishing back and forth in the water.

In the yard, by the lean-to, she found the black Dodge backed up to the log splitter. She found potatoes, carrots, yellow over-ripe cucumbers, and pumpkins still growing in the garden, but not Dad. *Mom's territory – bet Dad hasn't set foot in it all summer.* From the unattended garden, she walked to the summer kitchen. The empty room, also Mom's domain, looked fall busy. It smelled ripe. Large pots of water on the stove waited their reheating. Canning jars – those not already sealed and in the cellar, sat on the shelves.

Where's he hiding? Leia followed the mowed path from the summer kitchen around the house. Almost a hundred yards north, up the hill and in the trees, sat the old smoke-house. It had been a long while since the smell of smoked catfish had breezed down the hill and time had transformed the shack into an inconvenient tool shed. The grassy path gave way to dirt as it entered shade at the incline. Jon, up the hill, stood off the path and near the shed. Leia called to him – almost. *What's he doing? Peeing? No – thank goodness – but – what IS he doing?*

The dry dirt quieted her measured and curious uphill approach. She watched with trepidation, *He's not right.*

"Hi, Dad."

Jon turned slowly, excruciatingly slow, like a machine, a robot on a gear. "Hi, Princess."

In his belt, a shiny blade glinted.

She shivered. "What-chu' doin?"

"Just . . . taking a walk."

Jon rolled in at 6:30 Thursday morning and the lot could only have been emptier if Bill's metallic blue Impala wasn't sitting in the middle of it. Otherjon said, "Pull close."

Bill's year newer Impala looked like Jon's. Same tail lights, same body panels, and similar grill, but with smaller openings. Today, Bill's blue Impala took honors, considerably more appealing than Jon's old-man-tan version with missing grill, bent bumper, and smashed header. "Kill Bill," Otherjon suggested again. "Is he in there?"

"I thought we talked all this out last night?"

"Quit being so reticent. We don't want to pass up any freebies, do we, like if he happened to be walking across the lot? It's early, kinda dark; he could accidentally get run over. What a lovely sound that would make."

"That'd put the kibosh on the agenda, now, wouldn't it?"

Jon looked at the razor-blade in the ashtray, it looked sweet.

"None of that this morning. Get in there, managers manage, plan, execute."

"Plan . . . Gotta go, make sure Bernice fixed the sign like I told her."

"Ooh, it smells like vomit down here."

"It's Bill, he's dead!" someone yelled from the shower.

Bill slumped in a wet pool, eyes blank, staring.

Gene held his breath and went in. Bill's chest rose and fell. Gene turned the shower handle. Cold water spattered in puke. Bill slithered forth and moaned, "Where am I?"

"He's only death warmed over. See if Malcolm's in yet, and grab some towels. Where's Bill's locker?" Gene asked.

Mark gave Gene a hand; together they helped him up and held the deadhead under the shower.

Bill's head bobbed. "I killed him, I fuckin killed Rawling!"

"Good job, bout time somebody got the bastard," Gene said, looking at Mark, over Bill's baldness.

Mark laughed, "Sorry Little Buddy, swing and a miss."

"You just killed him a little."

"He's under a thousand bushels."

"We got him out, zapped him, alive and kickin. He's already in – saw him in the office. Probably at his desk right now, figuring how to squeeze blood out of a turnip."

"More benefit cuts," Gene added.

"What, he – he's at his desk?"

Gene and Mark nodded. "Probably," Gene said.

"Not *Weekend at Bernie's*, right?"

"Rawling's as live as you." Gene helped Bill get his puke shirt off. "More so, I'd say."

"What should I do?" Bill wiped at residual vomit on his chin, half a lunch washed down through chest hair and dammed above protruding belly.

"How bout we sneak you out? Call Bernice as soon as ya get home – tell her you're sick. You're sick, right?"

"God yeah. It's a bad one, *owha* my head."

"Looks like your lunch came up with Stillman."

"You guys aren't going to tell, are you?"

"Tell what? Bill killed his boss, got drunk on product, passed out, puked in the locker room, slept in it, snuck home, called in sick. Naawh, boring, SSDD. Oh, but we saw your smashing handiwork in the control room. Now there, you might wanna say 'sorry boot dat', and you'll pay for damages, maybe, huh?"

"Oh, God, I almost forgot about that. I'm gonna get fired, ain't I?"

"Don't worry your bald little head about it," Mark said.

"I don't think so, tell ya what. Mark and I'll go smooth it over with Rawling."

"If we can get past Bernice," Mark added.

"We might just catch him at lunch."

Bill looked at his shirt half plugging the shower drain. "I don't keep anything in my locker."

"I got a shirt you can borrow. Let's get him out of here, Gene."

"Got your car keys?"

Bill nodded.

"Here, take a towel to sit on."

There wasn't much sneak to it. They escorted Bill up the stairs, hung a left, and pushed him out the southwest exit.

Mark's white shirt-tail covered Bill's wet ass and he moved slow, head down, eyes squinting in the morning sun.

"See ya tomorrow," Gene said and half waved.

Bill shuffled between the growing corn piles and circled out of sight. Mark closed the door.

"We going to talk to Rawling?"

Gene crinkled his eyebrows, hinted a smile and motorboated an exhale through pursed lips, "Bbwhf-bwhf-bwhft."

"Well, what do ya think about that?" Bryce asked, slowly passing behind Teri with his lunch tray.

Teri sat with Monica and Nancy from production. Flattery felt Thursday at Cold Spot had been short-lived, but with yesterday's bonding, she might give him the time of day. "Think about what?"

"Come on. Don't tell me you didn't see it? Our illustrious leader and the sign in the entry, the status quo, Bernice didn't change it. Forty-five days, no accidents. Lord help us, Kernel Corn." . . . Bryce sat down, shaking his head.

Teri stood. "Save it." She looked at the girls. "Enjoy."

A red service truck sat in the north lot under midday sun. Printed on the doors, Dezers, and the truck's hitch held an open trailer. Seven full rail cars waited a mile down the spur line. Henry talked Jon into spilling ten thousand bushels out Bin Two's base relief. Corn poured from it.

"We're good," yelled A *Dezers'* employee, and he waved from the top of Bin Two.

It was Henry's turn to signal 'cut it' with fingers across throat. "Gilbert," he yelled, "Shut it."

Gilbert struggled, sealing the never-used purge. A great spill covered the lot, edging under *Dezers'* F450. "Go get the payloader," Henry shouted.

Gilbert waded through the relief from Bin Two and went for the *Cat*.

Henry met Jon, Bobby, and *Dezers'* specialist at the front of the truck. A clipboard rocked on the hood as *Dezers'* man filled out the work order. Henry said, "Won't take long, Gilly'll get this cleaned up and dumped in the farmer piles on the other side."

Jon kicked the gravel and looked at Henry.

"He'll have to skim it." Henry shrugged. "We'll lose about a thousand bushels."

Jon turned his attention to Bobby. "Let me know the minute they have it fixed."

"Of course," Bobby said.

"Can you cover for Bill . . . without mucking it up?"

"I could do it," Henry said.

Bobby had a tough time believing Henry could run a toothpick, but had to admit, the guy had responsibilities and, thick or not, was capable in his department.

"I'm sure you could," Jon said. *If Bill had a month to show ya.* "Bobby's run it a little, and if *Dezers* would be so kind to stick around until we get a rail unloading, see we're operational, I would . . ." Jon fought through a short coughing fit . . . "We would appreciate it."

Bobby asked, "Did you see Doctor?" He shrunk, realizing *Dezers'* man knew nothing of yesterday's events.

Jon shot him a look, shook his head. "I'll be fine, just the dust."

Not uncommon to find the mercury pushing ninety degrees in the production area but with the west-end expulsion fan on the fritz, the temps topped a hundred. A floor fan's dust-embellished blades pushed stale air around Henry's cramped office. Small to begin with, his desk looked student-like, and Henry, in a chair fashioned to it, sat with knees higher than his belt.

"You're going along with it?" he asked.

"And why wouldn't we?" Bernice drew a handkerchief from her stretchy pantsuit, dabbed beads of sweat forming on her face, then tucked it down her strait-top blouse where it might continue to work.

Hard thinking initiated, Henry's eyebrows lowered.

"Do we have a good thing going?" She waited.

"And do we need any investigators snooping around?"

Henry's posture rose with his eyebrows. "Yes, no." Riddles solved, and with good news, he continued. "I told Jon we'd lose a thousand bushels in the lot today. It'll be more like five-hundred."

Bernice cocked her head and reached, scrunching his nose with her fingernail. "Or maybe fifteen-hundred."

Five in the cubicles listened, a few whispered, looked to Rawling's closed door, and whispered some more. The coughing rose and fell in waves. Ten minutes in, Teri knocked and entered. Jon stood hunched, one hand steadying himself on the window frame.

He looked her way, then back out the window. "I'm fine. . . Just heartburn."

Teri handed him a cone of water she'd brought from the cooler. "Here, this might help."

"Thanks, you're a sweetheart. Is Bernice out there?"

"No, I think she's making the rounds."

Like a blind man, he felt his way to the end of the shelving and to his hanging suit-jacket. He draped it over his arm. "When she gets back, tell her I had to leave early, could ya?"

Jon parked in front of their white fence, shut the Impala off, but waited to exit. Heartburn turned to heart-inferno. *Anything for relief.* Chest pounding and coughing didn't do it. He laid across the front seat, stretching arms overhead. It seemed to help. He got out, pushed the Impala roofline in a runner's stretch, cleared his throat, and breathed deep inhalations. *Better*, but the burning oscillated; he momentarily clutched at his heart. A jog down the stone stairs to the river did the trick. Marked improvement settled him, *try the couch*.

"You're home early."

The coughing subsided and dinner went down without grievance. Rebecca cleaned up. Jon changed and went out.

Not a single decent target floated on the river. He left the dock with a box of shells in one hand, polished handgun in the other, and walked around looking for something to shoot . . .

. . . The pistol barked, shattering country evening calm. Rebecca jumped; mother's little helper spilled in her lap. She craned to look out the kitchen window. *Crack Crack* . . . *Crack Crack*, and from a rickety sawhorse, a row of pumpkins, ripe squash, and zucchini exploded. At twenty yards, Jon shot eyes in an elongated orange pumpkin sitting at center. He reloaded and sprayed lead at pumpkin head. Rebecca bristled and refilled her wine glass.

Quarter to eight, Friday morning, Bernice said, "You're in bright and early."

"And you. Any more problems with the schedule?"

"They've come around. I made a couple of adjustments, accommodations for Deb, and Gene finally got his people figured out, and Bobby's in the control room for now. Bill called in sick again, said he'd try to come in at noon, if he's better, sounds fritzed out. You know, he busted the window and monitor in the control room?"

"I know, if he comes in, try to settle him down. Tell him everything's AOK as far as *Core Fuels* is concerned. Bobby said he'd steal a monitor from another area for now. The window can wait. Run an ad for maintenance help. Part-time, low level – we supply the broom."

Teri and other office staff filtered in. Jon greeted them, everyone did their thing.

At ten, many went on break.

From his office, Jon watched. Bernice and Henry sat in her outer cubicle communicating in low tones, body language disseminating secrets.

Jon questioned the meeting's validity. *What ta'hell are they up to?* He let it ride, *as long as Henry isn't pestering Teri.* But closer to the door than his desk and Jon moved to the file cabinet, where travails to garnish confidences might continue. Bernice shifted, noticed the encroachment, and sent Henry packing.

Core Fuels employees worked their last regular eight-hour shift before next week's tizzy.

CHAPTER 15
Henry's Figs

Teri watched from the corner of her eye as Henry loitered at the soda dispenser. She glanced at Leia and rolled her eyes. "That guy creeps me out. He always has an excuse to stop in the office and bug me. Tries to be funny, hittin on me. And believe me, he was born without a funny bone."

"Oh, is that him? Old Henry, right?" She paused, looked him over, and thought, *not that old, though. Maybe forty.* Leia offered up support, "Big creep. Looks like he should be on *All Star Wrestling*." She took another peek. "His arms are bigger than my legs."

"I think he spends a lot of time fondling weights."

"And reading books?" Leia quipped.

"Right, Moby Dick."

"Is he wearing work boots?"

"Oh yeah."

"What brand do you think they are? Chick Magnet?"

"Classy, *NOT*." The girls laughed.

"Looks like he's by himself."

"I'd bet a whiskey-coke he overheard me talking to ya on the phone today. This is no coincidence; he knew we'd be here."

Under her breath, Leia let out, "He's comin over."

"Crap. Play it cool – watch this."

Henry approached, but before he could open his mug, Teri nonchalantly turned and met his eyes. "Oh, hi Henry. What movie are you going to?"

"*Uncle Buck*. I bet you gals are too, aren't ya?"

Leia slipped her *Uncle Buck* stub into a back pocket and Teri replied,

"Nope, we're goin to the new murder one, *Poolside*," and she pointed to the black and white poster of a belly-up, floating corpse. "Well, we gotta run. Ours is startin. See ya." She wanted to add, 'wouldn't wanna be ya'. Henry stood there, holding his refreshment. The girls scurried away quickly as they could, trying not to be too obvious that he was the plague.

Leia felt let down, *Uncle Buck* looked fun. *If Teri's that freaked out by the dude, what the heck. Poolside will work.* They were "Wing Girls" and when you're a Wing Girl, you work it.

POOLSIDE:
Feisty Heisty

One hundred fifty-two minutes later, they watched the credits roll.

"That was cool. What did you think?" Leia asked.

"I loved it, but what a long movie. I thought it was going to be a murder mystery, not so much a robbery."

"Well, it did say 'Feisty Heisty' on the poster."

"It did, but the floating dead guy threw me off. Fun movie, the drunk underachievers pulled it off. They reminded me of my parents."

"Your parents aren't drunk underachievers."

"Oh, come on, Leia. They aren't Irish, but they drink like they wanna be."

Leia completely understood where Teri was coming from; it was why most all the sleepovers growing up had happened at Leia's house. "Your parents are nice, they don't overdo it that often." *Kind of a lie.*

"Of course they do. There frickin pickled. But that's all right, I love em. They're my favorite type of alcoholics, working ones."

It was late and, leaving Theater 4, they both yawned, induced via an older gray-haired couple yawning in front of them. They turned and laughed at one another.

Leia's Mountain Dew had her back teeth floating. In the hallway, she said, "I'm going to the bathroom."

"Ok, I'll be right out the door." Teri needed a smoke. Every time she lit up, she heard her father's reiteration, 'Still got that monkey on your back, huh?' Her dad had a whole speech about why they still let cigarette companies 'sell those damn cancer sticks.' It was mostly about genocide, keeping the global population in check. Her dad was no dummy, but sometimes he was pretty funny.

Teri grabbed the bar and pushed open the heavy commercial EXIT door leading to the parking lot. *Click Clack*, it latched loudly behind her as she dug in her purse for cigarettes. With smokes in one hand and her pink *Grease* lighter in the other, she looked up and spied The Hulk, leaning against his Suburban. He was staring at her. Teri turned, tried the door latch. Locked, and the sticker on the door read, EXIT ONLY. She muttered a diminished "shit", then slowly turned to face the goon. *How do I play this? – Stall – Leia'll be just a minute – I hope.*

Through her, a prickle tinged. She tinctured white and faked her cool as Henry approached. Flame on high, fumbling with her cig, and she managed a light in the midnight breeze.

Lot lights cast three Henry shadows; long, long, and longer they reached as he meandered toward nervously-puffing Teri. He paced himself, moving slowly as not to scare off his prey. The shadows melted under security light scrutiny. He presented a pensive grin.

"How was your movie, sweet thing?"

Teri took a long deep drag. *I bet it took him all night to come up with that line.* She shrugged, looked skyward, and expelled an extended rivulet, mostly at him, trying to use it as a shield. She huffed and puffed again.

"Where's your sidekick?"

"Ladies' room, she's on her way. I rode with her." Teri wished she hadn't offered up even this much. She was cool handling oafs, but this was a new, scary situation she hadn't exactly visited before. Even Henry's foreboding size made her uncomfortable.

Leia, the last patron, left the bathroom. Vacuums echoed. The ushers had turned off most lights and locked her side-door shortcut. She headed for the lobby.

"How about you tell your sidekick goodnight? I have *Jack* in the glovie and ice-cold *Scores* chillin in the back. What you say we go for a cruise?"

Her skin crawled. *Of course, he has Jack in the glovie. What else does he know that I like? – What else does he know about me? – Freakin' stalker.*

Puff, stall, puff.

"Sorry, one date a night, and tonight it's all about the girls."

"Aw, come on, I got a great spot to show ya and the moon's almost full, you gotta see it."

R i g h t, like my first date with scary-man, any man, would be driving around drinking at midnight – Extra, Extra, Read all about it: Raped and Rotted Body Found in Culvert.

She did have to see him Monday. Firm, semi-polite, "No, I'm really tired."

Henry's big mitt clamped her bicep.

A yelp, and she tried to scream; fear swamped her. A weakness washed through her and she started to shake.

Leia walked through the lobby.

Henry growled, "Ya know, I'm really tired of you giving me the cold shoulder!" *If I can't get any the hard way, I'll knock some off the easy way. Maybe she likes wrestling.*

A monstrous shot of relief; Teri saw Leia rounding the corner. Now, with fire in her eyes and a surge of courage, she looked at Henry straight away. "Let go of me, Pea Brain."

"Pea Brain," he retorted, face reddening.

Her approach swift and Leia shouted, "What's goin on?"

Henry, not expecting her, (especially from another direction) turned and pulled Teri close, arm around her shoulder, securing his prize. "Your friend and I were thinking about going for a cruise, you could join us." Henry's mind swam in a great little fantasy.

I should put my cig out on the back of his hand. Teri refrained and tried to squiggle free. "I'm not going anywhere with you tonight, or any other night."

Henry looked confused and reached to gather Leia.

"Don't think so, big boy." With a shoulder feint, she slipped his grasp.

Leia, not a fighter, retained a single move from her one teen year in Tai Kwan Do. And she unleashed it spectacularly. A fuckin-full-fury front kick to the figs, a real nut-cracker. A kick sent down from ancient Karate masters. Whether by skill, or by-luck by-golly, the crotch-crusher brought Henry to his knees.

"Ooohhha," he sounded off like an antique car horn, clutched his groin, and sank to his knees. Leia punctuated her defense – another kick to a wincing face.

Bingo!

Blood dripped from Henry's nostrils, big tears forming in his eyes. The second kick hurt her foot; adrenalin masked the pain.

Teri gazed at Leia with wonder and adoration.

Before Henry regained composure, the gals were off. Leia's new thirty-eight-dollar starter synced with Jake's flipped ring gear. Lemonade didn't let them down.

"Your Monday might be interesting."

"Yeah," Teri quivered, trying to laugh it off.

"Fucking creep."

Chapter 16
First Kiss

"Would you like to come with?" Rebecca asked. A girl can always hope. The answer would be familiar.

"I'm going to take the truck – go try-ta find some parts for the car. And I have some work to get done around here, but I'll help you load."

On the table stood a line of canning jars, sealed, ready for the farmer's market. Another eight, open, near the cutting board, contained dill, vinegar, mustard seed, salt, pepper, sugar, red pepper, and chopped onion. Jon watched as she hastily prepared refrigerator pickles to accompany the other canned goods. She used the large knife from the butcher block to cut cucumbers lengthwise and some in thin rounds. As she cut, Otherjon also watched, hoping for an error, waiting for a cutlery mishap.

Rebecca topped off the eighth pint, spun the last cover, and gave it a shake. "Ready."

Jon placed jars on a flat. They carried the goods out and set them in the back seat of the Impala. "Would you back the car over to the summer kitchen?" she asked.

Cardboard boxes stacked under the short porch held her most presentable September vegetables. Jon helped load them in the trunk.

"I know it's kinda early, but I picked a few of the bigger pumpkins. Would you please set them in front, for me? They're so heavy."

Jon carried out two, one in each arm, and set them on the floorboard. The third, he wrestled with, leaning back as he carried it. *How did she manage this one?* The effort triggered another coughing fit and a pang in his chest. He made it to the car and set it on the front seat.

"Are you okay?"

The cough persisted. He cleared his throat and used a fist-wrapped thumb to thump his chest. Rebecca massaged his back.

"I'm fine," he said, suppressing the attack. "Surprised you could lift that one by yourself, should I buckle him in?" Jon coughed as he patted the great pumpkin in the passenger seat.

"I had to roll the big one." Rebecca slid a folded lawn chair atop the boxes in the trunk. She moved to the driver's seat of the injured Impala. "I should be home by two or three. Love you."

Jon handed her the Mason jar she used to make change. "Don't forget this. Have fun."

Elliot's kid, Buster Flat, ran Elliot Flat's Salvage. Elliot, blind in one eye, not able to see out the other, sat hatless directly in the sun on a boardwalk in front of the office. Baked, his skin looked leathery with deep furrows too deep to be called wrinkles. The pipe-smoking Oracle of Junk greeted customers from a greasy rocking chair repaired with a thin piece of disintegrating plywood across the missing seat.

"What-cha huntin?"

"Impala parts. Hit a deer."

Click, click. Elliot clicked false teeth loose from the roof of his mouth like an alternative hello. "Lots-a deer gettin hit this time-a year. What flavor Impala ya got, kid."

"Seventy-nine. Tan." He looked at Elliot, remembering forty-some years past, and his first visit to the yard – with his Dad – in the late forties. He was a kid, and Elliot, a younger man then, a mean junkyard dog with black hair, huge strong hands, and a 'don't-need-ya attitude.

Elliot struck a match to a groove in the chair's armrest where he'd struck ten thousand before. His pipe glowed orange, pulling in flame with each puff as Elliot thought inventory. "We got dat, go find Buster, she'll show ya."

Jon liked the sound of cars being crushed and watched Buster's kid pancake an F-150. Buster roared up a row, driving the pay-loader, a Buick teetering on the tines. She saw Jon and signaled her kid to idle down the crusher. The pay-loader moaned and the hydraulic hoses twitched as she placed the Buick in the masher, nestling it atop the flat Ford. Buster could have done it in her sleep. She moved the machine back, and with precision, pressed tines forward again, one tine kinking the post between the front and rear window. Glass shattered and mostly inward. She killed it and climbed down, one cowboy boot after another, then jumped to the ground with a groan.

"I think I know you," she said and used the bandana around her neck to wipe her mouth. She cocked her head back and pushed a dirty hand through dirtier hair.

"Hi, Buster, Jon Rawling, it's been awhile, actually, we were kids the first time I met you, we played cops in an old smashed police car about forty years ago. Right over there," and he pointed to a spot close behind the buildings.

"So we did, you kissed me," she said, tucking in her tee-shirt with nothing under.

He had forgotten but now recalled kiddy kissing. *Been a rough forty – Baby.*

Jon told her the Impala's need for grill, bumper, header, and accompaniments to hold it together. She sent her boy to show him parts on a t-boned match. A hundred, they agreed upon, and he could return in a couple of days to pick them up.

An out-of-view gruff voice asked, "How much for that pumpkin?"

Rebecca pulled her chair from the trunk and looked to the side of the car. A morphadite farm-wife had spotted the big orange globe and taken liberties, opening the door to get a good look. Mrs. Mustache scooped it off the front seat, thwarting anyone else's chance at it. The big pumpkin brought three dollars and her first deal settled.

Talked down from four, and Rebecca asked, "I also brought some homemade skin cream, would you like to try it?" and presented two versions.

"I call this one *Cool Cosmic Cucumber*," Rebecca opened it and let her smell.

"So *fresh*," she said, less gruff.

Rebecca set the small green jar on the hood of the car and showed her the other. "This is my latest and greatest. I call it, *Keep Him Close*." Mrs. Mustache watched Rebecca spin the top off the cruse and rub a swipe between her thumb and finger. "Feel that . . . all-natural ingredients, and you can use it on any body part, know what I mean?"

"Mmum," Mrs. Mustache (who turned out to be Ophelia) said in her most feminine response of the meeting and took one of each. Rebecca found change in her jar for a ten.

The Farmers Market held social value for Rebecca. Unless she was at a rummage sale, eighteen dollars wouldn't buy a decent skirt. Profit measured in fellowship. 'How much did you make today, Mom?' Leia once asked, and she replied, 'I prefer only losing fifty cents a jar on the canning.' Horticulture and grace were attributes she shared with the town-and-country ladies and she did grace with flare. Always well received and today, a star, at least in one way; the rearranged Impala made for lively conversation.

Not coin, but friendship and community, and news not on the radio – the off-air remix. Of course, there would be gossip making the rounds. She tried to put herself above the juice. This Saturday, that proved easy, whispers circling out of earshot.

Clara Stoke's buns, the best in the county, and a jar of blueberry jam chopped take-home pay to eleven bucks.

The thirsty four-forty needed filling. Yutan station had choices, the pure dope or ethanol blend. Jon lifted the ethanol nozzle.

Mr. R caught him in the open door's side mirror. "Put that back!"

Jon froze between pump and Dodge, gas cap in one hand, hose in the other. Through the driver's door open window he looked at Otherjon, and shrugged.

"Put the good stuff in. Who gives a rip? Let em look. Hell, give'er some premium, Blackie wants octane."

The low-lead ethanol spout returned to its slot and Jon hailed the premium nozzle to fill the tank, then a gas can in the box. Across the lot, a squirrelly fellow in aviator glasses unloaded a bulk truck's content into the underground tanks. One-two, the men finished. Both went in.

The driver, first through the station door, handed paperwork across the counter. 'Little early,' Jon heard Ed say.

Ed sold gas, but his station was much more. The plus-size convenience store had taken over all facets of Yutan consumerism. Ed's recently re-sided box enclosed an abbreviated hardware section, groceries (celebrating seasonal produce), non-perishables, a coffee nook for fellowship, and hotdogs rolling in a cooker. A cooler kept milk, butter, and beer, and from the cooler – beer proved the best seller. (The town kept a municipal liquor store, two bars, and in moral balance, supported twin churches. Attendance – best at the bars). The tight store's narrow aisles also kept a sporting goods section. Tackle, archery, unchained guns, ammo, and ball sports basics.

Thirty-eight special shells came in boxes of twenty. Jon carried two to the front along with a hefty tin of reloading powder. He lingered at the magazine rack, examining a cover adorned in pictures of handguns. He skimmed an article, waiting for new customers and the bulk truck driver to clear the checkout.

Coffee in the morning. Beer in the afternoon. Seven farmers, in low-back booths, sat in the coffee nook, complaining price and lying or bragging about yields. He recognized most of them and a few held contracts with the plant – Jon nodded, *Hello*. Few folk in Saunders County small towns didn't recognize *Core Fuels'* manager. Farmers facing him nodded. Then others, back to him, turned to nod or tip a hat.

He approached the counter and stood behind the bulk truck driver. A pissy discussion fell off . . . 'never during the day again.' Ed signed the clipboard and handed it back with an envelope and carton of Winstons. The driver said, "See ya next week."

Ed nodded dismissively, then attended Jon. "Hi, Jon."

"Hey, Ed."

"Not supporting the ethanol industry today?" Ed joked.

Jon had no answer for Ed.

Conversation fell silent in the nook; farmers stopped complaining and looked, those with backs to the counter turned, stared.

"No wonder that place is goin downhill?" one in a windbreaker said, and pinched his empty can, making a crickety sound.

"You'd think his job depended on it, wouldn't ya?" said another, wearing a Co-op hat.

"I would," said the first.

Grumbles amplified in the corner.

Jon paid in silence. Out the door, and he walked fast to the far pumps. He idled the full Dodge to the exit and waited with one foot on the brake for a two-car Yutan traffic jam.

Pudbang! And another, *Sputbang!* Tomatoes exploded off Blackie, one struck the rear window, the second, thumping the cab corner. Jon jerked, spun, and looked.

A few steps out of Ed's door, three farmers stood, yelling, shaking fists. A stout young long-haired agrarian in overalls chucked another; Jon watched it sail over the cab and splat on the street in front of him.

"Fuck you, Rawling!" one yelled.

Jon waited as the second car passed. He punched the pedal and dumped the clutch. Steep Dodge gears in the sure-grip rear spun back tires. Blackie squatted a second, smoldering tread, then lurched. In the pickup's box, the gas can slid, slamming the endgate. Jon crushed back in the seat and the truck screeched forward, leaving two solid black streaks.

"Otherjon, in the mirror, yelled, "Fuck you? Fuck them, go around!"

Instead of turning north, Jon held his foot on the floor, pumped the clutch, grabbed second, and turned south. The motile Dodge melted sideways onto the street and coursed in a somewhat southerly direction. The gas can slid to the corner of the box, shooting a gas plume from spout on impact. Smoke billowed from rear wheel wells, shells and powder slid off the seat.

The disgruntled farmers erupted in laughter.

"He's gonna blow it up," the one in Co-op hat cackled.

"Ha, ha, ha," they cracked up, and the two, still holding tomato ammo, slung with their all. Fruit arched through the afternoon sky. Ed watched from the station window.

Spat-poosh! One found its mark. Through open window, it exploded. Tomato insides spattered Jon and the windshield; more sprayed the interior, hitting seat, dash, and opposite door.

'*Whoohoho.*' The farmers howled, staggered, and punched at one another's shoulders.

Jon feathered the gas and held the truck in a power slide sixty feet to the station's other entrance. Pedal half up, he pulled the wheel hard left. The Dodge slid into the station's lot but slowed little.

"He's comin around," the one in bibs stated in disbelief.

"Whoa-wah!" yelled the Co-op hat lover.

Three farmers scrambled back. They had ventured many paces from the front of the building. Now, a perilous place.

Oil churned, pumped hot, and Blackie's crankshaft spun 5000 rpm. Unwrested 440 pistons screeched war, consumed air, and roared like a jet engine with your skull in it.

The hood's ram-head motif doubled for front sights. Sideways, the truck advanced. Jon leaned, and between pot-metal horns, zeroed in the three ducks.

The farmers stood scared a tick. Then one, one way, two the other.

Momentum, a beautiful thing, and Jon pressed pedal to metal.

The screaming Thor Missile angled in, closing gap. Three sodbusters looked, and through spattered windshield, saw Otherjon's happy-face, wild eyes, and focus – a termination determination. They thought they heard laughing in the roar, but too damn busy scrambling, they passed on a second look.

Ten feet a second and that far again to impact. Farmer Bibs tripped over himself, elbows scuffing, overalls ripping knee to concrete. "Ah, help!" No helping, every man for himself.

Jon closed an eye – left the other open for Mr. R., and they yelled, "Ethanol this!"

Two farmers on their feet grappled for the station door. The looser stumbled back and off the building's curb.

Twenty miles an hour, spinning, drunk on octane, the black Dodge slid sideways between Ed's station and first row of pumps. The long-box fleetside hogged the lane. Ahead of four screeching tires and Thor's inebriated screaming mill, Farmer Bibs rolled another direction, clearing the front, flopping to relative safety. In flash passing, Blackie's left tire grabbed a tuft from Farmer Bib's long yellow locks. A playful scalping for the recently jubilant.

The loser, near Ed's front door, braced for impact. *Boo-wham*, he ricocheted off the buddoinking box-side. Airborne and splayed, the flying stick man screamed higher than he flew. "Geeez-aaus." Erect, and air running, he tried to put feet under a mini moonshot. Rocket Man touched down, flailed in a Gumby cartwheel, and rolled to a sit. Less scathed than imagined, but dazed, and trembling.

In the mirror, Jon watched the man stagger to his feet. The Dodge hooked a pair of black marks out the exit and headed north. A pang of remorse settled in, not for the deed, but probability of repercussion. A small mirror adjustment brought Mr. R into view, and Jon said, "Another fine mess you've got us into."

He jigged from the usual route, used back roads home, and checked frequently for possible pursuing police, or axe grinders.

"Are these Clara's buns?"

"Yes, they are. She was late too, otherwise, I would've been out of luck."

"God, they're good."

"As long as she keeps baking em I'll keep buying em, eh? You know, her recipe made the Wahoo newspaper on the Saunders County Blue Ribbon Recipes page."

Clara Stoke's buns went well with pork chops and beets. Jon proclaimed future procurement of Chevy parts and Rebecca told pleasantries of her day at the market.

Rebecca cleaned up. Jon tried reading. Eyelid weights pulled and he reclined the *Lazy-boy* a notch. The book was back on the stand when Rebecca sat down.

"Wanna watch the news?" she asked.

Jon, half dozing, grumbled something. It sounded affirmative.

Rebecca surfed the remote to a station they seldom watched. News-music followed an extensive string of commercials. Then the hype, 'Latest stories' and 'On the scene,' and Jon dozed off.

The television glowed bright, and news anchor apparent, Otherjon, introduced Jon to tonight's headliner. And in a newsy news-anchor voice, announced, "Good Evening. Our top story tonight comes from the small town of Yutan, where three farmers tell us, 'We were nearly run down by a raging pickup not using ethanol.' Reporting, live from the scene, our very own Buster Flat, Buster."

Buster, in a trunk-found tweed jacket and hair held in a filth, stood with Ed near Ed's pumps. She held a WYKD mic. Behind them, on the station's curb, stout Farmer Bibs leaned against the Ice chest, holding a compress to his head. Buster pressed her ear and looked into the camera. "That's right, we're here with the owner of Ed's Gas Palace. Edward Ellingson. Ed, I understand you watched it happen from right there in the station window. Can you describe for us what you saw?"

"Well, it all started when Jon Rawling didn't use ethanol."

"WHO didn't use ethanol?"

"Jon Rawling," Ed repeated.

"He kissed me once," Buster said to the camera.

"Ed paused and looked at her curiously. An awkward silence followed, two staring into the camera. Buster looked at Ed for continuance.

"Three surly farmers stole an armful of tomatoes from produce, followed Rawling out and chucked em at his truck.

"And you watched it happen?"

'Sure did."

"Then what."

"Old Rawling did a big stinky . . ."

"A WHAT?"

"A big stinky, ya know, a burn-out, over there, and all the way around, smoked off a year's worth of tread."

Buster stepped aside to let the cameraman zoom in on black marks.

"That's a lotta rubber," Buster told the audience. The view wobbled as the cameraman followed her some steps to Jon's black Dodge parked near the end of the station.

"Look at these skins." Buster crouched next to the farmer in the Co-op hat who held a tread gauge in Jon's back tire tread.

The kneeling farmer removed his beloved hat and holding it, used the same hand to scratch his head. "Looks ta be about a quarter inch."

Farmer Bibs leaned in, confirming the degradation, and said, "He tried to scalp me," removing the cold-pack from the side of his head, showing the cameraman an oozing wound.

The camera focused on it, then backed away, letting Buster continue.

"What then, Ed?"

"He came around and tried to run em over, sent one a'flying, too. Now, I know Old Rawling should have been usin the blend, but those farmers had it comin, with the tomato throwin, swearin, and all."

Fast falling footsteps and the cameraman jerked from interview. He panned right and focused on the farmer who had been hit. Dissolute came the man, steaming across the lot. Arms up, Ed braced to fend off the offended. "Ugh." The farmer hit high, creaming Ed clear from Buster. Between black marks, on cement, they landed. Farmer blows fell heavy on Ed's face and Bibs joined the fray.

"Looks like these fellows have issues to resolve," Buster told her on-air audience.

Behind Buster, Co-op Hat entered the scene, adding kicks to Ed's ribs.

"Buster shook her head and smiled. "Buster Flat, reporting from Ed's Gas Palace, where the fun never ends. Now, back to the studio, Otherjon?"

"Well, that was . . . different," Otherjon said, all newsy. "Good Job . . . Joker!" and he gave Jon an on-air wink.

"Jon," Rebecca said, touching his shoulder. "Hey," and shook him. "I'm going up to bed, are you coming?"

"Uhm," he grunted, no.

She offered him the remote. Eyes closed, he adjusted his head, pulled the *lazy-boy*, and fully reclined. "I'll shut the TV off; you're sleeping anyway." Unfulfilled, Rebecca left him and climbed the stairs, wishing he'd join her between the sheets.

Chapter 17
The Clearing

Sunday morning, Jon pressed the Dodge back into service. Tight cowhide gloves felt good on the steering wheel, his blue jeans draped over boot uppers and Red Wings ran clutch and gas. He exited the yard, rounded smokehouse hill, and followed the road north. Half a mile to their property line, he passed the walking path that came up from the river. Not much of a road to begin with, and here it devolved into two dusty furrows with a grassy middle. A woodsy trail, with an occasional badger hole to dodge, or rock to straddle.

Near the clearing, he glimpsed a distant figure moving through the woods. A man, he judged by gait, and dressed in a field jacket, maybe. Jon squinted, *carrying a machete? Now, who the hell's in my woods?*

Not Jon's woods, but road-wise, they owned the only usable access to the undeveloped land. Another soggy trail skirted Kissin Cousins north shore but denied trespassers. Kids in jacked-up four-by-fours had claimed it, gouged it, named it, and *The Bog* discouraged access to St. Mary's parishioner-willed one-hundred-sixty-acre land bank.

Lemonade, running exceptionally well, didn't stall when Leia let off and turned onto the driveway.

Today's the day. I'm confronting her. No more pussyfooting around. Not just the wild ride home a week ago, there had been Wednesday's oddity.

Days to figure out how to start the conversation, and still, she didn't know how to bring it up. *She lives with him – She must know . . .*

She parked next to the disfigured Impala, went to the front door, and knocked. Waited. Knocked again. It always felt strange knocking on the door of the home she grew up in. She turned the knob and entered. "Happy Sunday," she called, and it came out like a song.

A high-pitched mechanical whine, coming from the kitchen, was the reply.

Dialed up, Rebecca's salad shooting gizmo ripped at a full head of lettuce, mounding it in a party-size plastic bowl.

At the kitchen door, Leia drummed a loud and cheerful, "Hi Mom, how are you?"

Rebecca jumped. Slaw spat across the counter, the wall, and sprayed a good portion of the kitchen window. "Oh shoot, ya scared the boo-gee-zees out of me."

They laughed and Leia hurried over. "Sorry. Here, let me help." Rebecca removed paper towels from a roll mounted below the cupboards.

"When did you get the new slim-a-lot?" Leia picked it up, jutted her hip, and resting her elbow near it, pointed the chopper skyward, imitating a sixties space-movie billboard. She only lacked the pocket-less gold jumpsuit and silver stiletto boots.

"Oh, that old thing," Rebecca said like she was talking about a dress.

"Looks like a *Lost in Space* weapon."

"Shoots green slime and all." Rebecca wiped her index finger through the patch on the counter.

"Quite well," Leia giggled, setting the weapon down. She hugged Mom, hello, and they went into cleaning mode.

Leia repeated, "How are you?"

"Good sweetie. Hope you plan on staying for dinner; I've got roast in the crockpot. How's it going with the new job – in the fast-paced high-intensity seed-sorting business?"

"It's *sooo* boring, but the people are nice and my supervisor's cool. When I started, Teri told me how lucky I was to get this department, cause he's fun and easygoing. Leia pulled paper towels from the roll and moved to the window.

"Oh, that's nice, what's his name?"

"Thomas." (To'mas) "He's Latino. His parents were migrants – worked fields in the '70s. After a couple of summers, they found year-round jobs and stayed. He graduated over in Kotes. Valedictorian, they say."

"Single?" Rebecca asked, always perusing a soul mate for Leia.

"Mom."

"Well, anyway, you've pushed the reset button. I'm happy you're back to work, eh." Rebecca paused. "Isn't Teri working in the same area as you?"

"Oh no, no, Mom. She finished her accounting degree. Got a job at the plant. She actually works for Dad now, sort of. She's doing really well, pay bump. Very good bump, compared to my job, and she's always been good at managing money."

"She works at *Core*? How do I not know these things?"

Leia shrugged. "I might go back to school next year, too. If you work at the company a year, they'll pay for it. You pay upfront but get reimbursed as long as you pass." Leia shook the paper towel over the garbage. "Didn't work out so well for them with Teri, though, she left with her degree for an opening at *Core*. But, yah, I think I'll be goin back next fall."

"Oh, that'd be great, your dad and I've been hoping you'd finish."

Leia took the opening. "How *is* Dad?"

"Good good, your Dad's doin good." Rebecca gave up on paper towels and tossed them. She budged close to Leia and ran hot water on a sponge. "A couple of concerns about work, that's no surprise. I think his back's been better. He isn't much of a complainer, but you know that. Not sleeping well, though. Up in the night, sometimes. 'Bad dreams,' he says.

"Did he say any more about the car, when we hit the deer?"

"Not that I recall."

"Mm . . . So, where's Dad now?"

Rebecca sidled close and looked out the window Leia was attempting to clean. On tiptoe, she scanned the yard. "Well, I'm not sure, but I think he's cutting wood. He was fiddling with the chainsaw this morning and I don't see the old truck."

"Oh, okay, good. Noticed anything different . . . odd, lately?"

". . . Not really. Well, maybe . . . quiet. We talk." The sponge worked wonders, and finished with the counter, she passed it off to Leia to use on the window.

"Quieter than usual?"

Rebecca laughed. "No one's ever accused him of being a conversationalist, have they? Stoic, that's what I'd say." Rebecca wouldn't share with her daughter that silent evenings and weekends, devoid of affection, let alone passion, had left her feeling lonely.

"Mom, Wednesday, when I went out to look for Dad, I walked around the house and took the path up the hill to the old shed. He was up there and I noticed him looking in the side window. But it seemed pretty weird because he wasn't looking *in* the shed, at least not like, looking for something. More, like, watching something inside, and he was back on the path, like five feet away. It didn't look normal. I hiked up pretty close and he didn't move. He was just staring in the window, or at the window. He didn't hear me coming up the hill, didn't even notice me until I was pretty close and said something. Then he just turned slowly, and said, 'Hi Princess'. You know, he hasn't called me that since I was fifteen. Mom, I think he was just standing there, staring at his own reflection."

"Oh? Well, I stare in the mirror once in a while wondering where the gray hair and stupid wrinkles come from. I'm sure we all stare at our reflection from time to time, don't you?"

"Maybe a bit, but not for five minutes without moving, not that long, Mom. It was weird. Who knows how long he'd been there. I'm not trying to freak you out or anything, but there have been a couple of other things that seemed . . . off. I think something might be wrong, kinda afraid for Dad." *Kinda afraid of Dad.*

"Well, I'm not trying to poo-poo your concerns, but I think your dad's just fine, eh?"

"Hmm." Leia paused, deciding if she wanted to press it further. "Ok, I'll let it go for now, but if anything else . . . seems strange, let's talk."

Leia wasn't going to just let it go. Only with Mom, and only for now.

Leia's words looped in Rebecca's mind. '*Something might be wrong.*'

(Wednesday evening, after the accident.)

Halfway between the shed and path, Jon stood, and watched, and waited.

"Hey, Hey!"

A new game – Mr. R, playing hard to get.

"HEY." . . . It was the first time Jon had to look for his accomplice.

Wind rustled through the trees. Branches swayed, moving leafy shadows across the window.

A pubescent smile filled the glass. "Just messin with ya . . . Joker."

"I'm ready."

"Ready for what?" Mr. R wanted him to say it.

"Rearrange things."

"Sometimes rearranging – gets messy."

"I know."

"Prune branches, trim ugly?"

"I can prune, and cut."

Mr. R chuckled, "You sure can. All that practice."

"Not funny."

"All the same, I'm your man . . . Joker."

"Let 'er wheeler."

"Well, we have some planning to do, then, don't we?

Half-an-hour Jon and Mr. R schemed. And as they were putting the stamp of approval on their blueprint, Leia, coming up the trail, interrupted. Mr. R cleared his throat and, with shifting eyes and eyebrows pointing, signaled Jon of an approaching daughter.

Jon turned slowly, de-trancing. Leia missed the smirk leaving his face, but it was the same she'd witnessed the night they mashed deer together.

"Hi, Princess."

Jon abandoned the trail. His Red Wing pumped Blackie's clutch and his leather glove coaxed the shifter into first. The Dodge crawled, weaving between gray stumps. Over gopher mounds, rocks, and deadfall, the Power Wagon jounced across the rutty clearing toward a stand of ash. Empties rolled out from under the seat and clacked. He kicked them back and teased. Back under there until the preacher's with.

The ash stood proud, but some listed lifeless as if to say, '*our work's done, take us down, for it's time to rest,*' and the standing dead he always took first. And soon, a cold house and howling winter winds would demand their cremation.

Tuned, and with a shiny new plug, the red saw waited to work. The fuel tank brimmed ashen oil in premium. '*93 the gas for me,*' Jon thought of Pistonhead's jingle, a commercial from his youth. He flipped the switch to "Run," set the choke, placed a foot in the handle, and pulled. First tug – the machine balked, and, as the two-cycle engine sputtered, it spoke to him. "I'm hungry budrup brrup." Another rip, and again, "Bu-budrrrup I'm hungry." *Third time's a charm.* The saw barked, started, and roared on high idle. Blue smoke fogged, hazing from the octane oil mix. The chain jerked between clutch and brake.

"I'll give you something to chew on." He revved it, and chose a leaning thirty-foot specimen.

Stricken by gravity and a kerf, the tree crashed over rotting deadfall. Jon removed limbs from the trunk and wistfully watched the twinkling line of razor-sharp links chew through deadwood. Clean chips of white, pink and gray, poured from the saw's bottom. With regard and sincere precision, he wielded the tool, practicing technique. A Gladiator in his prime. *I should have this baby at work.* And he cut, cut, and moving the hungry chain with hasty care, he thought. *Take that Knot-Head.*

A sore back later, Jon slammed the end gate. The over-loaded Dodge looked ready to drag ass home.

Drained, Jon shuffled to Blackie's open door, pulled a nipper from behind the seat, and took a bump. He climbed in, rolled his *Carhartt* into a pillow, and lowered his bristly weekend face onto it. He felt good about the precision cutting and the loading of the dead. With head on jacket and *Red Wings* hanging out the open door, Jon slipped away . . . off to Dreamsville.

He mowed through a stand of Core Fuels' softwood and stacked the cord of shit-sticks from Milling and Malting. A fine clearing it was. Past sawed-off ankles sticking up from the ground around him, he spotted Dale, his missing "yes man," growing like a weed. Jon sauntered over and gave his hungry saw a tug. It roared to life. He fingered the accelerator and the machine hummed in tasty anticipation, "Mmm, umumumm, Mmm, umummum."

With nowhere to go, Tree-Dale shook like a leaf.

Jon stepped close. "Time to cash in. Let's see, which hand did you write those checks with?"

Charismatic Dale's left limb popped up, tree moss hung from the elbow, and three stick-fingers involuntarily wiggled, indicating his guilty side. Dale tried to speak, but his mouth had grown shut. His communication was with the collective, the other people-trees in the forest, and they hoped for the best, as petrified Dale prepared for the worst.

"Oh, yeah, a leftie." Jon reached, and with an "M-um-um-mum–aaahh" the saw removed Dale's naughty limb with the sticky fingers.

Dale watched it drop. His non-functional knothole-mouth popped open for the first time, and he screamed a horrific scream. A sap tear rolled down his tree-cheek. In the pickup box, neatly stacked gray tree-bodies of felled Core employees popped their dead eyes open, and with their knotholes, announced, "Limb Down."

Jon crouched and took Dale below the knees, below two big knots on a pair of spindly trunks that had grown together the people-tree way. On the ground near the black Dodge, a pile of woody dead consortium members watched Dale teeter, then looked up at the 'stack in the box' and made their own sylvan announcement, "Timberrr!"

A *bing-bing-ting-tang* and thunder rolled. Jon's eyes fluttered. Heat lightning illuminated the black sky behind an indistinct figure standing at the cab's open door. The dude in army jacket stood, bapping the flat side of his machete blade on Blackie's roof.

Startled, half-conscious, Jon thought shadow-man looked awful tree-like. He kicked. The man leaned and the *Red Wing* whiffed. "Whoa, whoa there. Hey buddy, wake up, storms moving in."

"What?" Jon stirred from dreamland.

"Storms movin in, from the west."

"The wicked west," Jon said, sitting up.

Fat sporadic raindrops spattered the hood and windshield, a precursor of what was to come.

One man gained his bearings, the other, reached in with an open hand and introduced himself, "Clive, Clive Smivmore."

Jon's hand met Clive's. A sturdy handshake and he said, "Jon Rawling." Then, using Clive's grip, he pulled himself behind the wheel. He looked skyward and asked, "Give you a lift?"

"Thought you'd never ask. I don't mind the rain so much, but when it comes to lightning . . ." Clive shook his head, shucked his backpack, circled, and climbed in. "Long way back to my car." The pack, he placed on the floor between his legs, and the machete, on the seat between them. "Friends call me Smivy."

Smivy? – That's stupid. "But you go by Clive, too, huh?"

"Of course."

"Clive's good."

Clive wore a neatly trimmed beard, brown with a tinge of red, and he looked a lanky Lincoln. Jon noted Clive's new boots, blond leather with fresh scuffs and mud. He also took notice of Clive's machete. Easy to reach on the seat between them; he pondered if Clive was a leftie, like Dale. It, too, looked new with hickory handles. *Made in the good ole U. S. of A.* The blade looked sharp, with an edge that could shine in the shade.

"Well, Clive, what brings you out here? Haven't seen anyone in these woods in a *long* time."

"Inventory." Clive pulled a clipboard from the backpack to prove his mission. "It's called timber cruising – inventorying all the hardwoods on the acreage."

"Interesting, why?"

"Not sure. One of the companies I work for gets jobs like this; I usually don't get told much."

The sky opened and relieved its bladder. Jon flipped the wipers on high. The black Dodge's cargo sagged the rear like a fully loaded diaper, and in turn, made the light front end a challenge to steer. He eased onto the trail, straightened it out, and stepped on it. Tires spun in grassless groves and mud spattered the box sides. Rotted wipers left as much rain on the windshield as they removed. The driver's side streaker ripped itself a tail. It arced back and forth across the windshield, metal end screeching a groove.

"So how-da-ya like tromping around in the woods?" Jon let his hand slip from the wheel to feel the steel on the seat next to him.

"I love it, it's the reason I took up forestry. I go to the woods and hike about, and I get paid to be here. I'm an assessed, professed, and confessed naturalist."

"You don't say, I'm cutting it and you're counting it. And you don't know why . . . mushroom syndrome, they keep you in the dark and feed you excrement, eh?"

"Oh, I'm sure I'm counting it because *someone* wants to cut it."

Jon reminded himself that they weren't 'his' woods. "Oh, yeah, I suppose so. Now, where can I get ya to?"

Jon rubbed his thumb horizontally across the blade, testing its sharpness, and thought, *not bad for a machete*. He suppressed the urge to test it vertically.

"My car is off the highway about a half-mile, on a trail coming in from the west. I'm by a big slough, the road just went ta pot, so I hiked in from there. You know where I'm talking about?"

"Yeah, I know. That trail's impassable most of the year; there're lots of low-maintenance roads out this way, but that's a no-maintenance road. Better to cross on the frozen slough in January, not that it does you any good now."

Clive watched Jon fondle the steel blade between them. “Here, let me get that out of your way.” He returned it to a sheath strapped to his backpack. Clive didn’t think much of it, yet, felt something crawl up his back and jerk the hair on the nape of his neck.

The living room, cast in pale grays and black shadows, looked haunted. A gale blasted the yard and garden. Raindrops, big as nickels, stirred dust on the sidewalk. Fat drops slapped the dirty west siding and picture window, producing small muddy rings. Then the gusher hit and washed the mud-rings into blackened streaks. On the river, Baby Cake’s canopy ripped, whipped, and twisted on the boatlift framework.

Lightning struck close and the living room window flashed white. A reverberation jolted the house and glass rattled in frames. The lights flickered and went out. The TV fizzled. A glow from the picture tube faded in an outline of Arnold Schwarzenegger’s head. *The Terminator* partially ejected itself from the VCR. Leia grabbed it, a trail of tape dragging. She looked at Rebecca, and said, “I don’t think he’ll be back.”

“That sure snuck up on us,” Leia said. “Sounds nasty.”

“Would you grab some candles?”

“Are they in the hall closet?”

“Should be; look behind the light bulbs. I’ll grab matches and the transistor. Your father better be getting his buns home.”

“Hope he’s all right.” Leia looked out the window. “And the old truck started okay, always sounded weird starting, like *rur-rur-rur-rur*, turning over in slow motion.”

“Your dad said that’s just a Dodge thing, they all make that sound.”

“Should I check the roast?”

“I checked it, it’s done. Put it on low. He’ll be home soon.”

The last curve around smokehouse hill spelled trouble. Jon held the wheel, goodbye road, hello yard. He let off the gas, hoping for some gription. Tires skidding, lumber load pushing, and Blackie slid across the lawn. Momentum, a beautiful thing? Not today.

"Whoa, Nellie." Clive flailed, grabbing for any handle. The wipers wiped, one screeching. Jon spun the wheel. Blackie ignored him and angling tires scalped slickity sod. He pumped brakes gently as the deadwood propelled them toward the riverbank. Clive whimpered and Jon blew a slow exhale. Close and precarious, they rode the ridge. Tread spit grass over the bank and onto the path ten feet down, and ten more, to the river below. Truck slowing and tires catching, Jon eased the Dodge away from a plunge and wanton swim.

"That was scarier than a fair ride." A lightning flash illuminated the cab. Clive looked a shade whiter. "You'd think, with all the weight back there, it wouldn't slide around that much. Thought I was going to need fresh undies."

"Ever seen that film clip of those Army tanks sliding off the roads in Bastogne?"

"Can't say's I have."

"Freezing rain and thirty-ton Shermans were sliding right off the road on the thinnest layer of ice."

"Think those tank drivers were filling their shorts?"

"Yeah, when the German Tiger eighty-eights started landin on em."

Jon inched across the soggy turf, passing the garden, summer kitchen, and through the fence opening to the gravel drive. He parked close to the sidewalk and as near the house as the fence allowed. They sat in the squatting truck, rain roaring on the Dodge's roof, gusty droves sheeting off Jon's side window. "How about comin in for a little bit, should let up soon."

"Ya think I'll be able to get my car off that crappy road?"

"Maybe after it lets up, you can help me unload. We'll leave some on for weight and grab a rope, go see what we can do."

"I'd sure appreciate that." Lightning flashed. Clive glimpsed the pile of anally stacked wood in the lean-to not far from where they'd made their skidding entrance.

"Let's make a break for the door. Just leave your stuff in the truck." Twice, Jon laid on the horn, then pulled the door handle.

Clive let him lead and tried not to run him down as the elements broadsided.

They hit the steps and Rebecca swung the front door open. "Tornado warning, get in here!"

Jon stutter-stepped and stomped before slipping in. Clive did the same. Soaked from the brief exposure, they went in dripping.

Clive looked at Rebecca, then to Jon. *Son-of-a-gun. Jon's a lucky man.*

"Powers out?" Jon said.

"Um-hum."

"Phone?"

"I guess I didn't try it, yet. And who do we have here?" Rebecca asked.

"Clive, my sweetheart, Rebecca. Rebecca, Clive. Found him in the woods, or maybe, I should say, he found me."

"Nice meeting you." He shook her hand.

"Likewise," she said.

Their drippings pooled off the entry rug's edge. Jon knelt, removing his boots. Not wanting to add to the imposition, Clive stood, saturated, waiting for Jon to get out of the way.

Lightning flashed; thunder shook the windows. Except for the flashes, little light made it through the storm's cover. Candles added a few lumens to the entry and living room.

Jon set his boots aside and moved onto the polished hardwood.

Clive's turn, and leaning against the door, he untied the mucked-up cherries. He knelt, and finally sat to coax them off.

Jon watched his struggles. "They broke in yet?"

"Pretty good start, I'd say." Then Clive heard a new voice in the room.

"Here ya go." Leia handed Jon a towel. Another draped her arm for the visitor. "We were getting worried you broke down out there – or got hit by lightning or something."

To Leia, Clive, sitting on the rug in the poorly lit entry looked like a man-child getting ready for bed.

"The drive back was wet. Muddy and slow," Jon said.

"Almost scary." Clive looked up, stopped with the boots, and froze. He stared. Dim couldn't hide her sweet look, and he found Leia's concerned expression endearing in a girl-next-door Mary Ann way. His heart surged, and suddenly, he felt like melting candle wax, numbly dissolving – another puddle on the floor. *Wow – course I look like shit – the drowned rat.*

Rebecca saw it straightaway and watched, amused. *If I snap my fingers in front of his nose – will he come to?*

The boot came off, Clive scrambled to his feet, and stepped absently off the rug into the water.

He looks better standing. Leia didn't wait for an introduction and moved to hand him the towel. "Hello, I'm Leia."

Clive couldn't think. Not totally true; he checked her finger for a ring. Leia caught him looking and felt a flush rush. He had a boyish grin and some wise curl to his hair. She found his six-foot frame, healthy, and blue eyes, flittering candlelight, attractive. A younger version of the *Brawny* man.

"Thanks, friends call me Sm . . . Clive, I'm Clive. Good to meet you."

They didn't shake hands.

Lightning strikes crackled through Rebecca's transistor radio. The severe weather warning signal, *Beeep– Beeep – Beeep,* preceded, and they listened through grating static.

'We interrupt our regularly scheduled programming to bring you this Severe Weather Announcement: Saunders County, tornado watch until eight p.m., high winds, thunderstorms. Counties, Douglas, Sarpy, Cass, tornado watch until eight-thirty p.m., high winds, thunderstorms. Seek shelter. Stay indoors. Move to a basement or an interior room. Avoid windows.'

"Same warning they gave fifteen minutes ago – now they've extended it," Rebecca said.

"Let's not eat in the basement," Leia said.

"How about the dining room for a change, eh, and the basement stairway's right there," said Rebecca.

"Unlikely we get a tornado," Clive said.

"It'd be late in the year for one, but best not tempt fate," Jon said.

"And end up like poor Mr. Carl Holt," Leia added.

"Clive'll be joining us for supper," Jon said.

"Well, of course he is," Rebecca replied.

"Oh, no, I don't want to impose. I have granola bars and stuff out in my backpack." *Mmm, smells like roast.*

"Put'sa," Rebecca said. "I'm putting you to work, Clive. You'll have to earn your keep, eh? Go wash up now, and see me in the kitchen. Leia, show him around."

The rain definitely wasn't letting up, nor the wind. And the house grew dark, not as dark as night, but damn close.

Clive, returning from washing, smiled at Leia as he passed through the dining room. She returned him the smallest one possible.

In the kitchen, Rebecca lined candles on the window sill and readied the counter for Clive's help. Onion Slayer lay on the cutting board, waiting for him.

"Okay, what should I do, Mrs. Rawling?"

"Rebecca, please," she answered.

"Of course, Rebecca."

"Chop vegetables, slices, or any old way is fine. And if you can sauté em', I'll get the roast out of the crockpot."

"Gas stove, cast iron pan, nice," Clive said.

Jon took glasses out from the cupboard. He watched Clive work the blade and thought about the machete out in the truck. He passed behind Clive, and in the kitchen window, Otherjon came into view.

"His machete is right outside."

"And what would I do with that?"

"Well, chop him up, of course."

"And why the *hell* would I do that?"

"So he doesn't do your daughter."

"They're adults. Doing or not doing, not my monkeys."

"Little Princess, she's your monkey, you've got to protect her."

"She can take care of herself."

Leia opened the silverware drawer. Clive, stricken, watched her in the window.

Rebecca caught Leia in the act and shook her head. She pointed to the china cabinet.

Leia's jaw dropped, she rolled her eyes and tilted her head. With a bit of a stomp, she turned and went for the cabinet – the good silver. *She's making him inclusive before we even know who he is – might be a serial killer – okay, a cute serial killer. Not cute – handsome – kind of.*

"Plates, too," Rebecca sang and dug in a drawer for placemats. *If it could just storm every afternoon . . .*

Table set and they gathered. Clive waited carefree for the prayer that never came. Nothing mattered; he was sitting across from Leia and, imagined possibilities.

Rebecca, having it her way, poured a glass of wine for all participants.

"Well, isn't this romantic, eh?"

"Mom's from Canada." Leia's icebreaker.

You can take the Canadian out of Canada, but you can't take Canada out of the Canadian, Jon thought.

The big table candles burned bright. Leia could see the red in Clive's beard. *Bet he'd be more handsome without it.*

"This reminds me of how we met," Rebecca announced.

"And how would that – *Possibly* be?" Jon asked.

"We were having lunch, weren't we?"

Jon's eyelids dropped – he shook his head.

"I've heard it a hundred times," Leia said to their visitor, and announced, "I'll tell it." *Might be just a touch less embarrassing if Mom doesn't have the mic.*

"Oh, we don't need to bore Clive with ancient history," Jon said.

Rebecca held her hand up, and in the softest affecting voice Jon had ever heard, she said, "Let her *tell* it."

It went a little like this . . .

Chapter 18

Look at the Canuck

Jon's sights were aimed high at the prim new Canadian import. Rebecca wore glasses and walked with feet pointing out a bit. He liked the way she wore her hair up and her intelligently narrow specs. She looked like a young schoolteacher. Snug or loose-fitting sweaters on cool fall days, what was there not to like? Something about the teacher look did it for him, but mostly, she had a face that could launch ships.

Jon's smile greeted her in halls, met her on sidewalks, begged in parking lots. She was having none of it, and, though their eyes met on each occasion, not once did she reciprocate.

Painful weeks passed. No arbitration. Her friends were not his – and no mediator found. Finally, less her entourage, Jon found Rebecca alone at lunch. This rare opportunity would not be scuttled, and he sat at the table across from her . . .

"Mind if I sit?"

"If you must," Rebecca replied, curtly looking above low riding glasses and holding a pinned-open textbook on the table.

Ooh, that was cold. He forged on, "How's it goin, I'm Jon."

"Rebecca," was all she offered and with fork prodded her rubberized deviled egg.

"So what do you want to be when you grow up?" And as soon as it came out, he thought, *definitely looks grown-up today. Two hundred girls taking classes but this's the one. The Canuck, ya know when ya know. Ya know, when she's all you think about.*

Rebecca answered with a disinterested shrug.

I'm sinking fast. As soon as she finishes that damn egg she's gonna stand up, walk out, and never talk to me again.

Cutting past the book prices, the weather, the professors, the dorms, and the rest of the bullshit, Jon threw a Hail Mary. "Is there something you dislike about me? I'm just your . . . average Jon."

She let the book shut and pushed the plate aside.

"Oh . . . I think it's just about ev-er-y-thing," She dug it in for emphasis, but continuing, Rebecca ratcheted down her tone and sounded almost playful. "If you're looking for a little list, I'd be happy to indulge . . . Let's start with that funny nose, and maybe we could end with how all you football players get the breaks here in college, *just* like you did in high school."

"Ohhh, I see. All the breaks, like the flaccid grades I am getting in Chem, and E-Lit, cause all the time it takes to 'make the grade' for a coach. Don't ya think your enjoyable college experience has any connection to our winning season?" Jon sprinkled sarcasm dust.

"*Winning season?*" she said, shaking her head with a little jiggle. "What the heck are you talking about, Studley? Do you think any of the students around here care about *that*? We're here for an education."

"You could have fooled me, it looks like most of the girls here are husband shopping. And having some success, I might add."

"*Well,* Mr. Rawling, that might be the case for a few of the girls in the dorms, but I must say, they're the exception, *not* the rule."

A hint of hope welled up, *geez, I didn't tell her my last name. Why would she know that if she is so down on sports – down on me? Maybe she's playing this stand-off-ish thing up a bit*? He raised his eyebrows, held them there a second, and said, "Hmm... Maybe we should change subjects. Now, what about my nose?" He felt better. *At least I have her talking.*

Busy fending off a bushel of chaff, Rebecca had her sights set high, as well. Her heart set on a five-foot-nine Junior-All-American with a nose crooked during a high school football skirmish.

When Leia finished the tale of love, fifties style, Clive laughed. Rebecca and Leia smiled. Jon said, "More potatoes?" passing the bowl to Clive.

There was ample food, and Clive asked, "Who raised the beef?"

"The grocery store, right Mom?" Leia said.

"I think if I lived out here, I'd have animals."

"We have a cat," said Rebecca.

Don't tell him the cat's name, Leia thought.

"Mangy tom-cat," Jon said. "Not allowed in the house." And he had noticed cat hair in the house from time to time.

"When he was a kitten, Butterballs was Leia's kitty, but he comes and goes now, sometimes gone for a couple weeks at a time," Rebecca said.

Leia looked sheepish, *next thing, she'll get out pictures of baby Leia – getting a bath in the sink – God, Mom!*

"A cat unto himself," Jon said.

Butterballs? – I won't ask. Clive decided any informational pursuit pertinent to the naming of 'Butterballs' had to end in embarrassment.

"No dog?"

"We had Skill, til about a year ago, now he's in the pet cemetery," Leia said.

"Oh-ah."

"Skill had a good life, fifteen when he died," Jon said. "That'd be, like over a hundred people years."

"All this acreage, you could have horses."

"Not a fan," Leia said.

"Horses or riding?"

"Either."

A girl that doesn't like horses? What planet am I on? "Really, why not?"

"They smell – and bite, sometimes – and kick, too." Leia turned to Rebecca. "What did Grandpa call them, again?"

"I don't remember. Jon, do you remember what it was?"

"Hay-burners. He had some other choice names for his equestrian friends, too."

Rebecca changed the subject, "So how'd you bump into Jon?"

"I was out on the church property cruising hardwoods – Forestry."

"Oh, Forestry. How long did ya have to go to school for that?"

"A four-year degree and I love it, but the pay – not that great."

"Do you work Sundays, often?" Leia asked.

"I can pretty much do the work whenever I want, as long as I get it done on schedule, and it's hardly like work, to me."

"Working Sundays, what does your family think of that?" Rebecca pried.

"Single, don't have anyone I have to ask. It's great." *Not that great.*

"You're doing what you love, and what could be better than that?"

Only an incredibly attractive woman – like the one across from me – to come home to. "Not much," Clive said.

"Wooohoo," Leia said. And the lights were on.

They finished the meal talking of Jon's school and position at *Core*, the pros and cons of ethanol, Rebecca's upbringing on a farm near Winnipeg, Clive's meteorology knowledge, and Skill's inexplicable ability to bring home various species of live fishes.

Winds mellowed and the rain stopped. Rebecca and Leia cleaned the table, and Clive, not remiss, helped. Jon hinted it was time to wrap up the storm party. "Looks like we'll be unloading wood by yard-light. I'll back the truck over to the woodshed."

Rebecca bid their guest goodbye, purposely leaving Leia to see him out.

Leia wanted to offer him a ride home. Not that bold; she didn't.

"Goodbye, Clive the Forester." And to hold him there a little longer, she asked, "Where do you live?"

"Broken Down." He smiled. "It's an old RV; I've got it parked across the river about five, six, miles south in the Two Rivers rec area . . . but I bet that's not what you were asking. I'm from Omaha."

She left it at that, but now figured, *he doesn't have a phone,* and this – a one-off, chance meeting.

"Would you like to have coffee, sometime?" Clive asked.

"Yeah, that'd be okay."

"Could I maybe, get a number to call ya?"

She scratched digits on the newspaper, tore off the corner, and handed it to him. Her hand lingered on his. "I don't live here," she said and indicated the house.

"Oh, I thought . . ."

"I have an apartment in town."

"Oh, okay, I'll give you a call, soon." The number went in his pocket.

"Do you have a phone?" she said, again thinking about the RV.

"I'll find one." He felt like a teen and wanted to hold her, kiss her – they shook hands.

The pleased mother listened from the kitchen and abused the remaining wine.

Clive walked across the yard. The fresh smell of rain, new mud, and rotting leaves blended with the river, producing a pleasant fragrance, a woodsy cornucopia. It was good and he was high.

Above the woodshed's open side, three antler sets were nailed to the beam. "Those look like they came off some healthy bucks. You shoot em?"

Jon pointed. "That big one in the middle's been there forever. I shot the other two."

"They're all nice," Clive said, feeling sorry for deer he never knew.

Jon slid the top log from the pickup box. "We'll just pitch some off here next to the splitter."

"That looks like quite the deal-ley-o', where'd you get it?"

"I built it."

"*You* built it?"

"Mostly. Machine shop made the wedge and attached it to the ram. I did the rest."

"Looks like a beast." Even in yard light, Clive could see it wasn't commercial with a vehicle axle mounted under a suspension-less frame, belt-driven hydraulics, and powered by a Wisconsin.

"Watch this." Jon set the choke, wrapped a white hemp rope with wood t-handle on the missing recoil's exposed pulley, and pulled. One and done; it started. The entire apparatus shook on half-inflated snow tires. Puddled rainwater danced off the engine and frame. Steam rose from the muffler pipe. He wrestled a large-diameter log off the Dodge and placed it on the vibrating splitter. A control-lever-nudge sent steel wedging inches in. Jon let-off, and warned, "Stand clear."

Clive stepped back and Jon worked the lever. Dense ash split and, sounding a shot, tinted the air with the smell of hot friction. *Impressive.*

"Wow, wouldn't wanna get caught in that thing. Radical."

The men unloaded logs and the Power Wagon's back bumper rose. Jon found his elusive towrope.

At Kissin Cousins, they turned and drove the access road until they came up behind Clive's car. "Should we hook you up right away?"

"How about I just try it, first. I'm a good winter driver and this shouldn't be much different."

"If you get her moving I'll stay outta your way."

Clive eased his Maverick back, reversing on the denigrated road. Two wheels center and two on the edge, he straddled water-filled ruts. Jon backed out and his headlights lit Clive's way. At the good county gravel, they stopped and got out of their vehicles.

"That wasn't so bad, good job."

"Thanks so much, for everything," Clive said.

"No problem, Clive. Good meeting you." The pack in the truck was heavier than Jon expected. Clive handled it into his car. They said goodbye, and Jon, already missing the machete, backed his truck around.

Leia said goodnight to Mom. She passed Jon on the gravel heading home. They tapped their horns as they met.

Icing his sack wasn't the only thing he accomplished over the weekend. Saturday, Henry judiciously used the morning to nurse a hangover. Friday's nut-cracking escapade needed drowning and he initiated it as soon as he'd hobbled from the theater to the Suburban. Jack in the glovie drained into his tummy. Sunday he drove gravel roads, listening to Country FM in the Suburban, drinking the case of Scores, and throwing the empties at signs as he sailed by. A new booze-cruisin personal best, sixteen of twenty. "YEAH!" he cheered, after an especially self-satisfying over-the-roof strike, brown bottle shattering on a yield sign. Inebriated in Nebraska – Monday would be rough.

Chapter 19

Sin City

Harrison called Monday morning. The office-coveted cellular phone had no problem in Vegas – Vegas had a tower. In Saunders County, it was a worthless handful of electronics.

"Sheriff's Department," Ellen answered.

"Morning, good lookin." He sounded echoed.

"Roy . . . Are you using the cellular phone?"

"Yes, I am."

"From the car?"

"Yep."

"Cool."

"How long til you'll be back?"

"Not long, maybe a few days. Is O'Leary in yet?"

"He's in his office, I'll transfer you. Miss you." She hung on for a second, waiting for him to reciprocate.

"Miss you, too."

She worked the phone to ring O'Leary and announced Harrison.

"Harrison . . . Well?" O'Leary asked.

"He's here, all right. I followed him all weekend. He's playing it low key."

"Yeah?"

"Got himself a job, night janitor at the Nugget. Looks like he's going by Jacob now, that's what's embroidered on his shirt, anyway. Grew a beard, of course, glasses, too."

"Last name?"

"Don't know, yet," Harrison said.

"He's casing the Nugget?"

"For sure."

"And living with the great aunt?"

"Yep, he took her to church yesterday, and then they went out for dinner. Guess who paid?"

"Aunty?"

"Bingo. I thought that was rich. Anyway, give me some time, I want to see if he can show me the money."

"Unless he's sitting on it right there in auntie's house."

"Yeah, unless that. But if he isn't . . . and I take him, then what. Probably buried out in the desert."

"And if he doesn't talk, or things go bad – we never find it."

"Right, so give me a few days. I don't think he's going anywhere. Acts carefree, cool as a cucumber, just like Rawling said."

"You're staying at the Nugget?"

"Of course, moved over there as soon as I saw that's where he was working. I don't see a van, but you can bet he's got a plan, and the Nuggets gonna get burned."

"Are you getting any sleep?"

Harrison looked in the rearview mirror; disheveled, bordering scary. "Mostly in the rent-a-wreck, which is pretty sad, cause I got a waterbed in my room at the Nugget. It's like sleeping on an ocean of bliss." *Wish Ellen was here – Ellen in the lifeboat – nailed on the sea.*

"Okay, I think I better send Pearson down to help with surveillance. Then he'll be there to help you take him down. I'm not flying him, so it'll be a couple of days before he gets there."

"That works; I have Higgus's schedule mostly figured out. I'll try to call if I think I have to move on him."

At noon, Pearson left the station in a white panel-van. Hastily stenciled graphics painted on the sides read, "*Pudge's Plumbing*, Las Vegas, NV." And under that, an unreachable number starting with a Vegas prefix. O'Leary, pleased with his choices, grinned, watching it pull out of the lot. He pulled a cigar from his shirt pocket, unwrapped it, and ran it under his nose. It smelled like 180 grand.

Pearson made it across town, the first mile of twelve-hundred, then pulled in for burgers to go.

A consortium hard press, and with a degree of indifference, Jon put everyone on notice. Work the overtime, or stop in and see Bernice about your walking papers. Now, theory would be put to the test; plant utilization pushed to 100 percent. It looked good on paper, but he knew stresses on the employees and equipment would also be 100 percent. He stood at his office window. Otherjon said, "Masochist."

Henry dialed, hoping Bernice was doing the answering.

"*Core Fuels*, this is Bernice. How can I help you?"

"I'm sick today."

"You mad about the schedule?"

"No, really sick."

"Okay . . . See you tomorrow, then?"

"I'm sick tomorrow." *Click*.

Bernice leaned in Jon's office doorway. "Henry called in sick."

"Okay, thanks. If he's in tomorrow, remind him to bring load-out numbers up to the office."

Teri worked on payroll in her cubical. She listened with comfortable relief but waited anxiously for last week's totals. The something she'd started wanted more proving.

"Bernice," Jon said.

"Yes."

"After lunch, I need you for an hour or so. We have to get the ball rolling on specifics for the annual meeting. I want to make this year memorable, food, games, the whole shebang." *Shebang – nice ring to it.*

"Food too?"

"For sure, the owners are buying. We're going to make it a big Octoberfest. Who does pulled pork sandwiches well? Cater it in, baked beans, chips, dessert – pumpkin pie. Let's do it up, right."

"Sounds good." And for Bernice, it did sound good. He had her at pulled pork. "I'll stop in after lunch."

Instead of tromping around in the mud and a heavy Monday morning fog, Clive worked from the RV, mapping timber and planning the grid for his next trip. His mind was on the girl and how quickly his last interest had been plucked away. Don't let it wait. In the evening, he shared hobos on the grill with the Park Ranger, and after, asked to use the phone in his cabin.

Clive? – That was quick. Leia thought, hearing the phone ring. Never Mondays for her and Teri. They tried to start the week like good girls.

"Hello."

"Hi, how's it going?"

"Oh, Clive the Forester?" she said, feigning surprise.

"Sorry, yes, Clive. How are you, tonight?"

"Peachy. What did you do today?"

They spoke for the better part of an hour. The Ranger waited outside and split kindling until there was nothing left to split, then kicked back in a lawn chair and watched the sun go down, and worried about the cost of a long-distance call.

Clive could make her laugh. She wasn't feigning that and the more he amused her the higher he got. They wrapped it up joking about possible Saturday activities they might enjoy together.

First some nonsense about row boating on the Platte.

. . . "Maybe we could spend the afternoon riding ponies in the park."

"Funny boy . . . I had saddle sores once."

"Well, you're all toughened up then."

"Listen, Bucko, saddle sores suck. They're no laughing matter."

Clive never had saddle sores. He hadn't spent ten minutes on a horse in his life but wanting one or two seemed like a reasonable thing to aspire to, for an outdoorsy guy like himself. The new girl of his dreams obviously didn't share this obtuse vision and he felt an inner relief, letting the horse idea seep from his bucket list.

. . . "How about ten?"

And they decided on coffee at a downtown café. Then a walk – maybe.

Leia looked at the dirty dishes, overflowing hamper, and conveyed the address. *Not burdening myself with cleaning.* "I'll be waiting outside."

The river was up, lift down. It was Rebecca's idea to take the boat out Monday evening.

"You can be the Capitan; I'll be the cook."

"The days aren't getting any longer, are they?" Jon said.

Ready-to-go sandwiches preempted the cook's duties but she wanted more. *Baby Cake's* cozy cabin served multiple functions, including the galley with a two-burner stovetop. Rebecca rummaged through canned goods in an upper cupboard.

She called out, "I can make soup or French-cut green beans to go with the sandwiches. Or both."

"How about the green beans?" he suggested and turned the bow north into the current.

Rebecca struggled with the female-inimical can opener for a minute before bringing it topside. "Can you get this open for me? I can take the helm."

"The helm, huh? Where did you hear that? Been watching *African Queen*?"

The can opener proved not male-friendly, either. Jon muttered it open. "There ya go, I'll take the *helm*, so the cook can get to her chores below deck."

She bumped him with her hip and a splash of water spilled from the can.

They anchored a few miles north, between treeless riverbanks near

Newbridge Landing. The little cabin cruiser bobbed in Platte's current as they ate their heated beans and temperate sandwiches from waxy paper plates in the late-day sun.

"Are things going any better at work?" Rebecca asked.

"Much better."

"What did you think of Clive?"

Nice machete. "I don't know, should I?"

"I think he has designs for Leia."

"Humph."

"We could invite him for a boat cruise, the four of us."

"I don't think so."

"Why?"

"First of all, I don't know how we would even get a hold of him, and second, what makes you think, for a minute, that the two of them would want to be encumbered with us old folk?"

Rebecca pouted and said no more.

Tuesday morning, after breakfast, Rebecca asked, "So you're taking the pickup today?" Usually, if she wanted to use the car, she'd ask to trade. It wasn't that she couldn't drive a stick, but the pickup was clunky, not exactly what you might call – a grocery getter.

"Right, I'll be home late so don't plan supper."

"We can make a frozen pizza or something when you get home, and since I'll have the car, I was thinking about getting groceries today."

"In Yutan?"

"No, Wahoo."

"I thought we liked the grocery store in town. Shop local, right?"

"The new one's open in Wahoo. It's not like I'm going to China."

"True."

"Want me to pick up anything?"

"The tabs for the pickup are due. Would you want to stop at DMV? It's in the courthouse, up on the hill next to the sheriff's office."

"I know where it is, Silly."

He didn't have to tell her the keys were in it, the keys were in everything.

Bernice leaned in the office door. "Henry called in sick, again."

Jon shook his head. "*Nice* . . . Would you go let Gilbert know – make sure he has everything under control?"

Late morning, Gilbert portentously sat in Henry's dusty office and put a hand to the load-out report.

"Would you drop this off up front with Teri, for me?" Gilbert asked.

"Give it here," Malcolm said. He stood the folder between the Willie's Wax bottle and a metal tackle box he'd converted for tools and hardware. Mailman wasn't in his job description but Area Leads often used him as their personal courier.

The report limped around the plant with Malcolm until late afternoon. Jon had gone, but Teri, working her new schedule, remained.

"What's that?" Bernice asked, watching Malcolm's hand delivery. Malcolm shrugged.

Teri opened the folder. "It's the load-out numbers."

"We should have Henry check them when he gets back. Let's not trust Gilbert on those, yet. Why don't you give that to me?" Bernice said, weaving her way to Teri's cubicle.

Teri reluctantly gave them over and did her best to look apathetic.

Malcolm stood dull . . . Bernice stridently shooed him away. The report went in her desk. Teri pretended to stretch and watched.

Chapter 20
Daily Choice

Rebecca worked the garden, canned in the summer kitchen, and toiled at fall clean-up in the yard. Before going in, she ate ripe cherry tomatoes and drank water from the hose. At four-thirty, she looked at the kitchen clock and jerked, remembering the grocery list on the refrigerator door. Crap – I'll just run into Yutan? – No – Wahoo – it's got to be Wahoo.

Jon put miles on the gas-guzzler in a lengthy loop home. At Elliot Flat's Salvage, Buster's kid slid green Impala parts into the black Dodge's box while Elliot added bills to a fat roll he kept in his front pocket.

"Nice 'rool', wouldn't-ya say?" Elliot said, rolling the "R" in an Old Norwegian brogue.

Buster's kid struggled with the bulky five-mile-an-hour bumper. Buster dropped a big-block Chevy cylinder-head in the dirt and helped.

"Goin to put those parts on yourself?" Buster asked.

"I think so."

"Well, if you want, Tic can do it for ya – for another hundred. No painting, though."

Jon looked to Tic's Frankenstein Fastback and graciously declined Buster's offer. "You wouldn't happen to have any rescued gas for my thirsty Dodge?"

Another five wrapped around Elliot's 'rool' and steady drips fell on Tic's boot as he funneled five gallons of salvaged petrol from a dented Jerry can. Mad Max gas swirled down the Dodge's quenchless tube.

Elliot stowed his pipe, rocked off the chair, and made it up. He went to look at another dent. With the eye that couldn't see, not the blind one, the Oracle of Junk inspected the Dodge's box-side. "This wasn't here last time." He rubbed his purple hand over the indent where the farmer's hinder had connected. Elliot pressed along the edge of the dip and balled his other hand into a fist. *Boom*, he dropped a substantial blow on top of the bedrail and the dent popped, reversing the damage. He hobbled back to his chair and sat. A match flared from the armrest groove. He shielded the flame from a light breeze and the pipe glowed.

Rebecca turned the key and a swirl of dust rose with the trunk lid. More sifted down the drain channels and fell on the bumper. The dust mingled with a redolence of fresh asphalt and new stripe-paint odor wafting up from the lot. She repositioned the spankin new cart and transferred groceries.

"How do, Mrs. Rawling?" said Barry Ottos, rolling past with his window down. He cranked the wheel and pulled an old white-on-white Mopar into the neighboring slot. "Checking out the new low price leader?"

Rebecca waited to reply until he came to a full stop. "Oh yes, not a big fan of the warehouse design, though."

Barry exited his decomposing Chrysler and slammed the door. Rebecca watched rust flakes rain from the door's bottom and onto the fresh tarmacadam lot. *Won't look new around here very long.*

"It's all the rage," he said.

"*Daily Choice,* all the rage, eh?"

"Well, I'm happy to see something new around here. Seems like everybody's packing up and moving to the city these days."

"It all works out. And how are you, Barry . . . and the family?" She remembered his name, but for the life of her, could not remember his wife's. She knew they had a couple of young children and recalled they were late starters in the nesting department.

"Good. We're all good, and how's Jon doing after the accident?"

Rebecca paused. "What accident was that?"

Barry, surprised, and with a puzzled look, said, "The . . . bin . . . accident."

"Um, I don't think he, uh, mentioned it to me."

"Oh, really. Jon didn't say anything? *Shit.* I probably shouldn't have said anything, either." As if caught in the act, Barry raised his hands and continued, "Let's forget I said anything about it. Nothing to worry about anyway, all's well that ends well . . . Supposed to be pretty nice this weekend, uh?" He started a move for the store.

Rebecca manufactured a stall, moving her empty cart, gifting it to Barry. A rolling intercept and she said, "What is it that ended well, Barry?"

"Well, *suppose* I can tell you, but I'd appreciate it if you wouldn't mention to Mr. Rawling that it was hard-work'n Barry that told ya. Figured you knew, really shouldn't be comin from me . . ."

Rebecca nodded.

"Well . . . we had a close call, could have been bad, but it turned out fine. Just one of those little mishaps, and everything turned out fine." Stammering, desperate, Barry searched for his next sentence. He'd put his foot in it.

Rebecca wasn't sure she wanted to know, but, annoyed with Barry's squirming, she decidedly exercised her rights. "You're going to tell me about it, now, eh?"

Barry spilled his guts.

"No stopping in Yutan," said Jon to Mr. R.

Otherjon returned a smile from the side mirror as they passed Ed's Gas Palace where black donuts lingered on the lot. "Looks like Ed and his patrons will be reminded of you for some time."

"They'll soon forget about it, won't they?"

"Yeah, with something better to prattle about."

When he got home, Jon passed the parked Impala and drove Blackie through the opening in the white fence. He unloaded used parts in a neat stack next to the woodshed. Rebecca glowered from a window.

Teri sat on her bed, ready to calculate with the instrument from Texas. She peeled a sticky note from her checkbook's inside cover and crunched the numbers copied from Bernice's drawer.

Jon laid awake most of the night and at seven Wednesday morning, no alarm sounded. He had turned it off ten minutes earlier and showered.

Otherjon waited for him to dry off.

"How are you going to get the owners there, Johnny Boy?"

"Not sure, yet. I thought you had all the answers?"

"You get so testy when you don't sleep."

"Testy huh? I'll show you testy." Jon picked up a bar of soap and drew a waxy fresh-scent circle around Mr. R's face, then slashed a diagonal across the man in the mirror.

Otherjon leaned and looked out from behind it. "Pugh. What're you doing? Quit being so obstinate. You need me. Without me, you're about out of friends, I'd say."

Henry looked in the Suburban mirror and decided to steer his fading black eyes clear of Teri and company.

Core's timeclock, down the hall from the offices, was easy viewing for Bernice. She watched Henry punch in and go back out. *Now, where's he going?* She went to catch him.

Out, and already fifty feet west, Henry headed for the southwest door near his station.

Bernice called after him, "Hey, what're you doing?"

He stopped, retraced to meet her, and lied, "I was goin ta check and see if Gilly was out runnin the payloader, yet."

"Well, Gilbert did your Load-Out Report, yesterday, but I think it's full of mistakes. I'll get rid of it, so you need to get me the *good one* right away this morning. What happened to you?"

Henry rubbed his nose, and lied some more, "Oh this? Bumped into the edge of my bedroom door in the dark." This lie he'd been thinking about – he felt like Einstein.

Pearson rolled into Nugget's parking lot at ten-to-ten Wednesday morning and spotted Harrison standing next to his rental in the lot's front row.

Tear-drop sunglasses accented Harrison's light suit. Chest hair curled from his uncharacteristically open dress-shirt, and Pearson thought, *Good-god, what ethnicity does he think he is?*

As Harrison was climbing into his rental, Pearson pulled the white van tight behind him. Harrison checked the mirror and slid out.

Pearson reflected in Harrison's shades. He glanced at the exposed chest and said, "*Julio.*"

Harrison cocked his arms out, showing off the look. "Ya made it." He wore the shades low and had used the hotel room's blow-dryer to feather his hair. Livin large and undercover; Harrison loved it.

Pearson looked at the van's dash, paused, and said, "One-thousand-two-hundred and sixty-four miles."

"*Pudges Plumbing*, huh? That's a good one."

"Yeah, yeah, yeah, the only time O'Leary has a sense of humor is when the joke's on me."

Pearson parked the van next to the rental.

Harrison circled it. "I recognize the van. Nevada plates?"

"Stopped at the first Nevada town, Mesquite, I think. Junkyard there with an abundance of plates; all on cars that no one's missing." Pearson stepped out of the van. Dressed for casual travel, he wore blue jeans and a long-sleeve denim shirt. He unbuttoned the cuffs and rolled them back, showing off his forearms. Less flamboyant than his high-roller partner,

Pearson wore sneakers and noticed Harrison couldn't give up the cowboy boots, but supposed, they fit Las Vegas as well as anywhere.

"Works for me. Does that tin-can got A.C.?"

"Blows cold."

"Good, it's gonna be a warm one. Let's get lunch."

Pearson's subordinate ass felt like two numb bricks. He asked, "What about Higgus?"

"Higgus sleeps till noon, we've got at least an hour before we need to put our surveillance hats on. There's a good barbeque joint a few blocks down."

And dying to use the mobile, Pearson asked if he might, "Maybe I should check in with O'Leary?"

Harrison dialed for him but let him talk. Pearson drove Freemont Street and, from the driver's window, made friendly gestures to folks on the opposite sidewalk and to passing motorists. He held the handful of cellular in his left for the world to see.

Teri opened her desk drawer and, for a fifth time, looked at the pad she had mathed on the evening before.

"Here's the report from Henry," Bernice said.

Teri jumped, her hand jerked, the drawer rattled.

"Looks like Gilbert had it right after all."

Without looking, she gently slid the drawer shut and received the new report in her other hand. "Oh, good. I'll get them in the ledger right away. Thanks, Bernice, nice to have someone looking out."

A blatant suck up, and Bernice felt an internal temperature change, an uneasy imbalance in her not-so-little universe. "Well, get after it then," she pissed.

Exactly what she wanted to do, 'get after it,' and noticed new figures right of the decimal. *Tonight, we will see.*

It's hard to surveil a maintenance man but it helps when two detectives are staying where he works.

Higgus's shift ended; Pudge's turn. "Use the rental," Harrison said and handed him keys. Pearson followed Dale home to make sure he didn't detour. After he was confident Higgus was bedded down, he went back to the casino to compare notes.

"Look how many times he went by the manager's office," Harrison said.

"He checked his watch again tonight when they pulled the money out of the pit."

"Then he was back on second floor when they safed the cash."

"What do we do if he makes a move before we figure out where he's got *Core's* money hid? Do we take him down? We could be big heroes down here."

"No, we let him run. Give him the Yo-Yo treatment."

"What's that?"

"We walk the dog, put him in a brain twister, and then . . . the big *sleeepah.*"

"Those are things?"

"I'm just jivin ya. He'll take us to his pot-of-gold. Trust me, we'll be standin tall, all around."

Pearson hinted at something both had been thinking about. "Ever wonder how much of *Core's* money he has already lost – gambling?"

"I'd say forty grand would be a fair guess."

"You mean twenty at each casino?"

"Exactly."

After the evening meal, Jon walked the south path along the river. He wasn't looking for peace of mind, he was looking for a piece of steel. This path also looped, not back to the house, but around an eddy and into a small clearing. Otoe Creek ran through the clearing and fed the eddy directly, and the river indirectly via the washback. An olive green tractor sat abandoned in tall grass against an overgrown fence. The remains of a deteriorated manure spreader lay partially submerged in the back water. In the spreader lay the item of interest, the business end of a pitchfork, less shaft and handle.

Jon removed shoes and socks then waded out to retrieve the prize. River muck, weeds, itsy snails, and leaves covered half of the steel. Free from the compost, he submerged it and gave it a shake. After a healthy rinse, he brought it up for a look. A split and rotting stub remained in the mount. Below, in subsiding drips and calming water, Mr. R held one as well. The metal tines were four. Together, Otherjon in the river, Jon above, touched each tine and counted, "Eeny, meeny, miny, moe."

Otherjon waved – Jon waved back.

Farmers continued to haul and Teri spent the afternoon recording truck tickets, assigning bushels to contracts. At eight bells she slid the ledger onto her lap and opened her purse. Bernice rounded the corner in an untimely return. Terry deftly popped the ledger back into the drawer. Evening math test postponed.

Chapter 21
Onion Slayer

Knife Knife
Knife, knife what a life
too dull at best
too sharp to test
fun to fillet
fun to play
no cut too deep
artery seep.
Blade blade shiny in the shade
Steel steel it is made
cut the man, clean the blade
cut the woman, look what we made
slice the boy
slice the girl
bloody toy
bloody mural
what a picture on display
when the blade's allowed to play.

Jon ingested a six-pack and the recliner digested him. Rebecca tried again. "Come on, you'll be more comfortable in bed." He forwarded the chair's lever and she pulled him free. Incomprehensible grumbles followed her up the stairs. In bed, she pressed her back to his chest. Cool air descended from the cracked-open window and Jon snuggled her tight. He fell asleep and dreamed not of their wedding, but the day after.

Marriage consummated that morning, again, for good measure, and they were up now, coffee in hand, sifting through gifts in the living room. Together, they took inventory and notes in preparation for the writing of Thank-yous. Rebecca carefully adjusted her dress she'd put on to re-establish the wedding mood. The gifts, wrapped in white and gold, some with lace, others with shimmering ribbons, looked splendid around the coffee table. They made progress, Jon read names on wedding cards and Rebecca wrote, matching people to the gift list. A porcelain tea set; Aunt Lisa, blue bath towels; the Conwells, another toaster . . . all wonderful accompaniments to establish their newly-rented abode. Rebecca handed him a cutlery set.

"Who did we get the knives from?" Jon asked.

"I think it was someone on your side of the family, the card should be in the box."

"Oh, sure, here, under the bow." Jon opened it and read, "May all your dreams come true, The Butchers."

"I don't know any Butchers, but how funny is that? The Butchers give cutlery. Must be friends of your parents."

"I don't think so." He took the angled block from the gift box and set it on the coffee table between them. An irregular trio of wooden handles protruded. While he looked in the card, envelope, and package for more info, Rebecca slid each from the oak block for inspection. The outer two were small. The first, a dandy paring knife, short and sharp. The small handle opposite, guarding the big boy in the center, also held a five-inch blade, but handily curved. She drew the large center blade and read the imprint on the handle. "66S, Glad it says 66S and not 666, eh? Look at the size of this devil, for some serious onion cutting."

Rebecca admired the clean eight-inch blade. The blade new, so new and brilliant it reflected like a mirror. And in the mirror she watched Jon. A warped Jon, a Jon bent in the bend of the cutlery, another Jon. Otherjon didn't look the happy groom. He looked wild. Rebecca held the blade just so, mesmerized by his eyes, menacing, conniving. He looked mean. He looked nasty. Rebecca felt something dark seep in, and it scared her.

The blade's reflecting light flashed Jon; he glanced down and saw

Rebecca peering back. She jumped. Then hastily returned the blade, but taking eye from task to check her man, she allowed delicate fingers to guide knife in slot. The steel reached for bone as she slid it home, and the block, missing a bottom corner insulator, wobbled on the table with a sassy laugh. "Nuk-nuc-Nuk-nuc-nuk."

"Ahhh," Rebecca groaned. "Jon, help." Blood ran fast, dripping, spoiling lacy, white gown.

Jon stirred and rolled onto his side; dysfunctional rest continued and the dream branched anew.

On the kitchen counter, the butcher block sat, Onion Slayer missing.

"Now, where did 66 go?"

He remembered Rebecca's busy canning, 'putting up the pantry.' It must be in the summer kitchen. Under a full and hallowed moon, Jon wandered out of the house onto the dewy path to the utility kitchen. Faint, orange light flickered through front window panes. He pushed the sagging door open, bottom chafing an arc across dirty linoleum. Inside the small building, Jack-o-lanterns filled shelves and sat on every flat surface: on the counter next to the sink, on the overturned wash tub, on the old wood-stove, and on the canning racks. All glowed bright. Moans emanated from the mass. Flickering internal flames moved mouths, shifted eyes, and heat radiated from their life-giving hellholes. Above, a full shelf of petite pumpkin heads giggled at Jon's arrival. Ahead, on the cutting table, rested a fat daddy. A county fair blue ribbon winner with long, slender teeth carved into a frighteningly large mouth, but eyes alluring, and 66 imbedded in the side of his head.

"Hello, Jon, you're not supposed to be out here at night, are you?"

"Pumpkins don't talk," Jon declared.

Above, a shrill giggle from the little'uns, and one said, "We do."

And another warned, "Look out for the guts."

Jon lost footing, slid, and met the floor. Into an endless pool of pumpkin guts and slimy seeds he dove. His dip elated the moaners; pumpkins looked at one another, chuckled, and belched more innards for Jon's swim. First using the tub, then the stove, Jon pulled himself back to his feet. He flung slime from his arms then carefully slid to the towel rack. Again, slick linoleum nearly dumped him. Rag from rack, and he wiped orange mushy innards from his hands.

He stood, his back to Shredder, and Fat Daddy announced, "I've got a knife."

Jon didn't turn. He replied softly, "I saw that."

"You can have it."

"Is that so?"

"I'm done with it, trust me."

Jon told himself, it's just a dream, I don't need the knife – go inside – go to bed.

Shredder read his mind. "Sixty-six wants to be back with his little buddies."

In unison, the pumpkinettes on the upper shelf agreed, "Yeah, he wants to be back with his buddies."

Jon slid across slippery floor, easing toward Shredder's convincing eyes. Slowly he reached, hand passing terrible teeth, inching to knife. Pumpkin Head's upper lip quivered, docile eyes followed Jon's fingers.

Little pumpkins above, yelled, "Incoming!" Shredder spun, teeth reached, chomped, pierced the quarterback's precious arm.

Jon screamed, "You Con-knifing son-of-a-bitch!"

With his free hand, he punched the side of Shredder's head, and through. Shredder's monster candle spit hot wax and flame licked the withdrawing fist.

The room chanted a cheer, "Fight, Fight, Fight."

Pumpkin Head shifted his jaw and fangs sank deep.

Pain buckled him and Jon took a knee. He forced himself up, reached past sleepy eyes, and gripped 66. He pulled the hickory handle like the lever on a one-armed bandit. Another brutal tug sent a fissure across Shredder's cranium. Pumpkin Head's expression turned to a worried look of deconstruction. Again Jon pulled, down this time, all the way to the corner of its mouth. Shredder's candle burned bright, a road flare, a filament's last moment in a broken bulb. Fat Daddy split. An overweight cracking and puff of scorched pumpkin smelt the end for the Blue Ribbon Winner. Jon had the knife and his bloody arm back, too.

From the summer kitchen, he wobbled, checking his bleeding extremity. The arm oozed and dripped black in the moonlight. A trip to the emergency room looked the proper course of action. The Impala raced toward town and the ER. Highway center lines flashed. He pushed the Chevy hard. Distant police lights appeared in the rearview and the faint sound of siren touched his ear. He looked at the knife on the seat next to him. "There'll be less explaining without you!" So expensive to recover, but he rolled down the window and flipped it clear.

The patrolman pulled close and flashed his lights, beckoning him to pull over . . .

"Good evening."

"Good evening, officer."

"Late for the party?"

"No, Sir. Making a run to the ER," Jon said, showing the bloodied extremity.

"Looks tough, but I'll still need to see your license and registration. Then we can head in, get you patched up."

Jon opened the glove box to grab paperwork. Inside – 66's cameo. 'How the Hell?'

The officer examined Jon's license, shook his head, and said, "I'm afraid I'll have to ask you to step out of the car, Mr. Rawling."

Is there a problem, Sir?" Jon asked, exiting the Chevrolet.

"You're the guy we've been looking for. Had a complaint about you, Rawling. So you like to pick on The Pumpkins, do ya?"

"Sir, I don't think you get it, they're evil, and besides, they're . . . Jack-o-lanterns."

"Watch your mouth, I don't want to hear any of your racist bullshit."

"But . . .

"No buts, butthead, tell it to your lawyer. Now, turn around, put your hands behind your back. You have the right to remain silent . . .

One motion removed Onion Slayer from Jon's waistband; across the officer's throat, it slashed.

The Man-in-Blue dropped cuffs. With both hands, he grasped his neck.

To keep things together he tucked his chin. His eyes bulged in terror; red spwished out between fingers. He walked down into the un-mowed ditch, stumbled about, then turned to face Jon. His arms went limp and dropped to his sides. He looked up at the executioner, his gashed neck opened wide. The deceased tipped like a plank, dropping in a grounding thump. The cadaver stared face-down in long grass.

Now there'd be trouble. Slam-Slam-Slam! Pissed at the conflation, Jon made sure his car door was shut. He restored his mood and placidly turned the key. "I knew I should have gone back in the house, – but it's only a dream." Adamantly, the bleeding arm disagreed. Foot on the gas, he watched the squad-car lights fade in the rearview mirror.

Jon tailed an ambulance into the hospital parking lot and parked near the emergency room entrance. Apprehensive of who might be working ER, he let 66 tag along.

Under bright lights, he sat on the examination table. Jon held the arm tightly across his chest, protecting the wounded wing. In his left, he spun cutlery on an open palm. With each revolution, the blade flashed overhead lamplight like a warning beacon. 'Don't tread on me!'

The nurse looked at Jon's arm, then to the knife. "Is this the culprit?"

"It's the culprit, alright," and Jon read her nametag, "Ms. Quizzical."

"I'll set it on the stand while we tend to your wound. Here, give it to me."

"I don't think so, Miss."

She reached for the slow rotating knife riding Jon's flat palm. Tricky 66 resisted and fell away. His crusty arm grabbed the falling blade. He caught the handle as nurse Quizzical attempted her own scooping save.

"Oh Miss Q." 66 gutted her.

The Doc heard nurse Quizzical spill out, whimper, and drop. Over his shoulder, he eyed the scene and scolded, "Good Lord, Man, get some gloves on, you can't do that in here, and bare-handed? Did you even scrub?"

Chapter 22

The Big Bust

On Thursday, in the wee hours of the morning, gamblers at the Nugget were sparse. The Pit Boss unlatched a maroon velvet strap and let security in. Behind the tables, they gathered bills from cash boxes. Higgus watched, and from a Red, White, and Blue Lucky-Seven machine, Harrison watched him watch. Pearson watched them both from a distance. All three checked their watches.

Pearson worked his way across the floor and filled a seat a few machines away from Harrison. "What do ya think?"

"If it works like last week, Higgus's weekend starts today. I have a gut feeling." Harrison looked around. "I think one of us should follow the money upstairs, find a good spot, in case Higgus goes up. One of us can stay here and keep an eye on him, in case he goes another direction."

"God damn second floor, hard not to look suspicious."

Harrison, wearing the suit, buttoned his shirt. "I'll give it a whirl, try to look important."

Harrison didn't wait for the unenthusiastic guards to get to the elevator. With cash from the pit loaded and locked in their stainless-steel cart, they had but one place to go, second-floor security. He took the stairs and waited for the elevator to ding, then made an entrance. Down the hall he walked, timing his pace well, and slowed as the guards entered the windowless door marked security. They paid him no mind, and he thought, *I should have been a thief.* The glimpse inside proved basically what he and Pearson suspected. A guy in a white shirt with a badge-patch on his sleeve sat in a comfortable chair, watching monitors. Harrison couldn't see a safe or vault but that there was one, was no mystery.

For a better view, Pearson moved to the machine previously occupied by his partner. He offered it a twenty and it zipped it from his grip with surprising speed. A scantily clad sweetheart approached, and asked, "Can I get you something from the bar?"

"You buying?"

"You're playing, so the casino's buying. Something for breakfast – say, something with tomato juice and an olive?"

I'd like to take her to breakfast. "Would you have a coffee?" *I'd like to take her to bed fast.*

"Sure, coffee, Coke, or cocaine, twenty-four-seven at the Nugget." It sounded like more than a joke. Steeped in seriousness, it came with a promiscuous smile. "How would you like it?"

To Pearson, she suddenly looked thinner in an unhealthy way. From his seat, he now couldn't help but peer up her nose. "Black."

Watching her walk away was the next thing he couldn't help. *Wonder how much a vice cop makes in Vegas?* The reels spun on the Red, White, and Blue. They stopped silent on a losing mismatch. Pearson looked for Higgus – he was gone.

At the end of the second-floor hallway, another door operated on a red handle, and the attached metal flag read, Emergency Exit Only. Harrison worked his way back, trying each office door. The fourth, next to security, was unlocked. He slipped in and gently shut it behind him but left it cracked for viewing.

Guards exited Security, and Higgus, rolling a vacuum, entered the hall from the elevator. They passed on paisley carpet. Harrison watched.

Pearson abruptly stood, tipping his chair. An elderly couple looked embarrassed for him. His shirt un-tucked as he bent to upright the black, leather seat and he was pretty sure he heard the wife say pudgy something or another. With chair righted, he went for the stairs and used the railing to assist his assent. At the top of the flight, he huffed, catching his breath. Harrison waited in the empty office, peeking, listening. Pearson quietly entered the hall and waved tentatively at the cracked door. Harrison opened it farther, put a finger to his lips, and motioned him to come.

"He went in as soon as the Guards left," Harrison whispered. Pearson nodded. They listened and Huggus's vacuum hummed in the next room. When it stopped, Harrison switched places with his underling.

He whispered again, "You watch, I'm going to listen." Harrison moved to an open spot on the wall and pressed his ear to it. Pearson gave him a look, like, 'what are they saying'?

Harrison put his hand up, pointed two fingers at his eyes, and then pointed at the door for Pearson to keep watch. Pearson left his post, retrieved a foam coffee cup on the desk, and gave it over. Harrison pressed it between the wall and his ear and gave Pearson a thumbs up.

Higgus visited with the man next door. Harrison listened - tried to decipher.

"Mumble mumble payday . . . Mumble mumble ass-hole. . . Mumble share . . . mumble mumble combination . . . Share . . . mumble the damn . . ."

For the better part of ten minutes, Harrison heard mostly nothing, only interrupted by a few unintelligible sentences.

Mumble mumble full . . . Mumble mumble . . . outta here."

The security room door opened and Pearson motioned Harrison. They both tried to watch. Two right eyes, one blue, one brown, stacked vertical in the slightly open door, stared as Higgus pushed the vacuum down the hall and entered the last door on the left.

"Let's go," Pearson said.

"Stay here." Harrison slipped out and silently scooted down the carpeted hall to the door marked Maintenance. It was near the elevator and he loitered close, ready to press the button. Another five minutes of standing was too much for Pearson's aching knees and he started down the hall. The maintenance door opened and Higgus came out holding a black lunchbox and adjusting a baseball hat. The three converged at the elevator and Harrison asked the others, "Down?"

They waited. Higgus looked them over. "You work here?"

They tried to not look as if together but . . .

Harrison said, "No, out here for a little fun."

"Staying at the Nugget?"

"Yeah," Harrison said, as Pearson nervously shook his head, no.

"Second floor is employees only, guys."

Ding . . . and the elevator door opened.

"Sorry, I was looking for a restroom," Harrison said.

Dumbfounded, Pearson couldn't come up with anything. A sweat bead rolled from his temple and hung under his chin. Like a bobblehead, he shook neck up, and finally, "Gambling," tumbled out.

"Employees only, it's just offices on second."

Onboard and Higgus rode the elevator between the detectives. The three produced an obnoxious odor, Higgus's musky dust, Harrison's musky musk, and Pearson's nervous sweat, a pungent treat for the next occupants. The door opened and Higgus said, "Good luck."

"Thanks," – "You too," Harrison and Pearson said respectively.

The three exited in different directions. The elderly couple entered and stared at Pearson as they got on the aroma ride.

The detectives circled and met back at the elevator.

"I just wonder, that god-damn black lunch box, every night with that god-damned lunch box?" Harrison said.

"Guy's gotta eat," said Pudgy

"Yeah, but the Nugget has a buffet, and he's been in there almost every night, grazing. Don't you think the employees get plenty to eat? I bet the kitchen throws out hundreds of dollars of food a day." Harrison paused . . . "How much money do you think you can fit in a lunchbox?"

"How would he have got it in there?"

"Think about it . . . the vacuum."

Pearson shifted his eyes right and up. He nodded. "Of course, and he's splitting it with security?"

"Has to be. If the lunchbox is full of what I think it is, I bet he's going to take us to his stash, soon, maybe now." Harrison nodded confidently. "From now on, twenty-four-seven surveillance, we watch the house even if we think he's sleeping."

The elevator got busy. From their rooms, they retrieved handcuffs and the hefty cellular. Pearson clipped his revolver to his belt and made sure his shirt covered it.

They hurried out to the lot. The van's right rear wheel-well emitted a wisp of smoke as Harrison squealed out of the parking lot. "Pray he went straight home."

"I'm praying." And Pearson watched their hubcap race the van down the street. The tin disk jumped the curb, landed on the sidewalk, and did a Watusi.

***"Core Fuels,* this** is Teri." It was the first incoming call of her late start.

"Rawling in?" the caller asked.

"Let me check. May I ask who's calling?"

Jon's phone lit – he picked up. "Yes."

"I have Lon Peck on line one."

"Hi, Lon. How are you guys, how's Kristy, and how's Mick's leg?"

"We're fine. You winged Michael a good one, but he says he's okay. If the weather holds, maybe we can get one more round in, in October? Larry and some of the other guys would like to get out one more time."

"Yeah, maybe. What's up?"

"Well, the reason I'm calling is the consortium wants some time to make a presentation at the annual meeting. If you could set aside half an hour or so . . ."

"We can do that. What's it about?"

"We're going to be offering company shares to all *Core Fuel* employees. A great opportunity for them. This is huge. We're opening the door, a super-duper chance for them to be partial owners."

"Huge, huh?"

"Even Sherpt'll be there. It's like profit sharing, only better. Matching shares, too. Of course, I know you'll be on board. I'll have my gal send over an outline. Be ready to help us promote this. Oh, and one free share of stock for everyone that signs up for the program after the presentation. We don't want anyone left out of this incredible commitment we're making to their future. Jon, we're counting on your solidarity."

"Oh, of course, and you couldn't have picked a better year to be here. We're putting together quite the fun evening. Food, games, it's going to be a *blast*. And having owners participate, *wow*, this is going to be wonderful. Like one big happy family. You wouldn't mind if we put you at the end of the program, save the best for last?"

"That works for us. By the way, we heard the new schedule's been implemented. Congratulations, Jon, I'm sure we'll be seeing those production numbers going up lockstep. Anyway, pencil us in, we really are committed to their future."

"Great, looking forward to hearing all about it. And Lon . . ."

"Yeah?"

"Bring your appetites."

"Will do."

Jon shut his office door. Arms up and pumping, he jogged around the room in a triumphant Rocky Balboa salute. After a couple of laps, he stopped at the window and went into an air-boxing display opposite Mr. R. "How do you like them apples?"

"Give it to em," Otherjon replied.

Jon leaned on the desk. A coughing fit gripped him.

Harrison's bulging eyeballs could only have looked more cartoonish if his pupils had been replaced with dollar signs. He stopped scribbling and set aside his photo of now bearded Higgus. "Woa-wah, hot damn, get up here," Harrison picked binoculars off the dash, "He's out, and guess what he's carrying?"

"What?" Pearson scrambled up from a rumpled sleeping bag, ending his snooze in back.

"Look."

Pearson moved into the passenger seat in time to see a duffle bag get thrown into the back seat. Their van, parked near the intersection adjacent to the house, sat uphill a bit. For Harrison, the view was good. Pearson had a tougher time seeing through the doorpost and watched distorted images in the windshield's curved corner.

Higgus, in decent clothes, nice jeans, and a polo, looked fresh and quite improved from the green custodian garb. They watched him rummage around the back seat before surfacing with the black lunch box. Higgus got out, set it on the roof of the VW, and opened it.

"Where did *that* come from?" Pearson asked.

"Duffle bag, maybe?"

"What's he doing?"

"Don't know, can't see, counting?"

"Maybe, he's skimming off a little spending money before it goes into hiding."

The aunt was out now, as well, and carried a purse in one hand. A brown grocery bag, with paper handles, hung from the other. Aunty was slight, and even from their distance, Pearson saw her fragility. A sun hat shaded her face and her white blouse looked dated. Brown sixties knit slacks hinted at bellbottoms.

At the car, she said something uppity. Higgus looked frustrated and placed the lunchbox in the paper bag, then helped her in. He said something before closing her door, circled, and put the paper bag in the back with the duffle. The compact car tilted as he took the driver's seat. They backed out of the drive and drove away from the detectives.

Harrison turned the key. They idled down the street well-removed from the VW.

The car took a left.

"Quick, check the mail," Harrison said and pulled next to auntie's mailbox.

Harrison's pit stop and Pearson's quick grab took four seconds. Pudge's plumbing van eased down the street and Harrison held back some more, turning to let their target stay about a block ahead.

Pearson shuffled through the envelopes. "Jacob Pullman."

"Jacob pull-a-fast-one?"

"Not today," Pearson said.

"You got that fucking right."

The VW turned east on Charleston. Harrison, again, held up before turning out.

Pearson asked. "Whose name is the car in? Higgus? Pullman?

"No, it's his aunts, Hannemann."

"You don't suppose she drove to Nebraska and picked Higgus up?"

"God, I don't know, I've never even seen her drive the damn thing."

"I'm starting to get the feeling our little church goer's not all sugar and spice." Pearson pointed at the intersection sign. "They took a right, up there on 582."

Harrison pointed at another sign. "The old Boulder Highway. Should make for easy tailing."

Bernice went to lunch. Teri calculated. Gilbert's figures resembled production ratios in line with the numbers from a couple of years ago. She was convinced the discrepancy was on Henry, but it now looked like, Bernice, too, might be in on the manipulation.

Midafternoon, Teri returned from break. She still hadn't brought her findings to Jon. Bernice seemed married to her desk, and for all the days she wasn't a joy to be around, this day, Teri truly wished her away . . . it felt like Bernice was watching her.

Now, it was after four, and the clock wasn't slowing down. *Why today?* Soon, Jon would leave for the day. On her cubical wall, the clock's minute hand ticked past the six. Waiting was excruciating, and there Bernice sat, ready to scrutinize any deviation.

Why hasn't she gone on break? – Why hasn't she made the rounds? Teri tried willing her to rise. Like a hypnotist, she concentrated. *Cake – Go find cake – Mm . . . cake.*

It was Bernice that visited Jon. Teri had little success hearing conversations that took place in Jon's office, and it was no different today.

Coming out of the office, Bernice looked back. "I'll go shape em up," and then, with tasked gait, exited the offices.

My turn, and, without knocking, Teri entered and closed the door behind her. Emboldened with substantial proof in hand, she walked across the room like a prima donna and thrust the results in front of Jon.

"Look at this, Gilbert gave load-out numbers on Tuesday, but Bernice said she didn't trust them, and on Wednesday gave me new ones from Henry. She said they were the same, but I saw Gilbert's and they were a little different." Teri pointed at the sets of figures.

Jon sat thoughtfully for a moment. "In the hundredths."

Teri nodded. "And in resulting gallons."

"How much?"

Teri pointed again. "A thousand. Nine hundred sixty-eight – to be exact." And, though her confidence was bolstered, she felt herself perspiring, which she seldom did.

"Hum?"

She moved around the desk to his side and bent down to show him her work. "Well, yes. See, if you divide the . . ."

It was her hair that was distracting, today. He could smell the clean and it hung shiny near his face as she sidled close to show the alteration.

Jon listened and followed her equations to conclusion. He found no reason to doubt her work.

"What's the point?" she asked.

"That's the thousand-gallon question, now, isn't it?"

He looked at her, and she, with a concerned look, placed her hand on his shoulder.

"Thank you, Ms. Thompson," he said and dismissed her.

Teri, expecting more, returned to her cubicle. *Weird.*

At one minute to five, Jon lifted his suit jacket from the shelving hook. Instead of leaving, he walked the halls toward maintenance. At the control room, he slowed, stopped, peered in. Bill noticed. Their eyes met and Bill looked at him sheepishly, apologetically. The control room was well lit, but Mr. R's veiled reflection in the clean new window, spoke: "Save him for last."

In maintenance, Bobby stood at a bench, soldering. Jon came in, and when Bobby noticed, he unplugged the iron from the wall socket. He smiled, and made an announcement, "Four days now, notting broke. Knock on wood." Bobby pushed off with his butt, stepped to the table, and did the knocking.

"I'll knock to that." And on the opposite side, he did. "Would we have some good glue in here that I could borrow?"

"Sure thing, Boss. Would you like for wood, or steel, or . . .?" Bobby already had the blue-gray metal cabinet open. He rummaged out various tubes and bottles.

"Multi-purpose, got anything like that?"

"How about this one? Says, "Multi" right on the package. Two-part epoxy, grease y blanco, mix em fifty-fifty, dries mas rapido." Bobby handed him the small, rectangular, yellow box. Jon opened it. A cardboard divider separated two small tubes with white and black caps.

Bobby asked for them, felt and squeezed, to make sure they hadn't gone bad in storage. "Works good," he said.

Jon returned them to the yellow box. "Thanks, Roberto."

Bobby felt like a million, Jon gave him respect instead of the disparagement he received from most of his coworkers, and from the community at large, for that matter. He asked, "How's *Jefe* doing, now?"

"Remember what I said, it never happened, and I'm fine. Thanks for asking, though. And you?"

"Bien, Mr. Rawling."

Jon nodded. "Good. Okay, I'm going to give this a try, thanks."

Jon, almost out the door, and Bobby, feeling bubbly, said, "Don't forget where you found it."

Not looking back, Jon held it up.

In Henderson, the Volkswagen hung a left on the parkway. The detectives kept a couple of cars between them until the VW worked its way into the older residential section. Here, the afternoon traffic thinned; Harrison, with little cover, fell back.

"They turned again."

"I got him," said Harrison.

"Dogwood." Pearson read the street sign as Harrison hung a left. Three quarters down the block, the Volkswagen turned into a drive.

"I'm goin down to the end and hang a u'ey." Harrison slowed so they could get a look as they rolled by.

A Chevy conversion van sat in the drive, nose to the street. Behind it, a sedan was parked in a carport. The VW sat nose to nose with the conversion van and Higgus was helping auntie out. The duffle bag hung from his shoulder, resting on his hip and lower back. An elderly gentleman came out of the house and lifted his fedora to greet the company. Pearson noted his wispy hair and perfect white smile – undoubtedly removable.

"Looks like some old geezer's place," Pearson said and tried to continue watching in the side mirror as they rolled to the end of the block.

"I'll swing it around, park down a couple of houses on the other side." Under smoldering sun, Harrison parked but kept the van running. They hadn't missed much, but when the elderly man removed the brown, paper bag from the back seat of the VW, Harrison shut the van off. "This is interesting."

"Indeed." And with the engine off, so went the AC. Pearson's pores poured. Harrison's did, too, but he wanted to hear.

The old man slid the conversion van's side door open and set the brown bag inside.

"Nice van," Harrison said. "Looks like it's got the couch-bed in back."

Pearson was in a better position than at the last stakeout, but sat forward and leaned for a better look. "Captain's Chairs, too."

The man looked her senior, and the aunt asked, "Can I use your bathroom, quick, Don?" He waved and she went into the house.

Higgus slid the duffle bag in next to the grocery bag, and the old man said, "I'll go get mine."

Auntie was still inside when Don came out carrying another duffle. Higgus helped slide it in next to his and patted it.

"Shit, this is it!" Harrison hissed. "He's been holding the Nebraska cash."

"Old bastard," Pearson said.

Bags stowed, and Higgus stood. He noticed the van across the street and squinted. *That looks like those doofs from the casino this morning.*

Harrison watched Higgus whisper something to the old man.

"Get down," Harrison said.

The old man looked at *Pudge's Plumbing*, shook his head, and said, "I'll get Alice." Higgus looked concerned.

Pearson peeked over the dash pad. "What should we do? Ya think it's all there?"

"I don't know, probably. We aren't far from Hoover Dam and the state line. Let's keep it simple. I vote we take them right here and now."

"I say so, too. This neighborhood's dead, hardly a car since we parked."

"Plus, we don't need a van chase, do we? Get out like you're going in this house, here. Circle around back behind three or four, come out down there and cross over. His van should block you from view." Harrison pointed. "Then I'll pull the van up and block em in."

"How we gonna play it?"

"Whataya mean?"

"Well, do we take em all, we can't really arrest them in Nevada anyway without . . .?"

"We flip em our badges and arrest Higgus. Throw him in back of our van, confiscate the bags, and away we go."

"The aunt and the geezer?"

"Ta hell with them. They don't look like any masterminds, do they? What'uh we give a shit? We just want Higgus."

"What about the casino's money?"

"Combat pay."

"And we're taking him all the way back in the van?"

"You didn't think O'Leary had you drive it all the way down here just for surveillance, did you? What happens in Vegas is about to get expedited to Saunders County, Nebraska."

The aunt came out the front. Pearson, down a few houses, crossed the street. He moved closer and looked across for direction from Harrison. Harrison's spastic wave signaled him forward.

As if a director yelled, ACTION! Pearson pulled his thirty-eight, sprinted on short legs through the neighbor's yard, and to the back of the Chevy conversion. Harrison pulled the plumber's special into low and squealed from the parking spot. The van engine screamed with all its assets. He aimed at the driveway and mashed the brakes. Locked front tires screeched as loud as the rear had a few seconds before. *Boowumph,* into the Bug. The Volkswagen lurched ahead and *Pudges Plumbing* stopped a foot farther than Harrison's intent.

Negligible forward whiplash and Harrison quickly recovered. Pearson came around the conversion van like a bowling ball and delivered a strike. He crashed Higgus, pushed with both hands, and sent him sprawling. A glancing blow sent aunty stumbling to the travel van's side. She hit, wavered, then caught herself on the sliding door's back edge. She leaned and the door rolled in its track. The geezer reached, stuffing an arm in the opening, blocking the door's travel. It slammed his forearm and Aunty careened off the slider's back edge. Her forehead took the brunt of the impact. Bedazzled, she stepped twice and collapsed.

Harrison was out, and so was his little Walther; he pointed the PPK in Higgus' face.

Pearson wanted to say something. Something he'd wanted to say since the first day he dreamed of being an officer. He cocked the hammer on his double-action .38, pulled his shirt above his belt, showing the badge attached to the clip-on holster, and said, "The jig's up." He reveled in the saying of it and it had come out exactly as he hoped it might. In disbelief, Harrison looked at him. *Idiot.*

Harrison holstered Walther, flashed badge, and pulled Higgus up. "On your feet." He ignored damaged old folk on the ground and rode Higgus, smashing him on the Chevy van's passenger door. "You're under arrest. You have the right to . . ."

"For what?" Higgus interrupted, looking over his shoulder and squirming.

Amped up, Pearson raised his abbreviated .38 and pointed it at Higgus's head. "Don't try anything, Ass-fuck, cause stubby likes to go pop."

"Put that away," Harrison said and placed his hand on Pearson's .38, lowering it for him. And addressing Dale, "Robbery, you don't steal from the casino and get away with it, Higgus. You should consider yourself lucky, lucky we got to you before the Nugget's thugs found you out. You'd be a hundred coyote treats right now."

"Higgus, Higgus who?"

"Hi, Dale," Pearson taunted, this time with a pointing finger. "You can run but you *can't hide*."

"I'm not Higgus, Dale Higgus?"

"You should have left the country, gone to Mexico, and now, here you've dragged these two old folks into it. I guess you don't care if your aunty spends the rest of her life behind bars?" said Harrison.

"Into what? I'm *Not* Higgus, and she's my grandma, not my aunt."

The geezer helped aunty to a sit, and she said, "I told him we didn't need it."

"Aaah," Pearson said.

"She only gets three-forty-five a month from social security, and I'm not Higgus, I'm Pullman," Higgus whined, now looking over his other shoulder.

"Sure ya are," Pearson said, with a sloppy grin.

"Go grab the bags," Harrison instructed.

"Pearson took the two duffles out of the van and set them on the hood of the VW. They started to slide. He helped them onto the driveway and unzipped the first.

"Whatta we got?" Harrison asked, ratcheting cuffs on Dale.

"Depends," Pearson replied, pulling out a handful of content.

"Depends on what?"

"No, Depends, adult diapers, clothes, toiletry bag . . ."

"And?" Now Harrison joined Higgus, looking over a shoulder.

"Stay outta my stuff," the old man said. He had an arm around Alice and his fedora was off. His thin wispy-white hair stuck out to one side and watery waves hung in his eyes.

Pearson ignored him. ". . . And a pair of shoes, that's it in this one."

"Open the other one."

"Stay out of my grandma's stuff. You need a warrant," Higgus said, squirming.

"Dale!" Harrison said, pressing.

"For the last time, I'm not Dale."

Harrison shook him. "Dale . . . Shut up." Then looked to Pearson. "Open it!"

Pearson already had it unzipped, rummaging out old lady clothes. He stirred contents, looked up, and said, "Nope."

Harrison got rough and collapsed Higgus hard against the van door. With forearm, he held Dale's face to the window. "Where is it?"

Through mouth mashed between arm and glass, Dale tried one more time. "Please, I don't know what you're talking about, Sir."

The aunt shouted, "It's in the lunch pail!"

"Now we're getting somewhere," Pearson said and got on his feet, intending to go for it.

Harrison said, "My turn, you hold Higgus."

Pearson wanted badly to be first to fan some cash in hand but did as asked.

Harrison moved to the open van and looked at aunty. "Thank you. See how easy this can be?" He leaned in and dragged the paper bag across the tan pile carpet. Feelings of doubt were creeping in. Even if they found ten, twenty, or fifty grand in the lunchbox, he knew it couldn't be holding the hundred and some thousand they were there to recover. *Nugget* money wasn't *Core's* money. How, now, would they get Higgus to talk? With his back to everyone, he stood and stared in the bag, in at the black lunchbox. *Leverage – I need leverage.* Seconds ticked, and with each tick, a hundred thoughts raced through his mind. Thoughts from, The Good . . . *Kill em with kindness – a little late for that, now.* The Bad . . . *Threaten aunty with a gun to Huggus' head – and if she doesn't talk?* To the Ugly . . . *Threaten Higgus with a gun to aunty's head – and if he doesn't talk?* And finally to the Evil . . . *Drive 'em all out to the desert in this nifty van and make em talk, and if they don't, or do, we lock em in it and it catches fire.*

"Open it," Pearson said." His hold on Dale was slight and the detained spoke again.

"I'm not Higgus, he's my second cousin, I think, Dale Higgus, like I said."

Slow it down. Harrison decided to wait a minute with the lunchbox. He turned and sat in the open side door, hands back, fingers grooming cut pile. To the old couple on the ground, and to Higgus, in his peripheral, he spoke.

"So where did you all think you were going today?" And concentrating on the old geezer, he asked. "Don, was it?" Don, on the ground, holding Alice, nodded. "In Don's mighty fine unit," Harrison declared, patting the carpet.

"St. George," Don said.

Higgus looked over his shoulder. "Don't talk to them."

Getting nice was worth a try. Harrison ignored him and focused on aunty. "The three of you were going to St. George, to do what?"

Alice and Don looked at each other, then down, searching for an answer.

"I wasn't going anywhere," Higgus said. "They were going on a . . . a . . . vacation."

"A vacation all right," Pearson said.

"Just you two," Harrison asked the couple in the dirt.

Again they looked at each other and down.

"Alice?" Harrison waited for her to look at him. "Does your nephew have a problem taking things that aren't his?"

"Grandma! Don't!" Higgus barked.

Pearson slapped him on the back of the head. "Shut-ahp."

"Alice?" Harrison asked for her attention a second time.

She nodded, and said, "His name is Jacob."

"Okay, Jacob, Dale, whatever. Does he have a problem taking things that don't belong to him?"

She nodded, and whispered, "Yes."

"Do you know where he has been putting what doesn't belong to him?"

She nodded again, and squeaked, "I told him we didn't need it, we have enough money to buy the things we need."

"God damn-it, Grandma," Higgus whined.

Pearson cuffed Higgus again, letting him know he didn't appreciate the lack of compliance.

Harrison moved the paper bag to the ground in front of him. "I'm going to look in the lunchbox now, but before I do, I want to know something . . . if you will show me where the rest is hid?"

Don held her tight. "No matter what, Alice, I love you."

Tears ran from her gray, eighty-six-year-old eyes, and she said, "I can show you."

"Hot dog," Pearson said. Harrison lifted the lunchbox out of the bag by its black plastic handle. Up it came like an elevator on a cable and into the afternoon light. First the handle, then the lid. The sun touched the hinges in back. The latch hooked the paper bag's looping rope handle, and . . . *Flip*, so smooth; Harrison never felt it. The box arrived, latch sprung. Contents spilled out.

A thermos in the domed top pushed free its U-shaped wire hold. It caught the front, flipping the box's contents onto Harrison's lap. A plastic-wrapped container spewed on impact, covering his crotch with apple sauce. Two fat rolls of toilet paper flopped out, one settled on his lap between his legs, the other bounced off an immaculate boot and unrolled white across the yard.

Pearson watched in dismay. "Ass wipe?"

Harrison watched apple sauce soak into the roll in his lap and felt warm juices working their way through his briefs. He stood, used the back of his hand, and with one swipe sent the spill down the side of the van. "Don't anyone move." He sternly instructed Pearson to keep his gun holstered and not to say, 'one god-damn thing'.

To the house, he walked. Don's bathroom smelled like old people. After a pants-down washing, he went to the picture window and looked out at the scene. He scratched his head. *What a mess.*

In the kitchen, he first guessed the counter's end drawer, and this hunch he had correct. Harrison put kitchen shears to work on Don's phone line behind the living room couch.

He came out. Pearson had Higgus sitting in the open side of the conversion van. Higgus's hands, still cuffed, were behind him, and Pearson stood, leaning on the door they previously had Dale pinned against. Harrison pulled a dry spear of grass from a decorative Egyptian vessel on the landing and stuck it in his mouth. The yard party, waiting for him to say something, watched. He walked over to the *Pudge's Plumbing* van. Out of the glovebox, he retrieved his picture of Higgus. He returned, sat next to him, and looked at the photo. Although hauntingly similar, the man sitting next to him was not the man in the picture.

Higgus said, "That's Dale."

"Dale Higgus."

He nodded.

He showed it to the aunt and she nodded. "When's the last time you saw your nephew? Excuse me, your great-nephew?"

"I don't remember, exactly, about ten years ago, we went to his graduation party."

"His graduation party?"

She nodded.

"And where was that?"

"In California."

"And this, not-so-young man next to me, Jacob, your grandson, has been stashing stolen toilet paper, let me guess – in your house – under the sink – in your bathroom?"

"And some in the hall closet," she said.

"My, my, Pearson, what do you think we should do with this ring-a-bandits?

"What – ring?" geezer Don asked.

"Guilty, Don," Harrison kicked the roll of toilet paper lying next to his boot, it rolled out near the other one in front of the old folks. "Count em', two rolls of stolen TP, and we took them out of your van, right here in your driveway. Almost took stolen property over state lines, didn't ya? Next, you two love birds would've been illegally wiping away, carefree, up there in St. George."

Harrison took a deep breath and exhaled slowly. He took the photo with him back to the other van and grabbed the cellular. In plain view, he punched in most of Ellen's number and faked a convincing police call. When finished, he went to the VW and pulled the keys, then to the conversion van and pulled that set, as well.

"I have a couple of officers on the way, they'll take statements. It'll be up to the *Nugget* to decide if they want to press charges. My partner and I have to get going – my son's football game's starting about now. If you'll all climb into Don's van? – Help them up, Pearson. – I told the officers you'd be waiting for them right here. Now, I'm going to help you quell one dumb idea . . ." Harrison hooked the keychains together, and with an underhand toss, threw them on the roof of the house. "Your keys are up there, but easy enough Jacob can get them down after the officers take your statements. Now, the way I see it, you're in a little trouble, but not that much, so don't go do anything stupid to make it worse. Sit tight and relax. They'll be here in ten or fifteen minutes." Harrison un-cuffed Jacob, then helped Pearson seat the troubled and tumbled three in the back of Don's travel van.

"Shut it."

Pearson slid the side door with velocity, it slammed flush, and pushing the handle horizontal, he latched them in.

Harrison stared at Pearson. "The jigs up? Really?"

Chapter 23
Picks

"I want to get some work done before supper. Could we eat later tonight?" Jon asked.

For two days, Rebecca had been catching herself staring at him and wondering if he noticed. She'd been thinking about their mortality, his secrecy about the accident, and how much older he looked. Had the aging been sudden, or had it come on with a gradualness you don't think about? She was thinking about it now.

"That's fine. I haven't started anything yet."

Jon went upstairs to change.

When he came down, Rebecca asked, "Are you going to work on the Impala?"

"Oh – not tonight, got a couple of things I want to get done on the old boat."

"I could come down and help a little while before I start dinner."

"Don't really have anything for you to do. It's kind of a one-man show down there, ya know?"

She knew. *More alone time – that's what I get.*

Jon grabbed Bobby's epoxy from the car, then crossed the yard to the woodshed. Late-day sun fell bright on the bleached antlers. He looked them over and chose the left, an elongated eight-point rack. With a jerk, he pulled it from the beam.

In the boathouses, the two clear, incandescent bulbs glowed. The one above the workbench illuminated ingredients. He placed the antlers and epoxy alongside the retrieved hayfork.

Clamped solidly in the vice, Jon went to town on the pitchfork. One tine at a time and seven inches from their tip, he hacked. Each stroke moved the blade a bite through the quarter-inch steel and each pass emitted a wispy puff of rust. The tines sang like tuning forks under nipping blade, and each stroke produced a lower note. One *tinkle-tink-tink* after another, they dropped to the cement.

A forties medicine cabinet on the wall held dust, Band-Aids, peroxide, Q-tips, and other paraphernalia. Mr. R loitered in the mirror. Jon passed, going for leather gloves and a three-pound hammer. On the way back, he checked in. The content reflection refrained comment – Otherjon left him to his business, only humming quietly, filling the boathouse with a satiating ambiance.

Jon laid tines in a row on the cement floor. He chose one and, with leather-gloved fingertips, rotated the tine's arc off the floor. In straightening blows of four, the hand-maul landed. And, from Otherjon, a cadence developed. "Pick-ah pick-ah pick-a-pick."

Occasionally, a strike rotated the tine flat, and each time, Mr. R patiently waited for Jon to return the shaft to its arched position.

Blows continued, Mr. R persisted, "Pick-ah pick-ah pick-a-pick."

On the third tine, Jon joined in, lifting the maul with an, "Ah . . ." Together, they joyfully chanted, "Pick-ah Pick-ah Pick-a-PICK . . . Pick-ah Pick-ah Pick-a-PICK!"

Jon turned antlers in gloved hands, chose the four straightest points, and cut them off at four-inch lengths. Then, three inches into the antler's sawed-off end, he went with the drill's quarter-inch bit.

Together, they returned to humming as he mixed resin with activator. Jon dabbed each tine's hacked end in the gray epoxy and, with a pliers' help, twisted them into receptive bone handles. Lined up on the bench, they lay drying on a leather wrap.

Jon put tools away and, passing the mirror, stopped to confer with Otherjon.

"Like em?"

"Nice picks . . . people picks."

"A whole pack."

"A pack of people picks."

"Could be a tongue twister," Jon said. And together a limerick they chanted.

A Pack of Picks

Pack a pack of people picks,
people picks, he packed.
Pick a pick from the pack.
Pick a prick, pick a prick,
pick a prick to jack.

Part the pack to pull a pick,
pull a pick and pock.
pick a pick from the prick
pick a pick, pick a pick
pick a pick . . . Pop!

Rebecca rang the dinner bell.

Chapter 24

Lemonade Shines

The new schedule affected every department. It wasn't pretty. Five tens, or four twelves, with overlapping shifts, to brew up Core's production increase. For office personnel, it was as good as it got. No twelves, but staggered hours nonetheless. Now, a few days in and trying to adjust, the workforce was in a flap . . . and Teri needed a release.

Leia entered the apartment building and heard the phone upstairs in hers. She scampered up the flight, then quickly with the lock, and threw keys on the table as she ran to pick up.

"Hello."

"Thirsty Thursday," Teri announced.

"Thirsty Thursday," Leia repeated.

"Can you meet me at *Core*, I have to work till eight."

"Eight?"

"There's a big production push. It's all pins and needles here. Everyone's tired, mad."

"Sounds like a blast."

"Ya, that's why I'm so thirsty. Let's go to Goldie's. I haven't had a chance to wear my new blue outfit. Can you stop by my house and grab it? My mom's home.

Leia thought, *Thursday's supposed to be casual, Well, if she's wearing THAT, I'm not wearing this crap.*

"Okay, I'll stop and get it. You aren't going to change in the car, are you?"

"No, bring it in, I'll change in the bathroom, they're clean. Bernice's whip cracks and the cleaning crew jumps."

An uneasy feeling gave Leia pause. “I don’t know, I really don’t want to come in, ya know? What if I run into Work Boots?”

“Oh, don’t worry about him, he works in back. He hasn’t been up to the offices once this week,” Teri laughed. “You can come at seven-thirty, keep me company, not much to do, just sitting around trying to look busy for the boss.”

“My dad?”

“No, Bernice, silly. Your dad usually leaves by five, five-thirty. Your mom would kill him if he was late for dinner, wouldn’t she?”

“She’s not *that* bad,” Leia laughed, defending Mom.

Teri was envious; she could count the times her mother had cooked a real meal on her fingers.

Small talk at dinner scratched the surface of their existence. Rebecca tried to be interesting, but home all day and mundane tasks squelched her contribution. Dull – Insignificant – That’s me. She, unfortunately, never understood that her missing chatterbox was because she wasn’t a self-absorbed bimbo.

Jon helped her clear the table. There weren’t many dishes and clean-up looked to be a brief attachment.

Rebecca said, “Go relax. I’ll have this cleaned up in a shake.”

It was Onion Slayer, lying on the counter that held Jon’s interest. “I got this. You cooked, I’ll clean up, tonight.”

“I’ll dry.” More together time, that’s what she was looking for. A yearning for attention had set in. Worry over her recent discovery, and he, not sharing, added weight to an exasperatingly long day.

She picked tableware from the rack and dried as he washed. Anxious to be inclusive, Onion Slayer lay waiting among pans and dishes on the counter. A plate, a fork, a cup, another. Jon washed, anticipation to handle 66 mounting. *Work before pleasure.*

“You’re so sexy when you wash dishes,” she said and rubbed his shoulder. He returned her a masking smile and looked to his reflection in the kitchen window. Otherjon had joined them, washing joyously and whistling while he worked. Otherjon, in high spirits, looked him in the eye and winked. Then continued whistling a tune Jon recognized, but couldn't place.

Rebecca continued drying and circled the kitchen, placing dishes and glasses in their proper homes. Each time she returned, she gave him a smile or touch.

Mr. R and Jon washed pans, reaching closer and closer to the steel blade. *Blade blade shiny in the shade.* They washed it all. Alone on the counter, the knife beckoned. Otherjon stopped whistling and cast a long *trust-me* look at Jon. Mr. R smiled and slowly let his wistful gaze leave Jon's.

Together, they stared at the lonely cutlery. *Clowns and Jokers,* Jon thought, and now hummed the tune where Otherjon left off. He delicately picked up the knife.

Prompt at seven-thirty, Leia found Teri alone in the offices. "Looks like you got the place to yourself, tonight."

"Bernice stepped out. Dollars to a box of doughnuts, Ms. Piggy's in the cafeteria filling, filling her face again," Teri replied, trailing off, realizing someone might overhear.

Leia smiled and handed her the Penney's bag containing the blue outfit.

"Thanks for picking it up, I'll be in the bathroom right around the corner."

"Okay," Leia replied, looking to the hall and remembering the restroom location.

"I'll be right out."

Leia knew this meant, pull up a chair; it could well be half an hour. Teri had met someone; a new admirer that frequented Goldie's. Leia figured Teri wouldn't leave a single uncurled eyelash to chance.

With Teri in the bathroom, Leia roved the cubicles and stopped at Jon's door.

She flipped lights on as she went in and scanned Dad's office. Leia hadn't graced the space in years, but it was basically as she remembered. Shelving on the south wall; the middle shelf held business and other leather-bound books. Jon's tarnished trophies stood on the top deck. Lined up on the bottom shelf, Leia eyed a row of *Core Fuels* promo toys – including a scale semi-tractor, pulling a chrome tanker with *Core* decals on the door, and scrolled across the chrome tank. A similar scale, generic-looking, fifties-style pickup sat next. Its door also wore the mini *Core* logo. Behind it, a tin gas pump – *Ethanol* sticker across the front. Positioned smartly, its hose stretched, filling the pickup. On the end, a tacky porcelain corncob-shaped ashtray rounded out the lineup.

On the opposite wall, above beige file cabinets, hung plant certifications, Jon's diplomas, and, in a cheap black frame, a one-dollar bill, signed by the County Commissioner.

Two vertically-barred windows behind Jon's desk gave her pause . . . *Security? – Keep riff-raff out – or Dad in?*

Leia plopped down and rocked back in Jon's leather chair. She briefly checked out an antiquated picture of herself and Rebecca before placing it back on the desk. A shove off, and she spun like a big kid, rotating in Dad's high-back. Round and round she goes, where she . . . a few revolutions and she dragged feet, stopping front center.

She slid Jon's top desk drawer open for a peek. Pens and pencils lay in a narrow front tray; sharpener and keys to the left, paperclips to the right. Drawn to the keys, she grabbed them and looked around the office. File cabinets? The two keys, (identical on a small metal ring) didn't fit, but she found the cabinets unlocked. Boring.

She returned to the desk. The bottom left drawer held a lock. The key slid in butter-smooth and turned with a click. *And what do we have here?* A heavy something, wrapped in soft leather and with a leather tie strap. She lifted it from hiding. *Handgun.*

Shells dribbled onto her lap, interrupting the unveiling. She recognized Dad's drafting-class blocked letters neatly printed on each. The first read "Bryce" on the casing, with a sad face drawn on the lead head. The second, Mark, with a wee bolt of lightning that ended at the slug's tip.

With renewed care, Leia continued to unwrap the pistol and recognized the .357 handed down from Rebecca's father. She placed Grandpa's weighty revolver on the desk, then turned her attention back to the handful of shells cupped in the leather wrap. Artisan bullets brought a sick feeling, a roiling variant of the discomfort she felt when she'd found Jon staring at the smokehouse. The phrase *Goin' Postal* came to mind. She lined bullets up on the desk, and read, Lynn, Kerry, RIP, Gene, Henry, *Adios*, and Mick. The revolver's release was easy enough to operate. Leia pulled it, dropping the cylinder open. Empty, but one chamber, and pulling the single shell, she read aloud, "Mr. R."

Movement in the outer offices jolted her.

And her lips clamped. *Teri, ready? – Not possible.* Fear and guilt rushed in. *Careful klutz.* In her lap, she folded the pistol into the leather, tied it, and gently returned it to the drawer. Keys went back, as well. The shells she slid into the front pockets of her fancy jeans, her cutest jeans, the ones with the sparkly, 'look at this', stars on the back pockets.

She took a moment to adjust her face; clean the slate.

Not Teri's voice, but low and serious tones emanated from the outer office. She held back, then moved silently to the door, and waited to emerge. Leia listened. A low conversation came clear.

"What's the schedule?"

"I've got the driver lined up for Tuesday and Thursday. Did you get the new tires on?

"No, they aren't in yet, and we might have to skip a week. Needs to go up to Fremont for a clutch, too. It's slipping pretty bad. Works okay empty, but under load, you can really tell."

"Skip a week, you're nutso! With this increase in production? It's time to milk the cow. Two loads a week and they won't miss a drop. Momma needs a new pair'a shoes."

Ductile Henry looked to her for reassurance. "Where will we sell all that?"

"Already talked to the greedy bastards. They'll take all we can haul. And, they wanna know if we can tap into the bio-diesel, as well. So, wipe that skeptical look off your face and get with the program."

"You're the soup."

"Yeah, don't forget it, and keep your beak zipped, Dodo."

Leia recognized Henry's voice from the recent encounter with his figs. Not acquainted with many *Core* employees, she guessed the lady was Bernice, returning from the lunchroom. And who else could sound that authoritarian? Teri had recounted stories about the big gal on campus.

Oh-oh, wish I hadn't heard this shit. Wonder if Dad has a clue? Hope these bullets aren't the answer. And then, the realization that Teri would be returning, asking where she was. She needed out, a furtive exit to the lady's room.

Through the hinge of Dad's door, she peeked. The odd couple huddled in Bernice's cubicle. Shades of Leia's handiwork remained. Black had mellowed to a yellow and green aurora borealis below Henry's eyes.

Certainly, they'd see her leaving, but the cubicles were close, and the walls – tall enough – if she got small enough.

On hands and knees, she started a baby crawl, hugging fabric-covered panels, inching toward Teri and the hall bathrooms.

At the end of the row, she pivoted and held exit in sight. An easy twenty-five-foot crawl, but nothing could ever be easy for a Rawling, could it? The second of three cubicle openings gave Henry a direct line of sight. Leia, suspecting the possibility, went lower still and felt the bullets in her pockets as she pressed into an army crawl.

She tried to slither past.

Henry saw the little snake and barked, "Who dat!"

Made, she stood and dashed for the exit.

"Rawling's daughter!"

"Ya think? Get that little bitch!" Bernice screamed.

Teri, adding a finishing touch of eyeliner, thought she heard commotion. She shrugged, *now, who's Bernice berating?*

In the hall, Leia turned toward the front doors. Huge Henry emerged from the other office exit. She abruptly braked, breathed a yelp, and turned. A swiping grab needed dodging, and as she flew past, Bernice's long painted fingernails on short, chubby fingers scratched down her back. Few lights were on, and Leia raced ahead of the din in the dim. She hooked left at the first opportunity.

For a big girl, Bernice wasn't slow, but dreamy chance catching swift, young Leia.

"Go!" Bernice pointed. "Get her."

"Hmhm hahaha," Henry agreed as they crossed in the hallway.

"I'll go to the lot, find her car. She's not going anywhere."

With sporadic cognitive skills, Henry's bulb didn't flicker; zero Lemonade information forwarded.

Leia sprinted the hall west, across the plant, and to the adjacent passage. Vats to the right might prove useful to hide behind, but a short distance left, an "EX_T." The partially lit overhead light beckoned a welcome escape.

With a decent lead, Leia hit the outdoors. Ahead, two monstrous corn piles stretched across the lot. Covered in white plastic, they looked like a bust wearing a spatial bikini top. She ran between them, down the cleavage, and looked back for the Hulk. The door opened and light behind, cast Henry in a sharp, black silhouette. Leia veered left behind a pile. She heard soles clickity-clacking across the lot and peered over the retaining wall. The big gal, huffing and closing in.

Leia scurried along the arc, slipping, faltering in corn overspill. Her hand kept to the taut white wrap as she hugged the barricade. The corn pile blocked floodlights mounted on the plant wall. It was darker here, with pale parking lot light reaching as she circled. The overspill quieted her progress and she stayed low. A few yards and a stop, a few yards and a listen. Another pause, her chest burned from the sprint and she felt her body heat rising. Angry with herself for not being able to suppress it, Leia remembered a bad joke from high school. *After gym class, what do you call cute sweat pants? Pretty sweaty pants.*

Bernice glimpsed Leia's hair as Henry emerged from the door. She turned, followed, and pointed for Henry to run the pile in the opposite direction. Henry grabbed a heavy sweep broom and, like a twig, snapped the handle over his knee. He moved around the white hill, opposite Leia. He walked, smacking the stick atop the retaining wall. Sound echoed off the plant.

Leia listened and looked for another place to run or hide. Options nil, Bernice, or whoever, behind her, and Henry closing in. Fifty yards of open lot to the guard shack looked utterly daunting. (An empty guard shack at that – cost-cutting at its finest.) Twice the distance, and more dodging, if she wanted to get back into the plant. Decision time . . .

Leia hoisted herself onto the barrier wall. She climbed the pile a good distance and wriggled under a separation in the translucent white wrap. Squishing herself into the corn, she hoped to not show like a zit.

The cracking of Henry's broom handle intensified as he closed the radius, then went silent.

The pursuers' encirclement culminated directly below Leia and trying not to move a muscle, she went to long slow breaths.

"Where did she go? Weren't you right behind her?" Henry said.

"I was right behind her, she got by you."

"Bullshit!" Henry slammed his stick atop the barrier, and growled, "She didn't get by me!"

The sharp crack sent a lively gang of rats up the pile. Most passed by, others scurried over Leia. As they traversed, she watched their shadows on the white translucent tarp and felt them patter over her body. *Hold it together.* She held her breath – until – the runt of the pack scratched its way across her face. Beyond Leia's control, a squeal leaked out.

Up the pile they looked and discovered the improbable lump. Like children being handed candy, they turned and smiled at one another.

Jon picked the knife off the counter, lowered it into the water, and washed it . . . and washed it, and washed it a bit more. Rebecca felt an uneasy pang twist her guts. She stood, impatiently watching him scrub, scouring like he had picked it out of the gutter, and she thought, how dirty could it be? She'd only used it to cut up . . . onions.

The stalling ended; he looked up from the chore. Otherjon nodded, then tilted his head toward Rebecca. From the water, Jon lifted the blade and looked pastorally at his reflection. A long moment passed. Water dripped from Jon's hand, dripped from 66. Like a Gamma Ray, a flash of terror passed through Rebecca.

With concerted effort, Jon lowered the blade, placing it under soapy water and to his forearm. A quick slice across flesh and to the sink's bottom Onion Slayer flit. '*I thought you were going to help me with that.*'

'*I was trying.*'

'*I love my wife.*'

'*Sure, sure ya do,*' Otherjon consoled. '*But a memory can be as sweet as sweet can be.*' Mr. R lifted Onion Slayer, proffering it for another go.

Jon reached from the suds and pulled the cord, dropping the shade. Guillotine-like, it fell. *Shu-Pop* – on the sill. Rebecca jumped.

She looked down. Jon held his arm. Red drips tainted the water.

"Oh my, what've you done now, dear?"

"We slipped."

"Well, *we* will have to bandage that up." She flipped the faucet to cold. "Run it under here. I'll go find something to wrap it."

Rebecca distanced herself from uneasy intuitions.

"Now I get even." Henry climbed.

Bernice smiled and stood guard, surveying for unwelcome guests.

Leia listened as Henry's boots scrunched up the pile. His massive shadow blocked light, pitching her dim hiding place to blackness. Her heart stopped – her stomach knotted.

He kneeled, reached into the separation, grabbed Leia by the arm, and wrenched her out. Corn fell from her long hair as she franticly slapped at the Hulk. With little effort, he tamped her flailing arms, lifted the buck-twenty Leia, and carried her down the pile to the plump hand-wringing grinner.

"Hand'er down to me . . . Come here Missy, you nosey little girl. Now what are we going to do, with *YOU!?*"

Good question, very good. Bernice didn't know, and Henry, clueless, hadn't had it cross his diminutive mind. What to do with a little eaves-dropper, the little girly-girl that heard our nasty scamity-scam? How do you get rid of her? Can't just lock her away. Both were brazen enough to snap her neck, (Bernice out of intelligence. Henry out of ignorance.), but, maybe not if the other knew.

Bernice's mind, like a world-class chess player, filed through scenarios and settled on the tried and true car-in-the-river accident. All essential elements were in the immediate vicinity. A little recipe to serve up a tear-jerking, head-shaking, poor-baby tragedy. It read right out of the villain cookbook. Take one sweet girl, place in car, add water. Unfortunately for Bernice, this bake-off required Henry's assistance.

"Hold her."

Leia twisted in Henry's vice-grip as Bernice pillaged her jeans for keys. Leia struggled and Bernice answered with laughter. Shells fell to the corn as she pulled keys from Leia's fancy pants.

Until now, Leia hadn't perceived the danger as grave but it was sinking in and she yelled, "Help. Help mu . . ."

Bernice delivered an awkward left punch to the gut.

Leia gasped. She sucked it up and spit in Bernice's face. Her rear head-butt thumped off Henry's barrel chest.

Bernice rotated at the waist, arcing another blow; the volatile slap of accelerating mass spun Leia's head a violent twist. She dropped into la-la land, going limp in Henry's grasp. Bernice, surprised by her KO ability, said, "Nighty night, little princess."

Teri, waiting in her cubicle, wondered where her wing girl had up and disappeared to. Maybe Leia hadn't eaten? She made her way to the cafeteria to see if she might be grabbing a bite with Ms. Piggy. (Sport eater, Bernice was into . . . baking, boiling, frying, roasting, steaming, munching, snacking, bingeing, etc. She loved restaurants, her overeating meccas. Designs to eat competitively struck her as mmm-mmm-good and her palette preferences included two food groups – hot and cold.)

Bernice wiped spittle from her face. "Stay here, I'm gonna grab her car." She pulled a two-scarf belt from her waist and handed it over. "Gag her, in case My Pretty comes to."

Bernice slid Lemonade's seat back, squeezed her integument behind the wheel, and turned the key. The Futura spun but didn't fire. She aggressively pumped the gas pedal and tried again. The rust-bucket hit on various cylinders, coughed to life, and settled into a rough idle. To cool down from her exertions, she cracked the window. The incoming cold front puffed her hair and cooled sweat beadlets riding her upper lip.

Bernice rounded the pile and found Henry with his hand down Leia's shirt. She almost honked at the wolf, not so much that she was disgusted, but it didn't fit the plan. "Stop that!" She pulled close before lurching out. "You shit, this has to look like an accident, all buttons and straps in place."

Henry retracted, and not privy the plan, suggested, "I'll take her and lock her in my cellar."

Bernice thought, *he's dumb – and revolting – I'd watch*. "NO! She's going for a swim. Put her in the trunk. Wait, just put her in back. I don't dare shut this thing off."

Henry cradled Leia and Bernice helped with the door. "Tie her. Use the seat belt."

Henry's strapping results looked non-binding, but Leia was out cold.

Bernice dropped Henry off at his Suburban. "Follow me." She checked Leia in the rearview mirror and smirked. As they passed the empty guard shack with its busted window, she felt another wave of warm fuzzies. She'd presented the 'one less mouth to feed' to the owners. Idea, subsequently forced upon Jon. Pleased with herself, she was.

Teri walked past the production floor. Late shift was wrapping things up. An empty lunchroom left her miffed. *Where the hell did she go, now? – Did we have our wires crossed? – Did she head to Goldie's on her own? – Was I supposed to catch up? – Makes no sense . . . we go home right past the plant.*

A few short miles and the Suburban followed Leia's Ford over the bridge crossing the Platte. Some more and they came to the Missouri, the big river, flowing under bridge 31. At the *Boat Launch* sign, they pulled off and followed the gravel down to the fast-flowing Misery.

Leia twitched but remained unconscious. Bernice aimed the Blue Oval at the river, stopped a distance up the cement boat ramp, and beckoned Henry. She pried herself from the front seat, left it running in park, and asked her dull accomplice, "Got it, yet?"

"I get it . . . but what a waste."

"Calm down, Arrow Flynn, there's more snatch to catch. Your little guppy needs water. Now, help me get her behind the wheel."

Henry and Bernice moved Leia to the driver's seat and strapped the young Rawling in.

"Nice and tight. We don't want her slipping out, do we?" Bernice simpered.

Bernice pulled it in gear and Henry kicked the door shut. The incline took care of the rest.

Leia, torso strapped, head slumped and hair hanging, looked strangely ashamed as the rust-bucket headed down the ramp. Lemonade's porous Detroit body, passing through the Suburban's lights, looked like a confirmed sinker.

The Ford rolled fast, picking up momentum . . . and in for a dip, a tea party plunge. Bernice and Henry stood in the Suburban's lights, casting long, caricature shadows down the ramp and out onto the river. On the disturbed water, their shadows rippled evil. The car buoyed and briefly looked buoyant. The gruesome twosome watched Leia lift her head, and the car slipped under. Their eyes grew wide, and the shadowy pair looked at one another – *holy-crap*. They held back a few seconds, then burst into shallow inhale-exhales, 'oh ho oh ho' pie-hole laughing fits. Fine camaraderie.

Well past eight, late-shift stragglers were leaving Core. Teri shuffled out into the darkness with them, hoping to find Leia waiting in the lot. No Leia, no car, and Teri figured she'd bugged out. Thoughts churned, *there's plenty of fish in the sea, but Tom's mine – well he's going to be. She best not be flirting around.* Teri knew this was stinkin-thinkin. They were solid and had never pulled shit like that on one another, never, not even once. *Yet.*

Not knowing what to think or feel, she headed for Goldie's.

Clive lay in his camper. His book had fallen shut and he dreamt he was a knight, alone at an altar empty, his brethren laughing. Disappeared, his maiden betrothed.

For two hours, they drove in silence. At Mesquite, Harrison gassed up the van, Pearson changed plates. The Nevada tin went in the garbage.

A prevalent thought consumed Pearson, *Where will I work next?* He hoped Harrison might man-up and take the brunt of O'Leary's derision.

A couple of miles into Utah, he asked, "So, wha-ta-ya wanna tell the old man?"

"Nothing. But I suppose that won't do now, will it?"

"Something simple, that's what we gotta come up with."

"Short and sweet. Higgus . . .hm . . ."

"Was grabbed by . . ."

"Grabbed by . . . the . . ."

"No, no, no, Higgus flew to . . ."

"No, the van couldn't keep up to . . .

"The Bug?" said Pearson.

Sixty miles they drove mute.

Henry and Bernice waved good-bye, good-riddance, to little Leia and her little blue Ford. Back to Core in the SUV, and Henry clocked out. Office help didn't punch cards; Bernice gathered her purse and keys. And, a night, they called it.

Lemonade's carburetor sucked in a big gulp of Misery and locked up, running was never its forte, anyway. The confirmed-sinker dove, high beams leading the Futura to its soggy future.

Leia woke disorientated, eyelids fluttering in a bobbing head. One long blink, slow and deliberate. *Focus – Fuzzy – Sleep*. Again, she closed an eye, then the other. This time, pain brought her back. It felt like a swinging lead brick, hanging on a pole, sticking out of her forehead; squinting, she stabilized it, *Movie? Dream? Focus.* Reality set in. She slammed the brake, the gas, the brake again, *Where the?* A wave of desperation, and frantically she pumped the pedals, feet splashing pooling water. The cool liquid filled her shoes, procuring full revival, *No dream! – Water! – River! – Shit! – River Water!*

"No, No, No, No . . . Nooo – SHIT!" She shook and clawed the seat belt. It unbuckled and the car sank deep in Misery. Four fathoms down, Lemonade's nose bottomed with an aquatic *Thump*. Leia, loose the belt, crashed the steering wheel, smashing her breasts. "Ah-ouww," she whimpered.

They had reached the trough and the fast black water. Lighter in back, the current swung the vehicle into reverse, moving Leia downstream. Lemonade's front dragged bottom like a defective anchor, coursing bottom muck. The back skipped, buoyed by the slowly-leaking cab, four evenly inflated tires, and a big bubble under the trunk lid. Thanks to the seals, Lemonade held her breath – the little, blue sub that could.

A grim view, but headlights provided orientation and Leia acquired bearings. That is to say, she knew up from down, right from left, and hope from hopeless. *The river – cold – not frigid . . . it's not winter.* And in reflexive composure, she calmed.

Freed from the seatbelt, she climbed into the back, the high ground, and for now, dry ground. It'll work out. How could it not? *I swim – just going for a ride – open the door – float up.* Naïve. An understatement. Leia pulled the handle to exit – the door didn't budge.

Not thinking math, but her equation went something like this . . . One hundred twenty pound Leia, bumping shoulder against door – is less than – one hundred sixty square inches of door surface twenty-four feet deep in river. That's .432 lbs. of fresh-water pressure, times 24 feet deep, and multiply by the 160 inches of door surface area, giving her a staggering total . . . 1,659 pounds of Misery . . . pushing back.

Lemonade hit a rocky patch and lurched against a boulder. Jolted, and from the seat, Leia trampolined. *Crack* – skull on metal window frame and she fell back. Dazed and confused, Leia sat up, staring out of her head.

Small bubbles streamed from four door jambs and the headlights illuminated a murky behind. Zombie Leia swayed, reverse cruising the Misery's deep in her little, blue submarine. The lump on her head swelled, a trickle of blood ran down her forehead, into her eye, down her cheek, and from her chin, it dripped.

Nurse Rebecca sat Jon in his easy chair. "I think we should get that stitched up."

"No, no, you did a dandy job. It'll be fine."

"I don't know, we'll take a look at it in the morning. I'm going to make tea. Want the TV on?"

Lemonade filled incrementally as current pushed it a mile downstream to a bend in the river. The shallow turn grew wide and moon-lit rapids glittered on the outer shelf. Leia sat in a less buoyant sub, water swirling in her lap. A skip, a bounce, to the shallows, and the mobile practiced bobbers. A coffin deep, and Lemonade, in domineering current, ran the rapids. She bounced, spun, and Leia wavered; both weebles wobbled. Boulders bashed gaps in sheet metal. Lemonade gulped water.

Leia's bucket of wet rust mashed a big one, jolted, hoisting. Solid tight, it lodged between two mega rocks; a river icon, known to local fisherfolk as Big Baby Jesus and The Little Devil. Upright, listing, the car's top rested clear. Moonlight danced off the wet roof. Leia the Zombie, throat deep in chilly water, blankly stared. Empty Coke cans, a sandwich bag, gum wrappers, and the broken heel, floated around her. Lemonade's headlights flickered their last and went black.

Chapter 25
Search

Teri parked in Goldie's gravel lot. No Lemonade in sight ratcheted her concern and she went in to ask around.

"Hi Lilla, seen Leia?"

"No, but Tow Truck's here." Hands full, mixing drinks, she mischievously smiled and nodded at bathrooms in back.

"Tow Truck?"

"Tom."

Teri didn't know her new friend, Tom, as "Tow Truck", then making the connection, laughed. Tom, Jake's son, after moving home from North Platte, occasionally helped at the garage. More often, aging Jake tethered him via phone, to the lucrative recovery rig. Day or night, town or country, but usually Highway 92, and he'd hook a drunk, or college student, or that combination. A ditch rescue, then he'd send them back out on bald tires to try again – if they hadn't wrecked.

Teri looked around to see who else she knew; the click at the near table – a sure avoidance, girls she detested almost as much as they hated her.

"Thirsty Thursday, two for ones on tap, low balls, half off. What can I get ya?" Lilla said.

"Oh, sorry, nothing right now, I'm worried about Leia, and she *hasn't* been in?"

"Nope."

"Shoot."

Tom exited the bathroom. Teri, waiting, stood near the end of the bar, resting back, heel up, totally showing off. Worried for sure, but outfit, new and blue, and it couldn't hurt a thing to impress. "Hi."

"Hi, I thought you girls might stop in tonight."

"Have you seen Leia? Somehow, I lost her."

"Not yet. I've been saving up to buy you a drink, may I?"

"Not right now. I need to find her, she kind of went Gondi on me. Wanna help me look?"

"Sure." Tom, playing it cool, had resisted calling Teri another week. Now, he found himself happy to get into her mystery. He downed the remainder of his adult beverage, and not remiss, the big spender pushed both quarters back to Lilla.

"We can take my car," Teri said.

"I should grab my jacket."

In the lot, they walked to Tom's pickup. Teri thought of the petting that had taken place in it on a prior outing and felt a rising inner warmth. She would not let it show.

At her car, she handed him keys. "Would you drive?"

And getting in, she patted his hand, already on her shifter. "So – Tow Truck – Tom."

"Please, just Tom, okay? I get enough of that bull already." Tom started the Camaro and adjusted the seat. "Where do ya wanna look?"

"Well, she doesn't really go anywhere other than my place, and her folks, or maybe she just went home. Nothing seems right, though, we were at the plant and she would have let me know. I probably should have called her apartment from the bar. Let's go to town, see if she's home. Maybe she just didn't feel good."

"Back to town, it is. Maybe she broke down or got a flat or something."

"Yeah, that's more than possible, she drives junk and won't give it up. It's in your dad's garage as much as on the road."

She lit a cigarette. Another worry took hold. "There's something else. We had a run-in with this guy I work with. Last Friday, at the theater . . ."

At Leia's apartments, they checked the lot, the street, and traveled once around the block. No Lemonade and Teri said, "We should go in, make sure."

In the house converted to apartments, they climbed the stairs and knocked on #3.

"There should be a key up there." She pointed for Tom to check above the doorsill.

It was, and they entered the vacant apartment.

Teri looked in the bedroom. "Dang it, gittin a bad vibe here."

"I think it's time we call someone, don't you?"

"I'll call her folks."

Rebecca answered. Teri asked about her missing wing girl and Rebecca heard the underlying panic.

Tom and Teri drove around late into the night looking for Leia. Jon persuaded leery O'Leary that this wasn't young people shenanigans. An unofficial, low priority – 'keep an eye out for' – police search was underway.

Harrison and Pearson took turns at the wheel through the night. Like a brooding couple after a bad weekend at the in-laws, they said little.

Morning sun dried the car's roof and also attracted twins with fishing poles to the shoreline. Jay-Jay, first to spot her, instructed his sister, "Go tell Mom there's a lady in the Big Muddy."

The rescue unit had a time of it in the rapids. Near the car, the saviors called out to unresponsive Leia: at the window they watched minuscule ripples cast off her trembling body.

Twenty minutes later, the ambulance driver turned the key, put the hammer down, and hit the siren. Two kneeling responders swayed in back, performing a dichotomy; one held an ice pack on Leia's head, the other snugged a blanket over her shaking frame. The team leader opened her eye and used a penlight on the zombie. It dilated. She jerked. A semi-conscious maundering started, continued a few minutes, then the zombie stilled. The ice pack on her fractured skull cooled the swollen brain and her body temperature rose.

"How's she doin?" the driver called back.

"Comatose."

Jake backed the tow truck to the river's edge.

"That's good," yelled a man in yellow, fire-department pants.

Three men and their rescue vehicle remained on-scene to make sure Jake made it out alive.

Jake released the right winch, the longer of the truck's twin lines. Cable rolled off the drum and through the boom-pulley until the hook touched ground.

"Think you could help me drag out a couple'a extra chains?" he asked one of the wet rescue crew bucks. "I don't think my eighty-foot cable'll reach."

The strapping young man waded through the rapids for a third time. This trip, fifteen feet of chain draped each shoulder. He didn't offer to help when Jake dipped under rushing water, searching for a solid place to hook.

Ten in the morning, Rawling's got the call.

"We found her," O'Leary said. He tried to ease into it, attempting to explain the inexplicable.

He wanted to ask: might she have had suicidal thoughts, or depression, or ever eluded to hurting herself? Now wasn't the time.

Leia lay in a bed on the third floor.

A young Doc Brochette met Jon and Rebecca in the hall. He looked thirty-fiveish and trim in every respect. "She's stable."

Rebecca sighed in relief. Jon's concerns, less assuaged, recognized a deflecting poker-face and braced for explication.

"Can we see her?" they asked, in unison.

"In a bit; nurses are setting up the room. Please, come, let's go down to the conference room. I'll bring you up to speed." He ushered them down the hall and in.

Jon and Rebecca looked to one another with sad and sullen faces. Rebecca gave Jon's hand a languishing squeeze.

"Have a seat, folks," and he launched straight to it, "Your daughter has two compression fractures in her neck and suffered quite a blow to the head. Hypothermia, also, which slowed everything down. A good thing, considering. The contusion required staples, up here." He pointed at a line above his left temple, then continued, "There's pressure, swelling on the brain, and right now we have to assume . . . Leia has a brain injury, (He left out, 'traumatic'.). And she's in a coma."

"Huh," Rebecca inhaled.

"There is no easy way to say this, so I'm just going to say it. Damage could be permanent."

"No," Rebecca demanded.

"Her brain *is* functioning. Exposed to light, her pupils dilate."

Knee pumping, Jon nervously tapped his heel, put his bandaged arm around Rebecca, and asked the Doc, "What now?"

"Know she's in good hands. Unfortunately, now we wait, we watch, pray. I'm keeping her under, monitoring vitals. After a few days, I'll take her off meds and we'll see if she comes to by herself. It isn't up to us; now it's up to Leia. Listen, I do have hope for an appreciable recovery but must warn you to prepare. The degree of recovery is very unpredictable in these circumstances."

Rebecca's face washed ashen. She whimpered and dropped her head onto Jon's shoulder. "This can't be happening."

Jon held her and caressed her hand.

Doc Brochette reached across the table, placed his hand over Jon and Rebecca's, and said, "She's young. She's strong. Healthy young brains have a way of bouncing back from trauma. I want you to stay optimistic. I am."

The winch pulled snug and groaned. Jake let off and repositioned himself to the second set of controls on the truck bed's opposite side. In case something snaps. From his safer vantage point, he pulled the lever. The winch groaned and turned another revolution. The truck's front wheels lifted and they heard scrunching metal from the Ford in the river. "Look out!" yelled the dripping young buck. The rescue workers retreated, shying away in baby steps.

Hooked to its trophy, the taut line vibrated ominous tones.

Jake stopped. Looked. He spit. "Don't worry, boys. I've done this before." The truck postured like a Big Horn Sheep, front suspended, tires dangling at camber, and looking for something to ram.

He hit it again. "Come on, you *Mother.*" The truck reared another foot, fell, and bounced. In the river, Big Baby Jesus tipped as Lemonade scraped free. The babe rolled and swirled under the water. The Little Devil stood alone.

Jake dragged the battered Ford to town.

Untinged by her deed, Bernice practiced sympathies. She felt well, calm, with composure only unsettled by an obvious reality: across the plant, her accomplice had moon dust for brains.

Teri awoke lying on Leia's couch, her head snuggled on Tom's chest. He'd wrapped her in a throw.

She rose and immediately made calls. The Rawlings didn't answer. Ellen, at the Sheriff's office, gave them the low-down. Teri made another call – to *Core.*

"Bernice?"

"Teri? It's ten-thirty, where are you?"

"Have you talked to Mr. Rawling?"

"No, he isn't in, yet. Is something *wrong?"*

"My friend, Leia, Jon's daughter, she's been in an accident. I can't come in today."

"Oh *No!*. . . Is she *okay?"*

"She's in the hospital, maybe in a coma. I'm going to go see her right now. She was at the plant last night before I got off. We were going to go out. You didn't happen to talk to her, see her?"

"No . . . suppose I was making my rounds. If you see Mr. Rawling, tell him I have everything under control and he doesn't need to come in. Tell him how truly sorry I am to hear it." *Truly sorry.*

"What do you mean, not allowed? She's my fuckin sister!" Teri cried. Tom had accompanied her to the third-floor nurses' station.

The maltreated nurse held her ground. "I'm sorry, you're not really."

"Same as, we practically grew up together. I *need* to be there for her."

"She's stable," the nurse said.

"So, she's out of the woods?"

". . . I believe I've said enough."

"Tom?"

"Is there any way you can make an exception? Just her, not me."

"Absolutely not. Her parents are with her now and the doctor is only letting em in a short while." Addressing Teri, the nurse softened. "Calm down, and I'll tell you what I'll do. Give me your name and number, I'll ask the doctor for you. If he and the parents okay it, maybe you could come back this evening during normal visitation."

"You're back," Ellen said. "I didn't even know you guys were on the way."

Harrison smiled, removed his shades, and went straight for the Sheriff's office. His shirt lounged open at the top.

"Yeah . . . we're back," Pearson said, shaking his head, following his senior in.

Ellen caught a whiff; two oily-haired plumbers, ripe from Pudge's van.

"You're back," said O'Leary. "Got Higgus?"

"You wouldn't believe it; the funniest thing happened." A lengthy shrift followed. O'Leary wasn't laughing at Harrison's droll story.

"Uh-hu . . . I see." His face reddened. "Uh-hu . . . Interesting." His neck reddened. "Oh . . . Okay, mm-hmm." O'Leary blazed, head about to combust.

Recount endured, O'Leary's countenance returned. Color faded and enthusiasm effervesced as he foretold future paychecks eternally levied. Department reimbursement garnished a' la carte.

"I can live with that, Sir." Harrison hadn't called him Sir since the hiring interview. He was pleased with himself on two accounts. First, he didn't have to live with a lie. Second, O'Leary had taught him how to spot a lie, and even though he figured he could schmooze one off, Pearson would have melted, plunging like Icarus. They'd be poorer a while; not jobless, on guard, or sleepless. He felt, strangely – the hero.

Friday noon, Teri returned Tom to his truck. He gave her a caring kiss.

"Anything I can do?"

"Not much to do right now, I don't think."

"She'll pull through."

"She's like, my only friend, if she doesn't – I'll die."

He hugged her and placed another kiss on her forehead. "I'll call," he said.

She believed him.

O'Leary said, "Ya both reek, go home, clean up, then get back down here. Last night, we had another Rawling incident. Jon's daughter's in the hospital. I want you to look into it."

"What happened?"

"Found her in her car, in the river."

"Went off the road?"

"Don't know, she's unconscious. Could be an accident – drunk driving maybe. Could be suicide, foul play? Get me a timeline."

Harrison, relieved for new work, could push Higgus out of his mind for now.

Chapter 26
Nail Biter

Bad luck? Bernice believed Leia's fate absolute. No way could she have survived and it seemed so improbable, she pondered a possibility. Was the phone call a trick? Her mind raced. She waited nervously, hoping someone would proffer an alternate truth.

Innate composure waning, she watched the parking lot. A clip looped in her mind . . . Deputies cuffing her, parading her down the hall and out to the lot, where blubbering Henry would be signing a confession on the squad car hood.

At three, she made rounds to snoop and visit. She met Henry in Malcolm's squeaky-clean west hall.

"Have you heard any rumors?" she asked.

"Rumors?"

"Anyone talking . . . about Rawling's daughter, yet?"

"No, not yet, have you?"

"Teri called late this morning, said she's in the hospital."

"Teri's in the hospital?"

She cracked him.

"Listen, idiot. Teri said Leia's in the hospital, in a coma, maybe."

"No way."

"It might be some kinda trap."

"We watched it go under."

"Yeah? – Listen, if she did make it out alive and talked, we'd already be in jail. If she's dead, it's a trick to see who runs. If she – *is* – in a coma, we can't wait around to see if she comes out of it." Bernice went out on a limb, and asked, "Know what I mean?"

Henry slowly bobbed his head. He knew.

"They'll come asking questions, you can bet on it. Listen and listen good. You never saw her. You were in your little office working, right? I can be your alibi. Only if they ask, though. Don't just throw it out there. Hear?"

Henry nodded.

"Everything you wore last night, burn it, get rid of all of it." She pointed at his boots. Those too. Do you have others? Old ones would be good."

Henry nodded.

"Good, burn em. Don't buy any new ones for a couple of weeks, either. Everything we had on goes up in smoke.

"Have you heard how she's doin?" Jake asked.

"Stable. They're keeping her under," said Harrison.

"God, nice kid. Hope she'll be okay."

"Do you know her well?"

"A little. Customer, sweet girl."

"I was told they had her out before ya got there, but I'd like to look at the car."

"I left it on the back of the truck, for now. It's right around here." He led Harrison behind the garage. "Like to keep em out of sight or I got every teen and retiree in town pullin in ta gawk."

Jake leaned against the side of the winch-bed. Lemonade's front tires sat in the wheel lift with the car's front bumper four feet off the ground. The dripping Ford fed a mud puddle under it. Harrison walked slowly around the car, then back again, and said, "She didn't have a blowout."

"Nah, tires were all up."

Harrison kneeled near the mud and looked at the underside. "Don't see any tufts of sod. There's a bent tie-rod on this side."

Jake crouched, looked. "Eh, think my cable did that. I hooked just behind it, there."

Still kneeling, Harrison's inspecting eyes levitated to the driver's door. "Did you kick this shut?"

"Huh, No, looks like someone kicked it, though."

"I'll have to ask the rescue guys."

"Nah, wasn't them. See these scrapes, this dent, this whole area was up against a huge boulder, they didn't use *this* door to get her out."

"Don't touch, I'm gonna go grab my camera."

He took pictures and jotted down measurements, then looked at the car's contents, the garbage, and the steering column. "Keys are in the ignition. Still on . . ."

"Never touched em," Jake said before Harrison could ask.

Relegated to the waiting room, the Rawlings sat on a couch and talked little. Inconsolable Rebecca shook. Jon held her and blankly stared at a pair of cheap framed prints across the room.

Brochette's shift ended. Before leaving, he felt inclined to check his satellite patients. He entered the room and Jon helped Rebecca to her feet.

"Folks, her vitals are good . . ." he paused. Rebecca, with less color than her daughter, quaked as she stood. "Sit, please," he said.

The couple asked for details by saying nothing.

"You're welcome to stay all night, but I have to keep her under. For her own safety – till the swelling goes down, it might be a few days. You can go in and sit with her for a while, again, but please go home and rest after that. More comfortable than this couch. Oh, a friend, a Ms. Thompson has asked to see her. Is that alright with you?"

"That would be fine," Jon said. Rebecca nodded.

Brochette pulled a pocket notepad from his shirt and scribbled a prescription.

"To help you relax – sleep," he said, handing it to Rebecca. He eyed Jon. "If you feel a need, share at your discretion."

Teri was waiting near the nurses' station, they joined and entered together.

The phone rang a dozen times, echoing through Leia's empty apartment. Clive gave it up.

"You didn't expect her to be sitting home on a Friday night, did ya?" said the Ranger.

"Suppose not." Clive felt a jealous twinge. Why hadn't he asked for a Friday date? "I'll see her tomorrow."

"So you've said, a few times." The Ranger handed him a beer.

In *Core's* eight-o'clock exodus, Bernice walked out a few paces behind Henry, followed him to his Suburban, and climbed in the passenger side.

"What are we gonna do?" Henry asked.

"We're going to take care of business. You have an appointment for the truck tomorrow?"

"At eleven."

"Keep it. I'll go with, and later . . . we'll look in on little Ms. Muffet, bring her a treat."

"A trick or treat?" Henry smiled.

"I'm leaning, trick." Bernice's face contorted – a girl in the gallows improv.

The nurse changed the cold compress. Leia's eyelids fluttered and behind them, her eyes searched the black. It started in slow motion . . . floating in the night.

Below, a rodeo.

Tossed by rider-less bull, or bucked from bronco, clowns flew high.
High over fences, over gate. High, up a hundred feet to greet.
They came morbid, or surprised in night sky.
Silent, with a tear, with a wink, with fright,
reaching for help or with a vicious swipe.

One, with a high five, returning twice.
Then another, mouth open wide, breathed her in,
shook his head and growled delight.
Deposited in dim stables of long faces, some bridled, some not.
All wild, prancing, kicking, and snorting snot.
A Paint bucking she rode, and upon it twisted till falling in a splot.
Fans on weathered bleachers cheered
as she ran amongst her mind's four-legged lot.
More dodging, tripping, and slipping they watched.
A Gray kicked. It found a spot, and sprawling – a post she bought.

Spectators jeered.

Jason's Mrs. clapped and laughed and kissed stud in Stetson. She stood, "Whoot, Whoot." Pete's heifer rose next. To one another the ladies looked, and arms cranking, "Whoot! Whoot!"

Attendance waned while Leia lay in a grog.

"She needs staples," a Clown Doctor said. Hovering, face close, he reached up, arm stretching to moon, and adjusted the light.

Leia squinted. "Not in this unclean place, please."

"Unclean? You're unclean," said Clown, and picked up a piece of horse hockey. He rubbed it in the split and brought an industrial stapler to view. "This might pinch."

Crack! Crack! Crack! He planted staples over gash. Each echoed in her skull and sounded like Henry's smacking broom handle.

"Better," said Clown and helped her up. From behind his back, he produced an oversized vanity mirror, shaped in a fun-house wave. "See."

A child's line of staples zagged the cut. Some held stable straw tight, others, misshapen, crooked partially embedded. No blood ran from the wound. A coagulated placenta, bonded of manure and straw, pulsated.

Doctor Clown bent to kiss it, as did Rebecca bend, to kiss Leia in her room. They said, *"Goodnight, Sweetheart."*

A thirty-three-year-old Quonset on the abandoned Rothness homestead concealed the bulk truck. Henry removed a paddle-lock and slid the heavy twin doors outward on supported rails that extended clear the arching fascia. The Saturday morning sunlight poured in. On the gravel floor, the truck waited.

Past tattered corn cribs, an imploded barn, windowless chicken coop, and the windowless house, Henry drove. At the end of the driveway, he turned east onto the gravel. Bernice followed in his Suburban and in not many miles they were at the blacktop. They drove north on 77, then over the river to Fremont, where a new clutch waited on a mechanic's bench. Next to the bench, new tires sat in a stack.

Henry parked in the lot and went in to drop off keys. Bernice waited in the black Suburban.

Henry returned and Bernice slid to the passenger seat.

"When do we get it?"

"Said it'll be done Monday noon, but supposed to call before we come."

"I thought it was suppose'ta be done, today?"

"Said his guy's sick, gonna get greasy all by his lonesome."

They drove downtown Fremont.

"Tonight we'll visit Miss You-know-who. Drop me off up here." She pointed. Bernice shopped two stores on the same block. Henry listened to his radio.

Clive fidgeted fifteen minutes outside her apartment, then went in.

He knocked.

"Hello." And knocked again. "Hello?"

He waited, thinking, gauging the degree of loser he might be.

His accelerating imagination reckoned her on an extended Friday date; an overnight. Bare feet on another man's white kitchen tile. Another's morning caress. This man, this dashing man, handing her morning coffee. And she, mussed hair, legs bare, in white panties and wearing the man's open-hanging shirt, down, partially covering, she, on toes – kissing him.

"Hello – Leia," he called and pounded a short burst.

Dejected, he sat outside the apartment in his car. "Idiot!" He punched the roof and, leaving, coaxed a one-wheel-squeal from the Maverick's right rear.

The nurse waived rules and allowed Rawlings the day. Teri, also permitted, sat the afternoon. She recounted Thursday's mystery for the Rawlings, as she had that morning for the Detective. Harrison's questioning had garnered Leia's recent scrapes: Jason and Jason's bird-flipping wife, Bryce's brash antics, and Henry's re-arranged ball-bag. Harrison pressed Teri about Leia's mental well-being and Teri admitted her friend's sadness but left it at the breakup. She didn't mention losing a baby. The Rawlings received an abbreviated version of facts; Teri canned the run-ins and depression, only sharing those with Harrison.

Jon needed the restroom and left Rebecca and Teri with Leia. Malcolm pushed a laundry cart in the hall and nodded as they passed.

"Malcolm?" Jon said.

He stopped. "Mr. Rawling, how is she?"

"Same. You work at the hospital, too?"

"Not moonlighting, just weekends, Sir."

"Malcolm," Jon said, waving off the implication.

"I've been thinking of you guys – real sorry. I sat with her on my break, last night. Hope you don't mind, think I'm weird or something. We were friends in school." He held it a truth, anyway. Leia, but a sliver of the scholastic population never to disparage him.

"Of course not, thanks for your concern, Malcolm," he said, placing a hand on Malcolm's shoulder.

In the bathroom, Jon waited. Man in the mirror leaned forward. Their hands met flat on the glass and they stared.

"Somebody did it, from *Core*."

"Who would hurt Leia?"

"No, to hurt you."

"A stretch."

"Is it? Might even be little Limp Node out there."

"Slim chance, pun intended."

"Laugh it up, Joker. One week. One week – then – operation Clean Slate. You'll sweep'em up with the rest of the dirt."

"Lots to do."

"Managers manage."

"Don't know if we can make *this* right." He gestured toward Leia's room. "And I'm doin all the heavy lifting."

"That's because you keep me bottled up. Next time I hand you a knife, use it."

"Not a chance, you're fucked up."

"Come on, we don't need anybody. It's you and me, can't you see. Hmm, could be a song."

"You're a 'toon."

CHAPTER 27
Finish It

"Twenty minutes," Bernice said.

She climbed down next to the dumpster and Henry eased the Suburban away. Bernice strode through moonlight and shadow to the hospital back door. An empty corridor and, holding a sunny flower arrangement, she welcomed herself in.

Bernice knew a thing or two about insurance, and how fortunate insurance rep 'Brenda' had been Friday afternoon, milking Leia's details from hospital accounting-administration.

On third, she flung the vase, crashing it in the hall adjacent to the nurse's station. It lured the graveyard shift caregiver. For fun, Bernice picked up the nurse's hat as she passed the desk, fit it, and entered Leia's room.

Leia lay two covers deep, Rebecca's loving afghan on top. Bernice watched liquid drip from the I.V. into the tube, curl through it and disappear under the covers. A shielded fluorescent light shone dimly on the wall above her wrapped head. Amplified by a tube, her long, slow breaths harmonized with humming monitors.

Bernice reached into her blazer, took out three plastic hypodermic needles from a low inner pocket, and laid them on the girl. The trio, filled with Momma's insulin, rose and fell between wrinkles on the knit.

She lifted Leia's right arm from under the blanket and tapped her inner arm with two fingers. Attentive veins responded. Timed with a monitor beep, Bernice popped an orange cap off the first hypo. Leia's mouth twitched sad at the corners . . .

One vagrant rat ran over her pinned body. Henry held her shoulders. Bernice gripped her ankles. She screamed – Help!

A cement truck backed near, its drum turned, churning an organic mix. Bryce, in pajama bottoms, unfolded the delivery chute and swung it over her. The vagabond rodent on its haunches stood close and commanded Bryce, "Bring it!"

The tumbling sound rolled into the chute.

The needle pressed tender skin. Bernice adjusted the angle and pushed it in. She looked over her shoulder, and back again. For ten seconds she stifled an urge to hum – the plunger touched bottom.

The black surge rumbled. Blobs dripped, then black splashed from the chute. Henry and Bernice let go and scrambled clear as inverted spiders. The hot splash separated. Wooley balls un-balled, greasy hair stood on ratty backs. Beady eyes twinkled. Yet, more from the chute, uncoiling as they fell. The landed leapt from Leia's naked body, making way for the multitude.

All rats joined to ring around her – a circling black sea – and marched. On her tummy and between her breasts, only feces remained.

"Line Up!" said Master Rat.

The oily tide moved in unison, cocking cocky shoulders and shifting as they closed. Tight around her they stood, expelling warm breath. The damp rank engulfed her and her temp internal rose. Sweat beads formed on her entire body as a hot dew. Whiskered noses sniffed. Clear drops trailed down her sides and impure feces-steeped droplets ran, not clear, but tainted. They lapped and suckled her – no drop reached the ground.

Only gasps interrupted an erupting scream.

Over Leia's perspiring face, Bernice waved the second. "Ooh," she whispered, and softly said, "Here it comes, sweetie." The cap lingered in her bite. Needle Two went to the spot Needle One marked.

Dah-WonK! Malcolm clubbed her. The stainless bedpan dung a D. She fell forward on her game.

He shifted the laundry cart sideways and tight below the portly ass. Good leg back and gimpy blocking the cart, he reached across, gripped her blazer collar, and pulled. In she fell, bulk bending the top framework elliptical and sagging it on a side. One blue shoe flew as she toppled. He dodged it.

Malcolm removed the needle from Leia's appendage and gathered the two other paraphernalia. In the cart, they went. One tapered leg reached straight up; he folded it, her other, wayward, he coaxed in. The shoe went in next and he covered the freight.

One stood behind the desk holding the phone. The other, in front, pointed at the mess in the hall.

"Didn't you hear us paging?" said the nurse, and the nurse from second floor placed her hands on her hips and frowned.

"I'll be right back up," said Leia's angel. He wheeled dirty laundry into the elevator. The burdened cart jerked over the threshold. From under the sheets, Bernice's shoeless foot slipped. The door closed.

Malcolm rode the elevator feeling alive. *I'm a man*, and his body tingled in the D of Bernice's thwapping. But no doubt where the envelopes with crisp Jacksons nuzzling crisp Lincolns came from. And he decided to keep them coming, keep saving. Twelve thousand to fix his pre-existing condition. Then he would walk like a man, then he would ask Leia out; then he would tell her how he saved her.

Near the dumpster, the cart jittered, shook, and cocked, sending a black plastic wheel skipping across the drive. *A rat?* Henry thought, then he pulled past the dumpster.

Bernice tipped her three-wheel nest and landed rumpled in soiled bedding. A sphere of stars accented her staggering reorientation. They floated and popped around the black suburban, the dumpster, a hypo on the ground, and her blue shoe, peeking from sheets. The shoe, she picked up.

Henry ran the power window down. "What happened to you?"

Ringing eardrums distorted his voice. Bernice slurred, "Ta hell if I know." She touched her head. It hurt inside out. At the front of the truck, she leaned and checked fingers for blood in the headlight.

"How about the girl?" he asked, getting out.

"I don't know."

Henry helped with her shoe, then helped her up and in.

Sunday, Clive mapped the last Catholic oak. Dried Dodge tire tracks imprinted the trail. He stood looking south, contemplating moral boundaries, the pros and cons of trespassing, the constitutions of stalking.

He stowed it and asked himself, *time to move on?* Though, tarnished by jealous thoughts of Leia's alternate lover, her spell held.

"We'll make it through this. She'll get through this," Jon said.

Rebecca had to believe. Still miserable, and recovering from shock, she took solace in Jon's assurances – and Brochette's pills.

Her parents' voices echoed through Leia's subconscious.

"She'll get through this. She'll get through this. She'll get through this..."

"He doesn't have your good looks," said Jason's Mrs.

"But Leia's disposition," Jason said.

"Dead?" she asked. They laughed.

Jason removed the blue fetus from a bassinet beside Leia's bed. He laid it near her and, using his thumb, pressed its minute chest, massaging the peanut heart. It stirred. Jason continued to massage. Body becoming less blue, and its eyes opened. Pursed lips cracked and the fetus asked. "Why don't you love us?"

"Don't fret little feller, twasn't your fault. It's better this way."

Its lash-less eyes closed. Jason pumped faster.

Straps held Leia. One firmed a red ball in her mouth, others secured her head and body. She grunted unintelligible pleas beneath the sphere and strained to see.

Its eyes squinted open. In a wisped breath, the little one asked, "Happy now?"

"He is," pronounced haughty Mrs. Jason, embracing her husband from behind. The fetus's eyes closed. Cowgirl looked to Leia. "Steer clear, Bitch."

Leia strained.

Jason pumped the darkening fetus. It wrinkled gray, losing.

"Used up," Mrs. Jason said. "Let me." She took him from the bed and laid the withered handful on a stainless table.

Leia struggled.

Mrs. Jason removed a spur from her boot and spun it for Leia.

Leia twisted free from the gag and yelled, "Don't touch him!"

The tiny one on the cold steel looked to mommy and, with shriveled unborn fingers, clutched a jerky goodbye. The spur disemboweled him.

Sun setting, silhouetted they knelt at the dig. The shoebox of dry DNA, tied shut with old shoelaces, lay in the hole.

"Put me in with him," she told Clive.

"No. Live. I'm waiting."

"No one cares."

"I want you," he said, then helped her cover the box.

They stood at the grave. Clive's strength infused her. She did want to live.

"She has good color today," Teri said, smiling. She placed fresh flowers in the window and adjusted them to her liking. "I brought lunch." She had bolstered her mood for the Rawlings as well as for herself. She handed Jon a quilted bag and hugged Rebecca, then pulled a chair close to Leia's bed to sit a time and hold her hand . . .

Sitting and sitting was sitting. Teri asked, "Should we take lunch down to the cafeteria?"

After they ate, she went back up with them and squeezed Leia a Sunday goodbye.

Four in the afternoon, nurses came to clean Leia and sent the Rawlings home.

"Tomorrow's Monday," Rebecca said. "Are you goin to the plant?"

"I thought I should."

"Michael?" Rebecca asked.

Jon shrugged. "And you?"

"I want to sit with her."

"Of course."

By 8:15 Monday morning, the few who hadn't heard, knew. Jon met a barrage of shallow condolences – everyone pulling for her – regrets poorly articulated. Teri overheard much drivel but Leia's condition rang true in one commiseration – Bernice's. "Anything I can do to help, please ask." She reiterated how sorry they were; 'poor Leia, in the hospital'.

"How's she doing, Sir?"

The sound of her sincerity lowered his guard.

"She's still under. Looking better, though."

"Oh, wonderful."

The phone rang at ten, it was Lon. Teri directed the call. Bernice caught it and picked up to listen in.

"Tough times there for you and the missus, Jon. I'm really sorry to hear about it. The rest of the group conveys their sympathies, too. How is she?"

"The Doc's been keeping her under till some swelling goes down. She's looking better, though – we're hoping he lets her wake up soon. Then we'll see."

"Who's the doctor?"

"Brochette."

"He's good."

"That's what we heard."

"Michael's really taken back. I think he's got a sweet spot for your girl, he's offered to come in and cover for ya. A week or two – if it would help. Bernice could hold his hand until ya get back."

Sweet spot, alright – smack – in the kissa. "Ya, thanks, Lon. I guess we'll manage."

"All right. Did Bernice give you the outline for the shares program? We still want to present on Saturday."

"On my desk. I'll look at it this afternoon."

Bernice found Henry at his desk working on the load-out numbers.

"Get yer ass up. Time to go," she said.

"Truck's ready?"

"Yeah. And we need your Suburban, again. Meet me outside in ten."

Near Fremont, Bernice said, "When we get to town, we're going shopping before we pick up the truck."

"For what?"

"Decorations for the company party, Octoberfest."

Henry paid the mechanic in hundreds. Bernice kept her anonymity and waited in the Suburban.

"Take the truck straight to the plant, we need product."

"What about our driver?" Henry asked.

"You're the driver today, Henry, and your future depends on it. You fill, I'll watch the hall. This is all us, no Malcolm, no driver. It's just you and me this time." She looked out the window, a stiff wind was stripping leaves off trees. "Summer's over."

Bernice followed him in on the pocked north road, then parked in back next to Black Magic. She went in to do surveillance and Henry put on fifty gallons of Bio, as directed. Bernice followed him to the Rothness homestead, and thirty-five minutes later they were in the suburban, backing up to *Core Fuels'* front doors.

"Can we get some help, here? How about that cart, Gene?" Empty-handed, Bernice led Henry into the cafeteria. He carried two large pumpkins.

Her volunteers unloaded the Suburban; more pumpkins, straw bales (placing them on a cart), orange and brown streamers in clear plastic packages, other junk. Jon and staff watched the parade pass the offices. Henry trailed, carrying a well-constructed scarecrow. Bernice directed.

Jon and staff followed to the cafeteria. "Wow," Jon said.

"You said, do it up right. I stole Henry and his truck for a while. I knew you wouldn't mind."

"No, the consortium will be impressed."

He looked to Henry and Gene, and continued, "Could I see the foremen in my office at four? Bernice, tell Mark to be there."

At four, the foremen filed in. "Come on in, guys. Sit." Jon gently closed his office door and ushered them to three chairs on one side of an oak table. The men recognized the polished table and managerial seating from the conference room.

Gene, Henry, and Mark settled into plush leather. Four glass beakers sat at the center of the table – familiar production test equipment.

"I thought only board members sat in these babies," Mark said.

Jon gave him a passive smile, wheeled his high-back chair around from behind his desk, and positioned it across the table from the three. He leaned on the back of it and gave them a few seconds to get comfortable.

"Gentlemen, I'd like to propose a toast." Jon lifted a thick amber decanter off his desk. Its clear content neatly filled the pintsize beakers lined up on the table.

The men looked to one another. A most unusual meeting. For a second, Mark pondered, *Promotions?* Then a pall settled in.

Jon moved into his chair across from the three, picked up a beaker, and raised it in a favorable gesture. "Come, come." And nodding his head, directed them to join.

Apprehensively, Mark and Gene lifted their beakers. Henry, in the moment, joyfully seized his.

"Men, you've outdone yourselves. Production is *up*." And with the declaration, Jon put the beaker to his lips and sipped – the three across the table did the same.

They immediately recognized the brand of spirits served today. Once you've had Stillman, nothing compares and not exactly in a good way. Each, with their personalized twisted whisky-face, understood Jon likely had more to share.

"This plant's humming," Jon paused, "and there's something I think we can do to help promote continued success." He paused again. "We want to make sure everyone is recognized for their efforts at Saturday's meeting, and I do mean, everyone." He took another sip and indicated for the others to do the same. They followed suit.

Jon stood, strolled to the window, and took a swig. Otherjon mirrored him and raised his eyebrows.

With his back to them, Jon spoke, "You guys understand how important morale is. How important it is that every single person . . ." he turned and swept his hand in the general direction of the plant floor, ". . . be thanked properly? A celebration of accomplishment. A thank you from me, as well as the owners."

The men looked to one another, nodding.

"Now, I want to make myself perfectly clear, here. Some of the production," Jon took another sip and tipped his beaker at them, "at this particular plant, should be proscribed. That said, certain productions could continue. They could carry forward with no repercussions to those responsible for the high-octane embellishments discreetly bestowed upon us. I want to stress, that is if I see all in attendance for the meal, the presentation, and for the fun and games following. You do understand how important it is that we rightfully thank everyone for a job well done? For their sacrifices and ongoing support. And the owners have hinted at a nice surprise for everyone."

Mark cleared his throat. "I'll make sure all my people are there."

Henry, not comprehending exactly what was happening, went with it, sipped, and said, "Sack and Gilly's comin."

Gene fully understood. He knew Stillman had become a congruent part of operations at this juncture. "Everyone will be there Colonel, Cap . . . Captain." Gene, not much of a boozer, was feeling it.

"Good. Men, let's toast to the great time we're all going to have Saturday. Bottoms up, boys." Jon tipped his beaker, opened his gullet, and poured the gut-rot in; the pint emptied in seconds.

They guzzled. Gene, having trouble, lowered his half-empty beaker.

"Oop, oop, oop," Jon reached across the table and helped it back to his lips. "I said, bottoms up."

Gene gulped the piss down and the three were excused. They returned to the plant floor, dregs settling – bellies boiling.

Jon and Rebecca sat with Leia Monday evening.

"More flowers," Jon said.

"They came this morning, the card's on the table, from the owners. Lon, Larry, Sherbt, lots of em signed it."

Brochette entered. "Evening folks." He moved straight to Leia.

"Night shift, Doc?" Jon said.

"No, called in for an emergency. Thought I'd come up and see how it was going." He examined the monitors and listened to her heart. "I've taken her off the sedatives, it's up to her to wake up now."

"When do you think?" Rebecca asked.

"Tonight, tomorrow, a week? Really no way to know. A little hiccup yesterday, otherwise physiologically doing well."

Chapter 28

Henry's Turn

Two a.m., he backed the bulk truck from the alley and positioned it behind the hospital, near the back door. Airbrakes hissed and the shipment sloshed in the tank.

A wheel chalk from the truck's tool compartment worked well as a doorstop. Henry engaged the pump, pulled forty feet of hose to the corner of the building, and peered across the still lot, then doubled back. He went in and, at the end of the hall, opened the door to the stairwell.

Three long minutes, Henry watched bio-diesel cascade down the stairs as the truck dumped its fifty-gallon load. The basement puddle grew.

All set, and the fuel hose wrapped evenly across the truck's spool, gearbox whining the hose's retrieval. He went back in, walked the hall, and cracked open the stairwell door. Henry stared into the abyss. A farmer match flared. He flicked it like a cigarette.

Out of Henry's view, a blue flame spread across the basement's concrete floor. He clicked the hall light off and walked out. A glow flickered orange behind him.

Staff and patients heard a huff. Everyone conscious paused . . . then the alarm. Floor by floor, black smoke poured from elevator door seams. Floor by floor, sprinkler systems engaged.

"Run!" yelled the receptionist; no one was in the lobby. A feminine sprint through the indoor showers and she waited wet in the parking lot. Others from first floor soon followed. The night nurse on third stood at her desk in the rain. She moved through the squall to the stairwell door and peered through its narrow crosshatch window. Lights shrouded in black murk glimmered, went dark, and the crying started.

Down the hall, drops showered the comatose patient's face and soaked through her afghan. Monitors flashed, went dark, silent, and outside, sirens approached.

Leia opened her eyes.

An all-volunteer fire department battled the basement blaze as sprinklers squelched upper floor smoke. On third, wall-mounted emergency lights illuminated the all-white nurse huddled at her desk. She recused duties, shielded herself from the sprinklers with a clipboard, and bawled.

Leia's eyes reflexively blinked in spattering rain – what she looked at wasn't in the room . . .

Streams formed on the hillside, flowed, and washed the soil mound from her shallow grave. Mud-pies formed in her eyes. More rain exposed minty coins for toll. In them flashed the midnight storm and Charon, waiting on the Styx. Two bolts of white connected heaven to the silver coins and the ferryman melted with them. Through her eyelids, seeped the roux.

Leia opened shimmering globes to the night. She lay in the muck, listened to thunder, and watched lightning strike the wooded hillside. Electric bolts smashed trees and the air smelled of ozone mingling with her rot.

Fires grew. A fawn ventured from the smoking forest and stood on the road, waiting for Jon's hungry Impala.

The Impala slid sideways, smoke rolling off screeching tires. Jon got out. He closed the door and the Impala transformed into the smokehouse on the hill. Leia rose from the mud. The path up the hill lay before her and she stepped her decaying self forth. The fawn passed near, springing downhill away from blazing forest as Leia ascended into higher hell.

Jon consulted his reflection in the building's window as Leia drew near. Cinders swirled, flames freed themselves at smokehouse seams, and heat distorted her view.

"Dad," she said.

He turned. This father was not the one she knew, but the new one, the one she feared.

"Princess," he said, with eyebrows high and cocked; face, reddened from heat; hair, singed – smoking. The blade in his belt reflected the flaming forest. And flames, shaped like the ferryman, danced in Leia's chromium eyes.

He stepped closer. She stepped back.

"Does it hurt?"

"Yes," Leia said and rubbed her eyes.

"It's Charon, I can see him. He wants you."

"Of course, he does." Again she stepped back, and said, "He wants all of us."

"We'll take him out."

"No!" She turned to run.

The knife hooked her stale body. He pulled her down, pinned her with his knees and, arched up. His arms raised; one hand open, 66 detained in the other. PLUNGE, PLUNGE, and her eyes were out.

Silver globes scorched his hand and he threw them to the Styx. The river boiled and gave up the ferryman – and he went with the current.

"AAAhhhh."

The scream stirred the nurse and the clipboard shielded her from drizzle as she ran to Leia's room. Emergency lighting segmented the habitat by green hue and black shadows. Breathing tube, out, lay on the floor. Leia looked lifeless; eyes open, mouth open, and not a blink. Scratches; deep and bloody, vertically decorated her face. Her hands lay free of the blankets, fingers twitching.

Bernice listened to sirens and prayed for a well-done Leia.

Tuesday morning, she hummed, sat in the living room with her cereal-puffs, and turned on the early news. The fire headlined the morning report.

The reporter held the mic for Wahoo's Fire Chief. An outside generator droned behind them.

"Well, it wasn't luck that saved it. It was our response time . . .

Training and response time. Training, response time, and alarms, that's what saved the day."

"Thanks for taking time with us, Chief . . ."

"Sprinklers . . . training, response time, alarms, and the sprinklers, that's what saved it."

Bernice's celebratory mood waned.

"Okay, thanks, Chief." The reporter asked the viewing audience to stay tuned, and said, "After the break, we'll talk with the hospital's director." Timely advertisements interrupted; Bernice waited.

"Director Stengrim, thanks for taking the time. You've moved some patients to St. Elizabeth, in Lincoln?"

"That's correct, seven patients from second floor and two staff, smoke inhalation, not life-threatening injuries. We're operating in emergency mode for now, as we dry rooms and check equipment."

"Will you be able to stay open?"

"We'll see."

"And no burn victims, no loss of life?"

"We were fortunate . . ."

Bernice roared and slung the cereal bowl at the television. It caught the lower corner and splashed. The cat bolted, tail hooked as Bernice's spoon skipped past.

"Jon," Rebecca called.

"What?" he shouted from the upstairs bathroom. He gazed into the mirror. "Tonight," said Mr. R.

"Come down, right now!"

"Be right there."

"There's been a fire at the hospital. Everyone's okay, but they said no visitors on the radio."

"What the *hell?*"

The phone rang. "Hello," Rebecca answered, held her hand over the receiver, and whispered, "It's Teri."

"We just heard."

"Yes."

"No."

"Yes."

"That's what they're saying."

"I don't know."

"We'll let you know as soon as we find something out."

"Kay, bye."

"Jon . . ."

"Let's go."

"How's the Rawling girl?" Ellen asked.

"Still out of it. She scratched herself, and some smoke inhalation, everyone that was trapped inside has smoke inhalation," Harrison said, passing into their boss's office. Pearson, already with O'Leary, asked, "How's it look over there?"

He spoke more to O'Leary than Pearson. "Looks like the hospital's the patient on life support, operating like a M.A.S.H. unit. It's a miracle they didn't lose anybody."

"A disaster but not a catastrophe. It started in the basement, Chief said, probably a leaking diesel tank for the backup generator – said they should know more soon."

"I'd like to ask around all the same."

"I don't see a report on the Rawling girl's accident yet."

"Still lookin into it. She's still unconscious, you know."

"Why is it I always know what you know? Pearson, ask around at the hospital, see if anyone saw anything or knows more about the fire. Harrison, finish what you started."

Harrison *had* been working it but short on conviction. Ellen helped him narrow the boot print on Leia's door to a brand, but something bigger than a *ten* made for quite a pile of boots. Anyway, suicide was pretty high on his list. Henry Rothness was his favorite – foul play – suspect, but had an alibi, and the footprints in his dusty office were different. Who knows, the car door could have been kicked days, weeks before. Others he asked at the plant produced zip, and Leia's state – obviously a dead end. Clues were few, a couple of oddities he was keeping to himself. Why knock himself out? Surely, when or if Ms. Rawling woke, all would be evident.

O'Leary sent a deputy with Pearson to assist Wahoo police and help the hospital staff. Jon and Rebecca joined the families vying for information. Jon spotted Brochette leaving. He cut him off in the parking lot.

"She's okay, it's a mess in there, we can't let anyone in yet. Someone might get hurt."

"She's okay, okay?"

"Mr. Rawling, take the Mrs. home. Tell her I said not to worry . . . and go to work. There's nothing for you guys to do here. If anything changes I'll call you personally. LeAnn's alright, we're taking care of everyone."

"Leia."

"*Leia's* being taken care of. Trust me."

Tuesday. Core Fuels, a day lacking infamy.

Malcolm's cleaning avoided Fermentation.

Berry Ottos worked hardly.

No equipment blew; Bobby got after a dripping faucet and a running toilet.

Bill pressed correct icons in the control room.

Henry adjusted load-out numbers favorably.

Gilbert maintained the Payloader.

Sheila and Nancy forgot to complain about the new schedule.

Mark and Bryce alternated visits to Stillman.

Deb and Monica made it to the basement; Bryce poured.

Teri prayed her friend would wake.

The police didn't show; Bernice calmed and thought, *if Rawling's daughter didn't wake last night – maybe she never will.*

Jon read the consortium's stock scam.

Otherjon premeditated.

Chapter 29
For Shits and Grins

"Jon, come up to bed; your chair's digesting you, again." Rebecca offered a hand to pull him free. "It's after midnight."

She, too, had slept through the late-show and subsequent infomercial. The national anthem concluded and the broadcast went to test pattern.

"Go up, I'm going to have some toast or something." Jon gave her a peck, went to the kitchen, and Rebecca went upstairs.

At two in the morning, he checked on her.

At three a.m. he left.

The Power Wagon was black and had a muffler, not stealthy, but it was black and had a muffler.

Otherjon, riding shotgun, reflected in the passenger window. "Got the crowbar?" "Crowbar," Jon said.

"Got a dolly?"

"Don't need one."

"Got Dusty?"

"I've got Dusty – and the flashlight."

The black Dodge rumbled from the blacktop onto the rough lot. Ignition off and in neutral, he deadheaded it next to the platform. From behind the seat, he pulled Dusty Dan, the gopher-getter, with open sights and composite stock. The fresh lubed air-rifle smelled of 3-in-1 oil.

He pumped Dusty's front handle, jacking up muzzle velocity, then circled the lot, extinguishing perimeter lights. The fixture mounted high above the shed door and near the peak blazed. He pulled the trigger, sending one lead pellet. The bulb popped a hot hiss.

Through the open driver's window, Jon passed the rifle and laid it on the seat.

"Nice shootin', Wyatt." Otherjon handed him the flashlight.

Eyes adjusting to waxing moonlight and with a clean steel-blue crowbar in hand, he took the platform steps. At the door, he rested, coughing, and when it subsided, he inserted the bar in the U of the padlock and twisted the latch into next week. Wood split, screws ripped free. Jon hoped Mr. R appreciated the sound as much as he did. The *Masterlock* continued its business, keeping the hanging hook and latch together. No matter, the door swung open by gravity and the tin-clad shed's inclination.

He hung the crowbar on the open door and entered. Tanks lurked in the dark, waiting as emperor's guard. From his back pocket, he slid a red tube of *Eveready*s. *It worked at home*, he rapped the flashlight in the heel of his palm. It sucked the dark and he inspected troops of varying stature. Past acetylene, oxygen, and welding gas, his light landed on short and tall tanks with the labels he hunted, N.O.S. – Nitrous Oxide.

Jon whispered, "Dentist's best friend."

One by one he tipped them on edge and rolled them out. With an open hand, he guided them on top and, using his *Red Wing* inseam, he kept them moving with a gentle kick each step. Jon hadn't moved cylinders in years. Not a pro like the old guys working for the gas company, who could spin two at a time, but he was holding his own.

Otherjon, impressed, commented each time Jon spun another across the deck.

"Look at you."

"You da-Man!"

"Skills baby, skills."

Otherjon, stayed in the truck, watched and encouraged from a moonlit windshield.

Jon felt good, tonight they were getting along.

After half a dozen nitrous tanks, he helped himself to the acetylene.

A load made, and Otherjon said, “No sense leaving half empty.”

Jon woke on the couch, a wolf-print blanket wrapped him and his clothes lay beside on the floor. Rebecca stood under the kitchen archway, leaning, waiting.

“Where were *you* last night?” Before he had a chance to answer, she turned. She didn’t want to know and imagined an array of possible untrue responses. One thought rang in her mind, *sex*. Men think about sex – a lot, liked sex – a lot, needed sex –a lot, and if she wasn’t the object, whom?

Jon pulled his pants on. In the kitchen, cupboard doors and pans banged. He went up to shower. Rebecca returned to the living room, picked up his shirt, and smelled. She thought of the women Jon worked with. She didn’t know all their names but she knew faces and many were pretty, prettier than ever this morning. *A couple of ticks and I’ll be fifty, I don’t want to be fifty . . .*

To the stairs and taking each, in turn, she thought of those pretty faces.

Monica, and what a beautiful name . . . step.

Those two, possibly from production, or the office, a likely pair . . . up another.

Sheila, she knew that one, *so fucking divorced, word around town, watch your man, ladies . . .* two steps more.

Leia’s nurse – petite, small hands, caregiver, the white dress . . . the hat . . . another step.

Nancy, a Delilah if I ever saw one . . . Jezebel. Up a step.

Bernice, buxom, creamy white skin, luscious melons, smooth tapering legs, not a wrinkle . . . up two.

Teri, familiar, beautiful, slim, young. Available. Teri, sweet Teri, irresistible . . . candy!

Jon stood naked at the mirror.

"Lie," Mr. R said.

"Ya think?"

"Tell'er you tried to see Leia."

Rebecca, at the doorway, said, "Ya think, what, Jon?" He jumped, she continued. "Ya think I like being alone. Ya think catting around's going to bring you happiness?"

"Push her down the stairs," Otherjon said.

"I'm about at the end of my rope, Jon."

"See, now she's asking for it."

"I'm just a housekeeper . . . a cleaning lady . . . a cook – just your cook."

Jon tried to ignore both. He meekly reached into the shower and turned it on.

"You don't sleep. You're hardly ever home. What's going on? Talk to me."

Otherjon had let him down, they had been too busy, too busy to think up a good lie, white or otherwise, and telling her he had tried to see Leia might need extrapolation. He did his best, kept it simple. "I didn't feel good, went for a drive." Not looking back, he entered the water and slinked shut the curtain.

"Roll her down to 312. It's ready."

An orderly pivoted Leia's bed, aiming it at the door. The nurse steered them into the hall.

"Look."

Leia's eyes – open, and the nurse said, "She does that all the time now. Don't freak, more or less a vegetable, I think," and she pressed Leia's eyelids shut.

Harrison approached in the hall. "Is she . . .?"

"No, no," said the nurse, "She's fine, I mean, she's alive."

"Has she said anything?"

"Just that scream . . . the night of the fire."

"Nothing else?"

"No, poor thing, not yet. There's talk about the nursing home. But please, you didn't hear it from me."

Bernice returned from lunch and Jon asked, "How's party planning?"

"It's coming together . . . Teri's helping with itinerary and the games. Tomorrow, we'll type up the program."

"I want to see the draft, have an event to add. Planning a little treasure hunt, team-building exercise. I think at the end, should only take about a half-hour or so. Let's not get too crazy with the other games."

"Sounds *fun*, Sir." *Gag.*

"I'll make the rounds tonight, do a little scouting for the hunt. If you and Teri want to shove off early, six – seven?" Jon waited.

"Thank you, I'll tell her."

At twenty to eight, crews set equipment to auto or standby for the night. One by two, or three, employees left stations and gravitated to the locker rooms.

On the steps to the lower level, Bryce asked Henry, "What d'ya think, Big Guy?"

"These hours suck donkey shit."

"Surprised to hear you complain, ya lifer."

Henry shrugged.

"Live to work, work to live, huh? I'd punch your timecard for ya if ya wanted to leave early once in a while."

"I don't think so, heard about the last time you tried that little trick."

"Sheila flapped her flap, don't trust a chick."

"Heard Bernice wrote ya up – choked you out." Henry grunted a laugh.

"Damn near, wrath of Miss Stretch Pants. Like I said – don't trust chicks."

Henry moved to his side of the lockers. Others, changing or disrobing, sat or stood at theirs. On the opposite side, Bryce spun his combination. Terrance moved to the shower, exposing Malcolm at the flank. Malcolm, uninhibited, sat at the end of the bench with his shirt unbuttoned, contemplating a shower. A faint, sweet, metallic smell filled the air.

Behind Bryce, a row of white sinks hung on the wall, dividing locker room from showers. Horseplay echoed out of the shower side entrances. Laughs glanced around the room, shouts tinning off forty-five lockers. Soap jokes, more laughing . . . then singing . . . *Your smile set me free, you're the only one for me . . .*

Malcolm looked to Bryce.

Bryce's hate thawed, he shrugged and said, "Company policy, don't ask, don't tell."

Malcolm tittered.

The serenade traveled through ductwork. One floor above, groovy short-stack Sheila turned the water off in the ladies' stand-alone shower stall. From the construction afterthought, she reached for a towel.

Monica, at the mirror, stopped with her makeup. "Shhh. Listen."

In front of five complementing half-lockers, Nancy and Deb stopped cackling. Lefty-loosey valves leaked from two short tanks in the end amenity. Their tall cousins, draped under towels, hissed in locked lockers downstairs.

"Heads in a fog and loves got me shakin,." sang Barry and two from the Lab.

Sheila secured her towel between her breasts and joined . . .

"Settle down boy, there's a pill ya otta be takin."

Downstairs . . . *"Gonna love you so much more."*

Monica joined Sheila. *"I've heard that before."* Sheila danced.

Downstairs . . . "*Close your eyes and kiss me, baby.*"

Nancy rolled back on the short bench, slipped her shoe on, and timed '*baby*' with a kick to Deb's rear-end. The two answered, singing with Monica and a dancing Sheila . . . *"Press a little harder, honey bee."*

Barry cut the water and belted out, *"Gonna love you so much more."*

"So what ya waitin for!" sang four dancing ladies.

In the offices, Jon bade Bernice and Teri a later-than-approved, goodnight.

Stragglers filtered downstairs and to their lockers. Barry, drying his hair, emerged naked from the shower.

WHAP!

"Ouch!" Barry yelped. He turned to counterattack, and said, "Oh-ho-oh, you're going to get it now." He spun his thin company towel into a whip and advanced. Henry stood on the bench to witness from his side of the lockers. No one missed the snap-mark, growing red, on Barry's ass. Men giggled as ten-year-old girls at a pajama party.

"Get him, Barry," Bryce said.

Terrance, the giver of welts, attempted an escape. *Pop* – sounded the wet tip of Barry's uncoiling rebuttal. Terrance collided with exiting Josh, and dropping hard, they met the slick tile. Soaked and entangled, the bruised lay on the wet floor busting a gut.

Barry circled, spun his towel, and taunted, "Revenge – Oh sweet revenge." He snapped at the two-tone pretzel.

Nancy, Sheila, and Deb were *love-shagging* the next verse. Monica shushed them again; they listened. Bullshit and contagious laughter replaced the Muzak. Men below, women above, breathed locker-leaking merriment. The girls joyfully tittered and their male counterparts yucked-it-up.

A fresh observer descended and stood a step above *Core's* giddy bowels. Gene surveyed the laughing, pushing, towel snapping, and crawling. Ahead of wet snail trails, Josh and Terrance pre-ambulated from the shower into the locker room proper.

"Get up, you pussies," Bryce said. Jovial Malcolm offered a balled-up towel and Bryce threw it at the naked, wet and wounded floor urchins.

Terrance, looking back, cried, "Uncle," and lifted a forfeiting hand at Barry. *Whoo-tuh.* Barry snapped the wet towel, tip only missing Terrance's dangling sack.

"Whoa!" roared the crowd. Josh, made it to his feet and wrapped Bryce's unfurled towel around his waist. He looked up. Paused . . .

"What in God's name are you *FOOLS* doing down here?" Gene said. "It's eight-thirty, let's get going."

Jon listened. The laughing throng approached. He moved from desk to watch from his office door. They stumbled past the offices, a gang of intoxicated toddlers. A kerfuffle at the time clock and they exited the front. He moved to a south window and watched newly minted space cadets drift out to the parking lot to find their earth rovers.

Bill, at his car and fumbling with keys, watched Henry back out of the slot behind his. The Suburban accelerated across the lane. The back of Bill's Impala crumpled. Bill looked at the crack-up and cracked up.

Henry rolled down his window. "Whoa, girl." He reached for the shift lever, pulled it to L1, and mashing the gas, shouted, "Giddy-up." Tire smoke filled the air and a howling squeal pierced the lot. Henry slapped at the outer door shell, urging his black beast forward, then pulled right and down the row. Bill's kinked Chevy, imbedded on Henry's trailer-hitch, followed. Bill's driver's door and front fender caught the neighbor's car. Monica's rear quarter panel caved – taillight ripped free. Her back bumper hooked Bill's fender, pulling it to a ninety in an eye-for-an-eye thing. Most of Bill dodged the angling Impala; the front tire stapled Bill's foot with a crunch. "Ahuww," and Bill hopped back, dragging the pancake.

The lot erupted. Drivers, laughing under lights, ran for vehicles like the beginning of the Grand Prix. Monica inspected her damaged Mercury and made a feeble attempt to reset the taillight. Hobbled Bill came back to check her repair. It fell free.

She noted Bill's limp, swelling loafer, and cackled. Bill pointed; Monica had put shoes on the wrong feet. Her chuckle rose to snorting.

Analgesic nitrous permeated Bill's every cell and rocking on his foot, he said, "Doesn't even hurt."

Between air-gap snorts, the braying donkey said, "Get in with me, we'll get your car back."

Contagion experienced in locker room laughter relocated and malformed to outdoor disaster; smashing and crisscross crashing inundated the lot. Mark used his front bumper, bashing Bill's Chev free from the Suburban's grip. Sheila backed into a light pole, she held her neck. Bryce set a collision course with a carpooling couple from distribution. A Camaro and Ford hot-lapped the perimeter in a screeching oval. Josh stood on the roof of his sedan; he waved them by, yelling, "If ya ain't rubbin, ya ain't racin."

Jon smoked few cigs in his forty-nine years, but if ever there was a time? In Teri's desk, he found a pack and cobbed one. He struck a match on the windowsill, kicked back, and focused on the glass. Otherjon looked joyous – they smoked. Together, the impresarios watched the derby, and in blissful satisfaction, Otherjon said, "Aren't good times best shared?"

About seven minutes – the time it takes to do *Virginia Slim*, and it started winding down. Vehicles quavered out of the lot. All but Sheila's remained mobile under its own power. After backing into the pole, she complemented the effort, blowing the radiator on an adjacent parking barrier.

"I can pull ya home," Henry offered, hooking a chain to the steaming Marque's underbelly.

"I'll steer," she said.

"Good idea."

She leaned, looked in the side mirror and put fingers to mouth. Stragglers laughed at the busted lip. "Feels fuzzy," she giggled and, settling back, waved with both hands. Henry goosed it. The chain snapped brisk; semi-consequential whiplash and Sheila's loose head swiveled. She smiled.

Jon shut the door softly. He slipped his shoes off and positioned them on the edge of the rug. Rebecca sat on the couch and muted the television. She looked at the clock. "Really? So nice of you to come home."

"Had to work late."

"Of course."

"Annual meeting Saturday, planning, getting things in order."

"Any help?"

"Well, Bernice. I made her lead on lots of it."

"Um-hm."

Jon slunk.

"Your phones must be out." She lifted the receiver and listened. "Because this one's working *perfect!*" *Smash, Smash, Smash*, three times she slammed it home.

"Sorry, we got so busy, I shoulda called," he said, escaping to the kitchen.

She followed. "Anybody else in the offices, working late, tonight?"

"Well, Teri."

"Convenient."

She closed fast and he dodged as she went for the stove. "Supper's in the oven, I left it on so it'd be *hot*." Her eyes flashed furious. "I bet you're hungry?" A charred thing resembling meatloaf dropped on a plate. Next, she used the potholder, removing a blackened potato. Steam-less remains clacked to the plate next to the charred thing and black flaking stuck to her protective mitt. She set the plate on the table. "There. *Bon appetit!*"

Jon moved to her, tried to hold her. First, she resisted, then relented and let him gather her. He wanted to say, 'Nothing's going on.'

She felt rigid and Jon's unobstructed view of the kitchen window reflected an ugly self. Mr. R was silent. Jon looked to the three knives in the block on the counter and to Rebecca's back in the window; he felt her melting. "They called," she said. "Brochette called."

He could feel her shoulders pulsating in silent crying. "When?"

"This afternoon."

"And?"

"We can see her in the morning."

"That's good."

"He wants to meet with us." And she pushed away with an audible whimper.

He let her go. “Okay . . . did he say what about?”

“All he said was, ‘Options’.” She shuffled to the counter and used a towel to dab her teary eyes. Her continence wavered and more sadness leaked out. “He’s given up . . . I give up.” Her knees buckled; she sank to the floor, weeping.

He helped her up. Distant, in dazed capitulation, she had no words. Jon drew a water and fed her pills. He carried her upstairs and placed her in their bed.

She closed her eyes. He closed the door.

Chapter 30
Aliens

Thursday morning they met with Brochette.

"Let's go to the conference room." As the Friday before, he directed them and in smoky-smelling chairs, they sat. Rebecca looked as wrecked as the Impala they'd arrived in. Jon, not good, either. Even Brochette looked less than usual.

"We *do* get to see her today?" Jon said.

"Of course . . . I have good news, but at the same time, disturbing. The night of the fire, Leia scratched her face. It looks tough, but she did it to herself. Do you know what that means?"

"She woke up?" Rebecca asked.

"Well, I don't think fully *awake*. I doubt she was conscious, but she moved, so something's going on upstairs. This is hopeful."

The couple perked up.

"And, we're here to talk about something else?" Jon said.

Brochette paused. "Yes, our liaison, Mrs. Berger, in lieu of the fire, is out of town – working with patients and families at St. Elizabeth. I have these for you." He slid a Kirkdahle brochure with forms across the table. "Leia is stable, and resource-wise, it's time to move her. I suggest moving her to Kirkdahle. They have a wing for . . . and room . . . they can take her tomorrow.

"Nursing home?" Rebecca said.

"Resource wise?" Jon paused. "What do you mean?"

Again, Brochette paused, and a long one it was. " . . . I'm here to help you decide what's best for her, moving forward."

Rebecca looked to Jon. Jon looked to Brochette. "What are you talking about? She needs to be here."

". . . not really . . . As you can see, the hospital's a mess. We need all the usable rooms." Jon looked at him, doubtful.

Brochette removed a pen from his shirt pocket and clicked off a couple of clicks. "Remember when I said it was up to Leia and her maker? Well, it still is, and there's little we can do here that can't be done in a less costly bed." Over horn-rimmed glasses, he peered at them. "I'm not sure you know this, but Leia is uninsured."

Jon thought about roll-backs imposed on his employees and the six-month wait for sign up. Of course, *Seed Genetics* followed the downward spiral, benefit cuts spinning west from Omaha, keeping businesses and owners insulated from rising premiums. He did the math. Leia had worked four, maybe five months.

Rebecca asked, "On the phone, you said we needed to talk about options?"

"Options, right. There *are* other nursing homes. And if you could find the help, a good nurse or nurse practitioner, let's say, – some folks in this situation might elect to take her home. I don't recommend it. Even with assistance, it's an unbelievable amount of work. If she goes to Kirkdahle . . . well, she's an adult, expenses go to county, or the state, maybe. If you take her home," he shrugged, "there might be other agencies – I'm a doctor, I don't know."

"You're saying tomorrow; we have to decide by tomorrow?" Jon said.

Brochette clicked his pen. Trained to give bad news, yes, even death, but this, this was bullshit and delivering degrading announcements based on patient finance, it stuck in his craw. He had tried; he had railed against it. Buttered the director, even tried to use the fire as leverage. 'Surely we can pad expenses under the hospital's insurance? In the name of patient care; in the name of decency.' Stengrim, the old bean counter, not only didn't see it his way and doubled down on whose responsibility it was to deliver the short-fused news with an indisposed Mrs. Berger. 'No payee, no stayee, Brochette, she's dead weight, I want that bed available by Friday. This isn't charity central, we have an accounting department, the one on first, you know, that makes out your check?'

Brochette cleared his throat, toed the line. "I'm afraid so."

It was a tough thank you to give; Jon forced one out.

Allowed their visit, Rebecca and Jon stood at her bedside looking at their daughter. Even in daylight, curtains open, and room well-lit, she looked like the poster child for a horror movie. Eight scabby scratches ran from bandaged hairline, through eyebrows, and resumed on high cheekbones. Four on a side and past her nose. The inner two, catching upper lip, lower lip, then all eight, down, off the jawline. A clear salve anointed the scabs. Red infection, fading to pink, festered below the glaze.

"Oh my *God*," Rebecca gasped and put a hand to mouth, muffling, veiling aversion. "Her wrists." Wrists secured to the bed rails codified the patient's disconcerting condition. Rebecca gently caressed Leia's tethered hand.

Jon exhaled, "Uhf."

Leia's eyes opened.

Her parents jerked.

"Jon!" Rebecca said.

Jon leaned. "Leia?" He said it soft, then louder, "Leia . . . LEIA?"

"It's Mom," Rebecca said. Leia didn't respond.

Jon stepped into the hall. "Nurse." She came promptly. "She's waking up." He escorted her to the bed.

Aliens examined her. An un-formed face said, "She's waking up." And she wondered when she had learned their language . . . or did they know hers? Large fuzzy heads moved above her, blotting out the light. Then came into focus. Not aliens, Bernice, Henry.

"I'm so sorry. She's not; she just does that." And using a bottle from the nearby tray, the nurse put drops in Leia's eyes . . .

Bernice held the needle, Henry her wrists. The needle, long, straight, thin, extended from a syringe. How deep could it probe? Very. Her eye, an access, a cavity to pass through, with plenty of additional steel to probe the gray depths. Bernice held Leia's eye open with her finger and thumb as she lowered the syringe. The steel filament came. For a moment, it depressed the cornea, then pushed through layers and entered the vitreous gel. Bernice adjusted, continuing at an angle, and it touched the retina. Through, spiking the frontal cortex.

"Oh!" Rebecca said. Leia's hands jerked, the bed rails shuddered, and her left broke free from the Velcro strap. A strike smashed the nurse, sending her back, tripping. She grasped the tray table on her way. Jon tried to catch her; she slipped through. Tray contents sprayed the room. Jon helped the petite nurse to her feet. Leia, arm free, pulled the bandage from her head and sent it to the wall.

A crash boomed in her head and an icy-white light filled her. Leia stilled and held her gaze straight, fearing the slightest movement of the cold needle in her brain. "What is it?" she asked. She could see Henry, smiling, looking across the exam table at Bernice, and Bernice said, "It's not what we're putting in Girlie, it's what we're taking out."

"We're taking the kick outta you," Henry said.

Bernice laughed and Leia felt the probe jiggling as she chuckled. Bernice pushed – the syringe bottomed out, and then . . . the sucking sound. Bernice pulled at the plunger, Leia felt her essence draining and desperately fought the pull with her mind.

The nurse re-secured Leia's wrist and retrieved a box of tissue from the floor. She closed Leia's eyes. Droplets ran down her face. The nurse dabbed at what didn't make the pillow. Jon righted the tray table.

Covers moved, her legs jerked. Rebecca reached, pressing them. "I've got her."

A kick, then another. Covers pulled, exposing Leia's gowned upper.

Then thrashing, and Jon helped hold the uncontrolled. He looked to the nurse and saw panic.

"I'll get the doctor."

Leia's body heaved, releasing afghan and blanket. Violent jerks and restrained wrists rattled rails. Rebecca and Jon, across from one another, fought to contain the jolting monstrosity.

Leia centered her energy and fought the needle. She concentrated on the cold white light that filled her and compressed it. Under pressure, it heated. Further, she refined it, until it became a marble-sized sun. Not done, she forged a nuclear pea, then a bb. She made it split and held them in her mind's eye. They orbited, compressing yet smaller, atoms, one matter, the other, anti-matter. No longer visible to her but she controlled them the same and it was time. She sent them spinning into the needle and out. Bernice's hold slipped. The plunger shot from the syringe. Atoms ripped from each other's gravity and shot to the attackers. Pore size holes wisped smoke from Henry and Bernice's foreheads. Their clocks ticked; one nanosecond, two nanoseconds. Their faces became fuzzy. Their heads exploded.

Kicking and thrashing ended. Parents relaxed, watched, guarded. The room was silent.

"Get her blankets," Rebecca said as she straightened Leia's gown.

Jon bent for the blankets. He heard the bed creak and looked.

Smooth, Leia sat up. Her wrists stretched the bands tight. Her eyes opened.

Jon stood. Rebecca stepped back.

Leia, in her own world, turned, stared through Mom, and said, "Bastards."

Leia sat up. "Bastards." She turned, gripped the syringe, and slowly pulled.

Muscles twitched below Leia's right eye. Her lower eyelid quivered and moved in a rolling bulge. For thirty seconds the Rawlings watched it spasm as Leia sat looking through them.

She pulled the syringe and felt the needle retreating, inching from the center of her brain, through frontal lobe, thin shaft moving through viscous-filled sphere. Out it came. She laid it on the exam table and collapsed.

Brochette entered, followed by the nurse. The four looked at the sitting girl, exposed staples on partially shaved head, her scabby face, and quivering eye. They watched as she fell back.

Rebecca returned to her. Again, she took Leia's hand and in a pitiful tone, said, "Baby."

Leia's eyes fluttered, then opened to thin slits.

Rebecca saw a difference. "Leia, it's Mom."

Jon, holding blankets, closed behind the Doc and Rebecca. The nurse stood at Rebecca's other side. Leia closed her eyes . . . seconds passed.

Over Brochette's shoulder, Jon said, "Sweetheart."

"Leia," Brochette commanded.

Leia's eyes opened to the same narrow slits, her pupils shifted right, then her head. Fuzzy faces floated unattached above fuzzy bodies.

Brochette used his stethoscope. Rebecca watched, looking for a response. The Doc gave none. He let the stethoscope dangle and slid a penlight from his coat. Gently, he opened further the recently quivering eye and moved the light above it.

The bands snapped tight; bedrails shuddered. In a raspy whisper, Leia pleaded, "No more needles."

"Have you seen Jon, yet?" Bernice asked,

"No," Teri said. "He didn't call?"

Bernice didn't answer and looked to the gals that started at eight. They shook their heads. She had her answer, but asked loud, "Has anyone talked to Mr. Rawling today?"

Bernice went to the window, looked for Jon's Impala, then to the restroom to pray for the worst. In purgatory, a locked stall, she sat on porcelain, hoping a dump might help her think. *What's there to think about, either we're screwed or we aren't? That charmed little bitch. And Henry, what a tool, my tool, swing and a miss. Outlandish at the time, letting Henry take Sleeping Beauty home when they had her – might not have been the worst idea. He would have come in smiling every morning.* She laughed at that. *How removed from those crimes would I have been, very well removed, thank you. How long before Henry would have tired of his underground pet, tired of a basement wife, then I could have cajoled the outcome from a distance? All husbands want to kill their wives, don't they, all wives their husbands? Lamenting doesn't fix the present – does it, Bernice Jorgan?* She thought about the lies she would tell, and about Dale . . . *if he could go missing why couldn't I?*

A wolf spider moved from the next stall into hers. She placed her hands on the close metal walls, made an angry face, and stomped it. She missed. It raced off, and she thought, *I can't kill an itsy bitsy spider or a Rawling for losing.* A dump did help. She felt lighter and checked her watch, the truck was on its way; she went to check on Malcolm.

The Doc checked her pulse. Leia blinked, and opening her eyes half-mast, looked to her surroundings. Necks began filling the gaps between shoulders and the floating heads of her bedside aliens. On its leash, her hand stopped well short of her parched lips and marred face, she tried again.

Rebecca saw fear in her daughter's eyes. 'We're here, it's okay. You're safe."

"We're here, Sweetheart," Jon repeated.

"Leia, I'm Doctor Brochette. Relax," he said, his voice hypnotic.

Without looking away from Leia, the Doc asked the nurse for the clipboard hanging on the bed.

"Leia, this nice nurse is going to check your blood pressure. Your mom and dad are going to give you a little hug so you know everything is fine, then I am going to ask them to leave for a while." She looked at him, expressionless.

"Just a hug," he said to the Rawlings.

They hugged their girl, and were told to wait in the lobby. The nurse closed the door behind them.

Brochette released Leia's hand and moved it to her face. "Leia, you had an accident. You have some scratches on your face; we didn't want you touching them in your sleep. Do you feel them?" He helped move her fingers over the scabs.

She took control and gently touched, then closed her eyes and let her hand drop back to her side. "I'm peeing."

Chapter 31

A Breath of Fresh Air

Malcolm Johnson rolled his cart past fermentation without hindrance and set up at the end of the corridor. He mopped his way from it and down the hall to the steel door. It was nice out when he arrived that morning, was it still? And a breath of fresh air, he desired. One look back before turning the knob. The door opened, pulling at his hand as the heavy, overheated production floor air rushed out. His shirt fluttered in it. It was beautiful and he took a step out, stood in the breeze flowing around the building, and breathed. He held the door and watched Henry filling the blue and white bulk truck. He watched the driver finish a cigarette and crush it underfoot. Malcolm thought it neither strange nor unusual. So what, he mopped floors.

Henry disconnected the hose and scanned his surroundings. He saw Malcolm in the doorway and froze. Henry stood confused and, in the long moment, the driver noticed Henry. The driver's gaze followed Henry's to the open door.

As they zeroed in on Malcolm, the timing and peculiarity struck him. Malcolm stepped a turning stride back through the doorway and face-planted Bernice's blouse. Her bosom, warm, and the perfume strong. Quite pleasant. Bernice shoved with both hands, sending him out the doorway. Malcolm shot into the lot, fell, and reaching back, a scrunch sounded in his shoulder. An elbow struck tar and his favorite maintenance shirt tore on contact. The driver settled his ass in the truck seat and watched in the big side-mirror. Henry flung the fill-hose onto the dock. Bernice followed Malcolm out and shut the door behind her. She wielded the thin man's mop.

Malcolm said nothing, not a yell nor scream, but his eyes pleaded. Bernice planted the mop in his solar plexus. The blow sat him up. Henry approached, knelt behind him, and without pause gripped his head. Malcolm's body lagged the slow powerful twist. His eyes went from pleading to terror and opened wide when his neck popped.

For a few seconds, she was mad as hell.

But there wasn't an angle with Malcolm, only money, and with no leverage, well, cash didn't buy insurance. Bernice chose relief over anger, and thought, *done is done* – and – *whattaya know – they could hurt a flea.* Then she had an idea. A fun idea.

A short wait in the lobby and the Doc met them. "She seems lost, not with us yet, but this changes things. I'll see we keep her another day. You can go back in . . . talk gentle, very gentle; if she doesn't respond or recognize you, don't push." They tried to pass Brochette. He moved to block them a second longer. "We've witnessed a small miracle, let's not jeopardize it. Ten mellow minutes, okay? It's important she stays calm. I've added something to her I.V. Don't be surprised if she falls asleep on you."

The Rawlings returned to third floor and approached the nurse's station. The nurse held the phone, waiting for her connection. Twice she flashed an open hand, indicating 'ten minutes', and mouthed the words to complement the gesture. A puffy discoloration on her cheekbone knocked her good looks.

The nurse's bruise didn't bother Rebecca in the least, and she mouthed 'thank you' as they went by. A low conversation behind them started with, "Hi, Buck? It's Nurse . . ."

In the hall near Leia's door, an elliptically adjusted laundry cart with one clean wheel held sheets and reeked of urine. In her room, Jon noticed Leia's soiled, ooze-side-up, bandage in the garbage and caught its bad odor. The room, a nauseating bouquet, still smelled smoky, of rot from the garbage, of cleaner, salve, and Leia's stale breath. The shade had been set low but the sun illuminated the room through it. Replaced bedding looked taut over and under the patient. The salve looked fresh and a new wrap bound Leia's head. The wrap, lower this time, covered the scratches on her forehead and ended above her eyebrows. She looked mostly mummy, a mummy attacked by tiger, but a living mummy nevertheless. Woozy, drowsy, but her blue eyes had consciousness in them, or at least partial consciousness. The road to recovery looked plausible.

"Oh, Sweetie." Rebecca tried to hug her best she could over the short aluminum safety rail.

Jon took her hand. "Hey, Kiddo."

They either saw or imagined a faint smile and quietly waited a minute, hoping for more.

"Good to have you back," Jon said, optimistically. "You took quite a bump on the noggin."

Leia looked at them blankly. She whispered, "Rats." It sounded like a warning or a secret.

The confused parents hung on the word and looked to one another. "The rats are all gone, no more rats," Rebecca assured, then tried a hug from a different angle. "We've been so *worried* about you."

In a most lenient voice, Jon asked, "Do you remember what happened?"

"Jon! Stop," Rebecca said, instantly pissed. "What does it matter now?"

He paused. "You were at the plant, you were going to go out with Teri, and then you were in the river, in your car."

Leia's groggy eyes scanned. "Rats," she repeated.

"Take your time." Jon nodded.

Rebecca wedged herself in front of him. "Stop right now, or I'll . . ." She didn't know what she would do, but it would be ugly, she knew that much.

Jon stifled. The mother turned and continued in soft loving avowals and Leia responded in maundering whispers. They made out a word here and there, but nothing made sense. Leia said 'Mom' one time in a short, incoherent ramble. Rebecca seized on it as a win.

The nurse peeked in. "Time to wrap it up, folks. It's been fifteen minutes, she needs to rest now." She waited for them at the door to say their goodbyes and love-yous.

The nurse walked them back to her desk and Jon asked, "Would you call us if she becomes more – coherent?"

"She'll get better, don't you think?" Rebecca asked.

"Give me your number," the nurse whispered.

Alone in her room and without audience, Leia said, "Thirsty Thursday."

The bulk truck's airbrakes released; Henry and Bernice looked. The driver eased the clutch out and lowered his shades for a last check. In the side mirror, their eyes met. Malcolm, head set west, also seemed to be watching him. Bernice stood with Malcolm's mop, she whistled, then waved him over.

The driver inched away and turned for the north road.

"Hey!" she yelled and waved again.

The driver pulled the shifter out of super-low and put it in true first.

"Son of a bitch's leaving," Henry said.

"*He's* next."

The driver thought twice, circled, and pulled up.

Henry lifted limp Malcolm into the passenger seat.

The driver cringed. "Are you shitting me?"

Bernice coaxed the shades off the driver, handed them to Henry. "Put these on him."

Henry stood on the truck's passenger step and handed the seatbelt across. "Buckle him in."

The driver shook. "Ooh, he gives me the *heebie-jeebies*."

Henry adjusted Malcolm's new shades and they fit well. "First time he's looked cool."

Malcolm's neck crunched and a bone deformed the skin as Henry turned the head to the driver. Henry tried ventriloquism, and, gripping

Malcolm's hair, operated the nodding. "Time to get rolling, eh Shaky?" Henry's lips moved quite a lot.

"Ooh, you *fucker*."

Leaving the hospital, they discussed preparations to bring Leia home, moving her bed downstairs to the den, and a Saturday morning retrieval.

"Let's go by her apartment and pick up some clothes," Rebecca said.

"And check her fridge, see if anything's going bad."

Rebecca filled a couple of bags with underwear, t-shirts, and pajamas.

Jon filled another with molding bread and items from the fridge for the dumpster.

High in his seat, coaxing shifter into gear, and he asked, "What do I do with him?"

"Take him with, show em around," Bernice said.

"Hell no; no freaking way."

"Yes, way. It'll be fun." She smiled, flashing him her baby-teeth. "And when you're done, put the truck in the Quonset, just leave him buckled in, we don't want him running off. Henry'll take care of the rest. See, you don't even have to touch him."

The driver's hand gripped the shifter, and Henry flopped Malcolm's cooling hand over Shaky's.

Henry jumped as the truck lurched; momentum slammed the door behind him.

Chapter 32

Beer Works

The Rawlings said little on the drive home. When they pulled in the yard, Jon said, "I'll leave you the car."

Rebecca checked the time. "You're still going in, eh?" She masked anger with her joy of Leia's waking.

"I should."

At 4:00 p.m., the ladies in the office took their afternoon break. Bernice used the seclusion to stroll down the hall and punch Malcolm's timecard.

In the cafeteria, Teri grabbed a coffee from the machine, then sat at a table across from Nancy and Deb.

"So, how's your girlfriend doin'," Nancy asked. "How is Rawling's daughter?"

"The same. Out of it, I think. Hospital's closed to visitors, cause of the fire."

"I think they're letting people in again," Deb said.

"Oh really? Cool. I stopped last night and they said it was still off-limits to the public. I'll call her mom when I get home, or maybe just go and see if I can get in."

"Did she really try to kill herself?" Nancy said.

"No. She . . ."

"That's what I heard," Deb said.

"No way, she . . ."

"That's what everybody's sayin," Nancy said.

"She never would do that," Teri said but thought about how sad Leia had been at *Cold Spot* only a couple of weeks ago.

"Where does she live?" Nancy asked.

"Rustad Apartments. You're the second person to ask that today. Bernice asked the same thing.

"Bernice probably wanted to pay her next month's rent," Deb said.

"Yeah, she's a big sweetheart," Nancy said and looked at Deb. Together they repeated their mantra, "No . . . She's – Just – *BIG*," cracking themselves up.

"Did they look for a suicide note?" Nancy asked.

"I went there that night looking for her. I didn't see any note."

"Did you *look*?"

Teri stared at her coffee. She didn't answer.

Deb said, "They made that place into apartments cause no one would buy it. They use'ta keep dead people in there sometimes, in the winter.

"That's creepy."

Jon adjusted the Power Wagon mirror. "She sounded bitchy to me," Mr. R said.

"Baseless anger. Late for supper. I didn't call, big whoop."

"Baseless?"

"Unfounded."

"She's got you figured out, Dog."

"Nothing to figure."

"Teri looks good."

"I didn't hear that."

"Swing through Leshara."

"Booze?" Jon asked.

"Nobody says booze."

"I do." They laughed.

"Take the scenic route."

"Shit to do, shit to do. You're the one that keeps reminding me: manage, plan, execute."

"Oh what, a drop-off and a pick-up? Short agenda tonight, lots of time. You got it all worked out, don't ya?"

"Right, what could go wrong?"

"Little Princess woke up, gotta celebrate that, don't we? Let's go see where they pulled her out."

"Just beer."

"Beer works."

Jon bought a six-pack. The first can supped empty on gravel-road-*Seven*, and he tossed it in the box as he turned right at the T. The Dodge cruised east and over the Platte and another road-soda emptied into him. Near the Missouri, he turned, turned again, and this road ended.

Ahead, the river looked dark; it was getting late, the sun low behind him. Lemonade's extraction had rutted the shore and matted the grassy incline. He parked up and away. In the river, the onyx Little Devil stood alone. Water rushed around the boulder with a white rapid near to remind folks that Lemonade killed Baby Jesus.

Two empty rings made a good handle for the remaining four soldiers. Jon glanced at the mirror. "Two for you, two for me." A short walk down to the water, and he found a comfortable spot to drink early supper. "Zip," he said, opening a can. The river failed as before, its magic current relieved nothing but the beer flowed. "I like drinking with you."

Another top popped. "Zippy."

He saved the last two for the drive and, pulling in next to Black Magic, polished off the second. A few stars glimmered in the darkening blue-slate sky, and the light above the north door was on. Jon went in.

"Hey, get busy," Mark said. "Captain Corn's comin."

Bryce looked from behind a vat, then ducked back to grab his hard-hat and clipboard.

Jon passed the unlit hallway leading to the west door. Cones sat at the entrance and Malcolm's cart sat unattended behind them.

Whispers and nudging preceded Jon's unexpected approach.

Half in the bag, and bladder pressure on the rise, Jon hurried past Mark's crew. Mark put his hand to his helmet. "Mr. Rawling."

"Hi," Bryce said, looking important, both hands clutching a paperless clipboard.

Gene's crew scrambled for helmets, safety glasses, and shoved magazines under machinery. Sheila adjusted her neck brace.

No one knew better than the foremen – Jon hadn't been in. Gene missed the scramble and stood watching the clock tick seven-thirty. "Let's wrap it up, guys," Jon passed as he turned. "In twenty minutes," he added, seeing Rawling.

Jon gave him the stink-eye.

Next stop, Henry. Jon quietly closed on Henry's office; he heard Bernice.

". . . and no more snap decisions, Bozo." Bernice laughed at her wordplay.

"Sorry, it happened so fast."

"I'll meet you at the Quonset and we'll put your little mistake to rest. Let me do the thinking, okay?"

Henry nodded.

"See ya later."

Jon cut to the production floor bathroom. No food, only beer sloshed in his belly, and he wavered drunk at the urinal. His bladder emptied in a heavenly-long piss.

At the sink, he turned the hot water on, winked at Mr. R, and said, "Surprising these assholes is fun."

"The real fun's coming."

"Don't you know it?"

"Bout time to go get the toys?"

"One more stop. Let's see how Bill's doin."

Bill didn't hear the control room door open behind him, only its loud closing. Cords ran from the back of his monitor to the VHS player on the shelf below. It played *Beauty Shakedown.* He reached under the bench fumbling for the eject button, and in his haste, hit reverse. Jon placed his hands on Bill's shoulders and watched the action. Intercourse on the screen sped in reverse. A sumptuous cop in an unbuttoned blue PD shirt awkwardly humped. She dismounted her prisoner, magically removed handcuffs, and had her police mini-skirt back on by the time Bill found the elusive eject button.

"What ya watchin there, Billy Boy?" Jon said, kneading Bill's shoulders.

"Oowah," came out, but Bill had no answer. His head shaded to soft red. He bypassed the VCR and pulled up vat levels.

Jon patted him on the shoulder. "There ya go, Bill, keep up the good work."

Bernice, already in the office, sat at her desk.

"Good evening, Ladies."

"Mr. Rawling," she said. *Where the hell've you been?*

"Hello," Teri said. Teri thought the same and thought she smelled product when he passed, but was it on him or *in* him? They did work at an ethanol plant. The women noticed his shirt caught in his zipper. He wore no tie and his hair wedged up. A shoulder caught the door jamb as he entered his office.

Teri wanted to follow him in and ask about Leia. Were they able to see her; was there any change? The load-out numbers in her drawer were waiting, too. She looked at Bernice, and at Jon's closed door. *Now's not the time.*

"Mr. Rawling looks tired," Teri said. "Wonder if he was at the hospital?" *Hope Leia isn't worse.*

"Looks hammered to me," Bernice said. *Hope Leia's worse.*

Teri, lacking a rebuttal, said, "It's eight, if there isn't anything else, I'm heading out."

Employees streamed by the offices and were clotting in the hall near the time clock.

"Yeah, get out of here; I'm going, too."

Jon gathered the promotion toys from the lower shelf and placed them in a cardboard box. First, the semi-tanker, next, the pickup, and last the gas pump. Only the corn cob ashtray with a *Virginia Slim* butt remained.

With box in arm, he made way his back through the empty plant. The sound of an electric screwdriver droned above. Jon looked to the west wall and up. High above, Bobby stretched from the catwalk, power tool in hand. A screw fell, binging off a pipe and the side of Vat III.

"Hey," Jon called.

Bobby jerked, almost lost his balance, and recovered. From the high vantage point, Jon looked fine. "Oh, Boss. You scare me."

"You're still here?" Jon set his box of toys down and started climbing the ladder.

Bobby, leaning over the rail, watched him from vantage, and said, "Wanna get bad fan off my list."

"It's past eight," he said and coughed.

"Everyone so sweaty, wanna get this working, Boss."

Jon made the catwalk and stepped from the ladder. Here, above the hanging inside lights, it was darker than on the production floor. He leaned on the rail with one hand and clutched his shirt with the other. The coughing continued, but he straightened and staggered forth. Sweat did roll down his face. His guiding arm jerked straight and bent with each step as he clutched the rail, easing his way out. Bobby watched, fearing for his safety. "*Peligroso aqui.*"

Between coughs, Jon smiled as one about to say goodbye to everything. Bobby inventoried the sight in front of him, including the shirt sticking out of Jon's fly. He wondered how much he had had to drink, how he might help him down, and thought of the one day Jon had looked worse, three weeks ago when his boss lay dead in the corn.

"How's it goin, then?" Jon let go of the rail and rocked forward.

Bobby started for him, Jon caught his balance. Bobby paused. "Everyone's gone home . . . you think, maybe we go down?"

"Of course, everyone's gone home. I wanna see what you're doin up here."

Bobby, reluctant and with an eye on his boss, ran the fan on low in a short burst. "Put in a new motor . . . and a rheostat."

Until it stopped, the unit vibrated particularly loud where the shroud lacked its fallen screw. "It works both ways." Bobby ran the dial opposite and the fan pumped cool night air in. Jon positioned in front of it.

"You were a good man." The buffeting air chopped at his voice.

"Thanks, Boss." Bobby's English, fair, and the past tense made him uncomfortable. He secured a thin nylon rope behind the old motor's pulley and lowered it forty feet to the floor below. When it touched he let the rope drop. Jon's coughing, under control, and Bobby went before him on the ladder.

Jon descended, coughed, and pounded his chest. "Rest here a minute," Bobby said. He returned with a glass of water.

Jon knew it probably wouldn't help the affliction but thanked him for a needed drink. "I'll lock up, see you tomorrow, Mr. Fix-it."

Bobby recovered the junk motor, rope, and took his leave.

Jon placed the cardboard box in the truck and grabbed his chainsaw from the bed . . . and went back in.

Teri's mom answered the phone, "Hello."

"Is Teri home?" Rebecca asked.

"Not yet, she works late. How's Leia, any change?"

"She's awake and said 'Mom' today; we're bringing her home Saturday."

"Wonderful. I suppose you were calling to let Teri know, I'll be sure to tell her."

"What time *does* she get home, then?"

"Around now, nine, ten, usually."

"Thanks, goodnight." Rebecca hung up. Upstairs, she took two pills with a gulp of wine, got in bed, and closed her swollen eyes.

Chapter 33

T Minus One

Friday Morning, Rebecca served Jon breakfast. At seven-thirty she broke the silence. "I don't know what the hell is going on with you, anymore."

At seven-forty-five, Harrison dropped Ellen off at her apartment and proceeded to the hospital.

"I don't think you'll get much out of her, Buck, she isn't making much sense yet." The nurse escorted him to Leia's room. Ample makeup covered her bruised cheek, and with available eyes, she passed him her number. "In case you want to talk – about the patient." Harrison helped himself to the note and slipped into Leia's room.

He pulled up a chair, viewed the scabby face in the pillow, and initiated the gentle inquisition. "Ms. Rawling, Leia, I'm Detective Harrison, friends call me Buck."

A blink and she separated chapped lips.

Harrison gently turned her head. "I'd like to ask you a few questions." Again, she blinked; it seemed an affirmative.

"Leia, we found you in the river, in your car. Do you remember?" He waited.

"You were at *Core Fuels* with your friend, Teri. You remember, Teri?" Again, he waited. He took her hand, hoping for a physical response, and tried another basic question.

"Is Teri your friend?" It wasn't out of the realm of imagination. *She could be involved, even responsible.* Harrison possessed clues, and these clues codified his belief. *Suicide? – I don't think so, Leia hadn't hurt herself.*

– An accident, the more I think about it, the harder it is to imagine. – Bad actors – ding, ding, ding.

"Teri?" Leia said, shifting her lazy gaze, searching the room, or another dimension.

The nurse was right. Lucid, Leia was not. Harrison adjusted the bed, bringing her to a lounging position. From his jacket, he brought two small plastic bags containing the intimations, morsels of interest he'd gathered from her wet clothing the morning they brought her in.

From the first bag, he slid two bullets. "Leia . . . I found these bullets in your jeans." He held up the first, and read, "Mick."

She looked at it and Harrison believed he saw concern.

"Rest In Peace," he said, holding the second between finger and thumb. He waited, she seemed to be studying it. She said nothing but squinted. He gave her a minute to digest. The other small plastic bag contained kernels of corn. A few he'd found in the back pocket of the waterlogged, fancy jeans, and others, he'd retrieved from her lacy panties. Harrison's investigating had brought him to *Core's* corn piles, and he had walked around them more than once but found nothing.

He put the bullets down, shook the kernels from the bag, and held them for her to see. She looked at them and he watched her; she appeared to be filling up.

"It looks like you were in the corn . . . why were you in the corn, Leia?"

Her expression changed from concern to fear and she slowly whispered, "R a t s."

The nurse suddenly appeared at Harrison's side. "The Doctor's down the hall, making rounds, he'll be here in a minute, you should go – I don't want to get in trouble."

Harrison ignored her and continued to hold the corn in front of Leia.

"Buck," the nurse pleaded.

"Just a minute," he said, holding up a hand in angry rebuff.

She went to the door as his lookout.

"Leia, were you hiding in the corn?"

Her eyes shut tight and she turned her head as if to hide.

"He's in the next room," the nurse hissed and pointed.

"Leia, Leia." She didn't look and he tried to turn her head back to him. She held fast, burying her face away. He let her be and asked again, "Leia, were you hiding in the corn?"

"Work Boots," she said, in a fear-infused whisper.

"Buck," the nurse repeated. She tugged at his shoulder. He stood. She whisked him out the room and down the hall. The escort ended at her station, and she said, "They're kicking her out tomorrow."

Other nurses kept fewer numbers. Other nurses didn't call detectives. Other nurses liked to talk; few talked like this one. First, she'd contacted the detective, now she indecorously called another number.

The *Wahoo Daily* garnered stories from the wire, reported church bazaars, local sports, and printed the dwindling population's obituaries. Stories, good stories, were hard to come by. Not this year; embezzlement, tornados, and a hospital fire. Wonderful headlines and easy trailers filled the *Daily*. Was Leia's waking groundbreaking? A girl in the river, saved, unconscious for a week, coming to? It was something – icing on a reporter's three-layer cake. A few inches of column on the front page under a picture of the girl in her hospital bed and, on page six with a picture of her wrecked Ford, he'd finish the sentimentality.

". . . that's how you keep readership and bring in the advertisers. Would you help me? She should be sitting up. There. Could you help her look at the camera? No, stay, of course I want you in the picture," the reporter told the petite nurse. She angled a mite to shade her ghoulish bruise and smiled.

Bernice said, "After lunch, tell Malcolm to start cleaning in here, and to use the machine. I want it spotless, waxed, sparkling. After break, he can set up the riser and line up the chairs."

Bobby, sitting alone at the table, stopped chewing, looked up. "I haven't seen him today. Maybe sick?"

"He hasn't called." And with hands on her hips, she stood close, lording over him.

Bobby shrugged. "Don't know where he is."

"Well, you'll be *busy* this afternoon, then, won't you?"

He swallowed. "I've other things to do."

"Like what, look for a new job? Get someone to help, then, one of the girls, or that lazy shit, Bryce, he needs something to do. The owners will be here this year . . . Spotless!" In a partial arc, she swung her foot across the composite tile and stared. Bobby stared back for a couple of seconds, buckled, and agreed.

Teri watched Bernice join the lunch line; she returned to the office to grab her math and catch Jon.

The door was open, and she went in. "Hi."

"Teri."

"How's Leia?"

"She's awake, but still disorientated."

"Oh, wow, great!" Teri folded her hands and held them to her chest. "I went to see her last night, but didn't get in – got there too late. Would it be okay if I left at seven tonight, so I can visit?"

"No problem. You do have your presentation ready?"

She answered a nervous, "Yes."

"I brought you this." She slipped him a yellow note from her pocket.

Jon read silently, *eighteenth through the twenty-second, one-thousand fourteen gallons.* Teri watched him, then said, "Turn it over." Again, Jon read to himself, *H & B?*

Teri was leaving when he looked up.

The cafeteria transformed throughout the afternoon.

On the polished floor, rows and rows of chairs. The riser was in place. A lectern on it stood off-center next to a small table. The table held an overhead projector. Monica snapped the lens over the new bulb, and said, "Try it." Bernice flipped the switch. A trapezoidal shape glowed, lighting

Bobby's back and the wall behind. He pulled the screen down from its containing tube.

Monica adjusted the projector. Bobby knelt, nudged the tripod, squaring screen to light. The scarecrow, hay bales, and pumpkin decor sat to the right of the riser. Bryce set three tables end to end at the back of the room for caterers. Bernice perused preparations rather satisfied. She checked her watch. "Bobby, Jon wants to see you in his office."

Harrison had work boots on the brain. Rats, too. Rats – rat rats – or – people rats? It took him twenty minutes to walk the plant's perimeter, including another trip around the piles. A section of retaining wall had been removed from the west corn-crest and its white, plastic bikini top had been folded back. He watched Gilbert scoop a payloader bucket of corn from it. Harrison waved him down and, in highly maintained cowboy boots, cautiously crossed kernels strewn across the tar.

Gilbert spun the wheel and the yellow monster twisted in the center, then stopped. "*Now,* what's this son-of-a-bitch want?" Harrison approached, arms out for balance. Amused, Gilbert watched from his seat. He idled the beast down, opened the door, and secured it with a bungee.

Harrison climbed the payloader ladder and, standing on the second rung, eyed Gilbert's boots. Two more rungs and he stepped onto the perforated platform. Bent, and leaning in, he offered his hygienic hand.

"Hi," Harrison said over the running diesel.

"Detective Harrison, back again?" Gilbert said, pulling off an engineer's glove. Gilbert, not fond of work, disliked *Core,* and cops, too. He hated interruptions and shaking hands, he squeezed meanly. Harrison winced and disengaged.

"I just wanted to ask a quick question. With all this corn about, do you guys have any problem with rats?"

"Rats? I seen em, after dark more, hardly ever in the day, but once in a while. Smashed a couple with the bucket." Gilbert skipped his palms together indicating the smear, then grinned at his prowess.

"Wearin boots runnin the payloader, I see."

"Y e a h?" Gilbert said, slow and bewildered. "How's those spiffy shit-kickers you're wearin do when you gotta chase somebody down?"

"Detectives don't run much. We think, mostly, but if they went with the suit, I'd be wearing a pair of those, look comfortable. What kind ya got on, there?"

Gilbert wondered if Harrison thought he was being tricky; he lied to screw with him. Harrison made out partial footprints on the dirty pay-loader floor and ruled Gilbert a non-combatant.

Jon closed the door behind Bobby, went to his desk, sat, and opened a black vinyl folder. Bobby recognized the large company checks within and took the front-row seat.

"I've got some good news and some bad news, Bobby. What-da-ya want first?" And with quick scribbling strokes, he filled in blanks.

Bobby smiled, suppressing apprehension. He suddenly felt clammy. *A joke set up? A bonus? Not a bonus, not at Core.*

"Roberto, Bobby, I have to let you go. . . It's not you, more cutbacks. Orders – from the top, my bosses." Jon offered a white envelope. "This is a reference letter. Trade you for that ring of keys on your belt," he said, pulling the letter back and holding out a hand. Bobby unclipped the keys and gave them over in exchange.

"I think you'll find the letter glowing. I well covered your attributes." Jon folded the check at the perforation and tore it from the book. "The very good news, ten thousand, your severance."

Bobby looked to the check. *Ten thousand? – Fired? – They'll be out of commission in a week – a day.* The memo in the lower left, read, FOR *One good man.* He looked at Jon in disbelief. "I'm really fired?"

"That would be the bad news." Jon looked at the clock. It ticked to five. "Effective immediately." He held out his hand. "Good luck, Mr. Alvero."

Bobby carried a bag of personal items and his silver lunchbox, check enclosed. Only a little bitter, more miffed than angry, for he had never felt as wealthy. He walked the hall, chin up, to exit *Core Fuels* for the last time. At the door, he met Harrison. Bobby held it open for the entering detective that had visited him but a few weeks earlier.

"What kinda boots ya wear, Alvaro?" Harrison asked, pleasantly surprised he remembered the man's name.

Bobby looked at him a second, processing the question. *Good day to you, too.* He lifted a foot to look at the bottom. "I don't know?" Sole, thin, soft, worn smooth, and if the brand had ever been stamped or embossed it was visible no longer.

"Never mind," Harrison said. "Have a good weekend," and passed, leaving him balancing, backside holding open the glass door.

Harrison strode past the offices like he owned the place. Jon's door was closed and office folk scarcely noticed him. A loop took him through the plant's interior. He said little and took notes. Bernice, holding a roll of streamers, watched from the cafeteria doorway. Harrison's last stop, Jon's office.

"I'm going to get right to the nitty-gritty, Mr. Rawling. I have come to the mind that what happened to Leia was no accident."

"Same," Jon said.

"I know I already asked if anyone for any reason might have had motive. Anyone at the plant? I'm looking for a connection, someone working here that's linked to her past, that doesn't like her, or begrudges their boss . . ."

"Hates me?"

"You or *Core*."

"They're *all* disgruntled."

"Hmm, okay, wouldn't expect less."

Of course, he wouldn't – Feckless prick. Jon gave him a hard stare.

Harrison flinched, then continued, "Well, sometimes I tend to obsess on one idea, doesn't always work out the best. Let's expand possibilities. Other than at the plant, anyone else? Say, a past rift, new acquaintance?"

"She's been working at *Seed Genetics*. You asked around over there?"

"Ya, and I spoke to her supervisor. Your daughter's well-liked, no disputes he knew of."

"Teri – Ms. Thompson's her bud; if there're new acquaintances, she probably knows."

"Ms. Thompson gave me a history lesson. Romance stuff. Not much there in my opinion." Harrison contemplated his next question. "Did you know they had a run-in with your big fellow, Henry Rothness? At the theater, a while back?"

"No, what happened."

"Apparently, he wanted them to ride around with him after the movies, drinking. They didn't want to and he got a little grabby. Ms. Thompson said Leia kicked him . . . in the balls."

Jon smiled. "Hu-mm, doesn't sound like her, but okay. Rothness must be your prime suspect, then?"

"He was, but I've kind of ruled him out for a couple of reasons. I'm just asking, brought it up to see what you thought of the man."

"I knew he liked Ms. Thompson. A big mutt, thick, a little slow, but never seen him mad, certainly not violent. He was in my office, Monday. He didn't act funny, not so sure he'd be capable of acting."

"You've read *Of Mice and Men*?"

Jon, at the window, looked out, "Hard to tell how a man works, what's in his head." Mr. R gave him a look.

"Anyone else you can think of, Rawling?"

"We had a guest a couple of weekends ago. A forestry fellow. Met him in the woods, it started storming so I gave him a ride. He was at the house an hour or two, till the storm passed."

"And Leia was there?"

"She was. The wife seemed to think he liked Leia. Clive, Smivy, Smivmore, I think. He was working for the Church, sort of, inventorying wood on their property north of our place."

"Know where I could find him?"

"No clue. He said he was from Omaha, so if he's still in the area working, who knows? Maybe ask at St Mary's."

"One more question. Does Leia know anyone named Mick?"

"One of the owner's sons goes by Mick, Michael Peck."

"Oh, Michael Peck."

"What about him?"

"I don't know, just a name that came up in passing." Harrison moved to leave.

"Leia comes home tomorrow," Jon said. "She's coming around."

"I heard. I talked with Dr. Brochette, he's letting me see her this evening. If she's better, we'll have answers."

"She's getting better. I'm sure she'll remember, soon."

"Somebody's going down, I promise you that," Harrison said, going out the door.

Promises, promises – like Higgus? Jon thought.

"Could I use that phone of yours one last time?" Clive asked, his steps, heavy, mostly dragging on the Ranger's plank sidewalk.

The Ranger sat on the porch, watched him approach, and asked, "Last time?"

Clive stepped one foot up on the decking and presented a warm six-pack for admittance. "I'm packing it in tomorrow. Vacation's over. Time to move on, find some work," he lamented.

"Ya know where the phone is, knock yourself out."

"Thanks."

Clive dialed. As expected, the ringing continued, and he stood counting. Ten rings; he decided to wait for a few more. Fifty rings and he delicately placed the receiver in its cradle.

The Ranger heard no conversation, and, when Clive came out, he looked up at him sideways and conciliatory. "No luck?"

Clive shook his head.

"Better help me with these beverages, then."

"Aw, shit. Thanks, but I think I'm going to take a run into Wahoo."

A two-finger salute, starting from his eyebrow, and the Ranger said, "Good luck." Clive shuffled away and the Ranger shook his head, *pathetic.*

Clive drove past the old Rustad place, looking up at her apartment; light showed through thin, lacy curtains. He circled the block, parked, and crossed the street. Her car was nowhere in sight. Not seeing it gave him pause, but he went upstairs and knocked. Then knocked again, and, when she didn't answer, he searched one place for a key.

Indeed, and found it on top of the door sill. He rubbed it between his thumb and finger, then slid it into the lock . . . and paused . . . how he wanted to turn it. His better judgment won. He pulled it out, put it back, and returned to the Maverick.

He toured town and Yahoo's watering holes. *Murphy's,* with big windows, where happy people imbibed, joyfully celebrating the end of their workweek, *Blue Bar,* with dark windows and few cars out front, and *Cold Spot,* where Mark, Bryce, and others derided Core while hanging one on.

Not seeing her car, Clive went home to give up on love. In the RV, he struck a match and burned her number. He crawled into bed and filled his mind with anything but her.

Jon and Rebecca brought Leia's Saturday going-home clothes. They left them with the nurse who told them; Leia, with considerable help, had eaten. Rebecca clapped her hands and the Rawlings went to room 312. The bed, adjusted up, held Leia in a sit. She was free from monitors, wires, restraints, and tubes. Teri was with her and held her hand. She gave it over to Rebecca. Leia mumbled past them in her own world; a child's world of kittens, fishes, puffy clouds shaped like pirate ships, and her puppy, Skill.

"Every time I think I have her attention, she just goes into another one of those. It's all about nothing." Teri's caring smile faintly masked exasperation.

"Tomorrow we go home, don't we, sweetheart?" Rebecca said to Leia. She then turned her attention to Jon, mostly ignoring Teri. "She'll get better. She'll recognize home. We have a room all ready, don't we?" she said as if Teri was no longer inclusive. It was palpable.

Jon looked to Teri apologetically.

In a little girl voice, Leia said. "Mommy?"

Rebecca beamed and squeezed her hand. "Mommy's here, Sweetheart."

Jon moved close. "I'm here, too – Dad's here."

"Leia's eyes shifted to Jon. She studied her father and blinked slowly. She pointed and, in her childlike voice, made a proclamation.

"You're *crazy*."

The guilty truth exuded. Teri and Rebecca looked to Jon. They felt an unease as he tried to hide what Leia lay bare. He struggled to control the unmasking, and said, "Crazy… happy we're all together." His smile twitched and cracked of Otherjon. Leia withdrew her pointing hand, placed it over her eyes, and looked from between separated fingers.

Teri's level of discomfort peaked. She lied. "I have to go. Got a date. Goodnight." She left and Rebecca felt a small measure of jealous relief, hearing Teri claim a date.

"I'll be right back," Jon said, excusing himself for the lavatory. He dreaded the mirror in the bathroom and lingered in the hall. Harrison strode down the corridor and met him.

"Anything?" Harrison asked.

"Not yet. She thinks she's a kid, tonight."

"You guys take your time, I can wait."

Jon returned to Rebecca's side and listened as she spoke to Leia. Rebecca carried on, pretending her daughter's replies were pertinent.

After a few minutes, Jon said, "Detective Harrison is here to see her. The doctor said it's okay. I think we should go, let him ask his questions. I'll take you out for supper before we head out to the house. How's that sound?"

"I don't think he should be mixing her up any more than she is."

Harrison entered, and hearing her, said, "Don't worry, Mrs. Rawling, I'll take it slow and easy."

The Rawlings departed and Harrison, left alone, worked her over with volleys of questions. He interviewed in whispers, with pats on the hand. She looked at him dreamily. He shouted. She shrunk into the pillow. He said, "Rats." He said, "Workboots." He pinched her nose shut. "Who's drowning you Leia, who's DROWNING YOU?" He got nothing.

Jon walked Rebecca from the car to the house. She coaxed him to the couch and handed him the remote. "I'll make us some tea." Jon settled in but had "projects" on the brain. Rebecca returned with cups and sat close, shoulder touching his.

"Jon?"

"Yeah?"

"Can we get back to normal?"

He searched for words.

Rebecca tried to help. "Do you know how long it has been since you kissed me, like, really kissed me?" She waited.

"A couple of days."

"Weeks. Are you seeing someone? Have you fallen in love with someone else?"

"No," Jon declared, it sounded whiney. Instead of women, he thought of other adorations. *Onion Slayer – .357revolver – chain saw – people picks.* "I know I've been distant and busy. Tomorrow we bring our girl home and this work party'll be over. I promise, after tomorrow night, things'll be better, fixed."

He kissed her, and said, "But right now, I have to go out and get prizes finished up for the party. Go to bed. It shouldn't take too long. When I get back in, I'll come up and snuggle in with you."

Rebecca, placated, held him for another kiss. A softer kiss. A kiss searching for sincerity and the love she deserved; she pretended, then let him go.

In the boathouse, people picks lay on the leather wrap. The bench grinder whirled. *Zzzit zzzit.* Yellow and white sparks sprayed. Jon rotated metal tips on spinning stone, then cleaned the shafts on a wire-wheel opposite the stone. *How long since my tetanus shot?* he wondered. From the medicine cabinet, he returned with rubbing alcohol and dipped a pick.

With a tightly gripped antler handle in his right, he placed his left, fingers spread, on the bench. He stabbed between fingers. "Pick-a Pick-a Pick-a Pick." Slow at first . . . method and confidence established, accuracy proven; speed increased. He chanted, "Picka Picka Picka Pick." Faster, close, near the crook of his fingers he played. "PickaPickaPicka . . ."

The unlatched medicine cabinet door creaked open. Jon looked. Mr. R wasn't amused.

"Stop that!"

The descending strike glanced off wedding band and pierced webbing between fingers.

"Pop," Otherjon said.

"Ouch! Now, look what you made me do." Jon removed embedded steel and examined the puncture.

"Made you do, alright. We're out here to work and you're playing your little games." Jon enfolded the pics, rolled the wrap tight, then tied the pack with a thin leather strip. He pushed the small bundle aside to make room for more goodies, and after pouring alcohol on the wound, went to the medicine cabinet to close the door.

"Leave it," Otherjon said. "Best I keep an eye on you so you don't go and blow yourself up."

"If you're so concerned, why don't you come over and help?" He removed the door and set the mirror against the wall across from him on the bench.

On the span between them, he lined up contents from his box: Semi tanker-truck, one-twenty-fourth scale. Fifties-style pickup, one-thirty-second scale with gas pump. One full canister of black powder. Mechanical-over-digital alarm clock, from nightstand. Garden hose. One cymbal-playing toy monkey. Farmer matches. Wire. Tape. Glue.

They worked.

Jon looked at his watch. "It's Saturday." Reconfigured promo toys sat volatile on the bench between them.

"Fourth Quarter, Joker."

"Think they'll like their prizes?"

"I think they'll be excited."

"Hope so. Trying to be all-inclusive."

"No worries, Johnny Boy. Win lose or draw, it'll be a scream."

Chapter 34

Bring Her Home

Sunshine framed the curtain. Rebecca woke, back tight against Jon's chest. His arm held her and she reveled in the moment. Today they'd bring Leia home. Today would be a new beginning and she felt confident, with mom's nursing and familiar surroundings, Leia's recovery would be rapid and appreciable. She moved his hand to her breast and pressed her bottom to him. He woke, smelled her hair, and massaged her gently a minute before withdrawing.

"Let's go get our girl," he said.

It wasn't all she wanted. "Alright. I'll make breakfast if you wanna shower first." She hoped he would ask her to join him. He didn't.

In the bathroom, Mr. R said, "You goin gay on me, Joker? Not holding up your end of the marriage bargain very well."

"Mind your own business."

"You just don't wanna share?

"Stop."

"I'll share Teri."

"Shhh."

"We'll work it all out after tonight. Huh?"

"You're lecherous."

"Yeah?"

A hectic crew painted the hospital lobby. They worked behind a wall of plastic and rolled white latex over the smoke-scented enamel. Guests took turns at the bedraggled reception desk.

"We're here to pick up our daughter, Leia Rawling," Jon said.

The receptionist typed and checked her monitor. "If you want to take a seat and fill out the release form . . . They should be bringing her down in a few minutes."

Rebecca filled out papers. Jon watched obscure painters behind the wall of four-mil sheeting. Beyond the reception desk, the elevator doors opened, and a nurse rolled Leia out. A half step behind, an orderly carried flowers from her room, a vase in each hand. Leia wore pajamas they'd brought the night before and Rebecca's afghan lay folded across her lap. The Rawlings stood to meet the entourage.

Leia's ripe scabs protruded. Dark brown, dry, and thick, they striped her face, only skipping two sunken blue pools ringed by gray shores. The southern topography sat below her white wrapped crown, the polar cap. Her head looked the model of a distant planet – a battered celestial sphere, and in the southern hemisphere a hollowing sinkhole, as her mouth hung partially open in a gumpa. She gazed with minimal intent.

Folks in the lobby winced at the damaged mummy about to be unleashed, freed to their lands. Some stared, some tried not to. A child on her grandma's lap yelped and burrowed for protection.

"Leia's had a busy morning, haven't you, dear?" said the weekend nurse in baby-talk. She looked at the Rawlings, and then to the orderly for confirmation. The orderly nodded in agreement. "This morning, when no one was looking, she got out of bed. Wanted to go to the bathroom like a big girl, didn't you." The nurse patted Leia's shoulder.

The Rawlings welcomed the news; not the audience or lack of discretion. Rebecca suspiciously looked to the nurse. She knelt and took Leia's hand, put it to her cheek, and held it. A small gauze muffin, taped near the crux of her forearm, was new. Anger stirred in Rebecca and her energies surged, suspecting injected sedatives.

"Let's get you out of this nightmare of a hospital," Rebecca said to Leia, and then glared at the nurse. "Jon – get the car."

Jon surrendered the release papers to the receptionist, muttered a thank you, and went for the Impala.

Rebecca seized flower vases from the orderly. She placed them on Leia's lap and moved her daughter's hands around them. "Hold these," Rebecca said, and not in baby-talk. She decided it was about time for adult time. Spineless was getting old. Time to fight for Leia. Fight for her man. Fight for dignity. The nurse shuffled back as Rebecca, unapologetic, moved to the wheelchair handles. She had what they came for and asked for no more.

"Let's get you home." Rebecca pushed the wheelchair through the lobby, ignoring the audience. All watched, even the painters looked on best they could through hazy plastic. A moment's wait and the automatic door slid open. The wheelchair juddered over the threshold. A vase slid from Leia's lap, smashing on the walk in front of them. Rebecca circumnavigated to meet the arriving Chevy. Jon helped load Leia in the front and buckled her in.

Screw dignity. Rebecca leaned into a push and gave the chair a send-off. It crashed an entrance pillar, spun, and tipped to the bushes. She barked, "*Goddamn third-world institution!*"

Late Saturday morning, Clive folded lawn chairs and stowed them in the Maverick's trunk. It was time to go, time to pull the plug on a week of misery and stalking, whittling and walking. Tonight he'd be in Omaha, at home home, with the folks. He'd sleep in his old room, in his old bed. And with a little luck, Sunday, Mom would cook a real meal. Monday he'd call contractors, find work, mind-consuming work.

He hit the key. Broken Down cranked a slow revolution and stopped – solenoid clicking. He checked the dash, ejected his Barry Manilow cassette, and turned the radio off. Out with the jumper cables, and he stretched them from the idling Maverick. Ten minutes, and he tried the RV again. Broken Down started and he revved it a minute before moving the Maverick. Lined up behind the RV, Clive hitched the car to a tow-bar. At the ranger station, he let the camper run and went in to check out.

The Ranger sat behind the counter, tipped back in a chair, reading the paper. He lowered it and, landing the chair's front legs, looked at Clive. "Takin off?"

"It's time; vacation's over. What's the damages?"

The Ranger felt sorry for the unloved and rounded down. Clive paid.

"Thanks for staying, partner. If you're ever back in the area, come again. I'll have a cold brewski waitin with your name all over it."

They shook on it. "Thanks," Clive said but with a conviction to stay well clear of Two Rivers and Saunders County.

Clive went for the door and the Ranger back to his paper. "Hey," the Ranger said.

Clive turned. "Yeah?"

"That girl – wasn't a Rawling, was she?"

"Yeah . . ." he said, crossing the room to see what the Ranger was about. "Leia Rawling."

The Ranger turned the paper on the counter, presenting him the article. Clive adjusted it, looked at the Ranger. A whirl of excitement crossed his face and the Ranger wondered if Clive pudded himself.

Clive studied the grainy picture. Leia lay in a reclined hospital bed. A nurse stood next to her. Clive looked close. *Was it her? – Sure it was. – Had her head gone through a windshield? – A barbwire fence?*

He read.

Unconscious Woman From River Wakes!

Leia Rawling, 26, regained consciousness Thursday. Rawling, rescued from her car in the Missouri River, Sept. 22, arrived at the hospital unresponsive and had been in a coma for six days. Ms. Rawling woke Thursday evening to a jubilant staff and relieved parents. Rawling's harrowing hospital stay included a close call Monday night when fire broke out in the hospital's basement. *See – Patients scheduled to return from Lincoln, page 2.* Management at *Seed Genetics*, Rawling's employer, stated, they miss her and hope she will be able to return soon. Leia's nurse said, 'Rawling is in good spirits, on the mend, and anxious to go home.' *Continued on page 6.*

Clive flipped pages, stopping at the picture of Leia's battered Ford hanging from Jake's truck, and continued reading.

Rawling's car; recovered from the river after Rescue Unit carry Ms. Rawling to safety. 'It was kind of a miracle,' said Jared Koss, the rescue team captain, and went on to say, 'How she ended up way out there in the river, it's a real head-scratcher? That's one lucky girl.'

Saunders County Sheriff's Dept. is investigating the event. It's purported that Ms. Rawling has no recollection of the incident. Rawling has a clean driving record and weather didn't appear to be a factor in the accident.

"I gotta go."

"Git," said the Ranger.

The gas gauge read an eighth and seemed to drop each hill Broken Down climbed. He rumbled past Mead and its fuel station. A mile ahead, Rawling's damaged Impala closed on the intersection west of town.

"My dad used to work at the munitions factory," Jon said, pointing at Mead's second water tower, south of the village. He looked to Leia to see if the familiar axiom might register.

Rebecca said, "You remember Grandpa Ronald, Leia." Leia gave a slight nod as Jon turned north on Highway 77.

Clive, a half-mile east, missed it.

The Rawlings traveled north into the hills. Rebecca, in back, leaned forward. "I'll make us something tasty when we get home. Are you hungry, sweetheart?" The question hung. Leia clutched at the seatbelt across her chest and looked less groggy, but sat mute.

The RV chugged west toward Wahoo. The landscape leveled and Broken Down's flat front pushed air to beat sixty. Clive bopped the steering wheel and checked the gauge. In the RV's oil-burning blue haze, the Maverick trailed.

The Impala turned east onto the gravel. Leia looked at the freshly graded road and said, "Saturday."

Jon looked at Leia, at the road, and back to Leia. "Saturday. Yes, the grader comes on Saturday." Rebecca gripped Jon's shoulder.

Twelve-thirty, Clive pulled into Wahoo, camper running on fumes. At the hospital, he scored parking and went in.

"She was released about an hour ago," said the receptionist.

Clive slapped the counter.

Gauge on empty, he drove across town to the Rustad Apartments and parked the forty-foot train a block down on a side street. The sky had grayed and a warm dampness hung in the air. Clive, full of hope, walked up the block. *It's a great day to be alive.* Before crossing the street, he looked up at Leia's apartment window. The light was on and he was confident in what he saw; movement behind the curtains. *Finally.* He ran up the stairs and anxiously knocked. Again, with the waiting, *what if she's in bed, can't come to the door?* He listened. But who had he seen in the window? *A nurse – I could help her – I could nurse her.* Again with the knocking. *Come on.*

Who's not answering? He checked his breath and kidded himself it wasn't that bad. He listened and waited, fighting back 'loser.' Leia's key fell as he swiped the top of the doorsill, and how loud it jingled on the hardwood floor. Uncomfortable about going for it in the first place, sliding it into the lock elevated his consternation. *Not just a loser – soon a loser behind bars.* He turned the key, opened the door, and peeked.

"Sweet Jesus."

Tongues hung out of lace-less boots. They rotated slowly. Malcolm's milky orbs, fixed, and more gray than white, blankly scanned him as the body turned. The laces, taut and thin, almost disappeared directly under the light. Malcolm levitated a foot above the floor. A chair lay overturned.

Clive shut the door. Clive opened the door. Clive took a deep breath – and went in.

Malcolm scanned him again, rotating the other direction, and followed as Clive circled around to Leia's table. A long-stemmed rose lay diagonal across Malcolm's note. He moved the rose, read the note, and remembered the newspaper article. The phone book lay on the counter below the phone. He looked up the number and called the Sheriff.

"Saunders' County Sheriff's Department," Ellen answered.

"I'm calling to report . . . a death," said Clive.

"Can I get your name?"

"Clive Smivmore."

"The name of the deceased and the address?"

"I think the man's name is Malcolm, it's at the Rustad Apartments in Wahoo, on Elm."

"Oh, in town, I'll transfer you to the Wahoo Police Department . . ."

"Wait . . . I'm at Leia Rawling's apartment. The newspaper article said the Sheriff's Department was investigating her accident."

"Hold on a second, I'm going to let you talk to Detective Harrison." – "Buck, line two." Harrison told Clive to wait outside Leia's door.

Leia walked from the car to the house with her parents' help. They held and guided her up steps and onto the porch.

"Good Job, sweetheart," Rebecca said. "Let's have lunch out here, shall we?"

Low clouds shrouded the sun, but an appealing stillness and warmth filled the river valley. Jon adjusted Leia's chair so she could look at the water. From here, the bank blocked their shoreline view, but they could see the end of the dock and storm-tattered tarp, feebly protecting *Baby*

Cakes. The river looked mellow-gray and pleasing. Leia sat in blue flannel pajamas and gazed at the water.

"Remember how Skill used to bring fishes up and drop them right here on the porch?" Jon said. Leia's eyes brightened, hinted a smile.

"Floppin around, hardly a scratch on em," he continued. Leia gave a slight nod and looked clearer. She focused on the river, then looked at Jon as if waking, really waking, for the first time in over a week.

Her consciousness, starting from her youth, began rushing in. Eight years old, running with Skill, rolling, and fish-breath dog licks. Nine, the sting of the teacher's ruler across her knuckles. Ten, sitting on the dock, feet splashing water . . .

"Turkey sandwiches and apple sauce," Rebecca said, setting a tray on the table. Leia's memory disengaged, slipping into neutral. Rebecca draped the afghan over Leia's shoulders. "What would you like to drink?" she asked Jon.

"A beer." Rebecca gave him a look.

"I don't have to be in for a while, yet."

The good wife delivered.

Jon placed Leia's spoon in her hand and Rebecca moved her apple sauce close.

With slightly improved dexterity, Leia ate. Rebecca led Jon in conversation, recollecting all things Leia.

After lunch, Rebecca said, "Let's go in and I'll show you your new downstairs room. It's all ready for you. You can take a little nap while I tidy up, eh?"

Inside, Jon helped himself to another beverage from the fridge, and said, "I'm going up to get ready."

Rebecca helped Leia use the downstairs bathroom, then brought her to the den converted to bedroom, and tucked her in.

Upstairs, Jon shaved and dressed in a comfortable black suit. He returned to the bathroom and brushed his hair, then sucked beer with one eye on the mirror. Otherjon congratulated him on his appearance.

"Back in black. Perfect. Forget Joker, Joker. Tonight, you're – Undertaker."

"Good times at hand . . ." Jon smirked.

"Can't wait. Shits, shitting themselves."

Jon winked.

He met Rebecca in the kitchen. She adjusted his tie. "You're so handsome. Good luck, have fun at your party. Better peek in and say goodbye to Leia before you go."

Leia lay awake. Jon turned the desk chair and sat.

"See you later, Sweetheart. I've gotta go in to work, help Bernice set up. It's *Core's* company party tonight." Leia's eyes narrowed.

"Miss Piggy hits."

"What?"

Leia clutched the blanket over her tummy.

Jon thought . . . Then asked, "Did Bernice hit you, hit you at the plant?"

"Miss Piggy hits," Leia said louder, kneading the blanket.

Jon paused. "Why?"

Bernice's long red fingernails – the grab in the hallway, swiping down her back, flashed in Leia's mind. She twisted in bed.

"Was anyone else there?"

Leia's mind filled with Henry's footfalls, scrunching up the plastic-covered corn pile.

Immersed in the past, she stared at the wall, then shimmied down, pulled the blanket over her head, and said, "Shhhh, Work Boots."

"It's okay, Dad's here." Jon sidled close to his covered daughter and quietly asked, "Who wears work boots?"

The blanket shook where she gripped and Leia answered in a whispering rumble. "Henry, Old Henry."

Jon helped lower the cover. "Shh, shh, shh, it's okay. You're safe, safe at home with Mom and Dad."

Leia calmed as memories rotated out of queue.

"What's going on in here?" Rebecca said, looking in.

"She just had a bad dream. She's fine," Jon patted Leia's hand, "Aren't you – getting better."

Rebecca shimmied close and adjusted Leia's blankets.

Chapter 35
Stinky

O'Leary raked leaves in his backyard. His wife called him to the phone.

He met Harrison at the apartments. Clive sat at the top of the steps and stood as the men came up. He looked pale and greeted them with a single word, "Suicide."

They wanted to read Clive and brought him in with them. Malcolm and the smell of death hung in the room.

Harrison and O'Leary stood back, studying morbid.

Harrison said, "That's what I call, pulling yourself up by the bootstraps."

Not even his stern elder could help but smile.

O'Leary wiped the quip off his face, looked at Clive, and asked, "You didn't touch anything, did you?"

"Just the note, I read the note."

"Where did you call from?" Harrison asked.

'Oh, yeah, and the phone . . . and phonebook," he added.

Harrison shook his head.

O'Leary circled Malcolm, examining the slowly turning deceased. He prodded open pockets with his pen. Without looking at Clive, he asked, "Was the door unlocked?"

Harrison stared at Clive, waiting on an answer.

"The key was above the door. I just wanted to make sure she was okay."

"Stand over there," O'Leary said, using pen to point out the corner.

"She just got out of the hospital," Clive said.

"Her parents took her to stay with them," Harrison said.

"I figured that out, now, you think I could go?"

"No," Harrison and O'Leary said in unison. "Clive Touch-Everything Smivmore," Harrison added.

Harrison leaned over the table, and for O'Leary to hear, read aloud.

My Dearest Leia,

After I put you in the river I went to the bridge to jump, but I was weak. Fate decided it wasn't your time. Stupid fate. I should have joined you in your little car. Together now we would be.

You were kind but couldn't choose me in this world. Our minds and souls a match, but I understand, it's this unfortunate body you rejected. I now jettison the shell. Our bodies are nothing. Love endures beyond this world. Choose me in the next.

My soul waits you in the ether.
My soul waits its mate.
Find brave Titan hither.
Only you, My Love, I wait.

Malcolm

"What a chicken-shit pussy," Harrison said.

O'Leary shook his head. "Call the coroner."

"Ellen's already got the Meat Wagon comin." He picked up the faded rose, looked at Clive, and smelled it.

Clive cringed.

Harrison bushed the flower under a picture on the fridge, Leia and Teri, smiling at them in Polaroid. "Not so cute now. All scratched up. Nasty, doesn't even know . . ."

"That's enough," O'Leary said.

"So, who are you, Smivmore?" Harrison asked. "Let me guess, you're in love with Ms. Rawling. Not on the verge of slitting your wrists or anything? Cause, we need ya-ta come down to the station and give a statement, first."

"We *will* need a statement," O'Leary said.

Harrison took pictures. O'Leary radioed Ellen. They'd had dibs; it was time to let the police have fun. They could tape the place off, take Smelly down.

Rebecca cleaned the kitchen and prepped for a little project of her own. The smell of home and familiar tinkering sounds soothed Leia into a deep sleep.

Jon drove to the plant. Beside himself, his vehemence, and vehement other, frothed anew. He drove through Core's parking lot with gilded thoughts of Bernice and Henry's demise. Two big Shits with short futures. Managers manage, plan, execute. He drove past the corn piles and around the west end of the plant with thoughts of the owners, burning in hell. He drove past the fueling dock, then around to the north side, and parked between the north door and Black Magic.

Otherjon reached up and adjusted the mirror; Jon looked back, confused.

"I got this," said Otherjon. "There's two Jokers in every deck." Otherjon winked.

Jon, trapped, puzzled, and from the mirror, called out, "Wait, I thought I . . ."

"Come on, watch my back," Otherjon said, getting out. He leaned the box of mischief on the Impala's roof, waited a second, and slammed the door.

"Nice of you to let me tag along," Jon said. They went in as one.

Hours later, an exemplary titanic of femininity entered the cafeteria. Bernice said, "You're already here?"

Bernice's ensemble included: black slacks, black pumps, and a white with pink floral, spaghetti-strap blouse cut wide and deep. Fastened to her top, a novel gold broach celebrated her bosom. Pink polish on long fingernails matched the floral top. Gold earrings caught fluorescent light. She'd been to town; her hair was perfect.

"My, don't you look lovely?" Otherjon said. Jon had never touched Bernice. Otherjon put his arm around her waist, escorted her in, and asked, "Would you like to help me set up the punch bowl?" Bernice soared with the compliment; her last had faded from memory. Even his hand on her lower back thrilled. And he was there to help. She smiled. *I'm still killing your daughter.*

In its original box, Otherjon retrieved the punch bowl from the cafeteria kitchenette and delivered it to a cloth-covered card table at the back of the room. Bernice carried sheaves of small, clear cups and napkins. On a near table, his toy box, devoid toys, contained bottles of fruit juice, which he removed. He started pouring, and said, "Soda's in the fridge, mind grabbing some?"

"Coming right up."

Otherjon hoisted a fifth of Vodka from the box, cracked the seal, and spun the cap. He watched Bernice on her merry way and chugged. 'Glug-glug-glug-glug.'

Jon interjected . . .

Hush, hush you little lush
Here's your booze, down it in a rush
Stumble about, victim choose
Shame they have but one life to lose

Bernice, returning, watched the last of the bottle drain into the bowl.

"Loosen folks up a bit," Otherjon said.

"It's officially a party now." Bernice added the 7-Up. "Something to sustain them through your presentation."

They touched cups – sampled the nectar.

"Ok, Clive, lay it on me," Harrison said.

Clive sat across from Harrison at the Sheriff's station and recounted an abbreviated, less pathetic, version of his last two weeks.

". . . and something didn't feel right. I just had to go in." Clive's knees bounced impatiently; his chair squeaked. He wanted out. Things to do – and he'd rather not have to find her parent's place in the dark.

"Yeah, you're quite the hero, Smivmore. No, really, glad you went in, couple more days, *whew-wuh*. Would have been a real stinker." Harrison jotted fact and fiction, wished Clive the best, and released him on his own recognizance. Ellen and O'Leary got the gist, and rooting for love, bid him well.

"Bring your cup, Ellen," O'Leary said, passing with a bottle on his way to Harrison's desk. Into dirty coffee cups went double shots.

"Here's to wrapping something up," O'Leary toasted, "but let's wait on the coroner's report before you put it to print."

Harrison toasted, knowing full well what was on O'Leary's mind. The locked door was bothersome. Harrison wasn't fond of the typed note, either. Malcolm signed it, they checked his driver's license – did the signature really look like a match? And something else, those damned little boots. He sipped a shot from his Saunders County coffee cup. *Screw it – it's a wrap.*

Ellen poured the men another round. She abstained; on duty till eight.

"Who's calling the Rawlings?" Harrison asked. "It'll be all over the news in the morning."

"I suppose someone should really go out there and tell them," O'Leary said. He didn't look to Harrison; he knew who should do it.

"Yeah," Harrison said and, stalling, took a drink. *Jon's your old football buddy.*

"Shit, I'll just call out there," O'Leary said.

"Let your fingers do the walking." Ellen handed him the phone book.

Rebecca took the news and told O'Leary, "Leia's asleep and Jon's left for a party." She paused. "I can't say good riddance, feel sorry for the man more than anything. What was his name, again?"

"Malcolm Johnson, and Mrs. Rawling . . ."

"Yeah?"

"Your daughter's apartment will be off-limits for a few days, understand?"

"Yes, Sheriff, thanks for letting us know." She hung up.

"See you guys Monday," O'Leary said, and he was out, heading home.

Harrison asked Ellen, "We still on for tonight." He looked around the empty station and thought about doing her on a desk but phones ring and death clings. After hanging out with Malcolm, he presumed he wasn't the freshest daisy.

"If you still feel like it?" Ellen said.

"I feel like it."

"Me too, I'll call when I get home," she said.

CHAPTER 36

Social Hour

***Core Fuels'* lot** filled sporadically with employee cars. More exhibited damage than not. Some pulled in next to the vehicle responsible and some looked destined, sooner than later, for Buster's crusher.

In the cafeteria, Nancy and Deb sat on straw bales in front of the scarecrow.

"Smile," Gene said. 'Click,' and took their picture.

Bryce shadowed Monica to the punchbowl. "A little to your right," he said.

Shielded from the growing crowd, he smuggled a jug of product into the mix. Then rewarded his accomplice with the first taste.

Eyes wide, Monica said, "Mmm, punch with a punch."

Teri's speakers spewed stress-relieving soft rock. She parked the blue Camaro and hurried in. A little late, she had vacillated on hair up or down, how high the heels, and only confidently chose the new, blue Penney's outfit. The mundane presentation lay on her desk, and nervous, she practiced in the low-lit offices. She went to the lady's room, pulled stick from bun, and brushed her hair. She touched up lashes and softened overdone blue eye shadow.

Sherbt, Larry, and Mick caravanned in at quarter to seven. A setting sun and thick cloud cover tripped unneeded parking lot lights and the glow reflected off the consortium's waxed vehicles.

Larry's Grand Wagoneer carried five. He parked two slots right of the sidewalk, leaving the closest for the Bentley.

Larry slid the keys above the visor and asked, "What the hell are we doin here? Show of hands – who's excited to mingle with peasants?" Larry looked to Lon, then in the mirror, and surveyed the three seated behind him. "That's what I thought."

"Won't hurt ya to rub elbows with the working class one evening, will it?" Lon said.

"Won't be much mingling, social hour's about over," said an owner in back.

"Thank God for that," Larry said.

Sherbt's lawyer pulled just past the visitor's top parking spot and backed the Bentley in. Sherbt rode in the back.

Michael obliged himself and Corvette to *Core's* empty manager's spot. Mick's baked cousin toked a last toke, squeezed the roach, and asked, "Think they'll have a bar?" Mick shrugged and snorted a short, pre-packed straw of coke.

As a group, they went in. The entry and hall were well-lit, and next to the timeclock, the sign read, '61 days – No Accidents.'

Farther down the hall, Mick stopped to admire the expansive production floor, the machines in Milling, the web of pipes and shoots, and past, to the great vats in Fermentation. He wanted it, all of it.

Convivial Otherjon greeted folks as they entered the cafeteria. "Long time, no see, Sherbt." Through rhinestone shades, Sherbt briefly acknowledged Rawling and limply proffered a hand. He said nothing, then nodded at the flanking lawyer to care for an unnecessary cane.

"Here's a rising star," Otherjon said. He started a handshake from right field and clasped it firmly into Michael's hand. They shook on it.

"Holy shit, look at this place," Lon said.

"Looks like ya blew the budget tonight, Jon," said Larry.

"But you're worth it, Larry." Otherjon cranked his hand.

Under streamers, balloons, and on polished tile stood the consortium. Their entrance didn't go unnoticed. Curious employees gawked at eight men in tailored suits. In the center stood the ninth, Sherbt, wearing a lavender, brushed-velvet jacket and white dress pants.

"Look at that freak. Ya ever seen anything like it?" Barry asked.

"Only on that Lawrence Welk Show," Henry said.

"Ha, ha, yeah, he needs a trumpet," Josh added.

"Go ahead, laugh it up, you crackers," said Terrance. "He owns us."

Larry gave Lon's boy orders. "Get me something to drink, would ya, Kid." Mick glared at him. Lon tipped his head and using half his face, smiled, urging Michael's compliance.

Partygoers reveled in punch ladled from the clear, plastic cauldron. Bryce, chief connoisseur, served and argued convincingly a few cups quenched better than one. Bernice relieved him when the spilling started.

A line formed. "Seconds, Bill? And aren't you all spiffed up?" Bernice said, looking at his shiny top. Bill touched buffed scalp and stroked the tuft of hair above his ear.

From behind, Mark pretended to huff and polish Bill's dome with his sleeve. Bill took a sip. Mark put shorty in a joyous, one-arm headlock and reached for a refill with the other. "Come on, Bill," he said, taking Bill in his pit. Bill held his drink out front and, with one foot in a boot-cast, shambled. They tottered into the crowd.

Henry presented an empty cup. "Seven-thirty," Bernice said, filling it.

He leaned for a napkin and whispered, "What if they're still talking?"

"Pretend you have to use the restroom. Sit over there," she said, eyeing the back row.

Teri found the boss. "I'm a little nervous."

"You'll do great, flash that sexy smile and give em the good news," Otherjon said.

Barry asked for it and Sheila handed him her neck brace. "Go ahead, give it a try, chicken neck." She helped velcro it tight, then let her hand slide down his back, fingers mischievously catching a moment in his back pocket.

Gilbert noticed and jealously intervened. "For size, you should try me."

Sheila touched the back of his arm and twinkled, "It might be too tight for you."

Bryce slipped Mick's cousin a twenty. Mick's cousin slipped Bryce a baggie.

"Things must be going better," Nancy said. "We've never had a party like this."

"Quite the shindig," Mark agreed.

"Maybe they'll finally announce some raises," said Deb.

"Ha, ha, ha, and ha. With Kernel Klink running the stalag? No chance," Bryce said. It came out drunk-loud and turned heads.

"Maybe," Deb repeated.

Mark shrugged.

Monica sat on the edge of the riser, cackling at Teri. Teri pretended to listen and checked the order of plastic sheets she'd soon use on the projector.

Gene took pictures. 'Click . . . Click, click.' An arm around the scarecrow developed into a thing. Looping a lei of twisted orange and brown streamers, another. 'Click – click.'

Bernice left the punchbowl to run itself. At the podium she turned on the mic, tapped, and said, "We'll be starting in a few minutes."

Hint taken, some hit the bathrooms. Others filled their cups.

"Shall we," Lon said, moving to the reserved front row. Sherbt's lawyer passed and, with his briefcase, sat next to the other presenters, Teri and Bernice.

"I abhor these piss-ants," Larry said.

"You'll abhor them less when they start signing up for shares," Lon said.

"I'm still not convinced. The thing about shares is it has the word share in it."

"The thing about old money like yours, Larry, is the pile is so freaking big it grows by itself. I think you've forgot how to make money. Have a little faith; Sherbt knows what he's doin."

Sherbt's lawyer whispered, "Ya got that right."

Everyone settled in. Rawling adjusted the mic, tightened the stand, and looked them over. What a nice crowd, flush faces, rosy cheeks, malleable minds. Andy and Darryl – the Anderson brothers, down through the alphabet, to William Wiener – control room Bill. The icing, a healthy slice of the consortium, including Sherbt. He watched the lawyer next to Teri adjust metal frame glasses, *who doesn't like roast lawyer*?

"Welcome to our little party. Glad everyone could make it. Before we get into it, special thanks to Bernice for all her help getting this together." He clapped, stepped from behind the lectern, and indicated for Bernice to stand. Teri encouraged her. An inebriated applause rose from the audience. Bernice stood, soaking it in, and for a moment, truly looked amiable.

Chapter 37
What's Shakin?

Otherjon viewed the full cafeteria of faces. And started . . .

"Three *Core Fuel* employees walked into a bar . . . In back, they see a scarecrow sittin at a table havin a drink."

Rawling looked from his audience to the scarecrow, back to them, and continued, "The bartender says, 'What can I get ya?'

The first *Core* employee asks, 'What's that scarecrow back there, drinkin?'

'Corn whiskey,' says the bartender.

'Well, we work at a plant that makes corn whiskey, but they don't let us touch the stuff. Give me a shot,' he says. So the bartender pours him one, and the guy tips it back and downs it in one gulp. He gets this look of horror on his face and starts screaming and clawing at his throat and runs out into the street, and gets hit by a truck. The other two employees look at the bartender and the bartender says, 'He drank it too fast, some whiskey's for shootin and some whiskey's for sipping.'

'Ooohh,' together, says the other two *Core* employees.

So the bartender asks the next employee what she'd like to drink, and she says, 'I don't know if I should, but, I too, would really like to try some corn whisky, sees how we make corn whisky and never ever has a drop touched my lips.'

The bartender pours her a shot, and says, 'Careful *now*.' And she sips on it and sips on it and tells the other employee how tasty whiskey made from corn is. Then she drops the glass and doubles over holding her gut, stumbles out into the street, and gets hit by a bus.

'*Whoa*, gosh darn it,' says the last *Core Fuels* employee. 'No corn whiskey for me.'

The bartender shrugs and the scarecrow yells from the back, 'Bartender, two more corn whiskeys.'

The *Core* employee can't believe it, but he watches the bartender fill two more glasses for the scarecrow and the bartender says, 'He always gets two at a time. One for sippin, one fer shootin.'

Now, he figures he *has* to meet this corn-whiskey-drinkin scarecrow, so he follows the bartender back to the scarecrow's table and he says to the scarecrow, 'Two of my mates just drank that stuff, and now they're goners.'

The scarecrow lifts his glass, and says, 'Here's to your poor unseasoned mates, then. *La fermente' fatale,*' and takes a good sip off the top.

'But, how do ya do it? How do ya drink the stuff?'

And he says, 'Well, first, nobody with any brains would ever drink straight corn-whiskey, know what I mean?' And the scarecrow lifts his tattered hat, showing off his straw noggin.

'But you sure seem to like it,' says the employee.

'I acquired a taste for it when I worked at *Core Fuels*.' he says, taking another sip.

'You worked at *Core Fuels*, that's where we . . . I work.'

'So I heard,' says the scarecrow, and he sips the last of his first shot, and says, 'See, I learned to drink from Stillman.'

'Stillman? I don't know Stillman.'

'Well, he's incognito, but you can bet your timecards, he's still there,' says the scarecrow and he picks up his second shot and downs it in a hot gulp.

'Geez! I'd sure like to drink like you, Scarecrow,' says the guy.

'I'm tellin ya, if you wanna drink corn whiskey, you gotta. Find. Stillman . . .'"

Rawling's short story fell dumb on the front row. A pall settled over the rest.

Mark looked to Gene; they quickly broke eye contact. Glances shifted about. Henry stared straight ahead. Girls fidgeted. Gray folding chairs squeaked under twitchy asses.

They waited for the shoe to drop . . . Rawling stood fast, and they waited . . .

Bryce exhaled sharply – a nose laugh. Inhaled, then a real laugh, "ha . . . ha . . . ha, ha, HA." It rippled across the forlorn. Eyes shifted and more chairs squeaked as every person adjusted to see, who? "Ha . . . ha, Ha Ha ha HA Ha," mouth wide, it rolled out of Bryce, and again, "Hahaha, wahhaa wahh HA ha ha HA," laughter blast forth.

The realization filtered through the crowd – the Kernel knew, probably always knew, about Stillman. Then Gene, "ha, ha . . .Haha, ha." And Mark, and Sheila, and Terrance, all started, "Ha, ha, wahha, ha." They laughed, and pushed, and slapped knees. Bill joined, and Deb, and Josh, everyone, and finally Henry. Through the empty plant, levity echoed. The cafeteria erupted joy, a ruckus of roaring laughter, heads bobbing in a pond of mirth.

Otherjon smiled and left the stage for Bernice.

"Insane asylum," Larry said to no one.

Rawling sat in Bernice's empty chair and Teri gave him a curious look.

Hard hats and steel-toe footwear; Bernice talked safety.

Clive's five-block lift to the station had been in O'Leary's Bronco. He hoofed it back to the RV and drove downtown.

They were rolling up the streets in Wahoo. Clive parked Broken Down parallel across seven slots in front of the flower shop. *The dead guy's more romantic than me.*

"I'm closing," said the shop owner."

"This is an emergency. You'd stay for a good sale?"

"Hot date?"

"Two weeks in the making."

"Roses are in the cooler."

"Can't do roses," Clive said. *Dead guys give roses.* "I need something *huge*."

The owner looked on as Clive's eyes fixed to a bountiful arrangement on a glass shelf above the long stems. "This one," Clive said. A sequins-covered cross with a gold and white banner protruding from its center. It read – *Uncle.*

"I just put that together, it's for a funeral on Monday."

"But you could make another?"

The owner shrugged. "Thirty bucks."

Clive gave him cash and *Uncle* on a cross.

With a watchful ear, Rebecca canned carrots in the kitchen.

Leia stretched out and slept comfortably. Her healing face buffed the pillow and a few scabs worked free. She dreamed less comfortably . . .

She drove.

Jake sat on the fender with legs positioned in the engine bay and adjusted what she believed might be Lemonade's carburetor. The detached hood lay on the blacktop a half-mile back. They were lucky to have Jake. His tuning kept them ahead of Henry's tank.

"Faster," Teri urged.

"It's floored," she said and looked at her feet. Might they be the problem? Ruby-red slippers without heels ran the pedals. She decided she liked them, anyway.

Teri rolled the window down and yelled, "Faster, Jake," then looked over her shoulder and yelled again, "They're gaining on us."

Situated in the lower front hatch, decomposing Grandpa Ronald controlled the olive green war machine. He wore a leather helmet and goggles and laughed as he guided the tank over Lemonade's discarded hood.

"That's my scary grandpa," Leia said.

"The strange one," Teri said, and yelled at Jake, "Faster!"

Jake used an orange shop rag on his brow and kicked the engine.

Henry stood behind the turret and yelled something at the driver.

Grandpa Ronald disappeared into the tank, reemerged with a large shell, and hoisted it to Henry.

Block lettering on the shell appeared backward in Leia's mirror, she deciphered it. Made in Mead.

The car slowed, Jake asked, "Leia, did you remember to fill it up?"

Leia looked at the gauge – needle on E.

Henry loaded the shell into the breach.

"Look out!" Teri shouted.

"Noooo," Leia said. Lemonade rolled to a stop.

The girls crouched, looked over the back of the front seat. Henry fired. The muzzle flashed and a report sounded but nothing more – no explosion. They looked around – Jake was gone.

The tank passed and pulled tight, sideways in front of Lemonade. Henry swung from the turret, launched, and landed one foot on each fender, boots denting Detroit tin with a bang.

"I've got beer in the tank, girls. Wanna play?"

"Run for it!" she said. Teri agreed.

Leia exited quickly. Henry, quicker, grabbed her and lifted.

She faced the tank and pleaded, "Help, Grandpa."

Ronald Rawling slinked into the tank; a bony hand reached up and slammed the hatch cover.

Henry threw Leia. She rolled on the blacktop and stopped against the tank's track. There, she lay crippled, deaf and dumb.

Henry had Teri – she shook. A hopeless look crossed her face.

"Leia," she said.

Tight to her scalp, Henry grabbed the hair on the back of her head and effortlessly operated Teri, the Pez dispenser. Teri's mouth strained open, but her neck did the separating.

Leia woke and, shaking, pulled back covers – a moment of disorientation passed. She sat on the edge of the bed. Raindrops covered the dark window. Light from the kitchen filtered down the hall and into the room.

A desk, antique and tall, sat against the wall across from her. She looked at it, and she knew it. She stood, went, and opened it. The folded writing portion rested at a slight angle. Gently, she passed her hand on it and felt pinholes. Small marks, where, once upon a time, rubber bands strung on pins had rebounded marbles. Marbles propelled by ink pens used as flippers. She remembered the provisional pinball machine she and Teri made and played as adolescents. Yes, she knew it, and other things. An art book, pastels in a coop, and the economy blue stapler from school.

And more. English class with Mrs. Ward. Failing on monkey bars. Her shiny-new bike left in the drive, deformed under pickup's rear tire. Teri and her holding hands, trying to skate backward.

And on the bed, the quilt, Grandma's graduation gift, sent from Winnipeg. She thought of Teri's mom, handing her the Penney's bag. Artisan bullets. The sound of Henry's stick cracking on the wall, his boots scrunching up the pile. Bernice, punching her in the gut. A smoky hospital room. The dream.

"Mom?" Leia called.

In an instant, Rebecca appeared and took her by the shoulders.

"You're up," Rebecca said, looking at her fully conscious Leia.

"What day is it?"

"Saturday, it's Saturday," she said, hugging her.

"Where's Teri?"

"She's probably at the plant, with your Dad. It's their company party tonight."

"She's okay?"

"I'm sure she is," Rebecca said, then held her away again. "And look at you, up and with it! How are you feeling? Do you want a glass of water? Wait till Dad sees."

Leia, trying to rewind her dream, put a hand over closed eyes, and tipped her head. "I dreamt this guy from the plant killed Teri." Her memory filled with missing pieces. "Mom, people at Dad's plant hurt me, tried to kill me, I think. Henry, and the fat lady, I think her name's Bernice."

This conflicting story struck Rebecca as dubious. Little doubt O'Leary's facts were anything but. He wouldn't close a case on a hunch.

"And Malcolm? He tried to hurt you?" Rebecca asked.

"Malcolm? No, Henry."

"The Sheriff called while you were sleeping. He said it was Malcolm Johnson that tried to hurt you."

'No, I graduated with Malcolm, he's nice."

Rebecca bit her lip and helped her dress.

They went to the kitchen and Leia explained what she could.

Caterers filed in. They set roasters of baked beans and pulled pork on the tables in back. They carried boxes of fresh buns, trays of cake, and plugged the roasters' short, black cords into orange extensions. Last, they rolled in a cart, and on it, ice chests brimming soda and beer. Mouthwatering savors wafted through the cafeteria.

". . . and if you hadn't noticed, sixty-one days, no accidents," said Bernice. All eyes found Jon. "We're closing in on the record, just a couple more weeks. Thanks, and stay safe."

Bernice stepped down.

Otherjon skipped onto the riser and pulled the mic, "Great, thank you, Bernice." The 'thank you' drew apathetic applause.

"Next up, our favorite new accountant, Teri Thompson, with a short presentation on production. Ms. Thompson, show us those figures." He clapped and offered her an assisting hand aboard. Applause rebounded.

With high-heel care, Teri stepped up and waggled to the projector. She earned a whistle. It eradicated her smile. She bent to adjust the first slide.

Josh called it, "Nice figure."

"Stop it." Monica elbowed him in the ribs.

Teri blushed. She crouched, mindfully striking a less erotic pose, and flipped the projector switch. *Really Josh – a catcall? – I almost thought I liked you.*

Rawling checked seething, held his tongue, *just wait.*

What I'd do for a cigarette. She tried the mic, but started too close; it too whistled. From his chair, Jon showed her to hold it away. Teri proceeded, trying to emulate her best friend with the b-type personality, don't sweat the small stuff – and it's all small stuff. She concentrated on the slides and stumbled into her first secular presentation.

"Here we have last year's production numbers . . ."

On her way to help caterers, Bernice slowed and signaled Henry. Five minutes, she mouthed. He acknowledged but hated to leave. He wanted to look at Teri – listen to Teri. He liked her voice, liked to fantasize, dream about Ms. Thompson. He watched her work the stage and decided she was begging for a disrobing.

Henry Rothness lingered to enjoy her sweet voice and the slides reminded him how, with some help from *Core's* crafty queen, proficient he had become at skimming output numbers. Two truckloads a week, and Monday, he'd turn in a slick Bio-Diesel report, less the thousand gallons drained off momentarily.

The clock ticked south. The driver would be waiting.

Bernice stirred beans and gave him the nod. *Time to sell some Bio-Diesel.* An obscene cash stack grew at home. She'd find room.

Rebecca made tea. Leia spoke, surprisingly serene, and Rebecca heard unexpected clarity in her daughter's recollections. She listened and fixed the new truths in her own mind, then called.

Ellen answered, "Saunders' County Sheriff's Department."

"Sheriff, please."

"The Sheriff has gone home for the evening."

"This is Rebecca Rawling, the Sheriff called, a little earlier, about *stuff*," and she looked to Leia, "It's important I talk to him *right away*."

"Hang on, I'm going to put you on hold. Don't hang up, now. I'll try to call him and connect you."

"Hello, Mrs. Rawling, you needed to speak to me?" O'Leary said.

"It's about Leia. She says it was other people at the plant that attacked her. A guy named Henry and a heavy lady, Bernice. They . . . and . . . and . . . and hit her and that's all she remembers. It's the Company party out at the plant tonight."

O'Leary wasn't surprised. Leia's story rang true, and finding Malcolm in her apartment, it felt like they were being jacked off. Still, he had to ask, "She's not mistaken, I mean, mixed up."

"No, she's better. As clear as a bell."

"The party is going on right now?"

"Yeah."

"They would be there?"

"Yes, probably, I think it goes til about nine."

"Did you call Jon?"

"Not yet. I called you first. I doubt anyone would be in the office, anyways, eh?"

"That's good, I'd rather you didn't. Let's leave things on an even keel. I'll grab a detective or two and run out there. I don't think we'll have any trouble. You sit tight and we'll stop by later to talk with Leia."

"I'm so glad I was able to get ahold of you, Kelly – good luck, Sheriff."

Henry worked past other employees laying low in the back row. "Sorry, excuse me, gotta hit the head, sorry."

Teri switched slides and noticed Henry. "Local bushels came in at, at . . . at one million nine hundred thousand."

Jon followed Teri's distraction and watched Henry exit.

Henry moved quickly across the plant and out the west door. The bulk truck sat near the spur line, idling in the corner of the lot. Shaky hid behind his aviators and smoked. Henry waved him over.

"Been waiting long?" Henry fit the coupler to the tank.

"Nah, couple'a minutes." He got another Winston going, pretended to stretch, and took to leaning on the fender.

Henry drew from his shallow wit pool. "Malcolm gave ya back your shades."

The driver gave Henry the finger.

Bernice taste-tested a pulled pork sandwich.

Teri received an encouraging smile from her boss. Jon stood and Teri bravely continued as she watched him walk out.

Bernice wanted to follow, fearing it wasn't the bathroom Rawling was checking. If he went west, what might Henry do? She remembered the sound of Malcolm's neck, snapping, and how would she help? She'd only implicate herself. A caterer offered her cake. That did it.

O'Leary stood in boxers and waited for the wife to recover a laundered uniform from the basement pool table. "I gotta go," he yelled.

Ellen dialed. Harrison turned the shower off. His phone rang. He grabbed a towel, wrapped himself, and hair dripping, made it. "Hello."

"Hi, Buck, it's Ellen."

"You off, already?"

"Sorry, no, you're on the clock, again. Sheriff asked me to call."

'Now, what the fu . . ."

"He said, he wants you to meet him at *Core Fuels*; he just left and you're supposed to radio as soon as you leave."

"Oh shit, okay, see you tomorrow, maybe?"

"Roy?"

"Yeah."

"He told me to tell you, 'come loaded'. Please, be careful."

A mile out of Wahoo, the Bronco's needle climbed past eighty-five to an unregistered speed. O'Leary guesstimated 90 and change.

On the edge of town, Clive stopped for fuel. The gas station's lights illuminated mist in the air and he stood in Broken Downs side-door, watching gallons spin dollars to a lofty total.

He ran in.

"Ducky out there, tonight, huh?" the clerk said.

"Yeah, ducky . . . Got any get-well cards?"

"Rack'a cards over there."

Clive rifled through them. "Looks like ya got everything but."

The clerk shrugged. Clive laid gum on the counter, paid, and put his flat-front train on track.

Harrison buttoned his shirt, pulled the shoulder holster over, and adjusted it. Walther lay on the dresser. He checked the full clip. It felt nice clicking it into the handle and he slid the receiver, chambering a round. Come loaded. Safety on, he held the weapon away and pulled the trigger, checking, then holstered it. The blow dryer ran fifty-four seconds, he sat to pull on boots, then out the door to catch O'Leary.

"Sheriff? Harrison here."

"O'Leary picked the mic off the dash and let off the gas. The short wheel-base Ford slowed to sixty-five. "Where you at?"

"Just leaving."

"Step on it, catch me if you can, no siren, just run the lights."

"What's up?"

"Meet me in *Core's* parking lot. We're going to a party."

Otherjon had a strong hunch where Henry might be and cut through Milling, straight to the dark, west hall. The cleaning cart sat against the wall, and, moving past, he remembered Malcolm's weekend gig at the hospital. Rawling cracked the door and peered at an unsurprising sight. He pulled back. A stubby, round key on Bobby's keyring fit the firebox on the wall. Otherjon turned it, looked at Jon trapped in the framed glass, and said, "Fun Zone." They selected the fire ax and slipped out the door. The truck blocked his approach as he looped north in light drizzle. The idling diesel masked footfalls.

Parties require party *favors.* Harrison felt he might be short; he circled his block and ran back in to grab a box of shells. He looked at the phone and made a quick call.

"Saunders' County Sheriff's Department," Ellen said.

"Hey, Cutie, O'Leary tell you why we're headed to *Core Fuels*?"

Ellen paused. "Mrs. Rawling called. I accidentally listened. Sounds like two people at the plant were responsible for their daughter's accident."

"Who, did she say?"

"A Henry and Bernice."

"I know em."

"Everyone's supposed to be there for a party tonight."

"Um-hum, everyone huh? Do me a favor, get ahold of Pearson and tell him to . . ."

The driver sucked, and the Winston glowed. A shadow moved behind Henry and the grit dropped from the driver's bottom lip. Two steps more and the ax fell sharp on the loading dock's wood deck. The accurate swing severed the fuel hose. A gusher sprayed. The deck held the embedded ax; Otherjon struggled to release it.

Henry went for the boss. "You need to go – *AWAY!*" His boots slid in the slick and he went down. The driver monkeyed up the truck and ground first. The clutch pedal came up and the Fremont-installed disk bit. The truck lurched, juice sloshing in its belly. On the ground, liquid gold spread and met the Winston's filter. The diminishing cherry rejoiced, sparked, and ignited. A blue flame expanded across the spill. It closed on Henry, giving him few options. He leaped and grasped at the truck as new tires spun through the slick.

The driver let off the diesel, pumped pedal, and pulled second gear.

The tachometer bounced, returned to four grand, and the petro-coated duals spun again. He turned for the north road, putting the service vehicle into a slide. Henry pivoted, foot-loose, on the tanker's rear ladder – his oily grip slid on the rail. A twenty-foot umbilical cord hung from the tank. Henry watched it drag through the burning Bio and light.

The driver caught a glimpse in the passenger-side mirror. "Yee," he squealed.

Fire licked the loading dock; Jon and Otherjon struggled with their decision, stop the pumping fuel, or not. As fun as it would be, to let'r blow, it behooved the party plan to put the fire out. Mist did little to tamp flames, but with an at-hand fire extinguisher, they killed the burn on the edge of the platform and repelled the flaming puddle.

'*Whap*,' flat went the rail-crossing sign. One headlight down, the driver found the wipers and established the road's center. The truck gained speed. The burning hose left a fire trail.

From the dock, Rawling watched Henry secure himself to the tanker's rear ladder. Henry stared back at him. Otherjon waved.

From the truck's tether, bio-diesel ran unchecked, fueling the trail. The driver dodged potholes and hit many. The hose got to whipping. Flames spurted left, right and worked up the hose. It flagellated, flipped, and spit. Intermittent flames showered in every direction and the ditches kindled. A rain of fire splashed Henry's backside. "Ahaaa," he screamed and vaulted with the truck's subsequent swerve. Dropping and rolling, no problem, but velocity hindered stopping, and Henry came to rest, body straddling downed barbwire. Knocked out, he lay half in the ditch, half in corn stubble.

The driver jerked the wheel, desperately avoiding craters. Truck, rolling thunder, and its headlight illuminated the STOP sign ahead. Timed to a second, and he mashed the brakes. Every tire locked. As the proverbial falling tree, with no one to see, his moment of prodigious skill passed unwitnessed. The great machine screeched, bounced kittywampus into the intersection, and stopped. Shaky reached for the door handle. The flame reached for the tank of fumes.

The truck frame remained. Some yards down the asphalt, bowled the driver's dearly departed head.

Half a county away, O'Leary saw the lightning-like flash illuminate low nimbus clouds. Twenty-five years since Vietnam, but instantly, he recognized the explosion for what it was. He floored it and watched the needle wrap around to zero.

The Bronco's meats threw a misty cloud and the elements swirled in a hundred-mile-an-hour vortex behind. O'Leary wanted more. He got less. A tick developed into a rap. The rap into a knock, this ended in a bang.

"God damn it," O'Leary whimpered. The headlights dimmed and he guided the dead horse to the side of the road. An aluminum four-cell flashlight confirmed the impairment; a connecting rod stuck out the side of the engine block. Ten-forty oil pooled on the gravel shoulder. O'Leary slammed the hood. "Whatta Piss Cutter."

Broken Down drew its own misty cloud. Clive roared past, layering the Saunders County Sheriff in a blanket of wet.

Clive, oblivious, drove instinctively, negligently, daydreaming late-in-the-day daydreams and he imagined the most swell reveries.

Of course, her Mom and Dad will welcome me in, as for Leia, most likely resting. And what was Mom's name, again, Rebecca, yes. Good to know that. And I'll set the flowers next to the bed. And Leia, my wounded bird, I'll not even notice, pretend not to notice, your injuries. And she'll be so happy to see me. A man that cares. Her man that cares. And, oh, how gentle I'll care for her, tender, and dotingly nurse her. Because she'll want that. And soon she'll be better. And I'll kiss her tenderly, tenderly, then passionately. And I'll give her everything. But won't smother her, because that she would hate. And we'll date. And she'll be waiting for me to ask her. And I'll wait just a bit longer. And we'll get married. And live somewhere. And have boys, but no horses. And girls, too, maybe.

Chapter 38

Sell It

Teri finished strong. ". . . and this is how the new schedule has positively impacted production." The plant had put up impressive numbers, breakdowns and missing product notwithstanding. She assumed Jon to follow with congratulatory remarks, effectively excusing her. An uncomfortable short wait and she took it upon herself to do the cheerleading. "And that's how we do it here at Core Fuels. I think we should all give ourselves a big round of applause." Teri started them clapping, then stepped down without Jon's hand.

A missing MC paused the show.

"Should I go up and start?" Sherbt's lawyer asked Lon.

Lon saw Bernice returning. "Hang on."

The riser creaked under Bernice's crossing. She took the mic, pretended to search, and said, "Jon should be along in a minute. Hope he didn't fall in." She snared a good laugh from the room. "Last, we have the consortium's presentation."

She looked to Sherbt's lawyer. "If you'd like to start, we can *all* bring Mr. Rawling up to speed when he gets back." Implying it the crew's task, the improv received more chuckles and a few clapped.

Ellen called Pearson's number, but no answer. She knew the gal he was sweet on and tried the corner bar in Yutan. The barmaid, Pudge's fancy, answered.

"Hi, Ellen here – at the Sheriff's office. You wouldn't happen to have Detective Pearson hanging around there, somewhere?" Ellen thought she would give him a boost, asking for Detective rather than Deputy Detective, overweight rookie Detective, or, 'Where's my secret spy ring?' Detective.

"It's for you, it's Ellen from your office," said the barmaid.

Three rum-Cokes in, Pearson steadied himself, lifting from the barstool. He stretched the wall-phone's long, coiled cord and leaned on the end of the bar. "Detective Pearson, here."

"Buck asked me to send you out to the Rawling's residence to babysit. They think they know who Leia's real attackers are. It apparently wasn't that Malcolm guy. Buck and the Sheriff went to round them up but want someone to guard the house, just in case. You know where it is?"

"No, I've never been there."

"Hang on, I'll get you the directions. It's not far from Yutan, take the gravel north out of town and . . . and . . .

. . . and they're right on the river."

"Easy-peasy. Any description of her attackers?"

"I was getting to that. Man an'a woman. Henry Roth-something, late thirties, 'big oaf, brick shithouse,' Buck said, 'and Bernice Jorgan, mid-ta' late thirties, sandy blond, large gal, like three-hundred pounds, maybe?' He said you can't miss em."

Pearson soaked down a waiting fourth mixer; nobody walks away from a Yutan Mayor gifted drink.

Light rain soaked the paper taped across the van's advertisement. It ripped, flapped momentarily, and flitted to the ditch. *Pudges Plumbing* – back in business.

Flames simmered through another ditch and at Henry's clothes. He twitched, woke, and chose the plant.

The west door clacked shut behind Otherjon. He jogged through production and to the office. A box of goodies hid behind Jon's desk and, with it, he ran out the front door to the parking lot. Back inside, he wrapped chain through the inside door handles, and coughing, giggling, he secured them with a lock.

The Ordained, set to task, passed out certificates in a giving deportment. Two-color printer specials declared holder of 'said share,' a stake in Core Fuels. Michael, the face of salvation, shook each receiver's hand, and congruently said, "Congratulations." *Worthless paper – given for you.*

Michael completed his commission, and the lawyer said, "Thank you, Mr. Peck."

Folks slid their certificates from protective sleeves for a peek. Michael, again, congratulated the enveloped flock. *Blue and gold ink – shed for you.*

Sherbt's lawyer could sell . . .

"Folks, as Mr. Peck said, congratulations. Wow, those numbers." He smiled at Teri, shook his head, and started clapping. "Incredible."

The owners stood, turned, and clapped, as did Bernice. Encouraged, all joined. The consortium sat last.

"Ever think if you socked a hundred bucks into Kodak stock when it came out, where you'd be now?" He let it soak in. "Well, I don't know *where* you'd be, but I know what you'd be. You'd be a millionaire, that's what. Think if your parents would have bought up Montgomery Ward's stock, imagine the re-Wards, you'd be reaping, now.

"Friends, tonight is a watershed moment for the *Core Fuels'* strident family." He opened the briefcase and produced a manila envelope, and from it, slid the single share. "What you each hold in your hand is a gift. But not an ordinary gift, no. This is a cornerstone, a building block of financial security.

"These good men in the front row want to offer their family, this family, an opportunity to join them in ownership. An opportunity to be part of something organic, growing. Blooming. To share in a future of expanding advantage. As Mr. Falkher, here, enthusiastically said as we were taking our seats, 'Gosh darn-it, a family shares, and these shares are about sharing.' Tonight you are offered an opportunity, a generous and incredible opportunity, to sign up for a program that puts you in control of your future.

"An opportunity to accumulate shares – building blocks, if you will – to construct your tower of shower, a shimmering pyramid shedding coinage as it rises skyward." He lifted a hand as if presenting a monolith.

"And how do you get in, how does it work? Let me tell ya, this is so powerful, ingenious, and generous it's going to blow your socks off. Each pay period you elect to deduct purchased shares from your check, up to ten shares. These, at fifteen dollars each, are matched dollar-for-dollar by the consortium. Yes – free. Now, you don't *have* to take all ten shares, you could elect to take five, in which case, we match your five. Or even one share, and we would match that, but five to ten would be best. Think, for every fifteen dollars you invest in your future, you receive thirty dollars of value. Through this steady process, you own a bigger and bigger share of *Core Fuels*. And as *Core Fuels'* bottom line increases, your shares become more and more valuable. Now, here's the kicker, down the road, as the board adds dividends . . . well, ladies and gentlemen, that's how fortunes are made."

Jon pleasantly strolled into the cafeteria. Most in the back rows looked. Had he fallen in? Had extrication been a struggle? He excused himself to Henry's empty seat. He looked mussed, damp, and smelled like he'd been smokin in the boys' room.

The barker cleared his throat and continued.

"We all know how hard it is to save money once you cash that check," he looked shamed, raised a hand, and shook his head. "Guilty as charged, I know I have a heck of a time saving once that cash is in hand. Remember, as they say, what you don't see you don't miss. And who here hasn't worked overtime? We all know how annoying that is – when you're expecting a nice bump, only to find Uncle Sam has helped himself to most of it. I'd like you to think about turning that overtime into shares, it's a great way to get Uncle Sam out of your pocket. The consortium feels that's a break you deserve."

He paused. Sherbt stood and moved to the edge of the riser. The lawyer met him and leaned close. Conspicuously loud, the lawyer whispered, "*Free?*" He backed away, elation on his face, and announced, "The consortium will issue nine *extra* shares, that's a ten share total, to each person who enrolls tonight." The lawyer clapped. Rawling in back, and Bernice from the front, helped lead the congregation in another round of applause. The lawyer helped them direct perceived adoration to the kind and gentle owners.

"Are there any questions?" he said into the mic.

"What's in it for the consortium?" Mark asked the gift horse.

"Good question; I'm so glad you asked that. Very intuitive," the lawyer praised. "What's in it for these fine gentlemen? Well, two things, selling shares raises capital, capital for better plant maintenance, and capital for lobbying. We don't have any government spies in the room tonight, do we?" He scanned faces as if vetting, and got smiles. "You might not be surprised when I tell you ethanol subsidies go hand in hand with greased palms in Washington. And what do subsidies buy you? Job security, that's right, job security."

He looked seriously grim. "Let me tell you, I know firsthand, each man sitting here in the front row has surrendered a small fortune, greasing those Washington palms, protecting our jobs. . . . But all that aside, you know what else capital buys? More capital, you don't just waltz into the bank and say, 'Hey, banker, give me a loan. I want to build a new house.' Do you? No, you need capital, something down, something in your pocket to show you're solid, that you're worth the investment. So . . . what might *we* build?"

Again, he paused, adjusted his glasses, and as a great secret, dumped chum.

"Well, I'm almost done, but before you enjoy that delicious-smelling pork in back, let me leave you with a piece of steak. There's talk, and permitted to validate it, I'll convey it now. The consortium has been looking at locations to expand. Considering sites across the Midwest." (The first Sherbt and the rest had heard.) He reached in the briefcase and pulled out shares, half a ream, held them high, and said, "Holders of *these* shares," he let them slam the table next to the projector, "would be buying into those plants as well. A new plant opens, shares split. You know what that means? Dividends double. We open another plant, *Boom*!" he chopped an open palm, "your shares split, again. How many shares ya got, now? That's right, even the complimentary share you're holding in your hand has become four. Three *Core* plants, *Boom*!" he chopped, "eight shares. Four plants, *Boom*!" he chopped, "sixteen shares. More plants, more profits. I have a feeling, not far down the road, you'll be ordering safes for your homes. It's exponential, my friends. And the early bird gets the worm . . .

Meet me in back, folks. Sign up tonight and take home ten free shares."

Otherjon hurried to the front, escorted Bernice, and together, they joined Sherbt's lawyer on stage. "Something you forgot to mention?" Otherjon said.

As if suddenly remembered, the lawyer said, "Oh, we'd like it if you could please keep the building of more plants under your hat. Loose lips sink ships."

"Can we purchase shares tonight?" Bernice asked.

The lawyer looked to the front row and received feigned surprise, then an affirmative.

"You can, and how many would the lady like?" He fished out the signup sheet.

Into the microphone, Bernice said, "I'd like twenty tonight, and put me down for the ten every payday." From her stretchy slacks, she pulled three pre-planted hundred-dollar bills and forfeited them back into the briefcase, whence they came.

'Yes," the lawyer said, acknowledging Barry's raised hand.

"I want some too, but didn't bring my checkbook with."

Others grumbled.

"Well, what we can do, to be fair, is anyone that wants shares tonight can let me know and I'll just mark it down so we know ya want em," he looked to Teri, "Ms. Thompson, you could collect next Monday or Tuesday?"

She nodded.

Otherjon used the mic, "Put Jon Rawling down for all ten every pay period, please, and give me fifty more right now." He pulled a thick fold of green and gave it over.

Then announced, "Fifty shares to the team that wins the treasure hunt!"

O'Leary, ready to radio, saw police lights in the mirror and returned the mic to its clip. Harrison pulled in behind the Bronco and exited his cruiser. He drew in the cool mist and yelled, "What's up?"

O'Leary, getting out, barked, "Where the hell ya been?"

"Sorry – had to make a quick call."

". . . Ellen?"

Harrison shrugged.

"If there's any fussin or fightin, one of ya's gotta go." O'Leary reached back into the Bronco, unlatched his 870 Riot, and passed it to Harrison. "And then, I'd have to ask myself, who's essential?"

Harrison chose not to hear. "What happened to the Bronco?"

Waist in, O'Leary snatched buckshot from the center console. He tossed the box in his hand, weighing quantity.

". . . Blowed up . . ." Sideways, O'Leary looked at him.

"I didn't say a thing," Harrison deflected.

Bernice employed Mark and Gene to move tables from the wall. She slid the sign-up table near the end of the food line. What's taking Henry? The lawyer squared three-page fine-print contracts next to the stack of shares serendipitously paper-clipped in packs of nine. Underpaid caterers in hair nets mustered smiles, built generous pulled-pork sandwiches, and scooped steaming baked beans. The crowd assembled at the buffet. A greedy few forewent the line and secured shares.

Bernice filled her burgeoning belly.

Bryce, second through the food line, followed Terrance from the buffet.

"Mm," Terrance said, trying an escaped pork morsel. He set his plate on the sign-up table to make a commitment. "Aren't you signing up?" he asked Bryce.

"Maybe later."

"Free shares are just tonight," Sherbt's lawyer called after him.

Bryce didn't look back.

A few minutes later, Terrance laid the ten-pack next to Bryce's thin folder, set his tray on the table, and cozied up.

"What-a-ya nuts? Nine free shares? Aren't you the one always bitchin *Core Fuels* doesn't even have a retirement plan?"

Bryce looked thoughtful. "Ya know, I never cared for that little fucker, Malcolm."

Terrance, not good with hate, laughed anyway. "Yeah, so?"

"Don't see him, do ya?"

Terrance glanced around the room. "No? I thought *everyone* was here."

"I was in the locker room, getting ready for work a couple of days ago, and Malcolm's a few lockers down, ya know."

"Ya?"

"And I say something about the party and, Malcolm says, 'you won't see me hanging around *Core* on my day off,' and Sack says, 'big supper this year, free food.' And Malcolm says . . . 'Got better things to do, 'sides, nothin's free, free got me this leg'."

"So, now you're listening to the gimp?"

"I don't know. I didn't think much of it – kinda thought he was kidding, but then it hit me, he's not here. Then, the more that god-damn lawyer talked, the more I got thinking about Malcolm, 'nothin's free.' I don't know – I'll probably sign up."

'Ya, I think you'll regret it if you don't. What's gimpy know, anyway?"

Teri and Bernice rounded up folks as they finished eating and lined them up. The team-building games began. They handed out eggs, some cooked, some not – to keep it interesting. Pairs tossed and took a step back. Repeat till fumble. New groups paired off and, blindfolded, tied a short rope in a square knot to a partner's.

Bryce tucked his share under an arm and headed for the lawyer.

Sherbt's lawyer saw him coming. "Smart man."

In Bryce, the pork and beans traded places. One finger up, he said, "I'll be back in a minute." He detoured to the men's room and hastened to the far stall.

On the shitter, things moved quickly, then not so much. Reading material came in a sleeve. Bryce looked over his stake in *Core Fuels* and waited for thorough evacuation. The men's room, open for business, and feet shuffled to the urinals.

"I don't think I've ever seen anything like it," Larry said.

"What? Sherbt's lawyer or those dipshits lapping it up?" asked Lon.

"Both. You said, 'have a little faith.' Didn't know you could put so many idiots in one room. And Rawling, wow, hook, line, and sinker. What'uh fool."

"ROI, buddy, return on investment. Yeah, no, I can't believe how Rawling fell in line."

"I just wonder if he hasn't figured it out. If he knows your boy'll be sittin in his chair soon. I think he's just trying to prolong his stay."

"Well, of course, he is. No matter, change is in the wind."

Fwush, *Fwush*, Urinals flushed. Feet shuffled. Water ran in the sink. Feet shuffled out.

Bryce used the printed side to wipe. He let it float.

Chapter 39
Clive's Cleaver

They heard a vehicle and a door close. Rebecca, mid hospital-fire story, stopped.

She raised the shade. Broken Down looked large in their yard, and though she didn't know it, she did recognize the man.

"Is Dad home?" Leia asked.

"No, it's the lumberjack."

"Clive? Clive the forester?" She asked, getting up to see.

"Clive the forester. He's got flowers." Rebecca smiled.

"Get rid of him! He can't see me, I look like a monster."

Under mellow porch light, Clive, the prom-date dildo, knocked. He held the gaudy flower arrangement at the ready.

Van lights, coming up the driveway, went out. Leia, at the curtain, noticed. "Someone *else* is coming."

Clive heard the van and looked over his shoulder. Again, he knocked.

Not a second too soon, Pearson thought, pulling the van over. His clip-on holster with revolver lay on the passenger seat and he grabbed it as he climbed out. He darted ahead to Clive's Maverick, and shouted, "Hey!" In suede work boots, the figure on the porch turned. Revealed to Pearson, bold, gaudy, lurid flowers, and he thought *Sick Fuck . . . Gonna leave flowers after killin em.*

Rebecca opened the door.

"Mom," Leia whined, ready to bolt and hide.

Another vehicle? It dawned on Rebecca – *O'Leary in a van? Already? No way*, and safe they might not be.

"Stop!" Pearson yelled and drew. He fired a warning shot.

Clive flinched, dropping flowers, pushing for cover, and Rebecca pulled him. "Get in."

In a second, it'll all change and I'll own a hostage situation. And in a *split* second, he made his decision. Pearson leaned across the Maverick's roof and risked a dangerous shot. *SNAP.* Lead lodged in the door molding.

"Jesus!" Clive said, ducking, and in. *Talk about pissed boyfriends.*

Leia slammed the door. Pearson tried to think.

Bewildered, Clive looked at the women, and lower than the window, they crouched.

"They're after Leia," Rebecca said.

"What?" He looked at Leia. She nodded, reached up to hit the light switch, and Clive got his first good look. Scratches, dark welting scabs intermittently covered tender pink healing lines. Her gauntness and bandage on her bedhead registered as the lights went out.

"Come on out, we got the place surrounded," Pearson yelled.

"What should we do?" Leia said.

"You have guns?" Clive asked.

Eyes adjusting to the dark, Rebecca said, "Yes, but no, we're not having a shootout, eh?"

"They can't have the place surrounded, the car just came up the driveway," Leia said. "Let's sneak out the back."

"Go, I'll call the sheriff," Rebecca told them.

Leia led, Clive followed, and, crouching, they scurried through the house. To distract attackers, Rebecca flipped the living room lights on and off, on and off, and again.

Pearson stooped behind the Maverick, questioning the meaning, *bad guy must be in another room?* He made a break for the porch, running in the mist, both hands on his pistol and holding it low. A swift seriatim of steps and onto the porch he sailed. Full of booze, he slowly turned the doorknob.

Clive traded positions with Leia. She stood close. He squeaked open the back door and peered out.

Pearson cracked the front and peeked in.

Rebecca stood in the shadowy kitchen, holding the phone, wishing she could remember the number. Both doors opened and she moved to a corner, phone pressed to her chest.

Pearson's pistol appeared in the kitchen entry. Rebecca held her breath.

The back door clicked shut. The pistol pulled back. Rebecca listened as Pearson crept down the hall.

"Where?" Clive asked.

"Up there, there's a shed," she whispered. Leia took Clive by the hand and started up smokehouse hill's slickery path.

Bhuzz . . . bhuzz . . . bhuzz, off the hook, the timed out phone beeped. Rebecca held it firm to her breast.

Inebriated Pearson spun. *Bwam Bwam*, two rounds in the dark. Spent lead whizzed down the hall, through living room wall, siding, and exited the front of the house. The pistol's report rang in his ears. Pearson sucked it up and tried to listen. Rebecca jerked the cord, freeing the handset.

Forty yards uphill, they looked back. "No!" Leia yelled. She stepped toward the house. Clive pulled her and, as if a shot had struck her, she crumpled. He scooped her up and continued their retreat. Leia cried.

Pearson came out the back. Barren tree shadows dissected the yard light irradiating the path and he saw sobbing Leia scuttled uphill. Revolver raised, he wanted to fire another warning but saved ammunition and almost pleading, yelled, "Stop!"

Rebecca moved cautiously in the dark and upstairs for a gun. Jon's nightstand – empty.

Pearson took to the woods and counted previous shots. *Two bullets left*.

The rickety undersized smokehouse-door creaked and three-quarters open, caught dirt floor. As if cradling a new bride, Clive carefully carried her over the miniature threshold and stood her in the middle of the room. Then lifted the door closed and he helped it latch. Leia whimpered and slumped to the dirt. He circled the distraught lump on the floor, feeling walls for anything defensive, and thinking their shitty hiding place felt like a trap.

A short distance away, Pearson positioned himself behind a tree. He racked his brain. One watched video on hostage negotiation registered irrelevant and not one thing from it could he remember but hoped that it was something to do with keeping an assailant talking.

"Nobody needs to get hurt here, tonight, Right?"

Ya, right, Clive thought.

Leia moaned and Pearson heard her.

"Just give me the girl," Pearson called.

"No way," Clive yelled.

"Let her go and no harm'll come to ya."

"They tried to kill me, tried to drown me," Leia sobbed.

"Leave us alone, you pig," Clive said.

Son-of-a-bitch – I hate that. ". . . Come on now, do the smart thing, give her over."

"Go away, leave us alone."

Pearson fidgeted behind his tree.

Clive whispered, "Leia, is there something in here I can use – if he tries to break in?"

Only his voice located him in the black and she heard him patting the bench, feeling the walls, and then felt his hand on her shoulder.

"Leia, I need a weapon."

Did she care? Mom, dead or dying? And what, against guns? *For Clive's sake.* She gathered will and led Clive to the bench. With both hands, she pulled open a heavy wooden drawer. Clive's fingers followed her arm to the contents. "What?" he asked.

"Butcher tools," she whispered.

"Come on now, be sensible, let her go," Pearson repeated.

"Piss off!" Clive shouted.

"It won't be good if you make me come in and get ya." Pearson scampered across the path, stumbled on dead branches in tall, wet grass, recovered, and stood panting near the shed door.

Together, their fingers moved over the rusty trappings: A rectangular flat saw. Knives with worn handles; blades, curved, straight, short, and long. A small bow saw. And in the jumble, a square blade – substantial and with a wood handle – a cleaver. He laid it on the bench and took up a long knife. He placed it in Leia's hand, pressed her fingers around the handle, and whispered, "It's just us, now."

Pearson squared to the rickety door, stepped, and kicked. Boards smashed. At the door's center, a shoe, below pudgy calf, entered the black hovel. Knee deep, Pearson hopped and cursed, trying to extricate.

Leia moved fast, faster than Clive, and angry, and courageous, a doyenne she-bitch of war in the making. As brave as kicking Henry in the nuts, Leia attacked the fat-shoed worm squirming in the dark. The battered butcher swiped her rusty knife, slicing sock, skin, and a thin but fatty layer of meat – depth measured by shin bone. By instinct more than vision, Clive intercepted. "Get *behind* me," he bossed, jerking her roughly, blocking her away and to the side.

Pearson froze, digesting wound severity. A tremor shook him from within and he unleashed an insuppressible scream, "*Whaaaaa!*" He hopped once for balance, thrust his revolver forward like a punch, and discharged a round at the door.

The muzzle flashed, report sounding off the shack, returning to Pearson. The bullet carried fractional decibels into the smokehouse. Nine-point-five millimeters of lead lightning missed flesh, passed through the opposite wall, and returned to nature.

Pudge tugged his gory limb free. He hobbled a circle, cursing each stride, and stepped to kick again. "That's it, now you've done it."

The blow, the pinnacle of Pearson's stretchability, landed near the latch. *Crash*. The degraded door exploded. Boards and splintered wood fell at the couples' feet. In the dimmest of light, Pearson stood in the doorway, looking ghostlike.

He scanned the dark interior without scanning and with mind to imprint villain. For a soul needed dispatching, a girl saving, a hero making. And he fired anyway.

Handle over square blade, Clive's clever winked a lusty wink at the passing bullet. Handle over blade, blade over handle, chasing from blackness to less black, handle over blade, blade over handle, stopping in forehead. Clive's eyes crossed, trying to focus on the unfortunate event. He pointed, wavered, and pulling stubby's trigger, fanned the dark. The hammer clicked on spent cartridges. Ghost bullets sprayed the room. Clive held Leia.

Pearson tipped.

Part Three
EXECUTE

Chapter 40
Treasures

The caterers stacked roasters ruined of pork and beans and wheeled out. Pissed as a cat, Teri crouched in high heels and cute outfit to clean mishandled eggs. Less bendable Bernice pointed out another overlooked splash. Teri wanted to know, what gives – where's maintenance? Her guesses didn't include; Malcolm, lying on a cold tray, and tequila-infused Bobby, swallowing a tequila-infused worm.

Otherjon drew four tan packets from a mid-podium shelf and used the mic, "Ready for some fun?" He briefly explained the hunt. "An envelope for each team. Each team, a department, or two smaller departments together." He handed them out. "Fermentation, here Mark, and take Bill with ya. Milling, Gene. Here's loading, combined with office," he looked around, "I don't see Henry, Gilbert, wanna take it to start?" He handed the last packet to Lon. "And the lab gets to hunt with the consortium."

Michael leaned to his cousin. "Let's cut out."

Sherbt heard and looked over his shades at Lon.

Dad heard, too. "Everybody stays."

"We got the signatures."

"They could change their minds. You wanna run the place, you gotta show Sherbt ya give-uh shit."

"I give-uh shit, but it's Saturday night, and this is stupid."

"Hey, we're salesmen tonight. And let's win this thing. Show'em why we're the owners and piss-ants work for *us*."

Groups formed and Otherjon said, "Solve the puzzle and be first back to the cafeteria for bragging rights and the grand prize." He held up a hand, pausing them. "But, there're no losers tonight, we draw door prizes at quarter to nine, including a weekend getaway for two to Vegas! On your mark . . . Open your packets."

Four strings on four packets unwound in figure eights from securing red buttons.

"Now, we're not handing out hard hats, so let's play safe. And no running in the halls, kids." Otherjon chuckled, "Good luck, everyone."

Groups, in huddles, read clues.

Bernice read, "Big Guy – Small Desk."

Bernice knew. Gilbert, too, and said, "Henry's desk."

Larry read, "Boys – Singin in the Rain."

"The downstairs showers," Terrance proclaimed.

Gene blew into their packet and tipped out a Polaroid. Printed below the picture, the clue, and Gene read. "Fat Vat."

Sheila squinted at the photo. "It's an inspection port on one of the vats."

Mark slid content from packet. Two items and he passed them to the girls. Nancy held a timecard. Deb, the clue card.

"What's it say?" team fermentation reverberated.

"Bobby Supplies," said Deb.

"That's gotta be maintenance room," Mark said.

"Look at the name on the timecard," and Nancy read, "Mr. Right left Mrs. Right."

"Right, left, right? March?" JR said.

"March on a timecard? Means don't dilly dally. Let's go," Mark ordered. His crew followed Bernice's staff and *loading*, who followed the *owners* and *lab* techs to the westward hall. As the trifecta traveled, they wondered if all three teams might have the same clue.

Gene's crew cut through *milling* – straight to *fermentation*.

Departing the west train, Mark led his team into *maintenance*, and asked, "Where's Bryce?" Some shrugged.

"Hey, the floor's wet," Nancy said.

"Totally," said Deb.

"The wash sink's runnin over," Cecil said.

"The faucets leaking . . . Oh . . . it just didn't get turned off tight." Bill tightened the cold. He rolled up his sleeve and reached for the plug.

Mark reread the clue, "Bobby's supplies," and moved to the expansive blue-gray storage cabinet. He knocked on the tin door as if someone might let them in, then held Bobby's inventory-securing paddle lock.

"You think it's something else?" Bill asked.

"No, this has to be it, next clue's in here, I'd bet."

"Nancy looked at the black dial on the lock. "Who else knows the combination?"

"Mr. Right!" Mark exclaimed, pointing to the card in her hand. "Mr. Right left Mrs. Right – right, left, right. Go punch the card."

"Someone come with me," she said.

JR liked her; he did.

Gene followed Sheila's swing through dimly lit *production*. She delivered the group to the vats.

"Nothing," she said, looking in the first tank's portal.

At the second, Barry cupped his hands on the round window, reducing glare. "Hey."

Gene and company gathered.

"It's a note," Barry said.

Near the glass, attached to a line, the clue wavered in the mix. Barry read, "ADD WATER."

"Add water," Gene said, looking at several pipes leading from the floor to the tank. Waist-level plumbing right-angled, and on the short sections to the vat, valves beckoned. He palmed a tag on one and read, "RISING TIDE FLOATS YOUR BOAT."

He wheeled it open.

They smothered the window. A note swayed in the current. It began an ascent, as did the line hanging from it, and Sheila said, "It's going up."

Entertained, and with a good view, Bryce sat cross-legged in a dark corner of *production* atop Hammer Mill B. Out came the baggie. Deprived an Otoe peace-pipe, but flush with zigzags, he skillfully rolled a fatty and smoked Mick's cousin's best.

In the southwest hall, Sherbt, the dignitary, traveled at the center of the pack. Terrance led the bigots downstairs. Larry whined to Lon about following color.

"Smells bad," Michael said.

"It's the pits," Josh joshed him.

"What *are* we doing?" Larry said.

"Looking in the showers for the next clue."

They proceeded down the steps, past the lockers, sinks, and into the showers.

"What's in the drain?" Michael's cousin asked. "Is it . . ."

Josh knelt, wiped a smudge, and rubbed it between thumb and finger.

"Ish," said the cousin.

"It's wetcake," Josh said.

"Wetcake? Ewww, what's that?" Michael asked.

"Bi-product, its cattle feed, we make it from the spent grain."

"Oh, yeah," Michael said, as if obvious.

Short shower curtains and Josh's low vantage point afforded him a view; four drains full. He rose and slid a near curtain, exposing the discovery. "They're all plugged."

"What's it doin down here – so much? Guys been rollin in it?" asked Larry

"No, somebody must'a plugged the drains," Terrance said. He looked to Josh. "Bobby's gonna be pissed."

"He'll get Malcolm busy on Monday."

From the doorway and from Henry's office window, Bernice's group watched Gilbert rifle the desk. Bernice joined him and under the writing mat, they found a note. Gilbert sat back in Henry's chair and read their new clue,

"Slide the basement door – Read a little more."

The crowd in the hall goose-necked.

Teri, back of the pack, crossed the corridor first and aligned herself to the door's back edge. With her shoulder, she pushed. The heavy wood door ignored her. "When's the last time this thing's been closed?"

Below – Josh found a note in the end shower stall taped to the wall.

"What's it say?" Terrance asked.

Josh read,

"Forgettaboutit – You showered today!
Wash hands instead.

Try sink two for a good view."

A stance change and Teri redoubled her effort. Gilbert the Bruiser reached and placed a hand above Teri. The hefty door, hanging from unlubricated rail and casters, slowly closed. . *RrEEka–reek – rEEka – reek* – "What's that, noise?" Sherbt's lawyer asked. *Reeka – rEEk – Reeka – TOONK.*

Slack taken and a thin cable attached to the door's corner trolleyed over pipes near the locker-room ceiling. Taped to the cable, a paper slip withdrew from between battery and contact. The faux-woodgrain timepiece, strapped to an eight-inch pipe, hummed. Above the pipes, around a beam, over another and down, the line stretched. It lifted the end locker's handle. Number 45 opened.

In *fermentation,* Sheila hogged Vat II's portal. "Here it comes, another note." Barry looked as well, and they read,

"Did I say fill?
Dang me,
I meant drain"

"Shut that one, open the drain," Barry bossed their foreman. Gene spun valves.

In the basement, Terrance said, "The *door*, did someone just shut the door?"

"There is one?" Josh asked. "I never noticed."

"Go look."

Upstairs – the closed basement door exposed a clue. Bernice snapped free the sheet tacked to the wall, and read,

"Don't B.
Hammer Mill
A Holes
Rise up
Focus
C what you can see."

"Milling," Teri said.

"Wait, there's more," said Bernice, seeing 'Over,' and an arrow at the bottom. She flipped it. The group gathered. Again, Bernice read,

"If you're lucky, you'll catch'em in the basement.
They have easy clues.
Slow them down."

Below the print, a smiley face with a cocked eyebrow trolled them. Below that, a hand-drawn picture; a lock hanging by latch.

The group looked to the door. They found the same.

And at the bottom of the page, one more word,

"Hurry!"

"Oh, I don't think we should; that's not fair," said Teri.

"All's fair in love and war," Bernice said.

Josh ascended steps.

Behind Teri's back, *Click*, Gilbert latched it.

Teri protested, "But . . ."

Bernice, remissive, said, "They'll be *fine*."

A vertical hewn groove provided the lower level a handle. Josh's fingertips gripped the slot and he pulled. Nothing doing. He pounded. "Hey!"

"Seeya Monday!" Bernice sang. She laughed and, except Teri, the gathering joined.

"You guys're so mean," Teri said.

Gilbert led the group away. "It's just part of the game – she's kidding."

Teri shook her head and followed.

Josh reported, "The fat bitch locked us down here."

Out of the showers, the men loitered. Terrance stood, arm hanging on the open locker door, considering number 45's contents. "Look."

Disrobed its towel, a nitrous oxide tank, label out, teased. Josh reached in, turned the valve, and said, "Empty." He locked eyes with Terrance.

Terrance thought of Wednesday's grab-assing.

Josh thought, *parking lot dents*, and said, "Who, the hell?"

"Bernice?"

Josh shook his head. "No way. She couldn't 'av. This is all Rawling – *Fucker*."

Sherbt followed the cable up, through route, and to the clock. He pointed, elbowing the lawyer.

Lon held the shower note in front of the second sink. In the mirror, back-printed lettering across the lockers read, – 'Door Key – Locker 13'. "Hey, there's a key in locker thirteen."

They dismissed Lon and followed Sherbt's pointing.

In curious tone, the lawyer asked, "That isn't, some kind of, *bomb*?"

Others stepped back. The lawyer stepped closer, examining. Garden hose, wound tight, entwined two pipes, and strapped on top, upside down – the clock. Two wires ran from its bottom to piercings in the hose. Its numerated digits flipped. The lawyer held his head sideways. "11:29 . . . One minute?" he asked.

"The key – Thirteen!" Lon yelled.

Josh went for it.

Terrance led the rest, and said, "Everybody, get down."

The herd huddled low and tight between lockers and bench. The lawyer circled and joined them in a crouch. He checked his watch. "Thirty seconds . . . Run!" He stood.

Terrance pulled him down. "*Where?*"

Leia cleaved to Clive, face tight to his chest. Pearson lay belly down in the smokehouse doorway, clip-on holster and deputy badge in the dirt. Clive held Leia's hand. He stepped over the body and helped her skirt the dead. "Quiet now," he said, and slip-sliding, they worked their way down the muddy hill. Clive opened the back door.

Leia shook her head, "I can't," she whispered.

"Wait," Clive said. He went in.

Clive found Rebecca in the dark kitchen. She held the detached receiver in her armpit, hopelessly twisting severed wires. He sighed relief.

Otherjon intercepted Bernice and Gilbert's crew at Hammer Mill A. "I hate to interrupt your fun, but could I borrow Ms. Thompson for a few minutes?" he asked the group, then Teri specifically, "You wouldn't mind?"

"Sure," she agreed.

"We'll be okay without her, I think we got this," Gene said, patting Mill A.

Otherjon walked west with Teri at his side.

"What?" she asked.

"Come on." And he hastened the pace.

In the west hall near Malcolm's cart and out of treasure seekers' view, he stopped. Teri watched him look around as though he might bestow her a significant secret.

Animated as the day Jon met him, and with eyebrows jumping, Otherjon said, "They've cut the phone lines, the front doors are chained shut. I think they have the whole place booby-trapped."

"Who, Henry and Bernice?"

"I think so, or the owners. I don't know, but I'm going to try to make sure no one gets hurt." He pointed down the hall. "Can you go get help?"

With a jittery nod, she affirmed.

"The west door's open, find a phone – call the Sheriff."

Bryce climbed off the back-side of Mill B and hid in its shadow. Gene led, moving the group to Machine C.

Bernice repeated the note, "Don't B – Hammer Mill – A Holes – Rise up – Focus – C what you can see."

Gilbert, ten rungs up the contraption's side-ladder, stood waist-high above the mill's top as she finished reading. She looked at him, waiting for an answer.

"I don't know, not much, Gene's group, over at the vats. There's binoculars up here."

"C what you can see," Bernice repeated.

In seldom-worn dress slacks, Gilbert rested a knee on the dusty top and stretched for black field glasses. Fish line, tied to the strap, drooped off the opposite side, looping the mill's switch.

Gilbert procured the optics.

Inside the monster-mash, shafts, gears, and belts turned. Wires wound, too, pulling cotter pins from drilled bolts devoid of retaining nuts. The machine shook; Gilbert jerked. The ladder shuddered.

The group below him jumped as well, retreated a step, and laughed. Gilbert twisted, looked down, and laughed too. He shook his head. "God damn Rawling, not *that* funny."

Josh opened locker 13. "What the fu . . .?" Cloak hanger through its handle, Rawling's red chainsaw hung, waiting. He lifted the hanger's burden and to the crouched huddle he read a note tied to the handle,

"I love Stillman."

"Start it!" Larry yelled.

Josh flipped the Run switch ON, gripped the recoil, and pulled. And pulled again.

"Choke!" Lon yelled.

Josh set it. Pulled twice more.

"Five seconds," the lawyer said.

Almost calmly, Terrance said, "Get down."

Josh crouched near the others and they squeezed low. All held their breath. Some covered ears, some listened, and from silence, they heard – *Ta-tic.*

Panels flipped. 11:30

Nothing.

They waited. Josh cautiously rose and stood on the bench. Sweat dripped from his brow, found an eye, and out the other he stared at the inverted clock. ". . . In four minutes it spells 'hEll'."

Josh spun it and the cap hung from the chainsaw. He tilted the open tank to the light. "It's empty."

"Stillman," Josh said.

Terrance instructed the owners, "Stay down."

The two skidded into the cramped heater room, removed the defunct furnace's side panel, and exposed Stillman.

Cursive scrawled on the tank read, '*Drink up, boys*'.

Mean and clean 190 proof poured from the spigot and spilled into and on the steadied saw below.

"Eleven-thirty-one," Lon yelled.

"That's enough," Josh said, working the cap.

Terrance turned the spigot and tugged for the saw. "Let me."

Josh followed him to the bottom step. Terrance ripped the cord. Two, three, four times – the machine fired. He jerked again; it roared. Hot exhaust, nearly smokeless, smelled of spent alcohol.

Saw gunning, Terrance jolted up the steps.

Like a pack of nervous dogs, the owners squirmed. "Stay," Josh commanded. Up, he followed Terrance.

Out-of-focus binoculars adjusted, Gilbert spied on Gene, Barry, Sheila, and the others at Vat II. But not spying. Gene's crew turned to Mill C's roar.

Sheila said, "What's *he* looking at?"

"Us, I guess," Gene said.

At the base of the mill, Bernice shouted, "What'a ya see?"

Gilbert held his gaze and, releasing a hand from the binoculars, shrugged, "The idiots are just staring back at me. I don't know?" He lowered the field glasses and adjusted his stance. Rawling walked into view.

Gene, at the vat, greeted Otherjon's passing, "Meant drain, huh?" Gene chuckled, smiling.

"You got it." Otherjon gave him a thumbs up, a jaunty head-nod, and swiftly moved on.

Terrance stood, one foot a step high, the other, a step lower. His finger mashed the trigger – *WHAAAAA* – the saw screamed. He positioned and pushed. The chain spit wood, eating door.

"Go, go, go," Josh cheered.

And down, Terrance moved the hungry blade. Links sparked, occasionally hitting a nail. A metal edging sandwiched the layered door and near the metal framing he backed the saw out. Terrance picked a spot a couple of feet to the right and started a second vertical cut.

Josh heard Lon yell, "Eleven thirty-two."

"Go, go!" Josh yelled.

Terrance massaged the accelerator and again, squeezed tight. The links burned through, found more nails, and sparked. Progress slowed. Links, finding brads, dulled. Friction puffed smoke between door and whizzing chain. Terrance leaned into it. A foot, inches, and inches by halves – gnawing. The saw stammered, *WhAAaAAa*. Its boxy tin muffler glowed orange. The unlubricated piston scored. *whAAaa*. It slowed.

"No, no, no!" Josh yelled.

Terrance worked the trigger. *whAAaa – Whaa – whaa – aaa – Kwuh*. It sput. Burnt metal-smelling smolder rolled out muffler perforations. He looked at Josh.

"Eleven-thirty-three," Lon yelled.

Terrance pulled, choked, and pulled. Noncompliant internals rotated dead. He dropped the saw where it quit, hanging in the door. Josh raced down. Terrance chased.

They collapsed into the pack. A panic washed the lawyer's face white. He busted for the stairs.

Ta-tic . . . hEll

BOOM!

Halfway down the hall, Teri heard the muffled lower-level explosion. The floor vibrated. She stopped and looked back. Turned. Ran.

The west door opened for her. She tried shooting the gap.

In spatial light and dank night, Henry stood, and into him she careened.

Off the Hulk she thumped and tumbled to the tar, landing at Malcolm's memorial. Wafts of singed cotton, singed hair, and spent ethanol engulfed her. Whom she hit registered.

He watched Teri tumble in outfit and heels. Preoccupation postponed his Rawling obsession. "Where you goin, little mouse?"

Teri shook her head with clamped emotion, unnatural surprise covering fear. She faked a smile.

Henry weighed pleasures, then chivalrously announced, "I'll get you outta here."

She had no words for the smoking bear and looked to extricate. Bruised body gathered, she lifted herself to hands and knees. Eyes adjusting, she scrutinized Hulk's ripped and singed clothing. Casual smolder hinted reigniting fires. '*No*', she shook her head, backing away.

"What, you're gonna run from me again?" He teased a stomp toward her. Teri crawled back, keeping separation equal.

Henry's attention dropped to a smoldering tear near his crotch. In the shadowed opening Teri saw a smoke-veiled amber.

"Wh, wohh wo-ho," sharp breaths and he swatted his crotch, at glowing tighty-whities on his junk. Spanked embers went dark. He unzipped his pants and wisps of smoke trailed out. Aromas mingled, reignited clothing and singed scrotum hair. With an open hand, he gestured to the zone. "Looks like it's time for you to kiss my smokin hot rocks."

He rushed her. She scrambled away and to her feet. His Neanderthal arm wrapped her. Teri spun. Rough fingers hooked her new, blue blouse. Buttons flew – stitching ripped. She wriggled free of the sleeves. Henry pawed the gyroscope. She spiraled, stumbled, and touched a hand to tar, saving a crash. North, in heels, blue slacks, and skimpy bra, she sprinted.

Henry buried his nose in her blouse, smelling her sweetness. "Go ahead, run little mouse, run, but when I'm done with Rawling, you'll be," she rounded the corner, "suckin meeeeeee . . ."

Henry zipped up the smoked fly and spiked his own doffed shirt. His upper body glistened, muscles rippled; rain droplets and sweat clung to chest hair. He opened the door, looking for blood.

Nancy handed Mark the time card. "12:58."

A rumble. The floor shook. "What was that? Thunder?" Deb said.

JR checked the hall. "Rawling's coming."

"We should mop up this water," said Deb.

"No," Bill said.

They waited. Otherjon strolled into view, nodded, smiled, and passed.

"We *should* mop up this water," Deb repeated.

"Not just no, hell no. It's a time trap," said Cecil. "Are you dense?"

"You trying to lose?" Bill asked her, frowning at the mentally infirm.

Otherjon slipped into the control room, turned on Bill's new old monitor, selected four cameras, and kicked back. The follies were on. "Let the shit-show begin."

A moment to joke, Mark cracked knuckles and blew on fingertips. He spun the lock's black dial to zero. "Twelve right," he said, carefully turning the knob to the corresponding white hash line.

"Five left," Cecil said, possessing given timecard.

Mark looked over his shoulder. "And eight right?"

"Eight right," Cecil confirmed.

The lock fell open. Mark turned and held up a hand, waiting for a high five. Nancy obliged. He released the latch and opened the cabinet.

Fish line activated Otherjon's fuzzy, brown-haired friend. Plastic translucent eyes reflected. Rubber mouth, upturned at the corners, hinted happy. He started with a stretch.

"*Cute*," said Nancy, rubbernecking past Mark. An unwinding began. The monkey clapped tiny cymbals. *Chink.* Braided copper leads, riveted to miniature disks, conducted. Current found Mark's hold on the door, passed up his arm, and to the hand on his shoulder. Lightning split. Branched voltage grounded Mark. Stout amperage grounded Nancy. Substantial current twizzled the wet floor, exciting the crowd. In unified spastic jolt, they contorted.

Plant lights dimmed.

Nancy abled a release but stood in water. The thunderbolt clamped Mark's hand. The cymbals disengaged. Everyone sucked a quarter breath and Mark tried detaching an unresponsive hand.

Monkey, spring wound tight, clashed cymbals in half-second intervals. *Chink – Chink – Chink – Chinkspark.*

Mark led the jerking chorus, "Fu-ah – Fuc-ah – Fu-aw – Fawk." Together, jolting, everyone danced. *The Robot, The Twist, The Charleston*, and some went down. Sparks set the one-monkey-band ablaze. Mark's hair stood, his eyebrows smoked, and between bolts, he studied the evil creature's gaiety. He ripped free, fell to the puddle, and joined others doing *The Worm*. As a barnyard slaughter, moaning, cursing, writhing *Homo-sapiens* gnashed teeth and contorted.

The happy little feller paid flame no mind and played on.

Chink – Chink – Chinkspark – Chink – Spark – Chink. When would it end, some wondered – other minds went numb.

JR, on the puddle's edge, danced from the wet to the fuse box. Under a breaker, a glow showed him what to pull, and he did. Plug obtained, those still standing dropped. Animation ceased, time passing in a vacuum.

"It was jumpered," JR said, inspecting a glowing ten-penny. "Rawling!"

The shocked, roused. Mark didn't work. They helped him sit.

"Ewww, he smells like burnt toast," said Deb.

Spark free, the immolated monkey wound down. *Chink . . . chink . . . chinnnnkkkk*. Plastic eyes, melting, dripped sadly – show's over.

Mark's toasty vocal cords sluggishly scratched a brief phrase, "I – kill – Rawling."

They helped him up. Like Frankenstein's monster, Mark walked stiff, testing legs. Together, they faltered out of Electric Avenue.

Off locker 2, Sherbt's lawyer bounced. Time slowed, sped, synced. Men crawled from under toppled lockers. Pulsating heads felt swollen. Repercussion wavered sight. Fingers turned in ears. Jaws shifted.

"Water," Michael's cousin said.

Terrance shook cobwebs, spun to the sound of Niagara, and froze.

Two blasted pipes surged. Vat II's back-drain gushed from one. The other, the main, drained *Core Fuels'* water tower in a torrent.

Josh stood trisected in the few surviving lightbulbs' shadowy light. He helped Lon and Larry up, who in turn helped others perpendicular.

Liquid-filled shoes. Sherbt's lawyer lay face up, water closing over his neck. Owners splashed to him, lifted, and pulled him a few steps up. Someone said, "He's breathing."

Water covered the first step. They dragged the lawyer up two more.

"How do we shut it off?" Lon said.

"There's no shutting *that* off," said Josh

"We're gonna drown down here," Larry sniveled, water cresting knees. "It's Rawling, drowning us, isn't he?"

"Stop blathering, you're alive aren't ya?" Lon said, then, looking to Josh, asked, "With all of us, we could bust out, couldn't we?"

"Maybe, it's a hell-of-a door."

"Damn-it, is there anything we could pry with?" said the cousin.

Feet deep, and water over twice as many stairs, the two holding the lawyer moved him again.

Terrance climbed past them, freed the chainsaw, and threw it in the lake.

Room for four; Michael, Josh, Terrance, and Lon bashed shoulders against the wood. 'Help', their battle cry, repeating.

"Can't get a good hit, the angle sucks," said Lon and demoted himself.

Michael's cousin squeezed in. Results diminished.

A few steps down, Larry driveled to the others about hopelessness.

Sherbt ignored him but Larry's whining toasted Terrance's grits. "Let's use his head for a battering ram."

Josh agreed.

The tide touched light-switch copper. Near *maintenance,* Mark and company heard a breaker – *snap*. The basement turned cave.

The relentless rise crowded them onto fewer and fewer steps. Orientation courtesy lighted chainsaw slits.

"Help me. Help me lift him up," a voice struggled in the dark. Someone helped prop the lawyer to the door. The top step submerged. The door efficiently absorbed pounding and yelling.

"One, two, three, HELP." Josh led the chorus.

"One, two, three . . . Help!" they shout.

Water spilled under the door, climbed, and rushed from the silts. Aqua blades shot long and tall to the hall and water gushed from the door's edge. The leaks did nothing for them. Men on lower steps slipped to treading, their desperate cries, now, for a hand.

Three at the top remained standing, pounding, yelling. One-handed, Terrance held the lawyer up by collar and tie.

Above the slots and rising, water blocked the last light. Larry bobbed, coughed, and croaked, "If anybody gets out, kill Rawling for me." *Blub, blub.*

Terrance surrendered Sherbt's lawyer to the black tide.

Water five feet up the door and Terrance, chin in, formed hammer fists. *Bam, Bam, Bam.*

Nothing – and deeper – they all swam.

Kubwoooooossshhh. Pascal's law of hydraulics showed the stubbornly-proud door who's boss.

Fish in a crest, taken, *Swooowsh . . . Ahh, Whoa, aAhh . . .* cries surfed the rushing surge. And across the hall, they washed to a wall. Helplessly deposited, rolling and flopping, coughing and kicking bodies settled. Sherbt's lawyer choked, awoke, and burbled, "Where am I?"

Lon sat up, looked at Larry. "Now, you can kill him yourself – if ya can beat me to him."

A seething throng rose.

The explosion mitigated milling machine vibrations and, for a moment, Gilbert felt a calm under knee and foot. Bernice and crew, below him, felt the quake.

"What was that?" she shouted at Gilbert. He scanned as he could and shrugged. Movement at the top of Vat II caught Gilbert's eye. "Wait."

"What?" Bernice said.

Gilbert fine-tuned the lenses, and loud, over the machine noise, said, "Not good, I'd say."

"What?" the group below asked.

Gilbert studied.

Near the top of Vat II, the toy fuel-hauler drove up the side, inching vertically. Line from the tanker's front bumper, and pulling, ran over a blade secured at the Vat's upper rim. From there the line dropped inside.

Gilbert read, *Core Fuels,* scrolled on the plastic, chromed, tanker.

Gilbert scrutinized the blasting cap wired to its ass.

Gilbert read the card standing next to the blade on the vat's rim.

S. O. S.

Six inches to the top and climbing, up, up, it silently ascended.

"*Save Our Souls,*" breathed Gilbert.

Inside the vat, Otherjon's weighted float lowered, tugging the powder-filled toy upward as the massive cylindrical tank drained out eight-inch piping.

A minute to the top. A minute to a cut. A minute to a drop. Plus a second or two, and a massacre. And Gilbert wanted to see one. But Sheila, not Sheila.

"Get outta there," he yelled, waving at Gene's crew. "Get, get outta there." Below him, Gilbert's extras curiously watched the wailing man atop the mill.

Across the way, Sheila watched her portal and their new note sinking into view. "Here it comes, here it comes."

Barry's attention turned from portal to Gene and the others. What was Gilbert about, waving, shouting over Mill C's roar?

"Get outta there!" And wild, Gilbert waved. He pointed to death lurking above.

Gene looked up.

Bernice circled Gilbert's raging mill, shut it off, and returned.

Sheila read a soggy note,

"Captain Corn, says – RUN!"

She stood dumbfounded.

Atop quieted mill, Gilbert yelled, "Get the hell outta there!" He waved frantically one last time, then retreated to the ladder's top rung. Another rung down, and he swung, gripping to descend. Weight shifted outward, unsecured ladder bolts grated from mill, and scaffold tipped away. Gilbert's heart skipped. "*AAAAaah.*" Wide-eyed, he held tight, riding. The group below scrambled.

Gene snagged Sheila's sleeve. He jerked her from senselessness.

Both groups scattered. Gene's crew ran from Vat II terror. Bernice's dove from Gilbert on lattice.

The ladder scathed a few. Others cleared in the nick of time. He braced for impact and squeezed his eyes tight. With legs and arms about the rungs and back flush with the floor, Gilbert crashed.

Toy tanker's bumper met blade. The line strained – cut. The released semi went ballistic.

Further the better, Gene's crew ran the corridor south. Twenty, thirty, forty feet they sprinted.

Bah-Wam! Behind them, an explosion flashed. A deafening energy wave caught them, busting them like a cue ball.

Teri ran in drizzle thirty yards alongside the building to the north door before looking back. She stood partially naked in September rain under the entrance's fluorescent light, deciding. Enter and look for help, or not? Inside – would Henry intercept her at the first intersection? Or might he come around the northwest corner in a second?

She heard muffled yelling from inside and put an ear to the metal. Louder – people barking, shouting, and running too, she thought. She chose to look. But the door, locked, denied her. Again she placed her ear to it and listened.

Boom! The door resounded, resonating the stentorian blast – the ground shuddered. She scrambled back, shaking her head.

Twenty yards more she clipped to Jon's racked Impala. Hopped in.

No keys. Above the visor, no keys. She ran, heels – *Clickity-click,* close to the wall. Black Magic's door, like a good country church, seldom locked, and she slipped in.

The explosion's energy rippled from the vat's convex base. Plant pressure spiked. The steel vat stood unimpaired, only a sooty rainbow decorated its side. Smoke hung in the air and a calm settled.

Otherjon rocked back in Bill's chair and clapped a slow methodical clap. A mode change, facilitating a mood change, seemed appropriate. He fed the VCR and it sucked in *Beauty Shakedown.* Plant monitors illuminated. He placed the intercom microphone close to the speaker and cranked the volume near distortion. Throughout the plant, *Beauty Shakedown's* voluptuous starlet-in-blue moaned. She rode her prisoner, and without objection, the detainee bore police brutality.

Bernice, alive and well, led her group to count the dead. Gilbert limped, trailing at the back of the pack. Milling's monitor, behind them, played. The monitor ahead, in *fermentation,* played, and through smoky haze, they watched the screwing. Sable hair hung in the pornlet's eyes, she flipped it back, and from the intercom speakers, averred pleasure, "Yes – yes – oh – Yes!"

Gene and shell-shocked company scraped themselves off the floor; worse for wear and ears ringing, but without fatality. Saturated men, washed from the basement, helped the lawyer along. Three groups morphed into an ugly horde.

"No one leaves till Rawling's head's on a platter," Gene said.

The owners acceded and allowed Queen of *Core* to give marching orders.

"I need a few back over in milling to block, in case he comes outta the cafeteria. The rest of us'll go back through the hall, see if we can cut him off, check the offices, and that sex video didn't start itself."

Gilbert rested his crippled body onto a chair, and said, "I'd just slow ya down." He waved them luck. "Hey, when ya catch the bastard, I'd like a lick, too."

Away from the oaf, away from the melee inside, away from bad vibrations, sodden Teri gently shut the door behind her. She leaned her back against it and stood huffing. Then down to a crouch she slid and put arms around her knees. Lungs burning, and she thought, *'Damn Smokes – if I get outta this alive – throw em in the Platte – eat no fat – live'n beats die'n!*

She scanned the shadowed landscape – hand tools, equipment, cleaning supplies, and unfinished repairs strewn across a long bench. A stool, tall and rickety, she wedged against the door. And a hatchet, hanging on a pegboard, looked her size. She helped it down, and in shadow, ran her hand on its handle, deciding it felt red. No longer indefensible, she pondered, '*Now, where to hide*?' Teri looked at the grunge door concealing the foul, half-bath in back, *smelly idea.* She crawled under the workbench and wedged behind an industrial box of paper towels. The personal protector felt good in her hands and she wondered, *what's a hatchet do at an ethanol plant?*

Soon knees ached, her back, hips, ankles, neck, and bladder complained. Nerves compounded the pressure. Uncomfortable and cold, shivering started. Not helping; rain pattered on the tin roof.

Pip-pity pip above, and cold, led to looking. Her one creature comfort, Black Magic, her very own potty, how bad could it be? But in the dark? – Now *that's* scary. Henry and germs, both gave her shivers. Pressure great, and ready to leak, she moved to use the odorous throne behind door number two.

A deep breath held and in the small windowless cubical she adjusted her punch-filled bladder above the dirty ring. Not just a dark place, *what a relief.*

Chapter 41
Get Him

No monitor in sight, Mark's group stood in the hall outside maintenance, listening to rooky talent on the intercom. Mark jerked a Frankenstein arm and pointed down the hall at the probable source. They glimpsed a bare back enter Bill's control room and the door slammed.

Henry tried removing Otherjon's head. Neck bones musically cracked in chiropractic adjustment. Rawling spun on Bill's chair, and off, and flying, twisting, sending the seat crashing the door. Picked high, Henry airmailed him onto the counter. Otherjon crash-landed. Stunned, he gyrated and looked at the tipped monitor. His reflection obscured the humper on the screen, and Jon said, "Give him the ole one-two." Otherjon tipped off his perch and jabbed. The cross followed and Henry's head snapped back. Henry laughed it off, closed, and thrashed him to the control room window. Hands first, Otherjon landed. Face to reflection and again he found Jon looking back. "Let *me* at im."

"I got this," Otherjon reassured him.

Henry mashed Otherjon's face to the glass.

"Ya sure?" Jon said, lips pressed, one eye squinting.

"Um-hm," he affirmed, and under Hulk's control, jerked away.

By collar and belt, Henry used him to polish Bill's counter. Coffee cup, pens, and notepad fell. Henry lifted. Otherjon hung suspended. His bluchers churned air. Once, twice the Hulk rocked him, and on the third, tossed Otherjon as a late-summer bale. Faces met in Bill's new window. Mark's crew witnessed the ejection.

"G-g-get him," Mark stuttered, pointing with blackened finger.

Hands in glass, Jon pushed up. Blood dripped on shards. Otherjon, in a thousand pieces, strewn sunder. Jon knelt and in slow motion gently swept gems together. The splintered man below assembled on glass islands. A face, partial here, separate there, and the collage repudiated Jon's gallantry.

"*No*," Jon moaned.

In a thousand pieces, Otherjon longingly, wistfully, lovingly, looked, and said, "It was a good run, huh?"

Kite-high, Bryce placed the lawyer's briefcase on a bale, opened it, and gathered cash.The scarecrow adjudicated. Bryce, stuffing bills in pockets, said, "Thank you . . . thank you . . . thank you." Sign-up packets of ten, from tables, he lay in loose straw at the Scarecrow's base. Nails bent in two by fours as Bryce adjusted scarecrow arms, right high, left low. He hung Sherbt's cane and mauve jacket on the lower. Sherbt's bejeweled glasses, also left behind, he wedged on the burlap face. "Handsome devil." In the scarecrow's raised glove he balanced a cup of ladled punch. "Cheers."

Jon ran. Blood drizzled from cuts; the price of release and he missed his Other.

Out the door to finish it came Henry. The electrified bunch met him.

Henry, singed by fire, Mark and crew, singed by lightning, pursued one Rawling.

With a lawyer's pen, Bryce punched a hole in the scarecrow's mouthless face and into it, he turned a doobie. He found Gene's camera. *Click.* "Party Animal." *Too good for you, Frat Boy*, Bryce decided, and took it back. He splashed punchbowl dregs about the harvest, lit weed, then a bale, and enjoyed the flare. He kicked pumpkins from igniting bales into the burning shares. "Hot Party?" he asked stick-man.

Jon jiggled a key into the bottom desk drawer lock. He heard them coming.

Cecil in the lead, JR on his heels, and they hung a left into the offices. More folks followed. Bruised Henry, Soft-boot Bill, and Frankenstein's Mark trailed.

It felt wrong and he laid the wrap without rattle on his desk. *Who? How? When? Where* were his artisan bullets? He hoped for one happy shell and dropped the cylinder, looking for a Henry-stopper. Emptiness beheld, he snapped it shut and turned his attention to the two arriving at the door. He looked at rudimentary wrought-iron window treatments and listened – the mob approached.

The pack of people picks lay on the toy shelf – he grabbed it with his free hand. From his other, he slow-pitched the .357 to the doormen. JR fielded the high polish glint from low light and Cecil braced. Jon blasted through, people picks tucked in a quarterback keep. Three men tumbled, flattened a cubical wall, and ended within. The leather pouch puked people picks. Into corners and under a desk the picks rolled but their maker managed one. The linemen shook it off as an agitated b-team swarmed the office. Jon vaulted Bernice's wall, landed, and stood, baiting them closer. From Bernice's cubical, he owned the office south exit and used it. A roar resembling words rumbled and the growl-emitting bodies chased. He doubled back. A few saw why. Twenty-two tiles south, lock and chain secured the front doors.

Jon sprinted past the intersecting hall.

A distance down it, Bernice and horde watched Jon race past. She pointed and yelled, "There he goes!" The throng kicked it into high. Past maintenance and over Otherjon's shattered remains they thundered.

At the T, pursuing groups collided. Echoes of profanity showered Jon from behind. He looked back and watched incongruent melding. Bernice's horde fused with Mark's b-team under steam. An interspatial collision and charged particles bounced out of control in a chaotic scrum. Bodies careened off one another, and off the wall opposite. Some smashed and latched, grappling instability. Conflation belched Mick's cousin in a header. Palms slapped, unsuccessfully breaking the fall. He face-planted the tile. Teeth snapped. Jon looked again as the running of the bullies trampled the sorry sort.

Wanting is not the same as getting.

Extrication might be nice. Bodies blocked milling. Smoke rolled out of the cafeteria. He wanted the north door. On the production floor, the livid mob of speed beetles raced around equipment. Jon's sheep herded him. He deked his way through the mills. They blocked north. Options decreased. Bobby's key could open the southwest door, but no time to use it. Desperate, he ran from shrieking threats.

Henry found a head smasher; a pipe fitter's prize, nine pounds of pipe-wrench. Wild, boots clapping production floor, pains ignored, raging, he chased.

Jon coughed as he ran. A ladder to nowhere appeared, and like a fireman, or a man on fire, he climbed.

Henry made the base and looked back. Bernice pointed up and commanded, "Go!"

They had him. Bernice slowed, leading her group in a power walk of revenge. Tongues cursed. Feet marched. Heads nodded.

Henry slid the monster wrench in his belt and climbed.

Bernice touched the ladder, looked up, and said, "You want em, Big Guy? Go – *Get* em, Sic'm." Henry snarled and attacked the rungs. The seething congregated. They wanted up. Bernice guarded the ladder. The end of Rawling – this she wanted to witness up close and personal, and when Henry had a good start, *Core's* queen hoisted her heft. Smoke hung in hazy layers. Jon passed through two, Henry one. Mark jerked through the mob, tussled to be next, and tested his grip with a numb hand. He forced it to work. Up, and up, and behind Mark the ladder conveyed supplemental killers skyward. Through smoky haze, like pissed off ants, they climbed. An agitated mound stirred at the ladder's base. Not all could go; more bodies than skywalk – some crossed into milling to watch.

Harrison invented a parking spot at the end of the sidewalk.

"No, it was a hell-of-a flash. Not lightning, either. Something blew up," O'Leary said.

"Looks okay, here."

"Yeah, I don't know – sure looked like an explosion."

About to shut the car door, Harrison asked, "You want the shotgun?"

"Ah, shouldn't need it. You got your pea-shooter. They're probably all dumb drunk, anyway."

Harrison patted his jacket over Walther. Then whistled, coveting Sherbt's Bentley.

Mist giving way to rain, the men moved quickly to the building.

O'Leary tried *Core Fuels'* double doors.

Harrison tried them. "Locked."

They blocked reflection and parking lot light and peered in.

"It's chained," Harrison said.

"That's weird, I don't like it."

They looked again and down an empty hall. "Now what?"

Far to the west, a diesel woke, roared, and their attention turned. Payloader lights beaconed the lot as the machine swiveled, backing away from the far corn pile. It showed them its back amber lights, revved, belched exhaust, and rolled north around the end of the building, and out of sight.

"See where that's going," O'Leary ordered. "I think I'll grab the Wingmaster, after all. Be right behind ya."

Harrison tracked the payloader. O'Leary set buckshot on the patrol car trunk lid and positioned his foot on the rear bumper. He rested the 870 on his thigh, ignored rain, and fed the shotgun red shells.

Jon ran awkward across the catwalk, unzipping his fly. Past a short gangway reaching out over Vat I, past a second, over empty Vat II, and he jogged to the end, stopping above Vat III. He swung open the safety gate, whipped out dick, and started pissing in the fermentation vat. Urine streamed a long flowing arc and bubbled into the brew below. Queen of Core led ants skyward. Henry stepped from ladder to catwalk and pulled the pipe-wrench from his leather belt. Sweat dripped from his stringy hair. Wrench lifted in left and shirtless, he charged.

"Wait!" Bernice yelled, nearing the top. Henry obeyed, stopped, and stood with his feet apart as if blocking an escape. "I wanna see, I wanna hear it . . . when you crush his skull."

Blackened Mark followed her onto the walkway as others climbed. Jon continued relieving himself and turned to piss in their general direction. He whipped dick round and around, pissing everywhere. "Ho, ho ha ho," he laughed.

"Kill him," Bernice ordered.

Henry paused and set his arms in a Jesse Ventura pose. But there was no politician, no compromise in Henry Rotten Ass tonight. He kissed each bicep, then Henry the specimen, stepped forward.

"Smash him!" Bernice yelled. Mark jeered, as did those behind him. Cheers from the floor peppered Henry, too.

Henry's massive chest twitched. He cocked the wrench high.

Lon cleared the last rung, looked past the others on the catwalk, and shouted, "Take his head off!"

Jon tucked it in and zipped. He reached behind and gripped the pick protruding from his back pocket. Henry seemed to move in slow motion. How easy to insert tine in the naked belly before him but the pick he'd save for the woman behind old Henry. It was the bitch he longed to stick!

Henry roared, "You're done, Fucker," and swung the heavy metal with perfect aim and malice at Jon's melon. Jon stood his ground, almost letting the impact happen, only parrying the arc at the last moment. The deflected wrench grazed the crazed. Momentum pulled Henry hard and Jon returned low.

He used shoulder and shank. The pick hooked calf and his shoulder butted Henry's ribs with lift. Jon graciously helped Rotten Ass over the rail. "Have a nice flight."

"Waaaah!" Henry screamed and gripped tight the wrench. His head ricocheted off a cast iron pipe. A sweat shower splashed from soaked hair and the wrench took a new direction. Henry's flailing Jesse Ventura arms backstroked the quick trip down. Jon watched him fall, everyone watched him fall. Henry stuck the landing. A sack of rotten taters – no dead cat bounce. The thump echoed forty feet upward through a silent crowd.

The spectacle slowed the posse. Big and mean to the core as she was, watching Henry do a pike with half twist cooled Bernice's jets. She approached cautiously, minions in tow, her bazooka mammaries in the lead.

Jon leaned, reached for the Bobby-installed rheostat, and set it on high. The fan whirled. Cool-wet night air blasted in. Layers of smoke swirled. He bathed in night wind for a second and felt the blood, from yet another head wound, push across his face. He used a sleeve to wipe, then eased away, stopping precariously near the precipice.

Bernice stepped closer. Adrenalin rushed and her big, healthy heart pumped. She inhaled full, exhaled. A blouse strap draped off her shoulder. Sweat rolled, droplets cohered, zagged on her milky skin, and disappeared down much-exposed cleavage.

A flash from Jon's steamy dream shot through his head. Bernice rode him as Mrs. Claus, tasseled hat looping above as she swiveled, long red fingernails digging as she undulated . . . He puked a little in his mouth. He swallowed.

Through clenched teeth, Bernice said, "I'm goin ta rip you apart, you A-hole." Her voice buffeted in the fan's workings and her curls whipped.

A subsequent image flashed Jon – Bernice's obituary. And, *oh*, how she had checked the boxes; an obit torturously long. She would annoy in death as she had in life.

Bernice Goody-two-shoes Jorgen. How well she sniffed her snout up everyone's biz-n-ass. Blah, Blah, Blah . . . Active in the community – church council – city council – Blah, blah, blah . . . Blah, blah, blah. Bernice the pachyderm, crushed souls – took names.

Her mass approached. Jon felt tremors underfoot. The catwalk creaked, confessing strain. Bernice formed her hands – chubby tiger claws. She curled her lips – a rabid dog, baring two perfect rows of child-like teeth. "Grrrr."

Jon almost laughed. "Whoa, Cujo."

Bernice stepped an unhappy step. Low-grade Chinese decking broke at a Friday-afternoon weld. Under 286 svelte pounds, it gave way. A size six black pump shot through. Stretchy pants and skin peeled ankle to knee. She caught the railing with an arm and bellowed, "Aaaahoooww!"

Folks at the rails peered past one another, caring little if Bernice might be next, as long as they got in on the bloodletting.

Jon raised the pick and took a bead on her forehead.

"Nooo!" Bernice screamed.

Jon paused, felt a twinge of empathy – and there *was* that painful obituary hanging over his head. He diverted the plunge, sticking the pachyderm with restraint. The shank passed Bernice's forehead and sank full, between neck and naked shoulder, just below clavicle. *Pick a pick, pick a pick, pick a pick . . . pop!*

A scream, an octave higher than the last, she howled, "Aaawha!"

Jon thought, *maybe I'm not that crazy after all.* He turned the pick in its new home. "That's for Leia." The twisting engagement overloaded her nervous system, sending a shudder through Bernice. She stared up at him, quivering, blubbering.

For a long moment, Jon gazed into Bernice's watery eyes, then grabbed her chin and moved her head to the side. "I think that's gonna leave a mark."

He felt the antidote for chronic coughing coming on. From a lung, Jon hacked a green, swollen embryonic corn kernel encased in yellow mucus. He rotated it on tongue, inhaled, and hawked. The kernel led, pulling a clinging comet's tail of caramel mucus. Over Bernice, a direct flight path, and the gestation hit home. Mark winced, flittered back, taking it in the eye. "Aaah," he cried as if the infliction injured.

"Don't look so . . . *shocked,*" Jon laughed.

Mark wanted at him, as did others. Bernice-o-Saurus plugged the approach, blocked the mob. Jon's middle fingers flicked like switchblades, flipping them a double. He spun and cannonballed into the piss tank below. *Long way from Broadway – but – if you are going to give em a show…*

Six feet under, he felt the liquid concussion above, a wonderful splash, and figured it a nine or a ten. He emerged with a sidestroke, reached the rim, added a flutter kick, and pulled himself over the side. Rinsed in a vat of alcohol, the cuts on his head seared. Blood pumped from Jon's hairline. A diluted red veil washed down his face. Jon *The Red.*

Even hanging from the rim, his feet dangled far above the cement floor. He looked down, *a hell-of-a-drop*. The fall collapsed his knees and stung his heels. His wet ass met cement, smacked his coccyx, and the wind folded out of him. Still, he lay, as if it were the end. Then, the gang in milling watched Jon miraculously scrape himself off the floor and inflate to his feet. On slippery soles, dripping, and smelling like brew, he skated to the north exit.

He unlocked and behind him, the door slammed.

Chapter 42
Walther Works

An empty bladder helped, but there was something else that could really take the edge off. She dug the soft-pack from her pocket. Out came the lighter. She pulled a bent cigarette from the wrinkled pack, who could quit under all this stress?

Jon leaned into a reckless stagger and headed for the Impala. Beat down, rushing, he banged thigh on the Chevy's busted front clip. *Impala's revenge.* An alcohol-dripping shirt-tail caught the damaged header. With an angry twist of conviction, Jon spun, ripping free. As he turned, a flicker of light flashed in the shitter-shed window.

Teri slipped the lighter back in her pocket and enjoyed blowing a long exhale. *I'll crawl back under the bench as soon as I finish my smoke.*

Jon circled the car, opened the passenger door and glove box. Sassy 66 lay in waiting and he helped himself to it.

How long had it been, *ten, fifteen minutes*? Teri wondered. Not long, but cold, and her goose-bumps were growing. She wrapped her arms tight to her body and flicked ashes off the cigarette. Weary, impatient, she leaned back against the workbench. Lot-light angled through the window, casting her shadow across the room. She watched it take a drag and felt disgusted at her weak will. Into the melding black and grays, she dropped the cigarette, smashed the glow under a twist, and swore she'd extinguish the habit as well.

With renewed enthusiasm, Jon quietly danced to the shed and stood at the door for a listen. Black Magic blocked light. He pumped Onion Slayer's hickory handle. Shiny in the shade the blade flashed. He heard humming, *We Gotta Get Out of This Place.*

Not possessed, obsessed, he owed Otherjon, didn't he? *Get my fill. Carve something. Get it out of the system. And never cut thyself again. Pumpkin guts are for sissies, spill something significant.* He smiled at the clean flashing blade, suppressing laughter.

Jon turned the latch handle and pushed slowly. It creaked. The blocking stool chittered across cement and caught on a crack.

Bloody-faced, Jon peered. Framed in the window's light, Teri watched a protracted coagulating drip fall from a chin.

"*Aaahh*!" Her piercing oration of horror shot through Jon, taking him a stroke back from Shit Falls.

He pushed. Teri's engineering gave way and she watched the stool tumble.

He stood in full view. Wounds oozed dark trickles, down face, neck, under the standing white collar, and into a red and pink tie-dyed disaster – 66 flashed her. Again, Teri started a scream – recognized her disheveled bloodied boss, and the shriek tailed off.

"Jon, what happened to your face?"

"Small altercation with some subordinates."

"Altercation?"

"And the owners," he said, sliding 66 into his waistband.

"And the owners? – What about the plant, booby-traps, I heard an explosion, two of em?"

"A bunch of em were in on it, I think. Henry, Bernice, Sherbt even, and they framed me. Everyone thinks I did it. Pissed off hive of hornets and they're all comin for me. And you?" he asked, looking at her booby trap, top cupped in underwear, and trying not to over-inspect.

"Hiding from Henry, he's bad." She held her hand over a breast, concealing a cold cloth-covered nipple.

"They're *all* bad." And he reached for her free hand. "Time to get outta here." She took his. Together, they scooted for the car.

"Mr. Rawling, Jon, you shouldn't talk like that. They aren't *all* bad, a few – mean and greedy. Some misguided followers. There's some good people here."

"Good? Good for nothin sons-uh-bitches."

The north door burst open. The tattered two watched an angry crowd spill out, heard livid shouts.

He hustled her in on his side and she slid over. Keys from under the seat started the Impala. "They're coming!" Teri yelled.

Something thrown skipped off the hood.

Jon put it in reverse, looked over his shoulder, and backed fast. He cranked the wheel and hit the brake. The front slid ninety. Teri grasped air, pressed to the door, and bounced back with an abrupt stop against Jon.

Jon pulled the light switch. High-intensity halogen beams converged on the Impala occupants. They squinted. Teri raised her arm, shielding her eyes. Jon shielded his with one hand and selected D with the other.

Gilbert, in payloader, pounced.

Jon stepped on it – tried turning. Two, three seconds, the Impala sat in the rain, rear wheel spinning on gravel and spilled corn. "Hold on!"

Bucket low, Gilbert on the move scooped the car's front. For a moment, Impala headlights lit the inside of the bucket, then smashed black. Teri crashed the dash. Jon mashed the steering wheel. The hood buckled. Antifreeze sprayed from a gap above the fender. A metal-on-metal screech sounded under the hood. Gilbert had them. Payloader bucket off the ground and he pushed, reversing the Impala across the lot. A cheer rose from the mob. Jon knew who had them, as did the crowd.

Mid their merriment, Harrison rounded the corner and saw the applauding pack. In the rain and angling, he slowed, deciding where to go. He picked the payloader.

O'Leary opened the west door and leveled the shotgun. He listened, walked the west hall, stopped, and listened again.

'Awh, awh', faint moans waffled from the ether. He peered from hall to corridor.

'Oh, Oh, oh,' another voice, younger, moaned from speakers.

'Awh, ow, awh'. Louder. Not from speakers. He stepped to look up.

Bernice gripped the rails, neutralizing weight as her fatigued arms allowed. The antler handle angled out of her and blood trailed from two wounds. One spilled from clavicle to tributaries on and around her breast. The other soaked her sock, filling a shoe.

"Help, help me," she called, seeing O'Leary. "Help, I'm stuck."

O'Leary said nothing, waved, and inspected Henry's body from a distance as he passed. He looked at the monitor's lovers in changed tantric. Then propped the Wingmaster against Vat I and climbed.

Surprised at the vat and catwalk's elevation, he moved carefully across to Bernice.

Bernice, ripe and soaked, looked back best she could with a people pick in her. "Help, get me outta here, could ya? She asked as nice as she knew how, and her voice warbled in a shiver of shock.

"In a pickle, huh? Let's see what we can do."

O'Leary sat low on a leg, hugged her from behind, and used his other foot to step open the decking's break. First, he thought it funny, *Humpin a mammoth football*, then the smell, *sweaty mastodon.*

Before rising, Bernice lowered an inch. Jagged mesh walkway released and O'Leary opened farther its bite. "Owh," she moaned and lugged upward and her shoe hooked mesh. Forty feet it fell and spat blood on Henry as it smacked the tile. He didn't twitch.

They stood. He helped her turn and, face to face, he examined her deer-bone-handle appendage.

"Leave it, don't touch it."

He let it be, looked at her leg, at her clown-like mascara running down her ghost-white face. "How are we gonna get you down?"

She took a deep breath of determination, and exhaled, "I can do *it*."

Brave O'Leary went first, *if she falls – I die*. The old football injury hurt but he descended, nursing the shoulder. He watched her blood-soaked sock squish moisture on each rung above him. He prayed.

She moved, slowly, methodically, favoring pick side, moving left arm at the elbow. Both hands, both feet, touched every rung, and she expelled an 'Uhf,' on each.

Bernice touched down. She stood on the floor, favoring shoed foot, and held the ladder. O'Leary went for Bernice's fallen shoe.

"And who's that?" he said, returning, nodding back at the leaking splat.

"Henry, Henry Rothness . . . Rawling killed him. He's gone off the rails, ya gotta find him, arrest him."

O'Leary knelt. Bernice held a rung, lifted her foot, and he fitted bloody shoe on bloody sock. "I've got a bit of bad news, Bernice. Guess who came out of a coma today?" He stood, reaching for cuffs, and said. "You're under arrest for . . ."

Pick missing, Bernice's pock oozed anew. And here it came. In the same awkward fashion she punched Leia, she jabbed the tainted tine into O'Leary's solar plexus. She ripped it back.

"Oh, oh, OH YES!" the starlet on the monitor finished.

Eyes full of surprise, O'Leary dropped the cuffs and pressed hands to gut. "You sow!"

Arm swinging around, she stuck people pick in pig. O'Leary's carotid artery sprayed. He gasped.

Beauty Shakedown ended, monitors snowed, speakers *shushushed* dying O'Leary.

Bernice limped to Henry, curled the pick in his dead hand, and teary-eyed, said, "Henry Rothness, you sack'a shit."

Bernice hobbled down the west hall and out.

Gilbert accelerated past the bins, and on. Cocked slightly, the Impala's front fit well in Gilbert's steel bucket. Four great payloader wheels churned on damp lot, exposing dry September dirt beneath. A dusty cloud swirled behind the rain-spattered machine. Gilbert roared full ahead, soldiering them onward – backward. Winded, Harrison fell farther behind.

Teri, screaming, and Jon, shaking her, yelled, "Get ready to jump."

Gilbert ran the bucket higher.

Jon pulled the handle and cracked open his door. Teri tried hers. The Impala's buckled fender clamped it tight.

"Wait till he slows," Jon said.

Teri – frantic, pulled, jerked, pushed. "It won't open!"

Gilbert continued to lift; gravity worked against Jon's door, it hung heavy. *Should we buckle up?*

The front higher, higher, and the rear bumper touched ground. The car scraped, plowed, sound reverberating through chassis. Under the twisted hood, the battery slid; terminals shorted – sparks flashed. Taillights flickered. An ionization smell filled the cab.

Jon checked Teri. No longer frantic, she looked comatose. In the bright halogen, he watched a fear-of-dying tear run out the corner of her eye and roll down her face. The rising bucket draped the light – the cab went dark.

Gilbert drove them from lot to lawn. He slowed and lifted the Impala's front higher.

Harrison puffed, "Stop!"

He didn't hear, but the machine stopped; Gilbert had them in position and the car stood nearly vertical.

Harrison drew – aimed at the silhouette behind the rain-distorted glass.

Gilbert flipped the front of the bucket, sending his refuse tipping. "Bye, bye Bastard," he murmured. The Impala stood straight as a diver perched on high board.

Jon clung to the wheel. Teri compressed into the seatback.

Harrison fired.

The crowd jeered.

Ta-PinK. Gilbert jumped. The payloader's single wiper swiped over a bullet hole high on the windshield and water dripped down the window's inside. Gilbert rotated, found the entry hole in the cab's back glass, and through the wet window, saw a muzzle flash. He flinched. A miss.

The car teetered and tipped back to the bucket.

Gilbert crouched, nudged the machine forward, and working levers, he gave the bucket a better flip. The car stood vertical, balanced, then tipped in a slow-motion reverse dive. Jon squeezed the free-turning steering wheel.

Teri involuntarily placed hands on the roof and braced. Harrison moved a few paces closer and grounded himself in a trained stance.

As it fell, the Impala gained momentum, gravity pulling the weighty engine to earth. It smash-landed, pillars buckling, windshield crunching, 66 disappearing. Occupants crashed the roof – crumpled figures – knees in faces.

"Whoa, Yeah, Yes, Whohoo!" Like fireworks, cheers popped from the crowd.

The payloader roared, diesel smoke shooting from stack, and Gilbert lowered the bucket, pressing the Impala. He looked over his shoulder. Another muzzle flash. *Tang-pingk.* An outside cab light, glowing amber, went black. Again, Gilbert flinched, made himself small, and ran the bucket controls. The payloader's front lifted off the ground, bringing weight-to-bear on the car.

The back window shattered. Jon kicked at the door. The smothered dome light lit. He kicked again, and again – the doorframe pushed earth, mounding sod as it moved. One foot, two – and there, the pressing bucket planted the door. A hand reached in. Jon grabbed it.

Dazed, Teri croaked, "Help." Scrunched on her neck and shoulders, her legs worked like springing un-canned snakes.

The hand pulled Jon's. He slid in a half crawl, leg passing the dome-light, one arm out, one reaching back for Teri. She found it in the light.

Where did he come from? Gilbert swore, "Fuck you, Bryce!" and pivoted the great machine, swiping with his bucket.

Harrison steadied, one hand on the pistol grip, the other under, aiming Walther. He exhaled and squeezed off a round.

Tink-pwuck. Through the back glass, through Gilbert's silly striped polo, and the slug lodged deep in his shoulder.

That does it! Gilbert pivoted the yellow beast. Full throttle it roared at Harrison. Harrison stumbled back, fired, turned, and ran but moved half as fast as Gilbert rolled.

Bryce the hater, not a killer, helped Jon out. Jon helped Teri out. In the rain, they ran.

Most eyes fell to Harrison's scramble. Not Mick's. Heat lightning flashed and he glimpsed their escape. He punched Dad in the arm. "They're getting away!"

Lon jabbed Larry, tugged Sherbt's sleeve, and pointed. Four owners followed three runners around the building's east side.

Harrison, in full clamber, shot wildly over his shoulder. Walther PPK clip content sprayed. *Bank Bank* – Lead in the bucket. *Whizzz* – Lead through the air. *Tinka-splunk* Lead in the eye.

Harrison stumbled.

Gilbert slumped.

Payloader veered.

Gilbert's hole dripped blood between steering wheel spokes, on his good shoe, and to the dirty floor.

"Toro," gasped Harrison. He stepped clear and watched the massive diesel roar by. Bucket first, it struck Black Magic, pounding it from the foundation. In halves, the foul throne tumbled free toward the crowd. A healthy portion of Black Magic accompanied the payloader into *Core's* wall. Cab-deep in brick, it ended.

"Police are here," Jon said, seeing the squad car.

"What should we do?" Teri asked, slowing, looking.

"Get the hell outta here. Let them sort it out."

Teri jogged ahead. "We can take the Camaro."

"Where?" said Bryce.

Teri looked at Jon. "The hospital?"

"The farm," Jon said, opening the passenger door.

Teri's keys hung from the ignition. She pumped the gas and started the Camaro. Jon tilted the bucket seat forward, offering Bryce the back.

"You're welcome," Bryce said but backed away and started for his car.

"Ya sure?"

Bryce glanced, nodded at the plant. "Don't think I'll be seein ya Monday."

"No, spose not."

"*Cold Spot,*" he said. "Worked up a thirst burning those company shares."

"Thanks for saving our bacon, Bryce."

Teri's wet, naked back peeled off the vinyl seat as she leaned. *What can I say?* She looked out the open passenger door. "Thanks, Bryce."

"Yeah, I owed ya one." He waved. And hell-bent for a *Cold Spot* double, Bryce, in the lead, exited the lot.

They didn't yell. They didn't shout. Soggy owners slid into Sherbt's sweet Bentley. Sherbt backed around the cop car. With lights off, wipers on, they followed Teri's taillights. The Camaro crested a hill a mile east; Sherbt turned his lights on and pulled out of the lot.

Chapter 43
Home Sweet Home

Teri set the Camaro's heater on high. Jon found napkins in the Glovebox, cleaned his face, and pressed cuts.

"Are you sure? I think we should go to emergency."

"Looks worse than it is."

It looks awful. "I hope nobody else is hurt."

"The Sheriff's men'll get'em sorted out."

"Hope they catch em, figure out who did it. It's Henry for sure. Bernice and Henry . . . I know it. The stealing . . . Crap! My purse is in the lunchroom."

On the way, Jon told her what Leia had expressed; that Bernice and Henry had attacked her. And that Leia, doing better, should recognize her, be happy to see her.

Conscious of her top, she thought how but a few short years ago, she and Leia pranced around in bikinis, sunning on the dock, or lay on lawn chairs in the yard, and how she liked the way Jon had noticed her . . . her developments. She liked how Jon, trying not to notice, noticed now, even if he was a mess. She tried to concentrate on her driving. And not think about how fit he looked in his alcohol-soaked shirt. She tried to concentrate on Leia and how wonderful it would be to see her recovering friend. She tried to think about Tom, she hadn't forgotten Tom, but Jon . . . and the bloody, stained shirt didn't bother her in the least. It kind of turned her on. And she thought, *how ridiculous – He's like twenty years older – my friend's dad – married to my friend's mom.* And, rubbing thighs together, pushing forward in her Penney's slacks, she thought naughty thoughts.

The few unbroken cigarettes in her pocket cracked. A flush wave colored her cheeks and she turned the heat down.

"What's the plan?" Larry asked.

"Like the lawyer said, be part of something organic," Lon suggested.

"So there's no plan."

The Bentley rolled smooth, quiet, a wraith in the rain, and with one hand low on the wheel, Sherbt guided the phantom. Michael clapped his open hand with fist. Lon and Larry salivated.

Tar roads, valleys, hills, over creeks, past sloughs and fields of stubble to gravel road "R," Teri drove. Into and out of Kissin' Cousins curves the two cars traveled – a mile apart. Clouds broke, rain passed, and moonbeams sprinkled the fresh telluric landscape. Ahead, Rawling's mailbox.

Teri navigated the driveway, slipped past the plumbing van and parked near Clive's Maverick attached to the RV.

Sherbt shut lights off, slowed, turned, and idled down the drive. Halfway to the house, he parked the Bentley sideways across the road and popped the trunk. The men followed him out, quietly clicking car doors shut. In harvest moon moonlight, they watched him gear up. First a hunting vest. He zipped it and filled loops with shells, then placed a ridiculous plaid English hat on head. From a case in the Bentley's trunk, he slid out the long, sexy, Italian. An easy-to-swing Benelli Monifeltro 12.

"Fish in a Barrel," Larry chuckled. Sherbt winked. Then pointed the Benelli at his golf bag. Lon, Larry, and Michael helped themselves, each choosing from Sherbt's irons. Unabashed, they walked.

"What's with all the vehicles? Teri asked. "No lights on in your house."

A sinking feeling hit Jon. "I don't know . . . Something's not right. A guy we met a couple of weeks ago owns the Maverick and motorhome. Not sure about the van, not Darrin, not our plumber."

Teri recognized concern in his voice. "What do you wanna do?"

Jon's fear and anger wrestled. "Go in – see what the hell's goin on." He prepared himself for anything, from ax murderer to zombie daughter. "Maybe they're watching a movie or something."

Furtive approach – cautious – quiet, Jon figured, getting out. Teri slammed her door.

The owners watched and walked four abreast, like gunslingers in the dark. A hundred yards and closing, even strides scuffed wet gravel.

Larry, spinning a five iron, murmured, "There they go."

Michael heard Sherbt click the Benelli's safety off and, through clenched teeth, whispered to Dad, "This is nuts." Lon's eyes agreed.

Jon took Teri's hand. Yard-light defined Teri's scant, powder-blue bra against white skin. He towed her, and a half step behind, she safely accompanied.

Rebecca watched. "Oohw," she steamed. *Beyond belief,* and she hoped Leia couldn't see. Teri's top blinded reason. Emotions rushed, flooded, momentarily paralyzing her. She snapped out of it and left the kitchen window for the front door.

Clive saw them, too. "Your Dad's here."

Leia joined him at the living room window and Clive further separated the curtain for her.

"Teri's with," she said and moved to unlock the front door.

Rebecca put her hand on the knob. "No."

"What?"

Rebecca paused and not knowing what to say, looked down.

It registered and Leia said, "No, Mom, no. Teri's got a friend."

"It's been a long week, you don't know."

"Don't be ridiculous," Leia said, and Clive was getting it.

Jon shunted Clive's funeral florae aside with his foot. He rattled the doorknob. Teri stood behind him, shivering in night air.

In obstinate resolve, Rebecca shook her head.

"Mom! There still might be more of em out there, let em in."

Jon heard. "It's me . . . and Teri." Again, he rattled the knob, looked back at Teri, and shrugged.

Que sera, Rebecca crossed the dark room and collapsed on the couch. Leia unlocked.

Dim figures stood on the drive, fronts edging light, backs to night.

Sherbt signaled a frontal assault for his men, and how he would circle, post, euthanize escapees.

"No witnesses," Larry whispered. Sherbt gave him a callous smile and pat on the back. Nervous Michael dared not look at them. Lon, ready to shit his pants, shifted.

Three skirted Pudge's van, the Maverick, RV, and Jon's black Dodge. White fence to the left, white fence right, and unnoticed they approached the sidewalk. Sherbt and the Italian passed Teri's Camaro and followed the tree line around the house.

Jon led Teri inside.

"Did you see anyone out there?" Clive asked.

"No . . . what are you guys doing?" Jon asked, shutting the door.

Teri saw Leia's recovery – and Clive; she nestled behind Jon, hiding her nakedness.

"We were attacked," Clive said.

"Clive got one of em . . . there's a body in the smokehouse.

"Self-defense," Clive declared, and in a hopeful tenor, said, "Might have just been that one."

Jon tried to square this extended dystopian news.

What happened to you?" Leia said, checking Dad.

"Party turned into a fight."

Rebecca approached, shoved the folded afghan at Teri.

"Thank you," Teri sighed.

Jon reinforced Teri's gratitude, his wife's thoughtfulness, and also thanking Rebecca, he mumbled, "Thank y . . ."

Swap! Rebecca's palm struck his cheek with surprising intensity. "Some party, eh?" Bile churned. Rebecca suppressed an urge to spit, to spit on Teri, to slap her, to spit on Jon.

Minutes removed from squirming, pressing, coveting, cracking cigarettes in the car, Teri looked guilty as hell. She swaddled her top, not letting her eyes meet the ladies'. Jon's cumulative lust rebuked a pleading look of innocence. Leia constructed a brick wall of betrayal, projected it, and stepped near Mom. Clive stood alone.

"Are you kidding me? No," Jon said. "Teri's like a daughter. I, we, would never, it, nothing like that, ever, never."

Teri quivered and looked to Leia. "It was Henry. At the party. He attacked me."

Jon nodded an affirmation, then shook his head. "It got crazy."

Teri agreed.

Michael murmured two shallow words, "I . . . can't." The club slipped from his hand. He stepped back. Lon turned.

Larry turned. "Where do you think you're goin?"

"I can't," he repeated.

"Michael," Lon said.

"Come on, Dad, let's go." And he back-stepped again.

"Get back here, you fuckin pussy," Larry said. "Grow a pair."

"Dad."

Voice steeped in regret, Lon said, "In for a penny, in for a pound." The suffused lyrics hung in the moment. He picked up the club, offered it. Michael shook his head and with fingers apart, waved both hands in refusal. He spun and ran for the Chevy.

Jon reached for the light switch. They heard the Camaro door slam.

Rebecca, relieved, thought *O'Leary*. Jon paused. Clive separated the curtain and looked.

"Your car," he said, focusing on Camaro headlights. Movement, on the porch to his left, caught his attention, and farther he drew the curtain. "There's a guy . . ."

But to his right, like a diving Kingfisher, Lon's lucky seven-iron flashed, smashed, penetrating club-head deep in the tranquil picture window. *Puttoosh.* Glass shards filled Clive's eyes. Fright so acute he couldn't scream. His hands quivered in front of his eyes and he stumbled backward. Calves found the coffee table. Leia reached. Clive clutched. They toppled.

Wham. Larry bashed the front door, exploding latch from jam. Door, accelerating on hinges, smashed the wall. Larry came in swinging, yelling, "*FORE.*" Jon ducked.

Twunk. Rebecca's back stopped the club. She arched, pain stole breath, released her knees, and to them she dropped. *What's happening?* And she blamed Teri.

Lon was in. The congested living room contained seven.

"Ugh," Lon grunted, swinging club high-to-low in the dark. Lucky seven smacked Jon's shoulder. Jon grabbed, neutralized it, and started a tug of war.

He looked over his shoulder. "Run!"

Clive, under Leia, blinked, screamed, "*Aaaahhhh*!" blinked, and moaned, "aauuhh." Blood festered in sockets.

Jon climbed the club and kicked Lon out the door.

Larry struck again, iron catching the door's leisurely return. The bantam club-head detached, flew, and Larry held a poker. He thrust it, glancing Jon's ribcage a gouge as Bra Girl jumped him.

Teri saddled, jockeyed, scratched. Larry reared, spun, and shucked. "Off me, *you witch!*" and, with his free hand, he flung her. Teri sprawled atop Rebecca's odium, taking her to the mat. They wrestled up.

Jon propelled the door, thwarting Lon's re-entry with a strike. "*Run!*" he repeated. Larry slashed, club whistling, Jon dodging. Another, and on Jon's blocking arms it landed.

"Gonna whip you like a dog, you sumbitch." Larry slashed from the other side, and again, connected.

Down the hall in retreat, Rebecca separated from Teri, pushing her back. Leia pushed her ahead. "Can you see?" she asked, leading Clive.

"Sort of, not much," he admitted.

They heard a body hit the wall, plaster bust, then the television.

Rebecca paused at the door, ready to escape . . . but intuition whispered, *'don't.'*

"Go, Mom," Leia coaxed. Half-blind Clive scrunched Teri. Teri scrunched Rebecca. Rebecca elbowed.

Sherbt posted in the back yard, slightly uphill, behind a tree. He listened to house-ruckus and drips from trees on the autumn leaves that blanketed his surround. His damp shirt clung and transferred a chill into him. He shivered, leveled the Benelli, and aimed at the back door.

A grappling tussle took Larry and Jon to the den. Jon's punch separated them. Larry spun to the window, "uhf," fell, and knocked the sole surviving flower vase from sill to twin bed. Jon tipped the tall desk, *'Tilt',* and it crashed, part on Larry's legs, part on the bed.

Mean draining out of him, Lon picked himself up off the sidewalk. He stood, deciding if rejoining the fray was in his best interests. The bent seven-iron lay near. He adjusted his neck and stared at it. He thought about the four round Camaro taillights dipping into the ditch, rounding the Bentley, fishtailing back onto the drive; Michael disappearing west. *Smart Kid.* He thought about Kristy, naked, buoyant, in their new heated pool. He tried to remember, *did Sherbt pull Bentley keys – or leave'em in the ignition?* And finally, pondered his own swift death: Sherbt unloading the Benelli in him. *In for a pound,* and he picked up the club.

Larry struggled, half pinned under the desk. Jon shut the door and strode to the kitchen. Sixty-six, lost in the Impala, but Onion Slayer's short, sharp accomplices waited. From their hold, he slid them, and with a five-inch blade in each hand, one straight, one curved, he returned. *Cut the man, clean the blade.*

Larry worked free. The den door opened and opposite the felled desk, stood Jon. In abbreviated motion, *Tick-Tish,* Jon twice swiped the short blades together.

Anytime, Lon. And Larry decided – *Time to regroup.* He lifted the sash.

Palms left the raised window, and hands up, Larry snapped back. Sound followed motion. *Blam!* Pellet Head, Larry Lifeless, fell faceless up, in the lilies.

Jon chanced light, confirmed the grimness. Did Larry get his just deserts? Mess on the bed brought no joy – only weighted remorse.

Recoil tilted Sherbt's plaid hat. He adjusted it and smiled. *Arrivederci.*

Rebecca pushed the crowd back. Jon shut the den light off and met them in the hall.

"Larry's dead. . . We're going to run for it," and in the living room he picked up Larry's club turned poker.

"Lon's still out there?" asked Rebecca.

"Shotgun in back. We can get past Lon, take him." And looking at Clive's leaky sockets, he asked Leia, "Can you help him?"

Leia squeezed Clive's hand. "Stay with me, now."

Clive tried not to blink, and presently wished they'd never met.

"Here." Jon handed his bride the poker, and Teri, the straight-bladed knife.

Teri separated the curtain with it. "I don't see him."

The door had closed of its own accord. Jon opened it, looked, and listened.

"See em?" Rebecca asked.

Jon shook his head and turned with a finger on his lips.

"Here," Leia offered Teri a sweatshirt.

Jon thought, *Yard light*, and flipped it off. *We know the yard best, except Clive, and he can't see shit, anyway.*

The driveway and yard were well lit by moonlight, but where, where to go, where to hide? The Camaro was gone. The RV looked impossible, pinned by the van and with a Maverick attached. His Dodge – also pinned between the RV and fence. The plumbing van? An exposed run, and would there be keys? Or the summer kitchen, with one door? – *No, no, no, and no.*

And now, he had an idea, *Baby Cakes. Yes, Baby Cakes*, and if we might sneak around and down the bank, we could float away on *Baby Cakes*. Let the current take us to safety, let current assuage our woes.

"Easy, now, not a whisper." And Jon reached back for a hand to lead.

Rebecca slinked back. She might die tonight, but hell if she would take it, and she glared at Teri in the dark. Teri wanted to take it, but hell if she could, now.

Clive, one hand in Leia's, groped with the other and gripped it. Rebecca and Teri, with weapons, followed the three-link chain out the front. Jon steered and across the wet lawn they hurried.

"Five blind mice . . . see how they run," Lon said, cozy in the driver's seat. He turned the key.

Rearrearraerarr. The gear-reduced starter cranked.

"The Dodge," Leia said. Jon knew. The engine caught, revved, and the deserters froze. *Blam*, pickup lights caught five escapees in high beams.

"Hide!" Jon shucked Clive's hand, then stepped forward in the light.

Lon gunned the black Dodge. Jon spread his arms, inviting an attack. Lon revved it, this time clutching, slipping the shifter into gear.

Leia, Clive, Rebecca, and Rebecca's estranged stepdaughter ran.

Lon dumped the clutch and crashed Rebecca's pretty picket. White planks shattered. Jon moved slow, arms out, stepping back.

Sherbt heard revving, the crash, and left his post.

The ladies and Clive ran to the steps leading down to the river and stopped. Leia thought about the south path along the water. *Path to nowhere.*

Rebecca, rearguard, gripped the headless club and watched Jon's scramble.

"Where?" Teri urged.

Atrophied muscles, strength sapped, and Leia's weakness overwhelmed her; the boathouse looked good. "There," she said.

Sherbt walked the empty front lawn, following the commotion.

Jon zigged. The Dodge slicked left. Jon zagged. Lon cranked the wheel and the long-box Dodge, skimming wet grass, slid right. Lon chased and bearing down, Jon dove. The Dodge slid by and spun a slick donut. Headlights swept the nightscape, illuminating the shed, house, Sherbt, summer kitchen, and four heads moving beyond the bank. Sherbt spotted them and, when the light passed, watched moonlit figures enter the boathouse. He shook his head and smiled; soon he would finish it.

Jon, too, caught their poor choice as he waited on the circling Dodge.

"Careful," Leia said. Rebecca closed the door behind them. Teri flicked her *bic* and held it high. Leia set Clive on the stool. Clive blinked – whimpered.

Navigation challenges continued; Lon spun wheel and wheels. Grass sprayed. Jon played bullfighter, stayed close, and worked Lon past the woodshed.

Blham. Lead shot peppered the log splitter. Jon flinched, ducked. *Bwoof.* A blast filled the air and he felt the hot charge pass, looking for something to bite. The Dodge drove between them. Sherbt waited for another shot.

Lon squared an attack and Jon threw the paring knife. It snapped off the windshield. Lon chuckled, "See ya in the papers, Grease-spot."

In the spotlight, Jon feinted left. Lon adjusted. Jon glowed between the high beams and Lon could see the fresh grass stains on Jon's white and bloody-pink shirt.

Jon feinted right. Lon floored it, feathered the wheel, and cackled, "Nice try."

Jon back-peddled. Fell. Tumbled.

Lon listened for the smack and imagined Jon's skull exploding on the old chrome bumper. Headlights reached into the night, and the lawn went missing. His jaw dropped and the four-forty engine screamed a metallic freewheel.

Jon crouched on the path below, felt falling grass, and watched his truck shoot the moon.

Twenty feet down, and the headlights found something to light.

Lon inhaled to scream. The grill mashed soggy shore. Mr. Lonny Peck's head struck windshield, chest the wheel, sternum the horn. A blood-pool formed in a face-shaped safety-glass indent and Blackie's fading horn crooned, serenading Lon's fading pulse. Both stopped.

Blackie's spinning rear tires slowed and stopped as Jon ran south to the dock. He climbed stone steps and took a left on the path to the boathouse.

Sherbt pointed Ms. Benelli over the ledge at Rawling's crashed Dodge. It didn't look good. He called, "Lon, LON." He scanned the barrel over the dark path below and listened. Jon's strides echoed on the stone stairs. Sherbt walked the ridge south and, one, two, three, transferred shells from his vest into the gun.

"It's me," Jon warned the boathouse occupants before entering. As he closed the door, he saw Sherbt en route. He turned on the lights.

"Don't!" the girls gasped.

"He's coming, get in the boat."

Girls, bewildered, slow to move. Jon grabbed Leia, hoisted her, boosting her first. He helped Teri, Rebecca, and Clive in. "Stay low."

Sherbt couldn't remember when he had been happier. Light shone around the doorjamb. Close enough to hear rustling, he called to an imagined frightened herd, big game huddled, shaking, waiting to be dropped, "How's it goin in there?" He fingered the sexy Italian's trigger.

"Fuckin' *peachy*," Rebecca yelled. Jon looked at her. *Where did that come from?*

Leia pulled her adrenalin-drugged mom lower.

Jon dragged the bench in front of the side door and wedged his toolbox behind it. Then at the boat's bow, he unlatched the boathouse's double doors. On his trip back, he clicked off the antique light switch.

Sherbt fired. The blast echoed around the boat garage. A six-inch hole appeared and the doorknob was no more. His hat cocked and an earflap flopped. Sherbt tossed the cap. He replenished the chamber, keeping ready the sausage-maker.

Shoulder on stern, foot on back wall, Jon pushed. One sticky trolley wheel snapped free. The cart rolled forward, pushed easy on greasy axles, and Jon gave his all.

"Get down, now," he reminded the crew. "Hang on."

The bow divided doors and, riding high on rails, proudly nosed out. Sherbt heard scraping. Again, he fired at the side door, high and right, perceiving upper hinge. A second hole appeared as the blast echoed out the open front doors. An incandescent bulb exploded overhead. Glass rained. Boaters screamed.

Jon grunted, "Err," stepped, pushed, grunted, "Uh." Front doors swung wide.

Sherbt watched moonlight greet a boat. It looked empty and he held fire.

The stern passed the threshold and Jon felt the boat move of its own volition. Rails declined and he pushed with hands, instead of shoulder.

A Trojan horse? Sherbt calmly waited and trained his barrel on the emerging vessel.

A mellow angle quickly turned steep and Jon jogged as he pushed it free from the boathouse.

Sherbt had a target, a moving target, and he liked those.

Jon waited for a blast he might not hear, braced for death but embraced his effort. He ran, pushing, and now knew the boat's name, *Castaway*, and tried to stay behind the boat engine's lower unit.

"Ha, hu, ho, ho." Sherbt led the target and fired.

Everything on a decline, the load passed overhead.

Leia screamed, "Dad!" She watched Jon stumble and reach for the accelerating craft. Clive pulled her down. Jon gripped the stern, tried to run, to get in, but the speed, great, faster, and he fell to dragging.

Fine sanding dust swirled off the bow and the roller-coaster shed Jon.

He tumbled behind, down the bank, along the rails, and stopped prone in the weeds.

In a mighty splashing divide, the bow hit river. The crew buffeted together and Sherbt fired downrange. A subtonic splash off port and Clive stood to dive.

Jon rose, vaulted the rails, and ran. Sherbt ignored him, Jon wasn't going anywhere, but the *Castaway,* in current, drifted, transporting witnesses.

Clive dove.

The Benelli barked.

Leia screamed, "No!"

Sherbt, near panic, massaged the Italian's stiff trigger three times more, and *click.* One ripped into the bow, two spattered the river, and the girls were away, one-hundred yards and drifting.

Ironic quiet relief and loss filled the boat – mellow sounds of river surrounded. The smell of the water and sanded mahogany mixed under moonlight and the women sat on the dusty boat floor, speechless.

Sherbt reloaded. Jon ran to the dock, out to *Baby Cakes*, and released the lift. Cable unwound and the boat dropped.

Sherbt thought of the bridge on highway ninety-two, *Four? Five miles? Easy pickins.* The boat would pass under, he'd have time. The current was swift, but the Bentley swifter. First things first. *Bye, bye, Jon.*

Jon reached for *Baby Cakes* ignition. It disappeared. Then one of the two front windows went away. Another blast and, across the moon-reflecting river, Benelli's report echoed. Below the waterline, pellets ripped through the bow, and Jon heard diverted river rushing in. He ducked into the micro-galley, grabbed soup from the cubby, and peeked. Smoke leaked from the hot Italian and Sherbt filled her up as he walked the long dock. Jon disembarked breezy *Baby Cakes*, cans in hands.

Sherbt massaged the refilled shotgun, looked up, and slowly raised the barrel. "Don't worry, Jon. Rebecca's only going to be a widow for about ten minutes."

Jon drifted back, cocked, and *The Arm* propelled an eighty-mile-an-hour spiral.

Buhwam. Sherbt's sweet Italian orgasmed hot shot. Juicy tomato exploded and wayward pellets sprayed him. A dozen hot hornets pierced Jon's neck, cheek, chest, and shoulder. "Ahwa." He winced, spun, and transferred the second can to his throwing arm.

Sherbt watched him spin and waited for Jon to drop. He smiled. "It's going to be closed casket for you, Rawling." Cocky, he lowered the Benelli to his hip, ready to spray lead at Jon's head.

Stooped rotation, a thrusting step, and *The Arm* spent soup.

It came fast, true and straight. Sherbt tilted the weapon and fired instinctively. The Benelli gasmed – pellets whistling into the night.

Spa-Tunk. Above the left eye, Cream of Chicken struck a blow. The Italian slipped from his hands and fell to the dock. Sherbt spilled into the cool Platte.

Epilogue

Noon brought red-eyed Deputies, the Coroner, and the acting Sheriff.

Butterballs licked Clive's cleaver and heard them before he could see them. When they came into view, the cat looked up from Pearson's well-cleaned metal appendage and, guarding lunch, growled a low feline growl.

"Hey!" yelled the smocked man carrying a black body bag. A second man in white raced past the first and shouted, "Scat."

Like it was his decision, Butterballs slowly strutted into the woods, tail up, showing them his ass.

Deputy Newburg opened the den door. He stood, looking at Larry's faceless, leaked-out body, and his blood pool to the door.

Behind him, a camera-toting assistant tried to see. "What?"

"Twenty-gallon disaster."

"Ooow, where do I step?"

After Larry, they walked down to the black Dodge, where sticky flies sucked and laid eggs in Lon's flesh. Newburg's assistant found him extremely photogenic. *Click, click, click*, and a roll of 35mm film later, the men in white coats lifted Mr. Peck's face out of glass and removed him from steering wheel.

"Your turn," called Newburg. And with precarious effort, Jake winched Blackie up the bank. The *Wahoo Daily's* reporter stood on the ridge above the path, took his own pictures, and happily thought, *what a wonderful year.*

A deputy in street clothes cranked the lift and water poured from *Baby Cakes'* hole.

"They found somebody," another deputy said, holding binoculars, standing on the dock next to Sheriff apparent.

Harrison shielded his eyes from the sun. Downstream, two men in wetsuits pulled a body in not-so-white dress pants from riverbank branches. They rolled it over.

Eyes, blank, black, reflected sky.

The Rescue Leader cupped his hands and yelled upriver, "It's Sherbt."

Handcuffed to the rail, Clive lay in the same hospital bed Leia used, and down the hall, nursed by the petite one, Jon lolled.

Sunday afternoon, Harrison visited. "How ya doin?"

"Almost lost an eye." He raised a hand, touching the wrap, and with his other eye, Jon looked at him through the bandage opening.

"Guy down the hall almost lost two . . . Clive killed a detective."

"So I hear. Wife and Leia say it was self-defense. Dumbass never said he was *law*. Shot at em, too."

"We're lookin at manslaughter."

"I think you should keep looking. When's Kelly's funeral?" Jon said, checking out Harrison's Sheriff's badge.

"Wednesday."

Jon nodded. "Bernice?"

"Don't know, hoping you'd be able to help me with that."

A brittle smile, and Jon said, "Eating her way to hell . . ."

"I'm still a detective, Rawling. On one hand, I've got about fifty people saying you did it, killed Rothness – stuck Jorgen, too."

"Henry tried taking my head off, that's all I know."

"And they say you tried killing them, that you tried to kill everybody?"

Jon said nothing.

". . . And on the other hand, I got Ms. Thompson, telling me it was Henry, Bernice, probably Sherbt and company . . ."

Jon's eye stared at him between bandage edges, waiting. Waiting on the D+ detective . . .

"Found boots at Rothness' house, matched the print on Leia's car door . . . And a box of stuff in his vehicle, stuff he likely used to booby-trap the plant . . ."

Jon nodded. Brochette's drugs felt nice, Harrison's good works, nicer. He closed his eye and dreamed dreams he couldn't remember.

Teri went to the city, to Penney's in the mall, and another outfit, white, every bit as cute as blue, thrilled her. She tried it on and her dark hair contrasted perfectly. She paid with cash and the clerk slid it into a Penney's bag with the lacy, white brassiere. Two stores down, she found Leia a Teddy-bear. She browsed her way to the food court, and then, understood why he hadn't called.

The girl on his arm was cooing. Tom saw her, then pretended he didn't.

Leia found their old phone in the basement. Rebecca helped her remove the other and hook it up . . .

"Hello?"

"Hello. Hi, is Teri there?"

"No, she took our car. Said she was going to the mall and would stop to see how you guys were doing on her way home." Mrs. Thompson took a drink and looked at the clock. "It's past five, funny she isn't there, by now."

"We were hoping she might be able to take us to the hospital – if you don't need your car back right away." Leah looked out the window at Clive's clunkers. "We seem to kinda be out of vehicles."

"Of course, and hugs from us, too, we're thinking of ya."

"Thank you so much, see ya soon."

Teri sat in her mom's car, looking at the hospital, thinking about the last words she'd heard out of Bernice's saucebox. All's fair in love and war.

She went in.

Her hair fell on Jon's exposed cheek. It tickled, he woke, and her sweet smell registered.

Bad Teri pressed and her lips stayed.

The petite nurse entered. Curiously, she squinted and watched.

Teri's lips stuck, slightly tugging, slowly releasing Jon's as she pulled back . . . and she saw the nurse. She drew her hand from Jon's.

Caught, and not looking her in the eye, Teri said, "It was just a thank you kiss."

They ate lite, waited for Teri, and at six, Leia said, "Let's go."

"How?" Rebecca said.

"Maybe, Clive's Maverick?"

The key hung in the ignition and, next to Broken Down's driver seat, they found Clive's wrenches, tow-bar detaching tools. And the ladies did it.

"It's a stick?" Leia said.

"I'll drive."

"Help, this pack weighs a ton."

Rebecca helped Leia lug Clive's pack off the passenger's seat and lay it in the back.

Rebecca downshifted, pulling into the hospital parking lot.

Leia glimpsed a car leaving. "Teri? I think that was Teri."

Mom and daughter found Jon's bed adjusted up and he smiled when they came in. A Teddy-bear sat on the window ledge. Leia wiggled its ear. "Who brought this?"

"I don't know," Jon lied.

They visited pleasantly, avoided grit, and Jon directed conversation to Leia's recovery.

After a few minutes, Leia said, "I'm gonna go see Clive."

She liked that Clive couldn't much see her mangle.

"Leia?" he said. Un-bandaged, but face like balloon art gone awry and he tried to see through red puff. "I get out in the morning; my parents are coming." He moved his hand, clinking the cuff, "but who knows where I'm going?"

She kissed him, and said, "I like you," and Clive, again, was glad she did.

Leia walked to Dad's room. Mom and the nurse that loved to talk stood near Jon's door.

"Go say goodnight to your father, I'm ready to go."

As they slid into the Maverick, Rebecca looked at Clive's machete, and thought, *I could chuck it in the river on my way to Winnipeg.*

Harrison thought about it . . . and mid-October, Clive stood next to Leia near Elliot's crusher.

They watched Buster nestle Lemonade on top of the flattened black Dodge, placing it just back, avoiding the pickup's mud-encrusted ram-head motif.

"Wanna do the honors?" chittered Tic.

Clive helped Leia across oil, gas, and antifreeze-soaked muck to Tic at the controls.

Buster pressed Lemonade's window frame with the payloader's tine, breaking the driver-side windows. Most of the glass fell in the car, some pebbled out the front of the crusher. Buster smiled, adjusted her dirty red bandana on her dirty red neck, and gave Leia the thumbs up.

Tic helped place her hand on the control lever. "Pull it."

She paused, acknowledging Lemonade's travail. Then, mean, she pulled the lever. With her other hand, she made the sign of the cross on her front, deifying Buster's altar of latter-day transportation. "Rust to rust. Adios, you piece of *junk*."

And watching, but mostly listening, they enjoyed Lemonade's flattening – flex plate and all.

Elliot struck a match, puffed, and Leia waved to him as Clive backed around.

"Where to?" Clive asked.

"I want a Camaro, like Teri's, and a baby."

In his office, the new manager stood next to old trophies scrambled in a box on the floor. He threw a stupid corncob ashtray in with them and it broke. A tiny homemade leather tarp covered the '50s-style toy pickup's box. He pulled the miniature gas pump's nozzle from the toy. A farmer's match struck. Valves turned. Michael slid open the cabinet door below the shelving, looked at three green tanks with vinyl stickers, and read, 'Acetylene'. He heard a click, felt rain on his shoulders, and looked up. Office sprinklers sprayed and he smelled ethanol . . . and he smelled burning sulfur. Young Peck whispered, "Oh shit."

Knock, knock, knock. Dale looked out the peephole. In an airy summer-cut dress, Bernice waited. A bill-filled gray duffle hung from her shoulder. A hoagie in it sat atop her obscene stack.

Dale S. Higgus opened the door, stretching the lock-chain tight. "What you doin here?" He tried to see down the hall.

"Come to stay with ya a little while," and she held a card from the entry mailbox, and read it, "Ethan Al Stillman."

"Get in here!"

CPSIA information can be obtained
at www.ICGtesting.com
Printed in the USA
BVHW042321300522
638484BV00015B/73

9 781